BRANNIGAN'S LAND

Center Point
Large Print

Also by William W. and J. A. Johnstone and available from Center Point Large Print:

Dig Your Own Grave
Hang Them Slowly
The Morgans
To the River's End
Death and Texas
The Violent Storm
Dark Night in Big Rock
Taylor Callahan, Circuit Rider

**This Large Print Book carries the
Seal of Approval of N.A.V.H.**

BRANNIGAN'S
LAND

William W. Johnstone
and J.A. Johnstone

CENTER POINT LARGE PRINT
THORNDIKE, MAINE

This Center Point Large Print edition
is published in the year 2022 by arrangement with
Kensington Publishing Corp.

PUBLISHER'S NOTE
Following the death of William W. Johnstone, the
Johnstone family is working with a carefully selected
writer to organize and complete Mr. Johnstone's outlines
and many unfinished manuscripts to create additional
novels in all of his series like The Last Gunfighter,
Mountain Man, and Eagles, among others. This novel
was inspired by Mr. Johnstone's superb storytelling.

The text of this Large Print edition is unabridged.
In other aspects, this book may vary
from the original edition.
Printed in the United States of America
on permanent paper sourced using
environmentally responsible foresting methods.
Set in 16-point Times New Roman type.

ISBN: 978-1-63808-424-2

The Library of Congress has cataloged this record
under Library of Congress Control Number: 2022936631

BRANNIGAN'S LAND

CHAPTER 1

"What do you think, honey?" Ty Brannigan asked his oldest daughter.

"Just incredible, Pa. I don't know that I've ever seen a finer horse anywhere."

"He is something to look at, isn't he?"

"He sure is." MacKenna Brannigan lay beside her father near the crest of a rocky-topped ridge in the foothills of Wyoming Territory's Bear Paw Mountains, a spur range of the Wind Rivers, near Baldy Butte. Ty and MacKenna were peering down into the valley on the other side of the ridge. "I could lie here all day, just staring at him and his beautiful harem not to mention those six colts of his."

Tynan Brannigan, "Ty" for short, adjusted the focus on the spyglass he held to his right eye, bringing the big, impressive black stallion into sharper focus. The horse milled on the side of the next ridge, a couple of hundred feet up from where his harem languidly cropped grass with their foals along Indian Lodge Creek.

The big horse was watching over his herd, keeping an eye out for predators or rival herds led by stallions that might very well prove to be the black's blood enemy. He was having a good time performing the otherwise onerous task. The stallion ran along the side of the ridge then stopped abruptly, swung to his right and dashed up the steep ridge to the very top. He ran along the crest of the ridge first one way before wheeling, mane and tail flying, the sunlight glistening beautifully in his sleek, blue-black hide, and running back the other way before swinging down off the crest and galloping full out down the side toward where his harem lifted their heads and turned to watch him, twitching their ears incredulously.

Ty and MacKenna were several hundred yards from the big black, but Ty could still hear the thunder of the horse's hooves and the deep, grating chuffs the horse made with his powerful lungs as he ran.

The black slowed at the bottom of the ridge, near the stream, then went over and nosed one of the mares—a beautiful cream with a blond mane and tail. He nosed her hard, brusquely but playfully, then nipped the rear of one of the younger horses, a half-grown gray. The gray bleated indignantly. The stallion lifted his fine head and ripped out a shrill whinny. He put his head down, reared high, pawed the ground, then lunged into another ground-chewing gallop, making a mad dash up the ridge again.

MacKenna, who at seventeen was in the full flower of young womanhood, lowered the field glasses she'd been peering through and turned to her father, smiling. Her long hair was nearly as black as the stallion's, and it shone in the high-country sunshine like the black's did, as well. Her lustrous hazel eyes—her hair had come from her Spanish mother, but her eyes were the same almost startlingly clear blue-green as her father's—flashed in delight. Her plump red lips stretched back from her even, white teeth. "He's showing off, isn't he? He's showing off for the mares!"

Ty chuckled and lifted the spyglass again to his eye, returning his gaze to the black as the stallion stopped suddenly halfway up the ridge then turned to stand parallel to the ridge and peer off into the distance, ears pricked, tail arched, again looking for danger. "He sure is, honey."

Ty was glad he and MacKenna were upwind of the beautiful stud and his harem. If they'd been downwind, the black likely would have detected him and the girl and hazed his brood out of the valley where Ty and MacKenna, having a rare father-and-daughter ride alone together, lay on the side of their own ridge, admiring the lovely, charismatic, bewitchingly wild black stallion.

"They're just like boys, aren't they—wild stallions?" MacKenna said, playfully nudging her father in the ribs with her elbow. "Showing off for their women."

"Just like boys and men, honey," Ty agreed, chuckling. He turned to look at MacKenna who was peering through the field glasses again. "Would you like to have a horse like that, baby girl?"

MacKenna, named after Ty's long-dead mother, lowered the field glasses and turned to her father. Her thin black brows furled with speculation. Finally, she shook her head. "No." She turned to gaze with her naked eyes into the next valley. "No, a horse like that needs to be wild. Breaking or even gentling a horse like that . . . civilizing him . . . would ruin him." She glanced at her father. "Don't you think, Pa?"

"I couldn't agree more, Mack."

"How did you find this herd, Pa? I've never seen wild horses out here."

"Matt and I were hunting yearling mavericks on open range a few weeks ago, and we stumbled on several stud piles." Matt was the oldest of Ty and his wife Beatriz's four children, all of whom had been raised—were *being* raised, with the youngest at age twelve—on their Powderhorn Ranch in the shadow of several tall bluffs and mesas that abutted the ermine-tipped, higher peaks of the Wind Rivers.

MacKenna furled her dark brows again, curiously this time. "Stud piles?"

"Big piles of horse apples the herd leaders leave to mark their territory. Apparently, that big fella moved his herd in here recently. I've never seen stud piles in these parts before. Down deeper in the breaks of the Snowy River and in the badland country north of town, but never here."

"So, they're new in these parts," MacKenna said, smiling in delight and gazing into the next valley through her field glasses again. "Welcome, black . . . ladies and youngsters." She turned to her father. "Thanks for showing me, Pa. It leaves you with a nice feeling, seeing such beautiful, wild beasts, doesn't it?"

Ty smiled and placed a big, affectionate hand against the back of his daughter's neck. "Sure does, baby girl."

MacKenna shook her head again. "No, it wouldn't be right to try to tame a horse like that. Just like some men can't be tamed, some horses can't either."

Her eyes acquired a pensive cast, and she lowered her gaze.

Damn, Ty thought. He'd brought her out here— just him and her—to try to take her mind off her heartbreak, not to remind her of it.

"Oh, honey," he said, sympathetically. "He's not worth how bad you feel."

He meant the young, itinerant horse gentler, Brandon Waycross, who had once worked for Ty. MacKenna had tumbled for the rakishly handsome young man, five years her senior, one summer ago, and only a few months ago he'd broken her heart. Though they hadn't made any formal plans, and MacKenna had never confessed as much, Ty knew that MacKenna had tumbled for young Waycross and had set her hat toward marrying the young man.

"I hope he is, Pa. Or I'm a fool, because I sure do feel almighty bad."

"Even after what he did?"

MacKenna drew her mouth corners down and nodded, her now-sad gaze still averted. " 'Fraid so." She raised her eyes to Ty's. "I don't think he meant to betray me with Ivy. Some boys just can't help themselves."

"Don't make excuses for him, MacKenna. He's not a boy anymore. Brandon Waycross doesn't deserve you. You hold tight, baby girl. You're gonna find the right man—a good, kind, loyal man. That's the only kind to share your life with."

"Sometimes I feel like Ma got the last one of those," MacKenna said, then leaned toward Ty and planted an affectionate kiss on his cheek.

Ty smiled, sighed. "Well, honey. It's getting late and we've got an hour's ride back to the Powderhorn. Don't want to be late for supper or your mother will send us each out to fetch our own willow switches."

"Ouch!" MacKenna said, grinning. "She doesn't hold back like you do, either, Pa!"

"Believe me—I know!" Ty grin-winced and rubbed his backside.

He crawled a few feet down from the lip of the ridge, so the stallion wouldn't see him, then donned his high-crowned brown Stetson and rose to his full six-feet-four. At fifty-seven, having married MacKenna's mother when she was twenty-one and he was thirty-six, Ty Brannigan still owned the body of a Western horseman—tall, lean, broad-shouldered, and narrow-waisted.

Just by looking at him—into those warm eyes, especially—most would never have guessed he'd once been a formidable, uncompromising lawman in several formerly wide-open towns in Kansas and Oklahoma—a town tamer of legend. Ty had been the town marshal of nearby Warknife for three years and had cleaned out most of the hardcases during his first two years on the job, before meeting Beatriz Salazar, a local banker's daughter, falling head over heels in love, and turning in his badge to devote the rest of his life to ranching and raising a family.

It had not been a mistake. Ty did not miss wearing the badge. In fact, he treasured every moment spent working with his wife and their four children, now between the ages of twelve and nineteen, on their eight-thousand-acre spread, even when the work was especially tough like in spring with calving or when Ty was forced to run rustlers to ground with his old Henry repeating rifle and his stag-gripped Colt .44, holdovers from his lawdogging days. That Colt was housed now in its ancient, fringed, soft leather holster and thonged on his right thigh. The Henry repeater was sheathed on the coyote dun standing ground-reined with MacKenna's fine Appaloosa that Brandon Waycross had helped her gentle.

Ty didn't like wearing the guns, but they were a practical matter. Wyoming was still rough country, and over Ty's years as a tough-nosed lawman who'd sent many men to the territorial pen near Laramie, he'd made enemies. Some of those enemies had come gunning for him in the past, to get even for time spent behind bars or for family members who'd fallen victim to Ty's once-fast gun hand. When more enemies came, and he had to assume they would, he owed it to his family to be ready for them.

So far, the Brannigan family plot on a knoll east of the big main house, was occupied by only one Brannigan—Ty's father, Killian Brannigan, an old hide-hunting and fur-trapping mountain man who'd lived out his last years on the Powderhorn before succumbing to a heart stroke at age ninety. Ty didn't want to join his father just yet. He had too many young'uns to raise and a good woman to love. At age forty, Beatriz was too young to lose her man and to have to finish raising their four children alone.

"Come on, baby girl," Ty said, extending his hand to MacKenna. "Let's fork leather and fog some sage!"

MacKenna accepted her father's hand; Ty pulled her to her feet. An eerie whining sound

14

was followed closely by a resolute thud and a dust plume on the side of the ridge, ahead and to Ty's right. He'd felt the bullet curl the air just off his right ear before the crack of the rifle reached him.

"Down, honey!" Ty yelled, and threw MacKenna back onto the ground, throwing himself down on top of her, covering her with his own bulk then rolling off of her, pulling her on top of him again and rolling first her and then himself over the top of the ridge to the other side.

As he did, another bullet plumed dust within feet of MacKenna's left shoulder, turning Ty's insides into one taut, cold knot, sending icicles of terror shooting down his legs and into his feet.

"My God, Pa!" MacKenna cried when Ty had her safely on the other side of the ridge from the shooter. "What was *that?*"

"Keep your head down, honey!" Ty said, placing his left hand on her shoulder, holding her down, while pulling his stag-gripped .44 from its holster with his right hand.

"Who's shooting at us, Pa?"

"Your guess is as good as mine!" Breathless, Ty edged a cautious glance over the lip of the ridge and down the other side.

His and MacKenna's horses had run off, the coyote dun taking Ty's rifle along with it. Fifty yards beyond where the horses had stood was a wide creek bed choked with willows, cedars, and wild shadbark and juneberry bramble. The shooter must have fired from the creek bed, hidden by the bramble. Ty saw no sign of him.

Turning to MacKenna, who now lay belly down beside her father, her face blanched with fear as she gazed at him, Ty said, "You stay here, Mack. And for God sakes, keep your head down!"

Ty started to crab down the side of the ridge. MacKenna grabbed his arm, clutched it with a desperate grip. "Pa, where you goin'?"

"I'm gonna try to work around the bush-whacking coward! You stay here." He set down his gun to pat her hand that was still clutching his left forearm, and his normally mild eyes sparked with the hard light of a Celtic war council fire. Messing with him was one thing. Messing with his family was another thing altogether. "Don't you worry. I'm gonna get him, Mack!"

He remembered the bullet that had plumed dirt just inches from her shoulder.

MacKenna, as tough as the toughest Brannigan, which would be old Killian, hardened her jaws as well as her eyes and said, "Okay, Pa. Go get him!"

CHAPTER 2

Ty picked up his old but trusty Colt, crabbed down the sage- and rock-stippled ridge, then rose, turned, and hurried down the side at an angle to his right. A quick glance into the valley's bottom told him the ambusher's shot had cleared out the stallion and his harem of mares and foals.

The black would take no chances with his family. Neither would Ty Brannigan.

His heart thudding with the heat of his anger, Ty bottomed out at the base of the ridge and headed west. Just beyond the ridge lay another, brush-choked creek bed that connected the stream where the mares and foals were milling to the creek bed from which Ty believed the shooter had fired on him and MacKenna.

The big rancher followed a game path through willows into the creek bed, which was about five feet deep and threaded down its center by a narrow, shallow stream that smelled a tad skunky here in the late summer. He walked quickly along the edge of the murky water, heading north now, toward the intersecting creek bed.

He walked at a crouch, trying to make himself as small as possible, not easy for a man his size, the Colt cocked and aimed out from his right side. As he walked, prickly shrub branches and brambles reached out from the bank on his right to grab at his buckskin pants, blue wool tunic with laces halfway down the front, leather suspenders, and his neck-knotted red bandanna.

He kept a close eye on the intersecting ravine ahead of him, wary of more lead being fired his way.

He was twenty feet from the intersecting ravine . . . fifteen . . . ten. The brush-sheathed bank dropped away on his right, and he stopped, bent forward, peered off down the ravine through which the stream continued, the water following the ravine's course as it angled off to Ty's left, roughly fifty yards away.

This intersecting ravine was broader and deeper than the one Ty had just left, its banks peppered with rocks, Ponderosas, cedars, and junipers. As far as Ty could see, there was no sign of the shooter.

Had he pulled out?

The rancher began following the ravine's course, keeping the cocked Colt aimed out from his right side. The dark water trickled along its stony bed, spotted with dead leaves and cattail down. When the stream hugged up tight against the base of the embankment on Ty's right, he crossed it and walked along its left side, the bank on that side roughly ten feet to his left.

He'd just started to follow the ravine's bend

when he stopped suddenly, sniffed the air. The tang of horse and leather scented the nearly still, hot summer air.

He'd no sooner identified the aroma when a man shouted, *"Hyahh!"* and Ty saw a horse and rider burst out of a thicket dead ahead of him, not fifteen feet away. The rider whipped his rein ends against his horse's left hip and the horse reared slightly, whinnied shrilly, laid its ears back, and bounded toward Ty.

As it did, the black-hatted man in the saddle fired a revolver along the right side of the roan's neck. Ty felt the punch of the bullet in his left arm but still managed to snap off a shot just before the horse bulled into him and pitched him back into the shallow stream.

He landed on his back, splashing water and cursing then whipping up the Colt again, turning his body to follow the rider galloping off down the stream away from him. Ty cursed as he quickly lined up his sights on the man's back and squeezed the trigger.

The Colt bucked and roared.

The bullet puffed dust from the back of the rider's vest, between his shoulder blades. The man slumped forward in his saddle, rolled down the roan's right wither, struck the ground, and bounced several times before piling up against a rock. He rolled onto his back with a groan and a sharp curse, gave a spasmodic jerk, and lay still, his pale forehead where his hat shielded it from the sun glowing brightly in the late afternoon sunshine.

He'd rolled onto his hat. The dark green bowler peeked out from between him and the rock, its crown crushed.

"Pa, you all right!" MacKenna cried.

Ty glanced to his left to see his daughter scrambling down the bank through the thick brush, the branches grabbing at her black hair and pulling it back behind her. It ripped her black, flat-brimmed hat off her head, but she left it where it lay at the base of the bank and ran into the stream, splashing the water high around her long, slender, legs clad in blue denim and black chaps to squat beside her father.

"Dammit, you're hit!" intoned the hot-blooded girl of Irish-Spanish extraction, not minding her tongue.

Wincing against the pain, Ty inspected the bloody hole in his arm, up high near his shoulder. The hole was near the very outside of the muscular limb and a quick probe with his fingers, sucking air sharply between his gritted teeth, told him there was an exit wound.

"Not to worry, baby girl—it's just a flesh wound. Went clear through. Hurts like blazes, but I've cut myself worse shavin'!"

"I'll be the judge of that!" MacKenna lowered her head to closely inspect her father's arm, glancing at first the exit wound and then the entrance wound. She puffed out her cheeks and looked at Ty. "Hurt awful bad, eh?"

"Nothin' a few shots of Irish whiskey won't cure."

"Ma won't let you drink."

Ty smiled but it was mostly another wince. "I think she'll make an exception for this though she might accuse me of tryin' to get ambushed just for the whiskey. You'll have to testify on my behalf."

"Who's the bastard layin' over there?"

"Young lady, your tongue!"

"If Ma can make an exception for that arm wound, I think you can make an exception for my tongue . . . given the circumstances . . ."

Ty grunted his agreement with his passionate daughter. "Help me up, baby girl. Gonna go over an' have a look."

"Wait." MacKenna removed her bandanna from around her neck, wrapped it around her father's arm, over both wounds, and knotted it tightly.

Again, Ty drew a sharp breath against the pain.

"Cut yourself worse shavin', huh?" MacKenna grunted at him reprovingly.

She draped her father's right arm around her neck and helped hoist his big body up out of the water and mud. Ty stooped to retrieve his hat, which lay at the edge of the stream, the caved-in crown taking the shape of a horse hoof. He

21

reshaped the hat, set it on his head, glanced at the dead man, and turned to MacKenna. "You'd best wait here. You don't need to see him."

"I've already seen him."

Ty sighed and then he and MacKenna walked over to stare down at the bushwhacker.

He was obviously dead. Ty's bullet had plowed through his back and out through his breastbone, likely shredding his heart.

Ty crouched to closely study the man.

He was medium tall and slender, some would say skinny, and he had long, dark-red hair that hung to his shoulders. His face was round and pudgy, with a pencil-thin mustache that did not match the rawness of his features. He wore a small, silver ring through his right ear, and a cheap, spruce-green, three-piece suit with a wool, rose-colored vest. On his bare right hand, that lay beside him, fingers curled over the palm, he wore a gold ring on his pinky.

A gold watch lay on the ground beside him, a gold-washed chain trailing from the near vest pocket. Ty picked up the watch, ran his gloved right thumb over the leaf-scrolling on the lid.

"Dandy," Ty said. "At least, he was trying hard to be."

The dead man, who appeared in his mid-twenties, looked like a farm or ranch hand who, having tired of all day forking a saddle for the usual thirty-a-month-and-found, had decided to try his hand at the pasteboard and poker way of life . . .

MacKenna frowned up at her father. "Do you recognize him, Pa?"

Ty shook his head. "I don't recollect ever seein' him before. I think I'd remember." He dropped to a knee and, mainly using his right hand because his left arm was throbbing miserably, he went through the man's pockets. He found only two combs, one larger than the other, a small, pasteboard-covered notebook with only blank pages remaining, a gray canvas tobacco pouch, a pencil stub, and a deck of cards residing with a few lucifer matches in his shirt pocket.

"Nothing with his name on it," Ty said, sitting back on his heels. "And I don't know him by lookin' at him."

MacKenna stepped forward, placed a hand on her father's right shoulder, very lightly. "Don't mean he doesn't know you, though."

Ty looked up at her and drew his mouth corners down. She was too wise for her years. But then, her wisdom had come from the regrettable experience of knowing that men had come for her father before. Ty had never talked to her about it, but he supposed she'd lived with the fear more would come again.

And now one had.

Ty just wished she hadn't had to witness such a thing. None of his other kids nor Beatriz had—

he'd been alone when others had tried to trim his wick—but now MacKenna had been a witness to the violence. Ty wrapped his good arm around her and pulled her close against him. He didn't say anything, because there was nothing to say. Reassuring words would only sound hollow.

He rose and turned to her. "Why don't you see if you can run down our horses, Mack? I'm going to see if I can run down this fella's mount. I'll take him to town tomorrow, turn him over to Chris Southern." Southern was one of Ty's closest friends and the current town marshal of Warknife.

"You got it, Pa." MacKenna turned and started walking toward the embankment.

"You all right, Mack?" Ty called to her back.

She stopped, glanced over her shoulder at him, and gave him a crooked, reassuring smile, then turned her head forward and climbed the embankment.

Ty watched her with an expression of prideful admiration. She was tall for her age—tall like her father—and her figure was becoming more and more woman every day. A tough lady was Mack. "That one's got the bark on. Always has, always will."

MacKenna might have witnessed what had happened here today, and even nearly took one of those bullets herself. But the one Ty worried about was his wife, Beatriz. The woman was

24

strong, but she'd been born to worry. She'd worry about Ty now. He wished there was some way he could not tell her but with the bullet hole in his arm, that would be impossible. Besides, she hated when he kept secrets from her, and he didn't blame her.

Ty didn't have to look far for the dead man's horse.

He merely stuck two fingers between his lips and whistled. A couple of minutes later, the roan came walking around a bend in the ravine, reins trailing. Ty trained his own horses to come to a whistle, and he was glad the roan had been trained to do the same. He was doubly glad, in fact, because with the burning pain in his arm, he hadn't had the energy to run the mount down.

Not long after the roan had returned, MacKenna rode up to the lip of the ravine bank, sitting the saddle of her Appaloosa and holding the reins of Ty's coyote dun. Ty had just finished tightening the roan's saddle cinch. Now he crouched over the dead man's body, which he'd wrapped in the man's own blanket roll. He'd gone through the man's saddlebags and, as had been the case with the man's pockets, he'd found nothing that identified him.

Which likely meant he was just some nobody with a grudge—often the most dangerous kind of man. He'd likely tracked Ty and MacKenna after they'd left the Powderhorn headquarters earlier. He'd come packing iron and the determination to exact a reckoning for past injury.

What injury might that be?

Ty had no idea.

"Hold on, Pa," MacKenna said. "I'll help you with that."

"You stay there, Mack. This ain't a job for a seventeen-year-old girl."

MacKenna was already scrambling down the bank through the brush. "It ain't a job for a fifty-seven-year-old wounded man, neither."

"You're as stubborn as your mother!"

"Thank you. On the count of three . . ." MacKenna had already crouched to take the man's ankles in her hands.

"All right, all right," Ty said, resignedly. "One . . . two . . . *three!*"

They each grunted as they hauled the dead man up off the ground, carried him over to the horse, and then, readjusting their grips on the dead man's body, slung him belly down across his saddle.

Ty leaned forward to catch his breath and to wait for the pain the maneuver had aggravated in his arm to subside. He turned to MacKenna and said, "Now for the hard part."

She frowned curiously at her father.

"Tellin' your mother," Ty said.

CHAPTER 3

Ty leading the dead man's horse by its bridle reins, he and MacKenna rode through two separate Bear Paw Mountain watersheds before mounting the bright, windy pass above Mooney's Coulee.

As they started down the pass's east side, their own Powderhorn Ranch headquarters lay spread out before them in a broad, tawny bowl nearly surrounded by a slanting mesa and three haystack buttes peppered with cedars and pines and backed in the misty blue distance by three snowy peaks of the Wind River range. Natural troughs in the sides of the buttes surrounding the ranch yard were lush with wild berry scrub including strawberries and raspberries, which Beatriz and MacKenna and young Carolyn preserved every fall after they'd harvested and canned or pickled their garden.

The two-story log house, which had become somewhat sprawling after Ty and Beatriz had added onto it over the years as their family had grown, sat off to the right of the large, age-silvered log barn, the stable and its two attached pole corrals, and the blacksmith shop and wagon shed, also built of logs gleaned from the surrounding mountains and valleys.

The headquarters had been hand-built by the Powderhorn's previous owner, an old squaw man and borderline hermit named Leonard Cantwell. Cantwell had lived here with his Gros Ventre wife—in a much smaller version of the house, as the Cantwells had had no children—until the wife died from a cancer and Cantwell had a heart stroke and moved into a boarding house in the town of Warknife, which lay five miles to the north.

That had been nearly twenty years ago now, just after Ty had resigned his town marshal's job and asked for Beatriz's hand in marriage after sparking her against her banker father's wishes for over a year. Diego Salazar had wanted his only daughter to marry a wealthy businessman from a blooded family, not a former town-taming lawdog with murky Irish lineage. Despite the man's protestations, Ty and Beatriz were married in the Catholic church in the nearby town of Cutbank. The very next day, Ty purchased the Powderhorn from Cantwell.

That had been twenty years, four children, many cats, even a badger for a time (MacKenna), and a half-dozen dogs ago . . .

One of those dogs, the current one, came barking out from the trapezoid of shade fronting the blacksmith shop and ran, tail wagging, through the open main gate and under the tall wooden portal at the edge of the yard and the foot of the hill Ty and MacKenna were trotting their horses down. The dog's name was Rollie, a shaggy, black and white collie. Whenever one or more of the Brannigans left the yard, Rollie found a strip of shade in which to lay in wait and then to greet the returning party or parties with much delighted barking and tail-wagging, as though the returning family members had been gone for weeks instead of hours.

Rollie continued to perform the ceremony now as he ran up the hill to meet the current returning Brannigans and then to run along beside them in the bromegrass and sage painted here and there with late-summer wildflowers including the bright yellow balsamroot, the softer yellows of goldenrod, and the reds of Indian paintbrush.

As Ty and MacKenna passed under the portal, in the high crossbar of which the Powderhorn brand, a Circle P, had been blazed to each side of the BRANNIGAN name, Ty saw Beatriz and twelve-year-old Carolyn taking wash down from the clothesline on the near side of the house, which was shaded by two large Ponderosa pines and a dark-green fir. Wearing a blue day dress and a white apron, her black hair pulled up in a double bun, Beatriz glanced at Ty and MacKenna. She smiled, happy to see them, then turned away.

Quickly, frowning, she returned her gaze to her husband as he and MacKenna rode up to the hitchrack fronting the house.

29

Ty could tell that Beatriz knew something was wrong. Even if he hadn't been trailing the spare horse with a blanket-wrapped body lying belly down across the saddle, she probably saw the way he let his left arm hang slack at his side, that shoulder dipped slightly under the weight of the pain of the wound.

Then she probably also saw MacKenna's green neckerchief wrapped around the same arm. Ty thought his face was probably set stiffly, as well, and was no doubt a little pale. It had been an hour's ride from the Baldy Butte area, out on the open government range, where he and MacKenna had admired the wild horse herd, but with the throbbing burn in his arm, it had seemed like twice that long though he'd not let on to MacKenna.

The girl had been through enough for one day, and she was already worried about her father.

Turning full around to him, frowning with concern, Beatriz said, "Ty?" She dropped into the wicker basket at her feet the shirt she'd just removed from the line and lurched into a jog toward Ty and MacKenna. As she did, Carolyn turned to frown curiously at her father and sister, her brown-eyed, heart-shaped face also clouding with concern, her blond hair—the strawberry blond of Ty's hair—blowing in the wind caroming off the wild peaks of the Wind Rivers to the northwest.

Ty and MacKenna shared a dark glance and then Ty swung gently down from the saddle. Rollie leaped up against him, wriggling and barking, wanting to be petted, which Ty did half-heartedly with his good hand then turned to see Beatriz approach, the frown of concern ridging her black brows severely. "Ty, what's wrong? What happened?"

"Good Lord, you have a nose for trouble, woman!"

"It's your arm," Beatriz said, hazing the dog away and walking up close to her husband, canting her head to get a better look at his arm then lightly brushing her fingers across MacKenna's neckerchief. She returned her gaze to his, her eyes flashing anxiously. "You've been shot!"

"Shot?" echoed Carolyn, walking over from the clothesline and now breaking into a run.

"Who's been shot?" came a male voice from the other side of the yard. Ty glanced over to see his oldest son, Matt, leading a young clay-bank gelding around the breaking corral by a hackamore rope. Matt, who was good with horses though not as good as Brandon Waycross, whom he'd taken some pointers from, was gentling the bronc for a neighbor.

"It's nothing, son," Ty called. "Keep working the green out of that clay!"

"Poppa!" Carolyn cried as she approached,

31

her hair dancing across her shoulders. She was blond-haired and dark-eyed, and at twelve her body had not quite lost the plumpness of young girlhood and it did not help that Carolyn had a penchant for extra helpings of dessert following supper.

"Oh, hell," Ty complained.

"It's not as bad as it looks," MacKenna tried to reassure her mother and her younger sister as she wound her appy's reins around the hitchrack. "The bullet went all the way through Pa's arm."

"*Dios mio!*" Beatriz exclaimed, grabbing Ty's right arm and pulling him in the direction of the broad porch steps. "*¡Entra y déjame echarle un vistazo a ese brazo, hombre exasperante!*" Get inside and let me see that arm, you exasperating man!

Beatriz often slipped into Spanish when she got excited.

"Now, honey, please don't overreact!"

As she led him to the porch, Ty hearing running footsteps growing louder—likely Matt and his younger brother, Gregory, coming to check on their father—she turned and spewed another string of Spanish at him. When she could tell by his expression that she'd spoken too fast for him to follow, she translated: "Don't tell me I am overreacting when you come home from a ride with your daughter with a bullet in your arm!"

"It went all the way through, Ma!" MacKenna

repeated as she followed her parents up the porch steps, Carolyn and the excitedly barking Rollie hot on her heels.

As he and Beatriz crossed the porch, Ty cast a glance over his shoulder to see Matt, tall, dark-haired, brown-eyed and rangy and clad in trail gear including crisp cream Stetson and chaps, approaching them from the corral. Gregory, fifteen and with longish, dark-brown hair and his mother's even, delicate features and plump-lipped mouth, was halfway across the yard from where he'd likely been tending chores in the barn. A wheelbarrow full of hay and manure impaled by a three-tined fork sat in the barn's open doorway behind him.

The boots of Matt and Gregory thundered on the steps behind Ty and Beatriz, and Matt called, "Who shot you, Pa? Is that the jasper there, layin' across the roan?"

"Yeah, Pa—who shot you?" Gregory intoned, running up the steps beside his brother. He was not all that much shorter than Matt's six-two but unlike his rangy older brother, he was rawboned and somewhat lumbering. Both young men were breathless.

"Later, boys," Beatriz called over her shoulder as she led Ty through the foyer and into the big, well-appointed kitchen with a large, chrome range, stout food preparation table, many well-stocked shelves and cabinets, a wagon wheel

33

chandelier, and heavy ceiling beams. "MacKenna, you boil water! Carolyn, run upstairs for my medical kit and fetch several soft cotton cloths!"

"Oh, God, Ma," Carolyn cried from the kitchen doorway, "is Pa gonna die?"

Matt, coming up behind his little sister, swept her up in his arms, raised her high above his head and said, "One silly little bullet in the arm ain't enough to kill Pa, Muffin!"

He set her down and she tightened her lips as she wheeled to him and punched her older brother in the arm with her clenched right fist. "I wanna hear it from Ma!"

"Carolyn!" Beatriz fairly screamed at her youngest daughter.

"I'm going!" Carolyn screamed back and ran out through the kitchen door and mounted the half-log stairs.

Beatriz pulled out a chair at the food preparation table on which sat a bowl of as-yet unpeeled potatoes for supper, and turned to MacKenna, her voice sharply impatient: "MacKenna, are you heating that water?"

"Mother, I'm heating the water!" MacKenna shot back from where she was pumping water into a large tin pot, her own face flushed and mottled pale with exasperation and worry.

"Don't take that tone with me, young lady!"

Easing into the chair, Ty groaned, rolling his head around on his shoulders, and said, "Ladies, please do calm down! I ain't dead . . . yet."

"I was calm until we got home, an' now Ma and Carolyn are givin' me fits!" MacKenna exclaimed as she set the pot on the ticking stove.

Matt came around and hiked a hip onto the table near his father. "What happened, Pa? Who shot you? That the rannie you hauled in over the roan?"

"Yeah, is that the rannie, Pa?" Gregory said as he plopped heavily into a groaning chair on the other side of the table from Ty. Beatriz was unknotting the bandanna from around Ty's arm.

"Boys, please!" she scolded.

"Rannie?" Ty asked, beetling his brows curiously at his oldest son.

"Pa doesn't know who it is," MacKenna said, also walking over to the table.

"You don't, honey?" Beatriz asked, gazing with concern into her husband's eyes as she removed the bandanna from around his arm. "Do you think he was rustling?"

"I didn't see any signs of rustling in that part of the mountains. We weren't on our graze, so if he is a rustler, he was rustling Merle Miller, not us. Miller runs a herd near Baldy. The *rannie* didn't dress like any rustler I've ever met."

"Fancy-Dan," MacKenna said. "Ugly as a carp, though."

"MacKenna, don't insult the dead," Beatriz remonstrated her daughter, adding a little hesi-

35

tantly, as though after reconsidering, "Even if he did shoot your father . . ."

"Maybe he mistook you for Mr. Miller," Gregory suggested.

Ty was interrupted by Carolyn screaming down from upstairs that she couldn't find Beatriz's medical kit. After several screamed exchanges between Beatriz and her youngest daughter, Beatriz sent MacKenna upstairs to locate the medical kit.

Ten minutes later, Carolyn came down and set the leather kit and the cotton cloths on the table as MacKenna followed her into the kitchen. "I was the one who found it, after all!" she said, giving her older sister a saucy look.

MacKenna snorted.

"All right," Ty said, raising his voice. "I love you all but I'm startin' to wish that rannie had been a better aim and tagged me in the ticker. At least, I wouldn't have to endure all this Brannigan foofaraw! Everybody outside but your mother." He gave Beatriz's backside a playful swat with his good hand. "We want a little privacy, your ma an' me."

"Tynan, not in front of the children!"

"I wanna stay an' watch her doctor your arm!" Gregory said. The youngest Brannigan son had set his hat for being a doctor. "I never seen a bullet wound tended before. Is this the first time you ever been shot, Pa?" he asked, his light brown eyes flashing eagerly. "Does it hurt awful bad?"

"Outside!" Ty and Beatriz yelled at the same time.

"Come on, little brother." Matt donned his Stetson, rose from the table, and ticked the brim of Gregory's leather-brimmed immigrant hat with his finger. "You want me to pull that bushwhackin' rannie off his horse and lay him out in the barn, Pa?"

"No!" Beatriz said, cutting Ty's bloody sleeve away from his bloody arm. "That is no work for a—"

"Honey," Ty interrupted. "Matt's in better shape than I am. Besides, he's seen dead men before." Matt had seen his grandfather after Killian had died, and once in town, he and Ty had stopped for a beer in the Top Hat Saloon and witnessed a gambler shooting another gambler across the table with a pearl-gripped, over-and-under lady derringer.

He'd also seen rustlers hanging from trees on the range of a neighboring rancher—an uncompromising old Westerner aptly named Jake Battles.

Beatriz's only response as she continued to cut Ty's sleeve was a disgusted shake of her head.

"I'll tend his hoss, too, Pa," Matt said, and beckoned to Gregory. "Come on, squirt. You heard the man. You listen or I'll twist your ears full around again!"

Gregory gave an exasperated sigh, took one more look at his father's bloody arm, then heaved himself up out of the chair and strode in his clomping, lazy, heavy-footed fashion out of the house. Carolyn had been the first one to leave in a melodramatic huff. She was still sore after she and MacKenna had gotten into a shouting match a few minutes ago upstairs, when they were trying to find their mother's medical kit.

MacKenna came over and set a whiskey bottle down on the table before her father. She winked at him, kissed his cheek, and shrugged a shoulder at her mother. "I found this in Grandpa's room. For the pain, Ma. It's medicinal."

She kissed her mother's cheek and gave Beatriz a tender smile. "I'm sorry for yellin' at you, Mi Madre."

Beatriz tried not to smile but she didn't quite make it.

MacKenna swung around, and as she walked toward the foyer she intoned over her shoulder, "Just give a yell if you need any help!"

Beatriz was gently cleaning the entrance wound with a cloth soaked in the cooling hot water and whiskey from a bottle she kept in her medical kit, for disinfecting wounds.

Ty turned to her and said, "That's a boisterous

brood you gave me, you hot little chili pepper!"
Again, he gave her rump a playful swat.

Beatriz's eyes teared up, and her lips trembled. She lifted her head to Ty's, kissed his lips tenderly, and said, "I want one more, Tynan."

CHAPTER 4

"One more of what?" Ty inquired in surprise, jerking his head to indicate their children. "One more of *those?*"

"Si, one more of *those,*" Beatriz said. She'd resumed cleaning his wounds.

Ty gazed at her, pensive, incredulous, more than a little surprised by his wife's announcement. "Honey, I had no idea you were thinking of more kids." He decided to make a joke of it. "I mean, we've had four tries now and you see the hooligans we've produced. I don't know if we should risk it again!"

Beatriz looked up at him reprovingly from beneath her brows. "You joke."

At forty, she was still a beautiful woman with deep, soulful, dark-brown eyes, a clean-lined nose, and oval-shaped face. Her hair was thick and black with very few rogue strands of gray. She was tall, slim-waisted, full-busted, and long-legged. When Ty had first seen her working in her father's bank, she'd been only eighteen. Even at eighteen, she'd been an intoxicatingly beautiful, sexual, and sensual woman, with lustrous eyes and a ready smile that made her full, red mouth spread wide and her eyes lengthen and rise at the corners.

Even then, she'd been no woman to make angry.

Now at forty, she was even more beautiful than at eighteen, for the years, and having been a mother four times over, as well as being a wife to a tough but sensitive and passionate man, had added a ripeness and a deeper, more soulful and worldly sensuality. Rarely had Ty ever looked at this woman and not felt a glow in his heart and a hard pull in his loins. However, at forty she was even more formidable than she'd been at eighteen.

Not a woman to trifle with.

"My God—you're serious, aren't you?" Ty said, sliding a stray lock of her hair from her cheek and tucking it back behind her ear.

She glanced up at him as she wrung the bloody cloth out in the water.

"Did me getting shot bring this on?"

Beatriz dabbed at the exit wound. "It reminded me that we are here on this Earth for a brief time. It reminded me that you could be taken from me so suddenly. But, in truth, I have been feeling the urge to have one last child for months now. I guess I have been trying to fight it, because I knew how you would feel about it, but the pull is strong."

She wrung the cloth out again and glanced up at him. "I am forty. Very close to the end of my child-bearing years. I'm feeling old, Ty. This morning I found more gray in my hair. Having a baby inside me again . . . it makes a woman feel young."

"You're not old, my love. I'm the one who's old. I'm pushing sixty. When I turn seventy, the boy . . . or girl . . . will be only ten years old!"

"He will have his brothers and sisters. He will have me . . . and you, if you don't ride off and get yourself shot again!"

"I'm sorry, darling. I know this has upset you, but . . ."

"But, what?" she said, opening her medical kit and producing a needle and catgut thread.

"It doesn't feel right to me."

"You're saying you want no more children with me?"

Ty brushed his thumb across her cheek with affection and frowned. "If I were younger, of course. Don't you think those crazy owlhoots out there are enough?"

"No," Beatriz said, stubbornly shaking her head as she threaded the needle with the catgut. "I don't. I want one more, Ty. I want to feel young again. It will make you feel young again, too. You'll see, darling."

"No, honey," Ty said, resting his hand on her cheek and shaking his head. "It won't."

"That's your final word?" she asked, plucking a sulfur-tipped match from a china tray on the table, beside a green-shaded hurricane lamp, and

42

dragging it across the scarred wood until the tip burst into flame.

Ty took a pull from his father's bottle. "That's my final word."

"All right." Beatriz nodded gravely as she sterilized the needle in the flame. She took her time, sliding the needle in and out of the flame. The needle turned black and then red. Ty winced at the anticipated poke and burn when she started suturing his wounds closed. He sipped from the bottle again as she said, "I will respect your wishes and say no more on the subject." Making her lips round, she blew out the match.

"Thank you, honey." Ty leaned forward to kiss her cheek.

She leaned in close to his arm, bringing the needle toward the ragged entrance wound. Ty winced at the anticipated poke and burn. She might respect his wishes on the subject of another child, but she was going to make him pay.

His fiery chili pepper always made him pay . . .

He almost laughed but then she pinched up the flesh around the wound and poked the needle through.

"Oh, Lordy!" Ty grabbed the chair seat with his right hand and squeezed.

"I do believe you enjoyed that," Ty said when Beatriz had finished suturing the exit wound at the back of his arm, disinfecting it once more with her whiskey that was strictly medicinal, and wrapping a bandage around both wounds. Her face was flushed as though following lovemaking. Ty lifted the bottle of old Killian's Irish whiskey, and took a deep pull.

Beatriz gave him a crooked little devious smile and kissed his cheek. "I am angry with you now," she said, poking his chin with her finger. "But I am glad you are still alive for me to be angry at. That is enough whiskey, though. As much as you've had, you should feel no pain."

Ty gave a sheepish sigh and set the bottle down on the table and corked it. "How long's the anger going to last this time?"

"Maybe a little longer than usual."

"Cold shoulder?"

"And you'll be sleeping on the sofa in your office."

"Damn—that one I really hate!"

Beatriz gave him that smile again. "I am joking. You know I could not deprive myself of that big, warm body of yours, *viejo réprobo*." You old reprobate.

She removed her medical kit from the table. "I will be back in a minute to start supper. I am going to put my kit away myself so I will know where it is next time I need it, though I hope there will be no next time. At least, not one involving my life's one true love and an ambush in the mountains."

She ran her hand through Ty's thick, curly, strawberry blond hair and started walking toward the foyer.

Ty frowned down at the table. He was so deep in sudden thought that he felt the pain in his arm as though it were a long way away. Or maybe it was his dead old man's whiskey. He turned his head to look over his shoulder at his darling's retreating back and said, "Oh, hell, let me think about it!"

Beatriz stopped and turned back to him. She smiled, her soft dark eyes glinting in the sunlight angling in through one of the kitchen's big windows. She winked then turned back around and left the kitchen. Her footsteps had just dwindled to silence on the stairs when they were replaced by the rataplan of many galloping riders.

Ty frowned, pricking his ears, listening.

The rataplan grew louder, and then Rollie barked.

"What the hell . . . ?"

Ty rose from his chair and reached up above the kitchen doorway for the old Winchester he kept mounted there, a holdover from the days when he'd occasionally been harassed by bronco Indians, usually Arapaho or Sioux who would not go quietly into the night. Which is to say they would not stay on the reservations the Great Father in Washington had set up for them. Not that Ty had blamed them. They'd been hunter-gatherers and had ranged widely, following the buffalo and other game, warring with other tribes. But just as they'd been proprietary about their ancestral lands, Ty had been proprietary about his cattle and horses, which they'd occasionally tried to steal.

He doubted these riders were either Sioux or Arapaho, but he pumped a round into the Winchester out of old habit and moved through the foyer to the front door. He pulled on a light, doeskin jacket since his left arm was nearly bare to the shoulder. As he opened the door and stepped onto the porch, he saw that his visitors were not, indeed, Indians.

The dozen or so men who sat their horses in the middle of the Powderhorn yard, talking to Ty's kids standing before them—mainly to Matt and MacKenna while Rollie ran circles around the group, barking loudly and wagging his tail— were led by Con Stalcup, the foreman of Ty's uncompromising neighbor, Jake Battles.

Ty started to pull the door closed behind him, frowning curiously at the newcomers sitting under a haze of their own dust, when Stalcup said to Matt and MacKenna, "Your father in?"

"Here." Holding his freshly tended, stiff left arm against his side, Ty moved across the porch to stand at the top of the steps. "If you're not careful, you're gonna blow out them horses." He glanced at the sweat-silvered mounts whose saddles the Anchor Ranch riders were forking. "Jake won't be one bit happy."

Stalcup, a rangy, hard-faced man of medium height and with a thick, brown dragoon-style mustache laced with gray, and long sideburns, swung his sorrel around and trotted it over to the base of the porch steps. When he drew back on the reins, the mount lifted its head and fought the bit. "He ain't happy *or* angry. Not no more, Brannigan. He's dead."

"Dead? What're you talkin' about—*dead?* I just saw him out on the range—"

"Shot. Murdered. Last night around dusk. I rode out after hearing the shot out by Eagle Creek and found him lying belly down with a bullet in his back. Brandon Waycross was out there, crouched over the boss. When he seen me, he climbed onto his hoss and galloped away like that hoss had tin cans tied to its tail. We've been scouring the Bear Paws all day for him. You haven't seen him, have you?"

Ty glanced over at MacKenna, who looked pale and stricken. She held one hand over her chest, fingers splayed, as though to quell her quaking heart.

"No, I haven't," Ty said. "You sure Brandon shot Jake? I know the boy's a misfit, but . . . he's no killer . . ."

"Ivy invited Waycross into the house for supper. He and Mr. Battles must've got into it. Me an'

47

the fellas heard the old man yellin' all the way over in the bunkhouse." Stalcup gave the rancher a dark, knowing look.

It had been a complicated situation over there at Anchor Ranch. Brandon Waycross had agreed to marry Jake's daughter, Ivy, because, after getting her in the family way, it was the respectable thing to do. Jake could not abide a bastard grandson nor an unwed daughter with a child. Still, Jake had hated Brandon for what he'd done, and he hadn't made how he felt about his prospective son-in-law a secret. Still, Battles had wanted Waycross to marry Ivy, to make a respectable woman out of her. That probably meant especially much to old Jake since his only son, Cass Battles, was a known carouser, drunk, and whore monger who rarely did a lick of work anywhere at Anchor. That Cass was constantly in need of being bailed out of jails across all of Wyoming was an embarrassment to his proud old father, and had been practically since Cass had graduated from rubber pants.

Young Waycross was mild-mannered, but Jake Battles had pushed him over the edge and into several shouting matches others had witnessed. Battles had been uncommonly good at that sort of thing. Ty had been waiting for that powder keg over there to explode, but he certainly hadn't thought the explosion would entail murder. Waycross, a quiet, solitary soul who preferred the company of horses over that of men—but not women, apparently—had a known distaste for firearms and only carried an old carbine in his saddle boot for the wolves, grizzly bears, and rattlesnakes he often ran into on his notorious solo rides throughout his adopted and beloved Bear Paw Mountains—a remote range that served his need for solitude.

For a living, he gentled and trained horses. Waycross had never talked much about himself with Ty, even when he'd been working at the Powderhorn, but Ty had heard, probably from MacKenna, that he was originally from somewhere in Montana.

"Still, he's no killer, Con," Ty insisted. Despite Brandon's betrayal of MacKenna, Ty could not be convinced that Brandon Waycross was a killer. The boy he knew was a misfit, but not in a dangerous way. Hell, the boy was a lover and a poet. He was a near-recluse and a natural bronc gentler. He had a way with horses as he did with women. Before he'd betrayed MacKenna, Ty had hired him here at the Powderhorn to work with Matt on a dozen half-wild horses Ty had bought from a Colorado rancher, intending to make them plug ponies, or good ranch horses, and then turn around and sell them for a profit. Young Waycross and Matt had done just that.

That had been before young Waycross, undisciplined, moody, and half-wild himself, had betrayed MacKenna with Ivy Battles.

Ty had found himself wishing he could hate the boy for MacKenna's sake. But he hadn't been able to. The kid was likeable even at his worst. At his worst, he tortured himself even more than the people he hurt. Brandon was his own worst enemy, always at odds with himself, always blundering into one nasty situation after another.

MacKenna hadn't been able to hate him, either, for what he'd done to her. In fact, it was all too obvious to Ty that his oldest daughter still loved the roguish young horse-breaker/poet that was Brandon Waycross.

"I never pegged him for a killer, either," Stalcup said. "Lazy and infuriating, more wanting to make love to young women than put in a good day's work at the ranch." He cast a knowing look at MacKenna, who flushed and turned away. "Last night, though, I saw another side to him."

"So, you're out hunting him . . ." Ty glanced at the dozen or so other armed riders sitting behind Stalcup.

"Yessir."

"What're you gonna do once you find him?"

Stalcup shrugged. "I don't know. If he doesn't put up a fight, I guess we'll take him to town. Turn him over to the marshal. That'd be the legal way to do it, right?"

Ty looked deeply into the foreman's eyes. He

50

didn't believe the man. Stalcup was every bit as hard and tough and, yes, sometimes even as mean as old Jake Battles had been. But it often took a man like Battles and Stalcup to survive out here, this far off the beaten path, as long as they had. With as much range as they had, as well—a good twenty thousand acres of prime graze to the west and north of Ty's Powderhorn.

Battles and his own father, both greedy and power hungry, had established the Anchor out here when these mountains were still swarming with wolf-wild Indians. This was back when those tribes would as soon kill a white man in their territory as look at their cattle. Only men like Battles and his foreman, Stalcup, every bit as tough as the Indians they'd once fought, had survived here in the old days.

Ty didn't think for one minute that when Stalcup found Brandon Waycross he wouldn't shoot him or hang him. Stalcup rode for Battles' brand, and now with old Jake dead, Stalcup's own future, as well as the futures of all of the men sitting their horses behind him, were in question. Cass was old enough to take over, but Cass was notoriously useless. He and Ivy would likely have to sell, or they'd run the Anchor into the ground by way of mismanagement.

Ivy was a known flirt whom Jake had tried his best to manage by confining her to the house. Obviously, as per her relationship with Brandon

Waycross, that hadn't worked. Ivy was no more of a ranch superintendent than her fun- and woman-loving brother was.

With Battles dead, Anchor was a rudderless ship.

"We'll be on our way now, Brannigan," Stalcup said, pinching his hat brim to the rancher. "You let us know if you see Waycross, will you? I'd sure appreciate it." He gave his chin a dark, meaningful dip.

I bet you would, Ty thought, fingering his chin.

Stalcup neck-reined his horse around, beckoned to his men, and the wolf-like pack went galloping back out through the open gate and the Powderhorn portal.

MacKenna came running up the porch steps, her eyes bright with emotion, and threw her arms around her father. "Brandon didn't do it, Pa. I know he didn't do it." She pulled away and looked into Ty's eyes. "You have to do something!"

CHAPTER 5

"I have to admit I don't much care for Stalcup's jackals hunting that young man like he's some kind of animal, but I don't know that there's much I can do about it, sweetheart," Ty said, holding his daughter close against him with his one good arm. "I'm taking that dead bushwhacker to town tomorrow. I'll tell Chris Southern about Battle's murder. Since he's also a deputy sheriff, Chris will have jurisdiction over the matter and will likely ride out to investigate. I'll join him. I have to say, though, it doesn't look good."

"He was seen riding away from Mr. Battles' body," Matt said. He was still standing in the yard, beside Gregory. Rollie was standing up on his hind legs, his front paws on Gregory's chest, and Gregory was absently scratching the dog's ears. Rollie seemed to favor the youngest Brannigan boy, and Gregory returned the affection.

"That's what Stalcup says!" MacKenna fired back at her older brother.

"Said he was riding away like his horse had tin cans tied to its tail!" added Gregory with too much excitement.

"Gregory, you hush!" MacKenna remonstrated her younger brother, who drew his mouth corners down in chagrin as he continued to scratch Rollie's ears.

"Don't worry, honey," Ty said, giving his daughter an extra, reassuring squeeze, "Chris and I'll look into it tomorrow."

"Brandon might be dead by then." MacKenna released her father and turned wearily away. "The way those men looked, when they find him, they intend to hang—"

She stopped abruptly, her back to her father now.

"What is it, sweetheart?" Ty asked, placing a hand on her shoulder.

MacKenna hesitated. Frowning curiously, both Matt and Gregory turned their heads to follow their sister's gaze toward the opposite side of the ranch yard. With his back to her, Ty couldn't be sure, but she appeared to be gazing toward the blacksmith shop.

MacKenna glanced over her shoulder at him, shook her head. "Nothing. Nothing at all." She feigned a slight smile. "I was just thinking about Brandon is all. And Stalcup's jackals. I think I'm going to go curry the appy to distract myself." She glanced at her younger sister who sat on the steps beside where MacKenna stood with Ty.

Carolyn was gazing up at MacKenna with concern. MacKenna was not the only Brannigan daughter whose heart had been stolen by Brandon

Waycross. "Carolyn, you go in and help Ma. I'll be in shortly."

Carolyn drew her mouth corners down, sighed, and slapped her knees as she pushed to her feet. "All right. But I'm worried about him now, too!" The younger Brannigan daughter stomped into the house with an exaggerated show of emotion, as was her way.

"I'm gonna finish up in the barn," Gregory said, and started striding back toward where he'd left the wheelbarrow and pitchfork, adjusting the suspenders on his heavy shoulders. Wagging his tail, Rollie followed close on the boy's heels. "This has been one heck of a distracting afternoon," he continued. "First Pa's shot and then we find out Mr. Battles is dead. How's a fella supposed to get his chores done!" He threw his big hands out and let them flop back down against his denim-clad thighs.

MacKenna turned to Ty. "How's the arm, Pa?"

He raised his left arm, smiled. "Good as new."

"Does it hurt just awful?"

"It hurts, but I'll live. I'm gonna go in and have a little of that medicine you brought down, an' tell your mother about Jake Battles. Tend the appy then come on inside, honey. Your mother needs your help, too."

"I will, Pa."

Brannigan started for the door. He didn't reach it before the door opened, and Beatriz stepped out. She glanced from him to MacKenna and back again, her eyes dark with portent.

Obviously, Beatriz had heard.

When her parents had gone into the house, MacKenna cast her gaze to the hillside beyond and above the blacksmith shop on the opposite side of the yard from the main lodge, whose porch steps she was standing on now. When she'd turned away from her father a few moments ago, she'd glimpsed what she could have sworn had been the tail of a horse give a switch just before it had disappeared into a pine copse at the top of the low bluff behind the blacksmith shop.

Her heart had fluttered hopefully.

It still was . . .

Could Brandon be up there?

Maybe he was following Stalcup's men, keeping an eye on them and staying two steps ahead of them. Or behind them, as the case may be. Brandon was not only smarter than almost any other man MacKenna knew except maybe her father, he was cagey, as well. Unconsciously, MacKenna twisted her mouth into a fleeting smirk. She wouldn't put it past her former beau to have outfoxed Stalcup's riders.

She moved off down the porch steps and into the yard, casting a cautious glance at the house behind her, making sure no one was watching her through the windows on either side of the stout log door. Seeing no one, she hurried across the yard and passed through the break between the blacksmith shop and the breaking corral. She quickened her pace as she continued walking past haystacks then through cedars and high, tan bromegrass fringing the edge of the yard.

Casting another wary look behind her, she started climbing the bluff.

Several more times as she climbed, she looked at the house behind her and then at the barn where Gregory worked. Matt was in the stable, tending to the dead man and the dead man's horse.

So far, so good.

She kept climbing and then slipped into the concealment of the pines into which she'd seen, or at least thought she'd seen, the horse disappear. As she walked up the slope, wending her way through the pines, she scoured the ground with her gaze. She stopped suddenly, her heart quickening, then dropped to a knee and traced the print of a shod horse hoof with her right index finger.

Suddenly having the sensation that she wasn't alone, she looked up and gasped. Brandon Waycross sat roughly twenty feet farther up the slope, on a large, pale rock. He had his elbows on his knees, and he was twisting a long bromegrass stalk between his black-gloved hands.

He wore his customary low-crowned gray hat, red Spanish-style shirt with fancy green stitching down the front, black denim jeans under black, brush-scarred, bull hide chaps, and a long, green silk neckerchief. Brandon did not carry a sidearm—he'd said that carrying one only caused a man to have to use it—but MacKenna saw the old Winchester carbine sheathed on the beautiful pinto stallion standing behind and to Brandon's right, reins trailing to the ground.

"I didn't kill Battles," he said, staring expressionlessly down at MacKenna. He was darkly handsome, almost pretty in a feminine way. He had long, wavy, rich, auburn hair, and his eyes were the most striking amber. They fairly glowed like the sunshine of dusk reflecting off a mountain lake.

MacKenna felt her breath catch in her throat. He'd broken her heart terribly. It was as though he'd stuck a rusty knife between her ribs. Most of the time, her heart still felt impaled by that rusty blade. Still, she couldn't help but love him. She realized it now, seeing him after two months apart, now more than ever. It unsettled her.

Slowly, MacKenna walked toward her former beau, climbing the slope toward where he sat on the rock beyond the pines, in a strip of late afternoon sunlight. As she drew within ten feet of the young man whom she'd thought she would marry though he and she had never discussed it but had only professed their love for each other, she said, "What happened?"

"I was called in from the bunkhouse last night to have supper with Battles and Ivy. We were having a drink in the old man's office and he was tellin' me what he expected of me after Ivy and I married . . . what he expected of me on the ranch. He wanted me to earn the status of top hand and, since Stalcup's getting old, in a year or two he wanted me to graduate to foreman. I told him I wasn't no top hand and much less a foreman. I gentled horses. That got him all riled up and he went after me again—you know for . . ."

"Yes."

"He told me I wasn't good enough to marry Ivy, he didn't care whose 'bun was in her oven'—his exact words!—and then Ivy started screaming and crying, and Battles stormed out of the house. I got Ivy settled down and, since the night was ruined before it even got started, I decided to ride into the country, fort up for the night in the high-and-rocky. I wasn't far from the ranch when I heard a rifle shot. It came from just over that bluff on the north side of the house, by Arapaho Creek. I rode over to investigate and found Battles lyin' dead by the creek, belly down, a bullet in his back."

MacKenna raised her hand to her mouth.

Young Waycross continued. "I hear a horse and rider galloping toward me, from the direction of the yard. I look up and who do you think it is? It's Stalcup himself! He yells and claws iron and

I got the hell out of there. I could tell he meant business, and you know Stalcup well enough to know what kind of business, so, well . . . I don't know . . . I guess I panicked. I rode hell for leather out of there.

"A few minutes later, I reined up on a divide and see Battles' whole damn crew galloping after me. So, I high tailed it, holed up in the mountains overnight. I been followin' them followin' me, covering my trail. I didn't want them to corner me in town. They'd likely hang me for sure, and there wouldn't be anything old Chris Southern could do about it, neither."

Brandon swiped his hat off his head and whipped it angrily against his knee. "Dammit, anyway, MacKenna—my whole life has gone to hell!"

"And whose fault is that?" MacKenna couldn't help firing tartly back at him.

Brandon set his hat back on his head and looked up at her gravely. "It's mine. I know that. I know what you're thinking. I deserve what I get. After betraying you with Ivy. And you're right."

"That's not what I was thinking." MacKenna squatted on her haunches, rested her elbows on her chap-clad thighs, and set her hand on Brandon's knee. "Who do you think killed him?"

"I have no idea."

"You didn't see anyone else around the creek?"

"No one. By the time I got there, it was just me

and old Battles out there. They'll hang me for sure."

"Pa's gonna look into it tomorrow. He's going to go to town and fetch Marshal Southern, and they'll ride out to Anchor, probably look around where you found Mr. Battles and talk to the hands."

"Good luck talkin' to the so-called hands. They're mostly all hard-tailed gunslingers from Texas and Oklahoma. Old Battles hired 'em for their gun savvy. You don't talk to men like that, MacKenna." Young Waycross lowered his head, gave a weary sigh, and scrubbed the back of his neck with a gloved hand. "I came here hopin' to catch you alone." He gazed directly into her eyes. "I needed to tell you I didn't do it. I didn't kill Mr. Battles!"

"I know you didn't. You couldn't."

"Didn't like the man," Waycross said, chuckling darkly and shaking his head. "But I didn't kill him."

"I know you didn't, Brandon. Pa will help."

Waycross looked at MacKenna, blinked slowly, his mouth corners lifting a sad smile. "You're good people, you Brannigans. To help me after . . ."

"You broke my heart, Brandon. You truly did. But that doesn't mean I want you to hang for a murder you didn't commit."

He nodded, gave that vague little half-smile

again. "Like I said, you're good people, you Brannigans. If it means anything for you to hear me say it, I kick myself every day for what I did. It's you I—"

"No!" MacKenna threw up her hands and turned her head to one side. "I don't want to hear that!" She paused, her heart racing, her blood churning hotly through her veins. She turned her head forward to face the young horse gentler again. "You're marrying Ivy, so you love her, Brandon. And you love that child. It's yours. It rips my heart out to hear myself say that, but the child is yours and Ivy is yours. We're finished."

Brandon sighed and laced his hands together between his spread knees. He looked down, nodding, contrite.

Neither one said anything for nearly a full minute, and then MacKenna said, "Where will you spend the night? In the mountains again?"

"I reckon. Where else? I got nowhere to go."

"You should turn yourself in, you know. Tell Southern your side of the story. Let Southern protect you."

"It'd be my word against Stalcup's. Southern would turn the key on me. I'd go insane, locked up. I gotta . . ." Brandon looked toward the misty, dramatic peaks of the Wind Rivers and then up at the sky, narrowing one eye. "I gotta be out here . . . in the mountains." He glanced over his shoulder at the handsome pinto. "With ol' Rowdy."

The horse looked at him and switched its tail.

MacKenna studied young Waycross. Sympathy for his plight tempered her anger and heartbreak. He was like some wild thing. Some half-simple, tender-hearted wild thing. Yet he read and wrote poetry, having taught himself how to read and write since, having been orphaned at six years old in Arizona Territory, he'd had no opportunity to go to school. And he gentled horses. In fact, he was considered one of the top five best horse gentlers in this part of Wyoming.

Brandon could have worked anywhere, on any ranch for ranchers who could have paid him much more than what ranchers in the Bear Paws could afford or were willing to pay. But he'd ridden through this remote Bear Paw Mountain country four years ago, and the country had spoken to him, it had captured his heart, made his spirit come alive, so he'd stayed and gentled horses for half what he could have earned elsewhere.

Some would call him a romantic fool, and maybe he was. But he'd captured MacKenna's heart. Probably in the same way he'd captured Ivy Battles' heart, which wasn't fair, but there you had it. Despite what he'd done, MacKenna couldn't hate him.

"Tell me why you did it, why you turned to

Ivy," MacKenna said at last, forlornly, frowning at him curiously. She hated the heartbreak she heard in her voice. "You told me you loved me, Brandon."

CHAPTER 6

"Why Ivy? Good question, MacKenna."

Waycross chuckled dryly, shook his head. "I suppose I could tell you I turned to Ivy because she brought me lemonade every afternoon when I was gentling horses for her father. She'd stay and chat . . . and we'd laugh and kid each other . . . sometimes for a long time, especially when the old man and Stalcup weren't around. She made sure she looked nice when she strolled out to the corral. Put on a nice dress, wore ribbons in her hair."

"She's a pretty girl, Ivy."

"That wasn't the reason I turned to her, though. Not the whole reason, anyway."

"What, then?" MacKenna prodded.

"To be honest, I think I was afraid of settling down. Of feelin' bound to one ranch . . . maybe even to just one girl." Brandon drew a deep breath, let it out heavily. "MacKenna, you're just about as perfect as a girl could be. Your family is about as perfect as a family could be. I lost my family early on. I wasn't sure how to be in one. I think I was a little intimidated. That's no excuse; it's a reason. It's my reason, anyway."

"It's not a very good one."

"I don't have a good one. I'm sorry I hurt you.

If there was any way I could go back and undo what I've done . . . not only because Ivy's in the family way, either . . . I would. Please, believe me."

He looked up at MacKenna looking skeptically down at him, her arms crossed on her chest, one foot planted forward and out, as though with skepticism of his explanation. A very thin sheen of emotion shone in his eyes. MacKenna didn't think he was faking it, because he looked away quickly, flushing as though embarrassed. She also didn't think it was in Brandon Waycross to fake anything. He was a deeply flawed young man, but at least he was genuine.

"All right," MacKenna said at last, grinding the heel of her forward boot into the ground, turning the toe from left to right and back again.

Brandon rose from the rock, placed a hand on her arm. "Do you forgive me?"

"No." MacKenna shook her head. "I'm sorry, I can't. And I don't think I should. What you did was selfish and heartless. So, no, I can't forgive you. I'll never forgive you." She backed away from him, adding, "I hope everything works out as best as it can for you, though, Brandon. I hope my father and Marshal Southern can help. Good night."

She turned and started walking back down the bluff and into the trees. When she was halfway down the bluff, she glanced over her shoulder to see him standing there, gazing down at her, a sad and miserable expression on his handsome face. She knew it was not to her credit that his sadness was somehow satisfying to her. At least, he felt as badly about what he did as she did. At least, he seemed to. That was something, anyway. And she'd learned her lesson to not put too much trust in romantic young men.

Romantic they might be, but they were still men. Men would hurt you. She made a mental note of that for future reference.

When she glanced over her shoulder once more, Brandon and the pinto were gone.

MacKenna gained the base of the bluff and stopped abruptly. Her father stood before her, in the mouth of the break between the blacksmith shop and the breaking corral. Tynan Brannigan stood with his muscular arms crossed on his broad chest, his mule-eared boots spread a little more than shoulder-width apart. Even pushing sixty, he was a formidable figure, large and broad-shouldered, giving to his daughter even after he'd been shot earlier in the day a sense of great masculine power tempered by a kind and gentle spirit.

His broad, chiseled face was deeply tanned, his upper lip mantled by a thick, strawberry-blond, Dragoon-style mustache. His thick, curly hair, a shade lighter than his mustache and stitched with only a little gray, hung down past his shirt collar.

Tynan Brannigan was the handsome, thick-haired, hazel-eyed frontiersman MacKenna was proud to call the man who'd sired and raised her.

"Pa, I . . ."

Ty had put on a new tunic, this one hickory, and he'd knotted a red bandanna around his neck. His wounded arm was in a clean white sling. Suspenders held his buckskin pants up on his lean hips. He poked the brim of his high-crowned, brown Stetson up off his forehead, glanced toward the top of the butte above and behind his daughter, and said, "How's he doing?"

MacKenna frowned. "How . . . did . . . you . . . ?"

"I figured he'd come. Not this soon. I sent your sister to fetch you from the barn, but Carolyn said you weren't out there. Then I saw you come down out of the pines. It was him, wasn't it? Brandon."

MacKenna strode forward, crossed her arms on her chest again, and nodded. "Yes."

"How is he?"

"He's scared."

"He should be."

"He needs your help."

"Did you tell him I'd do what I could?"

"Yes, but I'm worried about him."

"He doesn't deserve your worry."

"Maybe not, but he doesn't deserve to hang for a crime he didn't commit, either."

"Do you believe he didn't do it?"

"Yes." MacKenna frowned. "Don't you?"

"No." Ty wagged his head. "The boy I knew wasn't capable of murder, but, then, I didn't think he was capable of betraying my daughter, either."

"He didn't kill Mr. Battles, Pa. I promise you he didn't."

"MacKenna, you don't know him the way you thought you did. That should be obvious to you by now."

She frowned pensively and stared off, feeling the cooling evening breeze caress her cheeks and slide her hair against her neck. Slowly, she nodded and turned back to her father. "You're right. I shouldn't be so gullible. I just found myself believing him again after he lied to me in the worst way a man can ever lie to a girl!"

She lowered her head and sobbed.

Ty stepped forward, wrapped his good arm around her, hugged her. "Now, now, Mack."

She looked up at him, studied him through a glaze of tears that reflected the dulling rays of the setting sun. "You'd never do anything like that to Ma, would you?"

"No, I wouldn't." Ty squeezed her tighter and planted a kiss on her temple. "But only because she'd beat me silly with a rolling pin and horse whip me to boot!"

MacKenna choked out a laugh, shuddering against her father's broad chest.

"Come on, my girl—supper's ready. If we don't get back to the house soon, we're both gonna get stuck washing dishes."

"All right, Pa," MacKenna said through another emotional chuckle.

Keeping his arm around her, Ty turned them both around and they walked back through the break between the blacksmith shop and the breaking corral. Cool, blue shadows stretched across the yard now, and a mourning dove cooed softly, lowering a gentleness over the previously tumultuous ranch yard.

As they walked back into the yard, MacKenna looked toward the house and saw her pretty, dark-haired mother standing on the porch, holding a folded blanket against her chest. Watching her husband and oldest daughter walk toward her, Beatriz canted her head to one side and frowned sympathetically at her obviously distraught daughter. As Ty and MacKenna climbed the porch steps, arm in arm, Beatriz clucked her tongue and unfolded the blanket and held it out.

As MacKenna and her father gained the top of the porch, Beatriz wrapped the blanket around MacKenna's shoulders, hugging her close against her and leading her through the lodge's open door and inside.

Behind them, Ty stopped and turned back around to face the ranch yard. He cast his gaze above and beyond the blacksmith shop, staring with a pensive expression toward the top of the butte where his daughter had met the man who'd betrayed her.

To say that the rancher felt conflicted about Brandon Waycross would be an understatement. Still, he'd look into Jake Battles' murder. If Brandon had killed the man, he deserved to hang. But if he didn't kill Battles, he did not deserve to hang though not long ago Ty had wanted to hang the kid himself from the nearest cottonwood.

There was still enough of the old lawman in Ty Brannigan to make guilt or innocence matter.

He gave a deep, ragged sigh, winced at the lingering raw ache in his bullet-plundered arm, and headed back into the house. He'd give his attention to his family for the rest of the evening.

Tomorrow, he'd haul the dead bushwhacker to town, try to find out who he was, and look into the matter of Brandon Waycross.

Despite a few furtive sips of his inherited who-hit-John from the bottle he secretly sequestered beneath his and Beatriz's bed, Ty had trouble sleeping. The whiskey helped but it was still hard to get comfortable enough to let slumber overtake him.

Lying there in the dark, a puzzling sense of apprehension grew in him. He frowned up at the ceiling, pricking his ears to listen to the night outside the house and then lifting his head from the pillow and twisting a look out the window behind him, sliding the curtains apart with his right hand.

A one-quarter moon cast blue shadows across the yard. In that weak, pearlescent light, he could see nothing out of the ordinary. The only sound was the occasional mournful wail of a distant coyote. Once he heard the eerie screech of an owl making a kill but then, after the echoes had dwindled, there was only the soft rustling sound of the breeze playing under the lodge's eaves, the scratching of a pine bough against the outside wall and, in the room across the hall, the muttering of Gregory in his sleep.

Often the boy muttered and chuckled in his sleep. So often, in fact, that the rest of the family had become inured to it.

Ty rolled onto his back, rested his right arm on his forehead, and studied the dark ceiling as if searching there for the answer to his strange malaise. He'd felt this way before for no apparent reason, back when he'd been a lawman and trouble was on the lurk. Even when he hadn't heard or seen anything threatening, occasionally his sixth sense would kick in and alert him to some badman trying to line up the beads of a rifle on him or furtively approaching his remote camp to shoot him in his sleep.

The feeling now might only be nerves carried over from earlier in the day when God knew enough trouble had come up to make anyone tense. That's probably what this was. Still, the feeling was too strong to ignore.

He glanced over at Beatriz lying curled on her side, her back to him, snoring very softly into her pillow. Slowly and quietly—he didn't want to awaken and worry her—he slid his covers back and dropped his bare feet to the floor. His clothes lay over the back of a brocade chair just beyond the night table on his side of the bed. He pulled on over his balbriggans his buckskin pants, shirt, and socks, then grabbed his Henry repeater from where it always resided at night, in the corner by the door. He grabbed his boots and walked silently, making the floor creak only a little under his two-hundred-plus pounds, through and out the door, drawing the door closed with a soft latch click behind him.

Hearing Gregory mutter in his sleep about how he'd caught the bigger fish—probably arguing with his fishing buddy, Dorsey Flynn—Ty made his way through the hall between the closed doors of his sleeping brood and down the stairs and into the foyer. He paused to step into his boots and don his hat.

Slowly and quietly again, he opened the door, stepped out, and drew the door closed behind him. Just after the latching bolt clicked, one of the horses in the main corral gave a low warning whicker. Hooves drummed and Ty could see the silhouettes of one of the horses running circles around the corral then stopping abruptly and lifting its long snout, which it pointed toward the same butte on which MacKenna had met Brandon Waycross.

Ty walked across the porch and stopped at the top of the steps, continuing to cast his gaze up the butte humping up against the one-quarter moon and the stars, a shadowy mass fringed with trees. In one of those tree fringes, a light flickered.

Orange light.

Firelight.

Someone had built a campfire up there.

Brandon Waycross?

Ty racked a round into the Henry's chamber, off-cocked the hammer, walked down the porch steps, and started across the yard toward the butte and the fire. He didn't think it was Brandon up there. The feeling of unease grew stronger inside him, making his pulse quicken.

No, he sensed danger up there. Brandon was no danger to him or his family. Brandon needed Ty now.

No, this was a trouble of a different caliber altogether, or that sixth sense of his had been corrupted and he was just becoming a nervous old man.

He'd find out soon enough.

CHAPTER 7

Staying as low to the ground as possible, Ty climbed the bluff.

He tried to stay out of the pale light slanting down from the high-kiting moon quartering in the sky to his right.

Steadily, the orange light of the fire grew larger above and before him. Soon, the smell of burning pine touched his nostrils, and he could hear the snapping and crackling of the flames.

When he came within fifty feet of where the fire burned in a slight clearing in the pines, roughly three-quarters of the way up from the bottom of the bluff, he slowed his pace, weaving between the pines, not looking directly at the flames growing before him because he didn't want to compromise his night vision. He knew the fire could very well be a trap. A man or men could be watching his approach, waiting to draw a bead on him.

Thirty feet from the fire, he stopped behind a broad Ponderosa and peered around its left side and into the camp before him. He could see nothing but the flames. No men sat around it. No gear was strewn around it, either.

There appeared no camp here. Only the fire abandoned by whoever had started it.

Slowly, staying out of the circle of flickering orange firelight, not wanting either himself or the Henry he held in his right hand, down low along his leg, to be revealed by the light, he circled the fire. As he continued to circle, setting each foot down quietly, tension was a dull knife embedded between his shoulder blades.

He peered into the shadows behind rocks, pines, occasional box elders, and cedars, sliding pine boughs aside with the Henry's barrel.

Nothing. No men. No sign of men.

Gradually, as the flames consumed the several blowdown branches that had been stood up and slanted together in a circle, fueling it, the orange light dwindled and the darkness slid closer around where the fire had been built in a ring of pale stones.

Ty circled the fire twice with painstaking slowness, squeezing the Henry's neck in his right hand, his left arm hanging at his side. He'd taken the sling off when he'd gone to bed and had not put it on when he'd risen. He might need both hands tonight. He'd bring the left one up, misery be damned, if he needed it to steady his aim with the rifle.

As the fire continued to burn down, he moved closer to it until, still concealed by the shadows sliding more tightly around it, he shouldered up to a boulder and stood gazing down at the now-feeble flames making soft crackling sounds, pale smoke skeining up from the pile of charred wood and gray ash.

The dying light glinted off something metallic on a log on the opposite side of the fire from Ty. He frowned, trying to get a better look at the object but snapped his head up when he heard a sound muffled by distance. It had come from uphill, maybe from the top of the bluff.

It came again, clearer this time—a man's laugh.

Another man said something in a mocking tone, chuckled, and then hooves drummed, dwindling quickly into the distance, down the other side of the bluff. Two or three riders, Ty judged.

What in holy blazes . . . ?

When the hoof thuds had faded to silence and the fire was only a small, copper glow in the mounded ash in the ring of stones, Ty stepped forward and around the near-dead fire. He crouched over the object that had a minute ago caught the firelight. He took his Henry in his left hand, reached down toward the log with his right, and pinched the object between his right thumb and index finger.

He held it up to his face.

A .44-caliber bullet. It had been purposefully placed on the log, casing down, bullet up.

A threat.

Ty closed his hand around the bullet, squeezed, his heart thudding slowly, anxiously. He looked down at the fire that was now three, fast-dying, firefly-like sparks.

He'd been ambushed earlier, then lured up here just now to be threatened with a bullet.

Someone was toying with him.

Who?

Someone was after him. Obviously, the man who'd ambushed him had been after him. Who else?

And why?

Old enemies. Had to be.

He cursed softly, opened his palm to gaze down at the bullet again. He dropped it into his pocket and began striding back down the bluff. Despite his lack of sleep, he wished dawn would hurry. He was more eager than ever to haul the dead man to town and to try to find out who he was . . . and who his partners—if the men who'd been here tonight were his partners—might be . . .

"Can't tell you who he is, but I saw him in town the other day with three others, Ty," said Warknife Town Marshal Chris Southern around nine o'clock the next morning.

He and Ty stood on Wyoming Avenue, Warknife's main street, outside Southern's wood-frame office near the Post Office and the Western Union office. Southern, a few years older than Ty, was lean, sharp-featured, and sun-seasoned with short gray hair beneath his gray Stetson, and

78

a trimmed gray mustache mantling his upper lip. His eyes, too, were gray. He wore a blue wool shirt under a corduroy jacket, a string tie, black whipcord trousers, polished black leather boots, and a wide black leather belt with a big, silver buckle.

He held a half-smoked quirley in his left hand, pinched between his thumb and index finger.

Southern had been the lawman here in Warknife for the past five years. A former rancher who'd nearly lost his shirt when the bottom had dropped out of the beef market nearly fifteen years ago, he was a good-natured, garrulous sort who also commanded respect. He was a tough old cowboy, and with the help of two younger deputies, he kept Warknife on a short leash.

Southern had crouched and lifted up the dead man's head by his hair to get a look at his face. Now he let the head slap back down against the belly of the dead man's roan.

"Three others, you say?" Ty asked, remembering the men on the butte the previous night.

"Yes, three. Tough nuts, especially their leader. I haven't seen 'em after I first saw 'em in the Longhorn Saloon the other night. They were drunk and getting into it with the Longhorn's new madame over one of her pleasure girls. Seemed as though the girl had had a previous run-in with the three and wasn't inclined to venture upstairs with them again. I got 'em settled down, but they were drunk and riled. It helped I had good Ol' Suzy with me, like I usually do."

Southern gave a devilish, heavy-lidded grin. "Suzy made an impression."

Ty smiled. "Suzy will do that."

Southern gave a smoker's husky chuckle and took a deep drag off the quirley. He was one of those smokers who made smoking appear a sensuous, almost erotic experience.

Suzy was Southern's double-barrel, ten-gauge shotgun. Most folks in the area knew about Southern and Ol' Suzy's cozy relationship. During his tenure as town marshal, Southern had blasted a half-dozen men to hell and gone with Ol' Suzy. When you blast a man with a ten-gauge, word of that sort of mess gets around. It makes men kind of squirrely when they find themselves in the same saloon or gambling parlor with Southern and his legendary ten-gauge, which he usually laid out on the table before him for all to see, beside the ever-present, hand-rolled quirley smoldering in an ashtray.

"What'd these other three jakes look like?" Ty asked the marshal.

"They looked alike. Nothin' like this fancy-Dan here in his gambler's garb. Two were big, beefy, moon-faced men. One was more average framed but with the same moon face and long hair. They were sort of Mex lookin'. Brothers, I'd say. The biggest of the three was bearded. He had a long scar running down from outside his left eye to the corner of his mouth."

Southern traced the scar's course on his own face with his finger.

"Looked like someone hacked him up pretty good. He was the main one the whore didn't want to go upstairs with. He was the most belligerent of the three though the one close to him in size was a close second. The smaller one was a little more subdued though he seemed to enjoy the big man's to-do with the doxie. Had a girlish sort of laugh, a little embarrassing."

"Hmm." Ty pondered the information. Not remembering any run-ins with three men fitting Southern's description, he said, "You haven't seen 'em around since the other day?"

"Not for the past two days, anyway." Southern frowned. "Any idea why this ugly little squirrel in the cheap duds was after you, Ty?"

Ty grimaced, shook his head. "No. It was bad, though, Chris. This time MacKenna was with me. We were out by Baldy Butte, watching a wild horse herd."

Southern stepped forward, concern showing on his face, and placed his hand on Ty's right shoulder. Beatriz had insisted Ty wear his wounded left arm in the cotton sling she'd fashioned from a pillowcase. The suspension helped with the pain and would likely make the wound heal faster, too.

"Is MacKenna all right?" Southern asked him.

Ty nodded. "You know MacKenna. She's wang tough." Mention of his eldest daughter reminded Ty of the trouble involving Brandon Waycross. "Bad news out at Anchor, Chris. Something else I needed to talk to you about."

"Oh?"

"Jake Battles is dead."

Southern lowered his hand from Ty's shoulder and widened his eyes in surprise. "Old Jake? *Dead?* I figured he was too mean to die. What happened?"

"Someone shot him in the back. Stalcup rode out to investigate and saw Brandon Waycross crouched over the body. When Waycross saw Stalcup, he mounted up and rode away fast."

"Brandon Waycross? Ty, I can't imagine that kid shooting anybody! I know he got crossways with Battles over . . . well, you know over what . . . but . . ."

"I can't imagine it, either. As mild as he is. Doesn't even carry a sidearm. But Stalcup can imagine it just fine. He and the entire Anchor roll are out scouring the mountains for Waycross, who showed up at the Powderhorn last night, talked to MacKenna. He holed up in the mountains the past two nights and is likely still on the run. Unless Stalcup caught up to him. Then he's probably low-hanging fruit on a cottonwood that otherwise don't *bear* fruit. I'm guessin' he's still on the run. He knows every nook and cranny of the Bear Paws. Loves those mountains, rides in them all the time. He probably knows that range as well as you and I."

"He should've come to town, told me the story. I would've kept him away from Stalcup. I swear Con's as mean an' ornery as Jake was."

"Yeah, well, he was taught by the best. Mac-Kenna said Waycross was afraid of being locked up."

"Well . . ." Southern took another drag from the quirley, dropped the butt in the dust, and ground it out with the toe of his boot. He frowned down at it uncertainly, blowing out the smoke through his mouth and nostrils, then looked at Ty.

"He's the wild-as-the-wind sort, ain't he? Can't say as I blame him for hating jail. I wouldn't cotton to it myself. I best ride out there an' get to the bottom of Jake's murder." The marshal shook his head, scowling. "Can't believe that old buzzard's gone. What the hell is gonna happen to the Anchor now? Ivy can't run it, and Cass— hell, he's never home. I heard Paul Buckman, the marshal over to Cutbank, has him locked up for pistol whipping a whiskey drummer he accused of cheating at High Low. Jake refused to make his bail."

"Cass's a bad one. I'd like to ride with you out to Anchor, Chris."

"I was gonna ask if you would. You were a lawman a lot longer than me."

"Not nice to remind a man of his age." Ty grinned.

Southern gave a rueful snort then absently toed the dead quirley butt in the street, pondering the killing of Jake Battles again, most likely. "Let me fetch Ol' Suzy an' my hoss, an' we'll—"

A female voice somewhere behind Ty cut him off with, "Mr. Brannigan! Oh, Mr. Brannigan!"

Ty turned to see a scantily clad young lady striding toward him along the boardwalk on the street's north side, just then moving under the awning over the boardwalk fronting the Crystal Palace Theater though there was nothing crystal about the place, only weathered wood and peeling paint. According to a large poster pinned to a cork board beside the front door, currently performing was PAWNEE BILL'S WILD WEST SHOW, with the subheading inside a large, black buffalo, THE ONLY GENUINE WILD WEST REENACTMENT TOURING THIS SEASON!

One of the several men standing on the board-walk fronting the place turned as the girl brushed past him, dropped his eyes to her derriere, and whistled with appreciation. The girl, holding a gauzy purple wrap around her pale, slender shoulders, long silver rings dangling from her ears and jouncing with her flaxen sausage curls, stepped off the boardwalk and into the street, approaching Ty and Southern. She wore little slippers and in addition to the see-through wrap, not much else except a very small black bustier, matching pantalets, and black fishnet stockings.

Her lower lip had been split, the cut now scabbed over. Her left eye was a little swollen and a sickly yellow color.

Ty was as male as any other man, and as his gaze swept the girl from head to toe and back up again, he felt a rare flush rise in his cheeks. He'd lawdogged in many craven frontier towns over the years and seeing a girl this girl's age so scantily clad hadn't bothered him until he'd started raising daughters of his own. The little whore couldn't have been much older than MacKenna. In fact, she might not have been as old as Mack.

Ty gave the wooly, fatherly eyeball to the men ogling her from behind, and they turned sheepishly away, chuckling self-consciously.

"Hello there, Miss," Ty said, pinching his hat brim to her. "What can I do you for?"

"Miss Hayes sent me to fetch you." The little blond raised a small, pale hand to shade her eyes against the climbing morning sun as she gazed up at the much taller man before her. "She'd like a word . . . ?"

Ty frowned. "Miss Hayes? I don't know a—"

"She said she knows you. Devon Hayes? She said to mention Abilene."

For a second or two, Ty thought he was going to fall in a heap. The street pitched around him, and the sun dimmed. Or maybe his vision dimmed.

Devon Hayes was a name from his distant past. One he'd never thought he'd ever hear again. A strange chill gripped him, the kind you get when a goose flies over your grave.

CHAPTER 8

Chris Southern's voice came as though from far away. "Ty? You all right, Ty?" The marshal stood before the rancher, slowly sliding a hand back and forth in front of Ty's face. "Ty? You've dang near turned as white as a sheet. You want me to fetch the sawbones?"

Gradually, Southern's voice had loudened in Ty's ears until he could hear him clearly now. His vision had clarified; Ty could see his old friend instead of a smudged image. A minute ago, he'd seen him as though through isinglass.

"I'm fine." Ty glanced around the marshal to see the little doxie gazing up at him skeptically. "Where is she?"

"The Longhorn. Has a suite upstairs. Follow me—I'll take you to her."

Ty looked at Southern, who eyed the rancher with open curiosity. "Chris, would you, uh . . . would you see to the . . . ?"

"You bet, I'll haul the bushwhacker over to the undertaker. Why don't I meet you over to the Longhorn in, say, a half hour?" Southern's expression turned hesitant, even more curious, uncertain. "Is that, uh . . . gonna be enough time, Ty?" he asked gently, furling his thick, gray brows.

"More than enough," Ty said curtly before turning to the doxie. "I'm right behind you, little girl."

The doxie swung around and Ty followed her up onto the boardwalk fronting the Crystal Palace and past the several men who'd ogled her a few minutes ago. Ty followed the girl, but he could only partly feel his feet touching the ground as he walked. He moved as though in a dream, stepping up onto and down from one boardwalk after another, passing folks he knew he should know but suddenly didn't recognize.

His mind had trundled back into the past. Way, way back . . . deep into a past he hadn't thought about in years. A past he'd never thought he'd plumb again. It was like dropping an anchor into a deep, dark lake that had no bottom, and somehow the anchor seemed to grow heavier and heavier as it sank, threatening to pull you down after it if you kept holding the rope.

Before he realized it, he'd followed the girl into the Longhorn's cool, dark shadows and past the bar on his left, behind which an aproned man with a handlebar mustache whom Ty knew he should know but could not put a name to just then was absently running a cloth in a swirling motion over the zinc bar top, glancing up and following Ty with his sheepishly curious gaze.

The rancher and the girl weaved their way through the tables, only a few of which were occupied this time of the day, most of the chairs tipped upside down on them. Three doxies including one half-breed and one very skinny colored one sat at one of the tables, sipping coffee and looking drowsy. They halted their desultory conversation and looked up at Ty with mute interest as he passed them.

He and the girl walked past the large open doorway, now dark, that led into the gambling part of the saloon and pleasure parlor, and then they started up the thickly carpeted stairs at the rear of the room, opposite the front door.

The Longhorn was a tony place with oil paintings and game trophies hanging on the lavishly papered walls, vases filled with bright, silk flowers mounted on pedestals. There was even an old conquistador's suit of armor, but Ty noted little of it as he followed the little doxie up the stairs and down the second story hall, stopping at the very last door at the hall's end, on its left side.

"This is her suite," the little doxie said, lifting a hand to indicate the door bearing a gold name plate in which "Devon Hayes" had been engraved. "I hope you have a good talk," she added thinly, maybe a little wisely, Ty vaguely noted before she swung around and walked away and into one of the rooms on the rancher's left, her door clicking back into place behind her.

Ty lifted his right hand. It was a bit of an effort;

it seemed heavy, as though made of lead. He closed his fist and turned his knuckles toward the door but before he could knock, the door opened suddenly.

"Hello, Ty." She smiled. "Been awhile."

"It's, um . . . yep. It sure has . . . Devon . . ." Ty's tongue felt swollen, making it hard to speak.

"Won't you come in?"

"I reckon that's why I'm here."

She smiled then turned sideways and waved her arm to indicate the room behind her—a parlor-like room with a fireplace and several fancy chairs and tables and a red velvet fainting couch running along the opposite wall, beneath a window letting in golden morning light that made the couch glow brightly. Almost too brightly to look at.

Ty stepped inside and removed his hat.

"Take a seat," she said, her voice sounding eerily familiar. "Anywhere. Would you like some coffee?"

He looked at her, frowning, unable to keep his surprise, his exasperation out of his eyes. She blinked slowly, lowered her chin, and a slight flush rose in her cheeks. "I've aged, I know."

How old was she now? Ty wondered. As he recalled, she was a few years older than Beatriz. Early to mid-forties. It showed in her face, but, like Beatriz, she was still a beautiful woman, long, curly red hair tumbling down over her

90

bare, pale, freckled shoulders. Her body, nicely revealed by the cream, low-cut silk gown she wore with a gauzy cream, see-through shawl, was that of an older woman, not the young beauty Ty remembered. Her bust and hips were fuller, of course. Still, she was lovely. Well-preserved, he supposed the saying was.

"I've aged, too."

"You have, I'm happy to see," Devon said, chuckling throatily, smiling up at him—that old, winning smile he remembered so well. "You're taller than I remember. Or did you grow . . . after we saw each other last?"

"Oh, I've grown." Ty patted his belly. "But not in that direction."

"You're lean. I'm the one whose grown in that direction."

It was time to stop the nonsensical chin wagging, as though their shared history was not complicated. And painful. Ty frowned at her, a little angry now as well as exasperated. He felt a little paranoid, suddenly, as though she were playing a trick on him, showing up here all these years later, when he was married. Happily married. Happily raising a family.

"What the hell are you doing here?"

"Ty, please, let's sit." Again, she indicated the chairs and fainting couch.

"I'll stand. Answer the question."

"I didn't follow you here, if that's what you're

thinking. I mean, I'd heard about you . . . in Cheyenne. I lived and worked there last, had my own place." By "place," Ty knew what she meant. "From overhearing idle conversation, I learned the legendary town tamer, Tynan Brannigan, was ranching in the Bear Paws. I did not come here because you were here. I came because I was given an opportunity to buy the Longhorn and to run the show here, so to speak."

Ty frowned. He'd heard that the Longhorn's previous owner, George Ellis, had put the place up for sale, but he'd never heard that it had sold nor who had bought it.

"I kept it a secret," Devon said. "I was going to be a silent partner and continue living and working in Cheyenne. I bought the Longhorn with an old friend, Jeff Legend. He should be here soon to help me run the place. I was going to stay in Cheyenne and let Jeff run the Longhorn by himself. Unfortunately, a fire burned me out and I had nowhere else to go." She shrugged. "So . . . I'm here . . . running the show."

"So, you're here . . . running the show."

"Ty, I didn't call you up here to have a row. In fact, I didn't intend to see you at all. I called you up here to discuss an entirely different matter."

"What entirely different matter?"

Devon stepped forward and placed her hand on his chest. "Your life is in danger."

Again, he scowled incredulously down at her. *"What?"*

"A few nights ago, two of my girls entertained some fairly brutish men. I kicked them out, but they returned the next night. Marshal Southern was here, and he managed to cow them, and they left. However, it came to my attention by one of the girls they patronized, Sara, the girl who fetched you, that she overheard them talking drunkenly about a man they'd come here to kill."

She pressed her hand more firmly against Ty's chest. "That man is you."

Ty stared down at her. However improbably the source of the information, things were beginning to line up. "I'll be damned."

It was Devon's turn to frown curiously, canting her head slightly to one side. "Were you aware . . . ?"

"My daughter and I were bushwhacked yesterday."

"Ah . . . thus the arm sling. I'd thought maybe you'd broken it."

"Flesh wound."

"I only learned of this last night, when Sara told me. Why she didn't mention it right away, I have no idea. These girls have a lot on their minds. I was just going to go over and inform the marshal, but then, coincidence of coincidences, I saw you standing on the street with him. Was the man . . . that dead man lying belly down across that horse . . . was he . . . ?"

"The man who attacked us, yes."

"What did he look like?"

"A ferret-faced man, late twenties, who fancied himself a gambler. Judging by appearances, anyway."

Devon drew a breath. "He was with the other three. The other three are considerably more rustic looking. I think they're all brothers or half-brothers or something."

"That's what Chris told me."

"According to Sara, while she pretended to be asleep to avoid more abuse—you probably saw her lip and eye—they sat around swilling whiskey. The one who fancied himself a gambler got to bragging about how the other three were only slowing him down and that he thought it would be easier if they stayed in town and let him take you down himself. Apparently, he also fancied himself handy with a gun. The others decided to let him go alone and placed bets on whether he would be successful or not."

"He wasn't."

"Lucky for you."

"Did Sara have any idea why they were after me in the first place?"

"No," Devon said, shaking her head. "But she could tell from the conversation that one—the big, bearded devil—had been harboring a grudge for years. He's why all four are here. It seems he really has it in for you, Ty."

Ty winced and turned to glance out the window, muttering to himself, "Then why in the hell did they only fool with me on that bluff last night . . . ?"

"What's that?"

"Nothing." Ty shook his head. "Never mind. Just thinking out loud. Thanks for the information. I'd best get going."

He set his hat on his head as he turned and reached for the doorknob.

"Ty!"

He glanced over his shoulder at her, frowning. She stared at him in wide-eyed, silent exasperation, her red lips parted as though she wanted to say something but couldn't find the words.

"What is it?"

She frowned, shaking her head. "Don't you . . . don't you want to know why I left . . . ?"

"Water under the bridge, Devon."

He opened the door and went out.

CHAPTER 9

"Tynan Brannigan, I've never known you to be so quiet," Marshal Chris Southern said when they were two miles south of Warknife following the trail that in turned followed the course of Whiskey Creek, which joined up with Indian Lodge Creek deeper into the mountains.

The first bullet-shaped buttes and sloping sandstone mesas of the Bear Paw Mountains lumped up ahead of them now as they rode. Meadowlarks and red-winged blackbirds piped in the brush along both sides of the trail.

The marshal's words jerked Ty out of his reverie. He glanced at his old friend with a sheepish smile. "Sorry, Chris. Just woolgatherin', I reckon."

"Are you gonna tell me who she is, or is it none of my business?"

Ty drew a deep breath, shrugged, let the breath out slow. "A friend from a long time ago."

"How long ago?"

"Abilene."

"Kansas?"

"Yep."

Southern studied him as they rode side by side on the two-track wagon trail. The Whiskey Creek trail was the main thoroughfare into and out of

96

the mountains. Finally, the marshal turned his head back forward and said, "All right—I ain't gonna pry. Curious as hell, but I ain't gonna pry!"

Ty glanced at him again and chuckled. "She and I were together before I met Beatriz. Devon Hayes sang at the Skylark Theater three nights a week. I attended one of the shows and was smitten. You have to understand, I was a much younger man, and I was single. I was thirty-four and never married. Married to the badge, I reckon, though I know that sounds maudlin as all hell. Well, I found some whiskey courage and sent a note to her dressing room one night, asking her to join me for a drink, and, to my surprise, she did. The next night, too. Till it got to be a habit."

Southern smiled over at him. "I think I'm getting the picture."

"I tumbled for her. I thought she tumbled for me. I asked her to marry me, and she accepted. Then, a month later, two weeks before we were to be married, she disappeared. I looked for her everywhere. I finally inquired at the train station. The ticket agent told me she'd bought a ticket for St. Louis earlier that day. She'd hopped the flier that had just pulled out of the station not ten minutes earlier."

Ty shook his head. "I wanted in the worst way to saddle a fresh horse and go after her, but I didn't do it. Pride, I guess. She'd obviously not felt about me the way I'd felt about her, so I let her go."

"Sorry to hear about that, Ty. Damned peculiar. And now here she is in Warknife. Just a coincidence?"

Ty nodded. "I think so. She had a place in Cheyenne that burned."

"I heard." Southern looked at him, brows arched. "Well, this morning did you get to the bottom of why she left?"

"Nope."

"Huh?" Southern asked in surprise.

"I don't care anymore, Chris. Those days are gone. I'm married to the woman I love, and I have a big, relatively happy family. It would, of course, be a whole lot happier if Brandon Waycross wasn't being hunted like a rabid wolf by Battles' men. MacKenna's worried sick about him."

Southern looked over at him again. "She can't still hold a flame for that boy, can she?"

"She can and she does."

Southern gave his head a hard wag. "I just wanna take that boy over my knee for MacKenna, Ty!"

"Believe me, I've considered it."

"Do you think he killed Battles?"

"I honestly don't know. If not, I hope we can find out who the real killer is before . . ."

Ty let his voice trail off. He and Southern

had just swung off onto the trail that an old, leaning wooden sign announced as the trail to J. R. BATTLES ANCHOR RANCH when a scream rose from just over the next rise straight off along the secondary trail threading a narrow coulee between brush-choked bluffs. They were in the Eagle Rock Country eight miles south of town, the large, shelving, sandstone and granite formation of Eagle Rock humping up steeply on their left. The turnoff to Ty's Powderhorn was a few miles back toward town and to the east of Whiskey Creek. His graze, much smaller than the venal Battles', abutted Battles' range.

"Whoa!" Ty checked his mount down.

So did Southern, who looked at Ty. "Tell me that was a bird's screech and not a girl's scream!"

As if in reply, the scream came again, louder and shriller this time. It was followed by the distant wail of, *"Please, don't hang him! Please, don't hang him!"*

"That was a girl!" Ty rammed spurs into his horse's flanks, and the blue roan, the second in his string behind the coyote dun, lunged into an instant, ground-eating gallop straight up the trail.

Southern followed suit and galloped up just off Ty's horse's right hip. As the old lawman rode crouched low in the saddle, the brim of his hat basted against his forehead by the wind, he leaned forward and slid Ol' Suzy from the scabbard strapped to the right side of his mount.

He rested the big, double-barrel gut shredder across the horn of his saddle.

Ty slid his sixteen-shot Henry repeater from its sheath, cocked it one handed as he rode, using the hand holding the reins, and off-cocked the hammer. As he and Southern shot up the next rise, crested it and started down the other side, cold snakes squirmed in Ty's gut.

Gun-hung men in cowboy garb were clumped up at the front of the long, low, shake-roofed log bunkhouse on the yard's right side. On the yard's opposite side sat Battles's surprisingly humble, neat, white, wood-frame house, which was flanked by the obligatory privy and buggy shed. The blades of the tin Gold Medal windmill standing between the house and the bunkhouse moved lazily in the slight wind, indifferent to the obvious chaos playing out near the bunkhouse. The Anchor men obviously had someone on the ground. Two or three were crouched over the man, and one was wielding a rope, the opposite end of which was held by one of the others.

At the same time, a brown-haired girl was on the ground near the windmill. That was Ivy Battles, Ty saw as he drew closer. She was clad in a dirty peach-colored day dress and she was trying to crawl away from her brother, Cass Battles, who had her by one ankle-booted foot. Facing the house, he had ahold of his sister's foot with one gloved hand and was trying to drag the screaming, wildly gesturing girl toward the house.

"Don't hang him, you devils! He didn't kill Pa! I know he didn't kill Pa!" Ivy screeched in her husky, raspy voice.

She turned onto her butt, pulling her one foot free of her brother's grip and driving her other foot up between Cass's legs, soundly connecting with his privates. Cass screamed, dropped his sister's ankle, and fell to his knees, bellowing, *"Bitch! Ah-oh, you little bitch, Ivy!"*

Ivy turned onto her belly, clambered to her feet, and ran toward where Ty, approaching with Southern through the open gate and the wooden portal, saw the Anchor men were knotting a hang rope around the head of Brandon Waycross. Young Waycross had lost his hat. His thick hair hung over his face. He sat back against the front of the bunkhouse, his hands apparently tied behind his back. His horse, a sleek pinto, was running broad circles around the yard and wildly shaking its head as though in aversion to the treatment of its rider.

Brandon grimaced as two men secured the noose around his neck while two others wrapped another riata around his feet, binding them tightly together. It appeared they meant to hang the kid from a ceiling beam poking out from beneath the roof's overhang and from which a tin water can hung with the handle of a tin dipper poking up out of it.

Con Stalcup, overseeing the procedure and not getting his hands dirty, turned his head and saw Ivy running toward him. He nudged the thick-set man standing beside him, and the thick-set man turned quickly, just in time to catch Ivy up in his arms and to start wrestling her back in the direction of where her brother remained on his knees, hands over his privates, barking viciously at his sister.

There was so much screaming and yelling that no one appeared to have seen Ty and Southern enter the yard until, his head turned toward the thick-set man and the girl, Stalcup saw them. The Anchor foreman turned full around and pulled his Colt .45 from the holster thonged low on his right thigh.

Chris Southern already had the drop on him, Ol' Suzy raised to his right shoulder, both rabbit ear hammers rocked back to full cock. His gray eyes were hard beneath arched, gray brows. "You think twice before you raise that hogleg, Con. If it comes up one inch, I'll blast a hole in you big enough to run a freight train through!"

Seeing the gut-shredder of legend bearing down on him, Stalcup winced, twitching his right brown eye and lifting the same left corner of his dark-mustached mouth. He held the .45 straight down along his right leg, opening and closing his gloved hand around the handle.

To get the other men's attention, Ty lifted the barrel of his Henry and snapped off three shots skyward, quickly pumping the cocking lever one-handed. Several of the men had turned to him and Southern but the others had been preoccupied with Brandon Waycross, one starting to take the slack out of the rope leading up and over the ceiling beam, causing Brandon to grimace and choke, his chin lifted sharply, cords of sinew straining out from his neck.

Ty barked, "You fellas hold it right there! Keep your weapons in their holsters. You with the rope—drop it!"

The man with the rope had turned to glare wide-eyed over his shoulder at Ty, keeping the rope in both of his gloved hands taut.

Ty snapped the Henry to his shoulder, aimed quickly, and shot the man with the rope through the pointed toe of his left boot. The man dropped the rope. As the hemp slackened, Brandon's chin lowered and the cords that had been protruding from his neck disappeared.

The man who'd been holding the rope now yelped and jumped, leaping around on his right foot while raising his raggedy-toed left boot and reaching for the wounded appendage with both hands though he couldn't seem to get his foot high enough nor his hands low enough to cradle the tender body part.

"Oh, you son of the devil!" he bellowed at Ty, waving his arms as though trying to fly. He dropped to his butt in a puff of tan dust. His dirty yellow hat tumbled off his shoulder. He bent his left leg inward and squeezed that foot, crouching over it, grimacing, his face red and puffy. He lifted his chin tufted with ginger goat whiskers, opened his mouth wide, and wailed at the faultless blue sky.

"When I tell you to do something, Rocky Jimson, you do it!" Ty barked over the smoking barrel of the Henry in his hands. He knew most of the men on Battles' roll. They all had reputations. That was why old Jake had hired them.

Con Stalcup raised his right arm and pointed an admonishing finger at the rancher. "You got no authority here, Brannigan! You're a citizen same as us." He turned to Southern. "As for you, Southern, you have no authority out here, either. Your authority stops at the city limits of Warknife!"

"You don't say?" Southern reached into a pocket of his corduroy coat, pulled out a six-pointed star with a nickel finish, pinned it to his right coat lapel, and poked it with his thumb. "That there is a deputy sheriff's star. It's all bona fide and legal. Even if it wasn't, Ol' Suzy here gives me all the authority I need to blow your damn head off your shoulders and make you even funnier to look at than you already are!"

In the corner of his eye, Ty picked up movement on the other side of Southern sitting his horse to the rancher's left. The pot-bellied, thick-set man who'd been holding Ivy suddenly turned the girl's arms loose and, believing he wasn't in Southern's field of vision, quickly reached for the Smith & Wesson holstered for the cross-draw on his left hip.

Ty's heart leaped. He himself wasn't sure if Southern was keeping one eye on the man. He got his answer when the gray-headed town marshal swept the shotgun quickly to his left and tripped a trigger.

Ka-boom!

The thick-set man grunted.

Ivy screamed, slapping both hands to her face, as Southern's double-ought buck picked up the man, thick as he was, and threw him straight back before he landed ten feet from where he'd been standing but not before tossing the Smithy up high in the air. It fell back down now and, adding insult to the thick-set gent's misery, konked the thick-set man in the forehead with a sharp smack.

It didn't much matter. The buckshot had chewed a pumpkin-sized hole through the man's fleshy chest, shredding his heart. He'd been dead before he'd reached the apex of his leap.

CHAPTER 10

When her shock over the thick-set man's demise had abated, Ivy gasped and ran forward and through the crowd of her father's riders, shoving them aside with angry grunts then dropping to a knee beside Brandon Waycross.

She sandwiched the young man's face in her hands, gazing into his dull eyes, and said, "Brandon? Brandon?"

Waycross only grunted. He'd been beaten up pretty badly. One eye was swelling. Blood trickled from one nostril, and several streams dribbled down from his fist-torn lips.

Ivy turned to Con Stalcup and barked, "He didn't shoot Pa! He couldn't have!" As she scuttled down the young man's body to untie the ropes from around his ankles, she looked up into his face again and said, "Did you, honey?"

" 'Did you, honey?' " Cass Battles mocked his sister, climbing to his feet with a grunt, his face still a shade paler than normal after he'd taken a hard one to the oysters. He pointed an angry finger at his sister. "You leave him right there, Ivy!"

Ivy probed Waycross's belly with her fingers. Young Waycross flinched and groaned, grinding his boot heels into the dirt. Ivy whipped another enraged look at her brother. "My God—you broke his ribs!" She looked at Ty. "He needs to see a doctor."

"We'll get him to town, have the doc look at him," the rancher assured the girl.

Cass Battles, tall but stoop-shouldered and soft-gutted, looked at Southern and Ty, and said, "This is Anchor business. We take care of our *own* business out here!"

"This is law business," Ty said. "I thought you were in jail in Chinook."

"I got out just this mornin', came home an' heard what that con artist done to Pa. Shot him in the back! That makes it *my* business!" Cass thumped himself in the chest.

"You got no call to ride out here an' shoot one of my men, Southern!" Stalcup said, taking one angry step forward, jutting his blunt chin at the lawman, squeezing his left fist down low against his side, wrapping his right hand tightly around the grips of the .44 he also, wisely, kept low.

Southern gave a caustic laugh. "He was gonna shoot me, so I sure enough do. I guess you don't realize that if you'd hanged that boy, you and your men would be murderers."

"It's called justice," Cass barked, walking around in front of the two newcomers' horses. He was in his mid-twenties with a broad, V-shaped face that might have been handsome if not for the cold, snake-like eyes. His face was clean-shaven, his nose broad as a wedge. He had his father's nose as well as Jake Battles' belligerent set to his features.

"Vigilante justice isn't justice," Ty said. He turned to where Ivy was now untying her betrothed's hands from behind his back, Brandon crouched forward, Ivy kneeling behind him. "Ivy, take Brandon inside and get him cleaned up."

"We'll be taking him to town," Southern said.

"Like hell," Stalcup said, narrowing his own flat eyes coldly. "He shot Mister Battles in cold blood."

"You don't know that."

"I rode out to the creek as soon as I heard the shot. Aside from Mr. Battles himself, Waycross was the only other man out there. He was riding away hell for leather and lookin' back over his shoulder at me. He had guilt written all over that purty face of his."

"We'll admit it doesn't look good," Ty said. "But Marshal Southern and I will look into it. Young Waycross's fate will be up to a judge to decide. Not you an' Cass and your hands."

"I'm the only witness," Stalcup said. "It'll be his word against mine. I been the top hand here at Anchor for the past fifteen years. A jury will believe me over that wolf in sheep's clothing!"

"We'll see if that's what decides it," Southern said. "In the meantime, I want you to show me and Brannigan out to the creek where you found your boss."

"What for? There's nothin' out there. At least, not anymore there isn't. We done buried the boss."

"Show us," Ty said, putting some steel in his voice. "While your men wait here."

He waved the cocked Henry at the men standing around glaring at him and Southern while Ivy led a dazed and battered Brandon Waycross toward the main house, one of the young man's arms draped around her neck. He could hardly walk, dragging his boot toes. He was in a lot of pain. Ty wasn't worried about him running off. You didn't run off with broken ribs, no matter how desperate you were.

Young Waycross's horse followed the pair closely, reins dangling. Ty took a second to marvel at the young horse gentler's close relationship with his handsome pinto. He doubted Brandon ever got as close to any man or woman as he did to his horse and all the horses he'd gentled in these mountains, after the three years of steady work he'd taken on after he'd settled here, having found a spiritual connection to the Bear Paws.

Ty didn't know about spiritual connections, but he knew young Waycross had an uncommon connection to horses. That was a copper-riveted, lead-pipe cinch. An admirable trait.

"I don't see the point," Stalcup said, "but . . ." He strode angrily over to a steel-dust gelding standing in a loose group with the other hands' horses and swung into the saddle. He glanced at his men. "Stay here, boys."

"If there's any more playin' cat's cradle with Waycross's head, there's gonna be hell to pave an' no hot pitch," Southern warned, aiming his two-bore around threateningly.

The human wolfpack eyed the older lawman wolfishly, hands down close to their gun handles.

Stalcup gave a dry chuff then neck-reined his horse and spurred it into a lope. Ty glanced at Southern and then they spurred their own mounts after the Anchor foreman, both casting cautious glances at the men turning to track them with their belligerent gazes.

Ty and Southern followed Stalcup through a fringe of pines at the rear of the ranch yard and then through some brush littered with abandoned wagons and wheels of all shapes and sizes, a couple of old plows, some discarded lumber, and haying machinery. They were following a footpath that led back to where Arapaho Creek chuckled along its stony bed between banks lined with cottonwoods.

At the cottonwoods, they swung left to follow the course of the creek upstream. The path was well-worn, likely by one man. It was probably a nice evening walk out here with the trees and the stream, maybe the distant yammering of coyotes, the somnolent hoots of owls. It surprised Ty in a vague sort of way that Jake Battles would be an appreciator of somnolent evening walks along a creek though he supposed even the fierce old Jake had had his sublime moments.

Likely hidden from any other man or woman.

No, Jake wouldn't want to let that be known. He'd have seen it as a sign of weakness.

"Right here." Ahead, Stalcup had reined his steel-dust to a stop, curvetted the horse, and pointed down at the trail. "Found him right here. You can still see the blood."

Ty swung down from his saddle and dropped the reins. Southern did likewise. Both men stared down at the dried blood crusted on the trail, and then Ty looked up at Stalcup still sitting his mount, his unyielding expression in place. "He was shot in the back?"

"Yep."

"Facing up trail or down?"

"Up."

"What time was it?"

"Close to eight. I was standin' outside the bunkhouse smokin' a cigarette when I heard the shot. Mister Battles—he always ate late."

"Where was Waycross when you first saw him?" Southern asked the foreman.

"Crouched over Mr. Battles. I came runnin', and yelled, and he hopped on his horse and galloped away. If that don't mean he's guilty, I don't know what does."

Ty looked up at the foreman and said, "Why would he be crouched over him if he shot him? Why wouldn't he just high-tail it? Why wait around and risk being spotted?"

"Why don't you ask him?"

"We will," Southern told the man. "That's a question we wouldn't be able to ask if you'd hanged him—now, would we?"

"It ain't gonna make a damn bit of difference! Now, if you'll excuse me, I got a man to bury and another to see if he's still fit to put in a day's work"—he turned a fiery glare on Ty—"since you blew his toe off!"

Ty thrust an angry finger at him. "You stay away from Waycross, you understand?"

"You go near him, Stalcup, and I'll arrest you for attempted murder," Southern warned. "You'll get ten years in Deer Lodge—mark my words!"

"Oh, hell. I don't see the point of wasting time. A jury's gonna convict him, sure enough!" Stalcup reined his horse around in a huff and put the spurs to it, galloping back in the direction of the yard.

Southern looked at Ty warily. "You trust him with Waycross over there?"

"Stalcup's a tough nut, but he's not stupid. He knows if he kills Brandon, he's gonna have to kill us, too, and I don't think he wants to get that deep in the muck. He'll leave it up to a judge now."

"I hope you're right."

"Me, too," the rancher said with a dry chuff.

Southern looked down at the blood on the trail, ran a gloved hand down his jaw, sighed, and looked at Ty. "Well, I reckon we know where he was shot and which way he was layin'."

"If we can believe anything Stalcup says."

"U-huh." Southern paused. "What else we gonna be able to find out here, Ty? I gotta admit, I'm good at arrestin' men, but when it comes to investigating crimes, looking for clues an' such, I'm still in school. Early days. Practically kindergarten, in fact . . ."

"Yeah, well, about all we can do is look around, see if there's anything to see. Why don't you walk up trail, scour the ground on both sides? I'll wander back in the direction of the ranch. Take your time, keep a sharp eye out for anything . . . I don't know . . . unusual."

"Anything unusual . . . all right," Southern said, wandering up trail, head down, pensively scratching his chin.

Since Jake Battles had been murdered, and obviously men and horses and even a wagon, judging by relatively fresh wheel tracks, had come and gone from the spot, the scene was badly corrupted. When Ty had walked back nearly to the main yard, perusing the grass and sage carefully along both sides of the trail, he pushed through the cottonwoods and walked out to the edge of the stream.

He walked upstream slowly, looking around. He had no idea what he was looking for. This was likely a waste of time. But he felt compelled to comb the murder scene as thoroughly as possible just in case there was *something* to see. In case something unusual stuck out.

Otherwise, the judge would have only Stalcup's and Brandon Waycross's testimonies to weigh. Stalcup's testimony would make young Waycross look damned guilty.

He had walked only a dozen yards before, his eyes scanning the ground, his heart skipped a beat.

A pile of horse apples lay just inside the cottonwoods and lilacs and wild berry bramble lining the stream bank.

The rancher stepped down from his calico's back and adjusted the sling on his grieving left arm, wishing he had a little whiskey to dull the pain that had kicked up when he'd had to use both hands on the Henry. He dropped to a knee beside the horse apples, chewed off his right glove, and poked a finger into the pile. Probably around three days old, he thought, judging by the moisture content. It hadn't lost all its green yet but was turning gray around the outside edges.

Yeah, about three days old.

Obviously, a horse had stood here. Not only were there apples but Ty found one fairly clear hoof indentation, and the blond bromegrass still showed the marks of a horse passing through here. The marks led out away from the lilacs and the cottonwoods to the edge of the stream. Ty followed the path, keeping his gaze on the ground.

At the very edge of the stream, where the water licked up against the moss, grass, and stones of the shoreline, Ty widened his eyes again as he scrutinized the ground. His gaze had landed on another hoof indentation. He spied part of another shoe mark evidently left when the rider had moved the horse off the bank and into the blue-green water of the stream.

"Hmmm, someone else was out here," the rancher muttered. "Sure as tootin'."

"What's sure as tootin'?" Southern's voice rose from the other side of the lilacs and cottonwoods; Ty heard the soft crunch of footfalls. "I couldn't find a damn thing up there but a whole bunch of overlaid horse tracks and . . ." The town marshal let his voice trail off as he crouched beneath a cottonwood branch and spied Ty staring at the ground at the edge of the stream. "Find some-thin'?"

"Yeah." Ty turned to his partner. "Hoof marks." He hooked a thumb over his left shoulder. "A pile of horse apples back yonder."

"I can go you one better than that!" Southern had turned his head to follow Ty's gesture to the horse apples then snapped his head to the right, arching his brows.

"What is it?" Ty asked.

Ty's eyes widened in surprise. "Well . . . I'll be damned!"

CHAPTER 11

Chris Southern took two steps toward the line of trees and brush, then crouched, extending his right hand between the base of a broad-boled cottonwood and a shaggy lilac to which the previous spring's dried blossoms still clung. He lifted his hand from the grass that was gently waving in the breeze, cloud shadows sweeping over it.

Between Southern's thumb and index finger was a brass cartridge casing. It glinted in the sunlight.

Slowly, scrutinizing the casing, the marshal turned to Ty. He held up the bullet. "What do you make of that?"

"I'll be hanged. That there is the somethin' I was talkin' about, Chris." Chuckling, Ty stepped forward.

"And it is *somethin'*, ain't it?" Judging by his toothy grin, Southern was equally pleased. He tossed the casing to Ty, who caught it in his right hand and stared down at it.

"Suppose that was the bullet that killed Battles?"

"I reckon it could be any bullet, but I'd say it has a pretty good chance of being the bullet that killed Jake. If it is, it means Brandon didn't kill

Battles, after all. If this was the killer's bullet and the killer's horse tracks and his horse's apples, the killer put his horse into the stream after he'd fired that killing shot. He didn't ride on ahead like Waycross did, according to Stalcup. The trail leads toward the stream."

"Yeah," Southern added, "I didn't see no bent grass between here and the trail. So Brandon didn't fire at Battles from here then ride out onto the trail to inspect the body, which is what Stalcup claims he saw him doing when he first spotted him."

"Exactly."

"So someone else killed Jake."

"We don't have clear proof, but it's looking a little better for the kid." Ty turned to the stream, looking around for a ford. Upstream about thirty feet was a beaver dam. "I'm gonna take a quick look on the other side, Chris."

"All right. I'll wait here."

Ty threw up an acknowledging hand as he walked upstream.

He stepped out onto the dam of intricately woven branches some particularly busy beaver had taken off the trees on both sides of the stream, and walked carefully, not wanting to fall and add more grief to his wounded arm. When he gained the stream's opposite side, he stepped down off the dam and walked back downstream.

He stopped on the shore across from where

Southern stood. The marshal had rolled a quirley and now he stood smoking, closing his eyes dreamily as he puffed, looking across the stream at Ty, his left thumb hooked behind his cartridge belt.

"Anything?" he called above the stream's sucking and gurgling sounds.

"Yep." Ty nodded, staring down at several more tracks clearly indented in the sand and gravel and then turning his head to gaze off down the curving trail of bent bromegrass. "He rode out that way. Looks like he angled along the base of that bluff yonder, heading northeast."

"I'll be damned."

Ty turned to his old friend. "I'd like to follow his trail, Chris."

"Why don't you do that while I get the kid to town?"

"All right." Ty walked back upstream toward the dam. "I'll help you fetch him from the house, get you started, make sure Stalcup and his men don't hassle you." When he'd made his way back across the dam and approached Southern who was just then taking another deep, luxurious puff from his quirley, he said, "Are you gonna arrest him?"

Southern blew more smoke out his broad, pitted nostrils and sighed. "I don't see that I have much choice, Ty. A prominent man is dead and Brandon was seen at the scene of the crime. We may have found a casing and spoor, but they could have been left by anyone earlier that day. One of Battles' men could have taken a shot at a deer, say."

Ty nodded. "You're right. We need to find out if anyone else from the ranch was out here around that time." He glanced off along the trail of bent grass. "And I'd like to find out who that rider was."

"Comprende, amigo," Southern said and closed his eyes as he drew on the quirley again.

The yard of the Anchor headquarters was eerily quiet and abandoned now in the late afternoon. On the lee side of the attempted hanging of Brandon Waycross, a funereal silence hung over the yard across which shadows were beginning to angle and turn deeper and deeper shades of blue. The only two men Ty saw around the place were two bare-chested men digging a grave up on a hill west of the house. Otherwise, none of the other Anchor men were around.

"Where do you suppose they're off to?" Southern asked Ty as the two men reined up in front of the house.

"Maybe they're actually off doing ranch work."

"Pshaw!" Southern quipped as he and Ty swung down from their saddles. "Jake's men never do a lick of ranch work!"

Ty snorted a laugh.

As the two men tied their reins at the rack and climbed the porch steps, Ty began to feel unease tighten the skin between his shoulder blades. What if they'd given Stalcup too much credit? What if he'd come back here to the yard, plucked young Waycross out of the house, and had ridden off to hang him elsewhere?

That thought began to fester inside Ty's brain until he felt his feet picking up speed as he crossed the porch. He knocked on the door once but did not wait for a response before he pushed it open and stepped inside.

Instantly, the tightness between his shoulders loosened.

Brandon Waycross sat in a chair at the kitchen table ahead and to Ty's right. The young man's shirt was off, exposing his broad, muscular shoulders and washboard belly. Oh, to be a young man again. The rancher vacantly lamented his own gone youth. Ivy Battles sat in another chair, close beside Brandon, facing the young man, and swabbing at his cut lips with tufts of cotton soaked in whiskey from the bottle standing on the table.

Brandon had turned his head to regard Ty as the rancher had entered so quickly. Now he gave an ironic smile and hooded his eyes as he slacked low in the chair. "What's the matter, Mr. Brannigan? Did you think I'd hightailed it?"

Ty shook his head as he and Southern entered

the house, both men removing their hats. "No, it wasn't that. The yard's so quiet I was starting to think . . ."

Ivy had not looked at either newcomer yet. She did not look at them now. She was a pretty brunette with a lush body and a heart-shaped face, but at the moment her face was expressionless, even dour, as she worked on Brandon's split lips and on the swelling over his left eye. "Don't worry, Mr. Brannigan," she said. "I have that shotgun over there, and I know how to use it. Stalcup knows it and so does my brother. They both know they're not wanted in here."

Now she turned to Ty and Southern, curling her upper lip, rage and defiance flashing in her brown eyes. "I'd have cut either one in half if they tried to do what they'd tried to do earlier to Brandon!"

Waycross glanced from Southern to Ty and said, "I reckon I owe you my gratitude, savin' my bacon like that." He studied Ty closely. "Why'd you do it, after . . ." He glanced at Ivy, whose suntanned cheeks turned a shade darker as she continued swabbing and applying salve to her lover's face.

"Because we're all due our day in court."

"But what about your court, Mr. Brannigan?"

"I don't have a court. I learned that a long time ago, when I had a badge like that one there." Ty jerked his thumb toward the six-pointed star on

122

Southern's coat. "Judge, jury, and executioner are three separate things, and I was none of those things. I just did the investigation and made the arrest."

Waycross turned to Southern. "You're taking me in . . . ?"

"How're your ribs?" Southern asked him. "Can you ride?"

"I can ride. They're just bruised." Waycross gave a grim little smile on his almost-pretty face. "I don't mind sayin' that the idea of being locked in a cell makes me squirt down my leg." He glanced at his future wife. "Sorry for the expression, Ivy."

"I reckon under the circumstances, you're due." Ivy glanced over her shoulder at Ty and Southern. "I'm going to be another minute, cleaning these wounds. Then I'd like to wrap his ribs before he rides. I don't think they're broken, but they sure are bruised." She glanced at the speckled tin pot gurgling on the range. "Help yourselves to mud, if you like. I made it before Stalcup's men came roaring in here with Brandon, so it's likely pretty strong . . ."

"That's how I like it," Southern said, walking around the table to the range. As he reached for a mug on a shelf above the wet sink and water pump, he glanced over his left shoulder at Brannigan, one brow arched in question.

"Why not?" Ty said.

When Southern had filled two thick, white stone mugs with the smoking, black brew for himself and Ty, the two men pulled chairs out from the table and slacked into them. Ty felt good, taking the weight off his feet and resting his arm. It had been a long day, and he needed a breather and a cup of coffee. He had some questions for Ivy though he couldn't help feeling an angry edge for the girl. She had, after all, taken a hand in the betrayal of his daughter. He knew her reputation. Ivy had likely seduced young Waycross despite knowing full well he'd promised himself to MacKenna.

Ty blew on his coffee, sipped, and said, "Ivy, you don't seem all that upset over the death of your father."

"What can I tell you?" Ivy said, keeping her attention on a long cut that trailed low on Brandon's left cheek as she dabbed at it with whiskey-soaked cotton. Brandon lifted his chin, grimacing against the burn. "He was a hard man. I have to admit I'm a little scared about what's going to happen to this place. It's been my only home for my entire life, but it's hard to feel grief for a man as hard as Pa. He was better to his men than he was to me and Cass. You can see how het up they are about him bein' gone. They pride themselves on ridin' for the Anchor brand!"

"Oh, I know," Ty said. Ranch hands were some of the most loyal men on the planet. They would live and die for the man and stretch of ground they worked for. It was in their blood. The way they saw it, they were soldiers fighting not only for a man and a stretch of ground but for a cause, a way of life.

"Who do you think might have killed him?" Southern asked her after he'd taken a couple of slurps from his own mug.

Ivy glanced at him. "Take your pick. There's not a man around who hasn't tangled with Jake Battles. I'm sure you've had your run-ins with my father, Mr. Brannigan."

"Oh, one or two," the rancher said and sipped his coffee.

He reflected that Jake Battles could be relatively pleasant one minute and the next minute turn around and insult the horse you were riding, your operating methods, or even your family. One time during roundup Ty had found himself watering his horse at the same spring old Jake had been watering his mount at. The men had exchanged pleasantries for about ten minutes before Battles had suddenly turned to Ty and said, "That youngest son of yours . . . what's his name again?"

"Gregory."

"Yeah, Gregory." Battles' moth-like brows had come down lower on his eyes. "Is he simple?"

Ty only frowned, not sure how to respond to the question. He'd been rendered speechless by the rude query that had come out of nowhere, without provocation.

"What do you mean, Battles?" he'd asked, anger building in him. Part of his brain wanted to believe he'd somehow misunderstood the man.

Battles had pooched out his lips and shaken his head. "Might be the Mexican blood. I'd never cover a Mex that wasn't a whore."

With that, he'd casually reined his horse around, clucked to it, and galloped off, leaving Ty staring hang-jawed after him. Many times over the years, reflecting on those comments, Ty had wished he'd pulled the old scudder off his mount and given him an old-fashioned thrashing. When he'd been younger, he'd have done just that. He tried to be a calmer, more composed man now in his later, family-raising years.

Ty pulled the .44 casing out of his shirt pocket and held it up between thumb and index finger, showing it to Brandon and Ivy. "We found this out by the creek. Has anyone been shooting out there lately—obviously besides whoever shot your father, Ivy?"

The girl frowned at the casing, shook her head. There were still bits of dirt and straw in her hair from when her brother had dragged her so unceremoniously toward the house. The flowered print dress she wore was torn and dirty from the dustup, as well. "Not that I know about.

Leastways, I hadn't heard any shots until the other night."

Brandon had come alive as he gazed hopefully at the shell casing. He slid his gaze to Ty and said, "Where'd you find it?"

"Near the stream. Behind where Battles would have been when he'd been walking upstream."

"I was ahead of him."

"The tracks attest to that," Southern said, adding, "Ty found horse apples in the cotton-woods and a trail through the grass where some-one had ridden a horse into the creek."

Brandon was sitting up straight in his chair while Ivy wrapped a foot-and-a-half-wide strip of torn sheet around his battered ribs that already were showing some purple. "That's the killer's trail. See—I didn't kill Mr. Battles!"

"Doesn't that prove it?" Ivy inquired, pausing in her work to slide her anxious gaze between the former lawman and the current one.

"Unfortunately, it doesn't, son." Southern was slowly rolling a quirley, leaning back in his chair. "We need to find that rider, ask him a few questions."

"He was there to kill Mr. Battles," Brandon insisted as Ivy resumed wrapping the long length of sheet tightly around his waist. "I know he was. Because I didn't kill him. Somebody else did. The man who left that casing and them apples and that trail through the grass.

You find him, and you'll find Mr. Battles's killer!"

Southern glanced at Ty. "Mr. Brannigan's gonna follow that trail while I take you to town."

"You're not still gonna arrest me, are you, Marshal Southern?" Waycross said, glowering at the man. He nodded at the casing now standing on the table near Ty's coffee cup. "That there casing should clear me!"

"I'm gonna take you to town, son. I'm gonna put you in a cell, but I'm gonna leave the door open. Make you feel better that way. Consider it free room and board. And protection from Battles' men while Ty and I look for whoever left that casing. Stalcup and Ivy's brother might have backed down today, but I know those two men well enough to know they're gonna get mighty antsy if you're not locked up and waiting for a judge. They'll come after you again, and I'm not gonna let 'em get you."

Young Waycross shared a silently conferring look with Ivy. He sighed and turned to the town marshal. "You promise you'll leave the door open?"

"I promise."

Waycross drew another slow, ponderous breath, and glanced at Ivy again. "I reckon I can't stay here now. After what happened. I don't wanna make trouble for you, Ivy. No more trouble, anyway."

"Stalcup and my brother wouldn't stand for it," Ivy said. "They'd get to drinkin', and there'd be trouble. I think you should go with the marshal, Brandon. You wouldn't be safe here."

"No, and you wouldn't, either."

"I'll visit you every day."

Waycross nodded slowly.

"Now that that's decided," Ty said, sliding his chair back, "I'm gonna follow that mysterious rider's trail while it's still relatively warm."

Southern snapped a lucifer to life on his thumbnail and stared up at the rancher. "Good luck, Ty."

Ty set his hat on his head, placed a hand on the marshal's shoulder, and headed for the door.

CHAPTER 12

As soon as Ty had put the roan across the stream and up the opposite bank, that all-too-familiar sense of danger splayed its cold fingers across his back. He'd learned the other night to ignore the sensation at his own peril.

Immediately, he reined in the horse and, looking around, slid the Henry from its saddle sheath. He looked back across the gurgling stream toward the Anchor headquarters and then along the cottonwoods and wild shrubs, looking for any sign of danger.

Finding none, he looked toward the north, the direction the possible killer's trail led, marked by a narrow swath of bent grass. The ground swept openly out toward a conical bluff sitting on a grassy pedestal and capped with rock and pines rising a couple of hundred yards away. The terrain between Ty and the butte appeared flat, but Ty knew these mountains well enough to know there were likely plenty of low spots and small hummocks of ground in or behind which a man could lie in ambush.

He gigged the roan ahead cautiously, pumping a round into the Henry's chamber one handed, off cocking the hammer, and resting the barrel across the pommel of his saddle. He was glad to find the trail still relatively clear as it led straight out to the bluff's west side. As the rancher had suspected, the rider had ridden around that side of the bluff and then headed northeast, through a shallow trough between a craggy dike—Rattlesnake Rock—rising on Ty's right and a broad butte with two separate, bullet-shaped peaks rising on his left. If the mysterious rider's trail did not switch course soon, Ty would soon be on his own range, for the Powderhorn abutted Anchor in the north and east.

Soon the grass gave way to sage and needle grass, and the ground grew harder, the topsoil shallower. Here the rider's trail was more difficult to follow but, leaning out away from his saddle and scouring the ground with his still keen-eyed gaze, Ty managed to pick out enough hoof indentations to stay on his quarry's trail.

Soon, he was on his own range. The white-faced cattle he was so proud of, the progeny of two bulls he'd had shipped all the way from England, peppered a distant slope.

As he followed the trail around a hillock from the very top of which a lightning-split cedar thrust its charred limbs toward various horizons, Ty spied something on the ground near a round, white stone and a small pile of deer beans. He checked the roan down once more. He stared down at the object in question.

A cigarette butt.

It lay near a hoof print—or half a print, the other half obscured by firmer ground.

Ty stepped down from the saddle and crouched to pick up the butt. Some of the dry tobacco dribbled out of the burnt end of the cylinder. It was a ready-made cigarette with the face of an Indian wearing a single feather jutting from a headband stamped near the end you drew on. Ty had seen that signature before.

Beatriz's father, Diego Salazar, smoked a ready-made brand called Indian Feather. This was one of those. Salazar had shared one with Ty one night when the old man had ridden his carriage out to have supper with his daughter's family even though he openly disapproved of the older and more rustic man Beatriz had married. He did, however, shower affection on his grandchildren, which kept Ty from totally disliking the contrary old Mexican. Ty remembered the cigarette had had a distinctly peppery taste and aroma. He thought it was a fairly rare brand, one likely favored by more moneyed men or men more conscious of social status. While ready-mades were becoming more popular, most men in these parts still rolled their own.

Ty didn't normally smoke. Beatriz didn't approve of smoking any more than she approved of drinking. Ty wasn't tied to her apron strings, but he did like to keep the peace, and that wasn't always easy when you were married to a fiery chili pepper. (He smiled now at the notion.) However, he smoked with his friends when his lovely wife wasn't present, and he rolled his own from a bag of Durham he hung around his neck by a rawhide thong, inside his shirt.

He wasn't trying to be sneaky. The lump was too obvious for Beatriz not to know it was there. It was just one of those marital dances that are required now and then when each member of the marriage needs to maintain some semblance of independence from the other.

Ty pocketed the stub then mounted up and continued following his quarry's trail. As he did, he continued to feel that cold, wet hand pressed against his back.

Trouble was afoot. He was certain of it.

Was the killer out here somewhere? Maybe the man had spied Ty leaving Anchor headquarters, taking the same route the killer had when he'd left the ranch after killing Battles. If so, that would mean the man who'd killed Battles likely worked at Anchor. Maybe he'd somehow stuck around after the other hands had ridden out, wanting to keep an eye on the current and former lawmen snooping around the murder scene.

Unless . . .

Ty had just remembered the men who'd led him to that fire set on the butte the previous night when what could only be a bullet whined louder and louder, ominously, before screeching through the air over Ty's right shoulder and spanging off a rock behind him.

"Ah, hell—not again!" The roan reared, nearly throwing him.

He was holding his Henry in his right hand, so he leaned forward and grabbed the horn with his left, wincing at the agony the maneuver kicked up in his wounded arm. When the horse dropped back down to all four hooves, Ty leaped from the saddle and narrowly avoided another incoming round as he ran to his left and dropped behind a rock a little larger than your average gravestone.

To his right, the roan buck-kicked angrily— some horses took to being shot at less kindly than others—and galloped wildly off to the east, tail arched, whinnying shrilly. Ty cursed again but at least he had his Henry this time.

He peered ahead to a low stone bench roughly a hundred yards away. Smoke puffed from the right-center of the bench. Ty pulled his head down low behind the rock, and the bullet screeched to his left and thudded into the turf behind him. Another bullet smashed into the side of the boulder only inches from Ty's head, peppering his face with rock shards.

He cursed angrily. That bullet had come from somewhere off his right flank, which meant there was more than one shooter out here. He turned his head to look behind him just as a big, broad-shouldered man in a flat-brimmed, bullet-crowned, black hat and wearing what appeared to be a long black duster stepped behind a pine that stood with a handful of others clumped together over there. Ty snapped the Henry to his shoulder, aimed quickly at the pine. He waited until the man behind the pine slid his head out from the pine's left side, and squeezed the trigger.

The man had seen him a quarter second before Ty had sent a round chewing bark from the very edge of the tree, where the bushwhacker's head had been a blink before. Ty's bullet had clipped the broad brim of the man's black hat and blown it off his head and into the short grass and sage maybe ten feet behind him.

That sense of danger Ty had been feeling really dug its claws into his back now. Sensing there might be more trouble off his left flank, he turned to see a rifle aimed at him from over a low hummock of grassy ground. Ty flattened himself down against the ground as smoke puffed from the rifle's barrel. That bullet screeched loudly just over Ty's chest and face to slam loudly into the rock only inches above his head, peppering his face with more rock shards.

Ty stretched his lips back from his teeth angrily, pumped a fresh round into the Henry's breech, and fired a shot toward the man behind the pine, then racked another round into the Henry. He aimed toward the man behind the hummock but held fire when dirt and torn grass plumed to the right of the barrel of the rifle aimed at Ty from behind the hummock.

Another, more distant rifle's report reached the rancher's ears a half second later.

Ty cast his gaze toward a low rise to the right of the shooter hunkered behind the hummock and maybe a hundred yards away from him. Two horseback riders were riding hell for leather down the rise, diverging, one riding toward the man behind the hummock, the other heading down the rise to Ty's right, toward the man who'd been shooting from behind the stone bench.

The rider galloping a broad-barreled sorrel toward the man behind the bench raised a carbine in both hands, down-canting his head toward the breech, aiming. Smoke and flames lapped from the barrel.

The man behind the bench shouted shrilly, "Trouble—pull out!"

Remembering the shooter behind the tree, Ty slid his rifle in that direction but held fire. The man had mounted and was galloping off through the trees, away from Ty and soon out of sight.

Ty slid the Henry toward the man behind the hummock, and again held fire. The rifle and the hatted head no longer shone over the top of the hummock. Then the rancher saw why. That man, too, had mounted and was now galloping up a low rise beyond the hummock, quartering toward Ty's left.

There was a brief exchange of rifle fire in the north. Ty whipped his head in that direction, and a few seconds later that shooter, too, appeared, galloping around the base of Rattlesnake Rock two hundred yards beyond Ty's position. Soon the rider curved around the far side of the rock and disappeared.

Ty turned to one of the two riders galloping toward him, saw the long, black hair bouncing on slender shoulders clad in a man's wool work shirt. Silver hoop earrings flashed in the sun where they jostled with the thick hair. The face beneath the brim of the tan Stetson owned the likeness of Ty's beautiful Mexican wife's fine, delicate features. Sunlight glinted off lake-clear blue-green eyes. The thuds of horse and rider grew louder and then MacKenna checked the Appaloosa down abruptly, curveted the mount, and leaped out of the saddle, holding her smoking carbine up and down in one gloved hand.

"Pa, you all right?"

Ty lay the Henry across his chest and scowled up at his daughter running toward him. "Young lady, what're you doing out here?"

"Pa, are you hit?" MacKenna said, falling to her knees beside her father and placing both gloved hands on his right arm, squeezing.

"No, no, I'm not hit, darlin', though not for them three's lack of tryin'. Who . . ." Ty turned to gaze toward the bench again, frowning curiously.

Then he saw the slender young man in the crisp, cream Stetson and hand-tooled chaps loping the sorrel toward him and MacKenna. Matt Brannigan held his Winchester carbine straight up from his right thigh. His tan-eyed gaze beneath the brim of the Stetson was cast with worry.

Ty raised his hand toward MacKenna. "Help the old man up, darlin'."

MacKenna rose, grabbed her father's hand, dug her boot heels into the ground, and leaned back, grunting, as she helped pull her father to his feet. Ty had pulled his left arm out of the sling to wield the Henry more accurately. Now, wincing against the burn in the arm, he slid it back into Beatriz's makeshift sling, muttering, "Ay-yi-yi!"

"Pa!" Matt said as he drew rein before his father and MacKenna, the sorrel chewing the bit.

"I'm fine, son. Just fine. A little worse for the wear but otherwise sporting no fresh bullet holes." Ty cast his smiling countenance from his daughter to his son whose young man's features were sharpening and broadening into those of a man—a handsome man, at that—and who remained mounted. "And I reckon I have my two eldest children to thank for that."

"Thank God you're all right, Pa! Who were those three jaspers, anyway? Rustlers?"

"Not sure, exactly," Ty lied. The less his children knew about the four men who'd come to snuff his wick for some unknown reason the better. He didn't want to worry them. He especially didn't want to worry Beatriz. "But maybe . . . yeah . . ." Best if they thought they were rustlers and not men out on some personal vendetta against their father.

Ty changed the subject. "What were you two doing out here?" he asked, casting his curious gaze between them.

"You wanted us to check that stock pond on the north graze, Pa. See if it needed to be dynamited out again." Matt hooked his thumb over his shoulder. "It's just over yonder. We heard the shooting and thought we'd best check it out."

"Well, I'm glad you did, I reckon. Just glad neither of you were hurt."

MacKenna stepped up to him, frowning with deep concern. She placed her hand on his right forearm and gave it another squeeze. Her eyes narrowed, drew up at the corners the way her mother's did when her mood was grave. It was such a direct, Brannigan-woman look that the rancher felt himself almost turn away from it. "Pa, what's going on? *We* were ambushed yesterday, and *you* were ambushed again today."

Ty sighed, wagged his head, hoping the act was convincing. "I don't know, darlin'—I reckon we have a rustling problem."

"Not missing any cows, last time I checked," Matt said. "Haven't seen any branding fires out here—you know, for running irons."

"No? Well—"

Before Ty could continue, Matt said, frowning suddenly, "Just before we heard the shooting, though, MacKenna and I were following the tracks of someone who'd crossed our range recently. We were thinking he might've been a rustler, wanted to check it out."

Ty's interest grew. Matt and MacKenna must have stumbled across the spoor Ty himself had been tracking. "Did you see where his trail led?"

"We didn't track it far, but it appeared to lead across this corner of our graze and up over Billy Goat Ridge. You know, on the other side of Billy Goat Ridge is—"

"Yeah, I know," Ty said, chewing his lower lip, pondering. "That's Glenn and Sonya Thompson."

Glenn Thompson, a man in his late thirties, had owned Sunrise Ranch, the small spread on the other side of Billy Goat Ridge, since Thompson had mustered out of the frontier army at nearby Fort Carlisle about ten years ago. Thompson had been a bachelor until recently when he'd married the daughter of a saloon owner in town, Sonya Cameron.

Thompson, a soft-spoken man with a farming background, and the former Miss Cameron lived together now at the humble little Sunrise headquarters, where they raised chickens and pigs as well as cattle. Ty stopped at Sunrise for coffee several times a year just to be sociable though they rarely visited Powderhorn singly or as a couple, despite several invitations over the years. The couple kept to themselves. They had no children for whatever reason, but they seemed content enough working on their ranch together.

"Those tracks were probably just made by Mr. Thompson maybe looking for his cattle on our land," Matt said. "You know how they're always mixing, Pa."

"Could be, but . . ." Ty let his voice trail off as he caressed his chin between thumb and index finger.

"What is it, Pa?" MacKenna asked, gazing up at him.

"I picked up that fella's trail—at least, I'm assuming it was a fella—back at the Anchor. I found a forty-forty casing near where Jake Battles was shot. Picked up the horse and rider's trail near the cartridge casing."

"You think you might've picked up the trail of the killer?" MacKenna asked.

"I think there's a chance."

"Brandon's trail?" she asked, her voice becoming tentative.

Ty shook his head. "No. Waycross's trail went west toward Whiskey Creek. This is a separate trail heading north."

"The killer's trail!" Matt said.

MacKenna said nothing but parted her lips

and drew a deep, hopeful breath, puffing out her chest.

"I followed it to see if I could find out whose trail, exactly. But, yeah, since he left that cartridge casing behind, I'm thinkin' it's the killer's trail." Ty had cast his gaze to the north, the direction the rider he'd been following had led him.

"Pa, do you have any news about Brandon?" MacKenna asked suddenly, imploringly. "I've been worried sick!"

Ty turned to her, hesitated. She didn't need to know about Stalcup and Cass Battles attempting to play cat's cradle with her former beau's head. "Chris Southern is taking him into town, honey."

"*Arresting* him?"

"Mainly to protect him. Chris promised Brandon he'd keep the cell door open unless any of the Anchor riders were spotted in town. This will give Chris and I time to try to figure out who the real killer is."

"You're starting to believe it's not Waycross, aren't you, Pa?" Matt asked.

Ty thought he detected a little hope even in his oldest son's voice, despite how enraged Matt had been—every bit as enraged as Ty himself had been—when he'd learned of young Waycross' betrayal of MacKenna with Ivy Battles.

"I have to admit I am. I'm gonna continue following the trail I picked up at Anchor. You two ride on home and stay there until I get back. I don't want you out here with those three bushwhackers running off their leashes."

"Pa, what about you?" MacKenna asked. "You're the one they're after."

"I'll be all right." Ty pulled his glove off and used two fingers to whistle for his horse.

"Pa, you weren't all right," Matt said. "You were outgunned three to one, and those bushwhackers had you surrounded. Mack and I rode in just in time to scare those scudders off, or they'd have kicked you out with a cold shovel."

Ty smiled. Matt had picked up the "cold shovel" expression from his father—an old one Ty had picked up in his town-taming days in Kansas and Oklahoma, dealing with one colorful character after another. That was the only aspect he missed about those years. The sundry disparate characters, including Buffalo Bill Cody and Pat Garrett as well as Wyatt Earp himself, he'd brushed elbows with. He'd even once been cussed up one side and down the other by one Calamity Jane Canary, in a rain of whiskey spittle flying from her lips.

Matt gave a crooked smile and, knowing his father's proud nature, raised his gloved hands in supplication as he continued with, "Now, I'm not crowin', you understand. Just stating facts."

"Matt's just stating facts, Pa," MacKenna

143

chimed in, a little defensively. She was only too aware of her old man's pride, as well.

"It's right humbling," Ty allowed, "but I know he is." The smile faded from his lips. "I do appreciate your help, you two. I was lucky you were out here today, and I'm impressed by your shooting and riding skills. You're Brannigans through and through."

They glanced at each other and flushed a little, with their own brand of Brannigan pride.

"That said . . ." Their father gave each of his offspring in turn a steely, commanding look. "I want you to get on home now. Not a word about what happened here to your mother, understand?"

He turned as the hoof thuds of his horse rose in the east.

CHAPTER 13

Ty sat his roan and watched his two children ride away from him, side by side, to the northeast, back in the direction of the Powderhorn headquarters. They each cast their father worried looks over their shoulders but continued riding until they disappeared into a pine copse.

Ty wanted them off the range until he'd dealt with the three men who obviously had a bone to pick with him. Not that he wasn't grateful for Matt and MacKenna's help today. He admired as much as loved those two kids, and he had to admit he was pleasantly surprised by the shooting prowess of each. He'd taught them both how to shoot to protect themselves, for this was still wild country, and men as well as some women needed to wield shooting irons.

Ty hadn't realized the good job he'd done. But then, he was a protective father and knew from his own personal experience that no matter how distasteful it might be, men and women residing on this wild side of the Mississippi often lived or died according to how well they could protect themselves with pistol and carbine.

That said, for the time being Ty didn't want his beloved family anywhere around him on the range, where his mere presence would no doubt provoke another attack. Those three stalkers might have been cowed today, but their return was just a matter of time. There was no way in this world Ty would ever let a bullet meant for him take down one of his kids. He still shuddered when he remembered that bullet plunking into the ground yesterday only inches from MacKenna's tender flesh.

Damn those three devils, anyway! As if he didn't have enough on his mind with trying to run down Jake Battles' killer, he had to keep an eye skinned for bushwhackers. He realized now that last night's fire and mocking laughter had been all in fun. All in fun for his stalkers, anyway. They'd wanted to bedevil him, rattle him. Taunt him with the knowledge they were gunning for him.

That meant they were confident. Maybe too confident though Ty had to admit they would have rendered him wolf bait had not his children heard the shooting and come to help . . .

Assured that Matt and MacKenna would continue on home and not pull a fast one on him and try to flank him to watch over their old pa, Ty booted the roan on up the trail, following the trail of the horse and rider he'd trailed out from Anchor. Matt had been right. The rider's trail led up Billy Goat Ridge, following a well-worn game path through brome and buffalo grass and peppered liberally with mule deer beans and elk scat though the elk scat was older. The elk usually moved out here from deeper in the mountains in the winter but spent the summers deep in the mountains or in the rugged, remote breaks of the Avalanche River.

When he'd gained the top of the ridge, he checked the roan down and sat staring down through pines at the humble layout of the Sunrise Ranch headquarters. The rectangular, shake-roofed log cabin sat with its back to the ridge, a couple of hundred feet out from the bluff's base. At work in the garden flanking the cabin was Thompson's wife, Sonya. She was on her hands and knees, working with a trowel, digging up something—likely new potatoes—and shoveling them into a wooden bucket on the ground beside her. A straw bonnet shaped like a rose petal shaded her face.

Ty couldn't see her clearly from this distance of sixty or so yards, but he knew she was a pretty, plump, round-faced, young woman with long, light-brown hair she usually wore down, and a shy demeanor that somewhat matched that of her husband. She wore a tan day dress and an apron, and currently she appeared to be working in her garden barefoot. She worked with a weary air, waving away flies and often shaking back strands of her hair from her face.

Every time Ty had visited, she'd seemed tired though cheerful. Likely overworked. Ty had the impression—mainly from working with

Thompson on roundup—that Thompson was a bit of a dullard. Congenial enough when cornered, but basically lazy. During roundup, he usually rode behind the other riders and almost always needed help in brush-popping his own herd-quitters. He usually hired two or three capable ranch hands who nearly always outshined him. He was not a good horseman; Ty had seen him nearly unseated several times. Though he'd been out here ranching for a good ten years, Thompson still hadn't seemed to have grown comfortable with his riding stock.

Surprisingly, he was good with pigs and he was good at calving, however—he and Sonya both could hold their own during calving season—and calving was one of the hardest tasks of a rancher. They'd persevered out here despite innate shortcomings, and that in itself was a victory. Ty was not totally without admiration for the man or his wife.

He did not see Thompson anywhere in the yard on the other side of the cabin, so he decided to ride down and speak with Sonya. He gigged the roan on down the slope but reined in again when he saw the trail of the man he'd been following angling off to his right, descending the steep bluff at an easy angle. The rider's trail appeared to be angling down toward the original cabin—the first one on the place, an old trapper's cabin built decades ago.

The current cabin was not large, but the original cabin—brush-roofed and with hand-adzed logs silvered with age, a rusty stove pipe angling up out of the roof—was half its size and all but consumed by tall weeds and wild bushes. It sat back near the base of the ridge and sixty yards or so from the more recent, larger dwelling, separated from the current cabin by several Ponderosa pines that had grown up over the years after the yard had been cleared by its founder.

Ty wanted to follow the rider's trail but decided to wait until later. He'd find out from Sonya where her husband was and speak with Thompson first in an attempt to get to the bottom of who had ridden from the scene of Jake Battles' murder clear over to the Sunrise.

Probably, it hadn't been Glenn Thompson.

But Ty had learned from all of his years as a town-taming lawman that you just never knew what cards any man was holding until he turned them over. Sometimes it took some doing to get him to turn them over.

When he was halfway down the butte, Ty called, "Hello, Mrs. Thompson. It's Ty Brannigan!"

He'd meant to warn her of his approach so as not to startle her. But he'd startled her, anyway. She lifted her head quickly and gasped.

"I'm sorry, Mrs. Thompson," Ty said, smiling with chagrin. "That there was what I'd hoped to avoid."

"Oh, Mr. Brannigan," she said, the flush of startlement leaving her face, anxiousness leaving her eyes.

Sonya Thompson climbed to her bare feet, straightening her lowcut, sweat-damp dress. She must have gained weight after she'd made the dress, for it clung to her revealingly, accentuating the womanly curves of her lush body. She glanced down as though self-conscious of how the simple frock's cambric was drawn taut against her bosoms, and pinched it out away from her flesh, loosening it, though it clung right back against her. Being damp and tight, it had little choice.

She glanced nervously at her bare feet, then, again nervously, she smoothed the skirt against her thighs. Flushed again with self-consciousness, she raised the hand that held the trowel up to shade the sun from her eyes and gave another embarrassed smile.

Strands of hair that had come free from the bonnet were sweat-plastered to her plump, pink, attractive cheeks. "How nice to see you again," she said, lifting her dirty bare toes from the ground, then setting them down once more, a cat-like gesture.

"Nice to see you, Sonya," Ty said, reining up at the edge of the garden, feeling a little bad about his interruption. He felt as though he were intruding on an intimate moment, which he supposed he was in a way, since she obviously wasn't dressed for company. "Nice afternoon for a little gardening," he added, raking his gaze across the several hills of potatoes, rows of greens, radishes, cabbages, squash, beets, pumpkin vines, and slender branches that had been woven to form a lattice for green beans to climb at the garden's rear. There were several rows of five-foot-high corn off to the garden's right side. Between the rows were deep troughs for irrigation water. "And a darn fine garden, as well. Is this all your work?"

"Oh, yes," she said with another shy smile, still shading her face with the hand holding the trowel to which dark, crusted soil clung. "Glenn tends the ranch chores. I tend the house and the garden."

"Speaking of Mr. Thompson—is he around?" Ty asked, casting another curious glance around the larger cabin beyond Mrs. Thompson and the garden, hoping to catch a glimpse of the Sunrise rancher.

The question seemed to bring a flush to her cheeks. "Oh, yes." She glanced behind her at the slender rear door of the cabin that had been propped open with a rake. "Glenn, are you there?" she called gently.

Inside, a man coughed, cleared his throat.

"Yeah," a deep, throaty voice called, echoing woodenly beyond the black rectangle of the open door.

Another loud throat clearing, a creaking sound as that of strained bedsprings. There was a staccato thumping sound as though of a man stepping into his boots. Footsteps rose, boot heels pounding and raking uncertainly across the wooden floor, echoing woodenly.

Thompson appeared in the doorway. He raised an arm as though to steady himself against the frame. His thick, curly brown hair liberally peppered with gray was badly mussed. He was clad in only baggy sack trousers and a longhandle top. One suspender came loose from his shoulder and fell down against his side. His salt and pepper mustache completely covered his mouth. It hadn't been trimmed in weeks.

He scowled up at the sun, squinting, then shaded his eyes with his hand and looked beyond his wife at Ty. "Oh . . . hello," he said, his voice still sounding thick and gummy. He hacked phlegm from his throat, spat to one side, then cast his own embarrassed smile across the garden toward his visitor. "Brannigan?" he said. "That you?"

"Yes." The rancher booted the roan around the garden and Mrs. Thompson, who turned her head to track him, and reined up near the open back door. "Good day to you, Glenn. Please pardon the intrusion." His congenial tone belied his befuddlement at Thompson's disheveled appearance so late in the day. Had the man been taking a nap? Glenn's washed-out eyes bespoke drink.

Don't tell me he'd crawled into the bottle, Ty wondered.

"Oh, no, no," Thompson said, hacking more phlegm from his throat and spitting it into the hardpacked dirt just beyond the door. "That's fine. What can we, uh . . . what brings you here?"

"I followed a trail here . . . from the Anchor headquarters."

Thompson frowned, flushed a little. "The Anchor headquarters?"

"Yes. Oh, I suppose you haven't heard." Ty glanced behind him at Sonya Thompson, who'd turned full around to regard him, her face suddenly a little pale. Turning back to Glenn, he said, "Jake Battles was killed."

The tanned skin above Thompson's long, slender nose rumpled more severely than before. He said nothing, just stood staring at Ty, his gaze flicking occasionally toward his wife behind the visiting rancher.

"Oh, no," Mrs. Thompson said behind Ty.

He turned to see her covering her mouth with her hand.

"Yes," Ty said, shuttling his gaze between the woman and the man. "He was shot on his place. I'm helping Chris Southern investigate. That's why I'm here. I picked up the sign of a horse and rider near where Battles was found with a bullet in his back. The trail of that rider led me here."

He frowned curiously down at Thompson and then cast his gaze over his left shoulder at Sonya. She still held her hand over her mouth. Her light-brown eyes were wide and round. The news of the death of Jake Battles, not a well-liked man if liked at all by anyone, had evoked more reaction in Sonya Thompson, and even in her husband, than Ty had expected it would.

Thompson said with a slow smile, "Well . . . you don't think I did it, do you?" He gave a self-conscious chuckle. His eyes flicked toward his wife again.

What was happening here? Ty thought.

"No, no," he said reassuringly, though he of course was sure of nothing. Their reactions were puzzling. "I just followed the trail, that's all. Have you had any visitors here, lately, Glenn?" He glanced over his shoulder at Sonya again. "I mean, besides me, of course . . ."

He grinned, wanting to put these two at ease.

"Heck, no," Thompson said. "We never get anyone out here."

"You haven't ridden out that way—across the northwest edge of the Powderhorn . . . toward Anchor . . . ?"

Thompson frowned, shook his head. "No." He jerked his head back. "My herd's up north now. Leo Divine an' I moved 'em last month." Leo Divine was a semi-retired puncher who lived in a boarding house in town and whom Thompson hired from time to time when he had more work than he could handle alone. Thompson's holdings were small. His herd was, too, so he managed to do most of the cattle work himself . . . When he wasn't working his cattle and tending his range, he was tending the other stock. Ty hoped the nap he'd interrupted wasn't a hooch-induced habit or these two were in trouble.

"Haven't been out that way in a long time. I ride out to hunt along Four-Mile Creek but that's as far as I've gone in a coon's age. I got all the work I can handle right here." Again, Thompson's eyes flicked to his wife, and there was a strange hardness in them.

Ty switched his gaze to Sonya, whose plump cheeks flushed again, and she dropped her gaze to the ground around her bare toes.

"Hmm." Ty gazed back up the ridge down which he'd just come. "Puzzling. Whoever the rider was must have ridden around your ranch headquarters on his way elsewhere." He glanced at Thompson. "Mind if I continue following his trail? Atop the ridge it angled down and over toward that original cabin back yonder."

Thompson just stared at Ty for several seconds. He looked again at his wife then shrugged. "Suit yourself, Brannigan." With that, he turned and strode lazily back into the cabin. Ty thought he heard a cork being pried from a bottle.

He reined the calico around and rode back around the side of the garden. He reined up before Mrs. Thompson. "Sonya," he said, haltingly, frowning with concern, "everything all right out here?" He didn't mean only Glenn Thompson's odd nap time and obvious day-time drinking.

She smiled a little too brightly. "Everything's just fine, Mr. Brannigan." Her brows ridged. "Why wouldn't they be?"

"Oh, I reckon I was just checking's all. You know where I and Beatriz live. If you ever need any help . . . anything at all . . . please let us know. We neighbors have to look out for each other out here."

"I will do that, and thank you mighty kindly for the offer, Mr. Brannigan. Do stop by again soon. We'll have dessert and coffee. I'm afraid you caught me a little unprepared today."

"I'm sorry to have surprised you." Ty pinched his hat brim to her. "Good day, Sonya."

"Good day, Mr. Brannigan," she said and waved.

Ty rode back over to the base of the ridge. He climbed to where the horse and the rider's trail had branched off to drop at an angle down the bluff. He followed it to the base of the ridge and followed the faint, partial hoof prints over to the back of the original cabin.

Ty frowned as he stared down at the ground. There were several piles of horse apples in the high brush and weeds. Several piles of various ages. He could tell by the well-trampled grass that the horse had stood here awhile on several separate occasions.

Ty swung down from the calico's back and dropped the reins.

He studied the ground closely for a time and then stooped suddenly and plucked another cigarette butt from deep in the brush and from beside several dry, flaking apples. One eye narrowed, Ty scrutinized the butt closely.

Sure enough, there was that feather protruding from the head band again.

Another Indian Feather ready-made.

Ty pocketed the butt, stepped up to the cabin, and peered inside through an unshuttered window. The place was a mess. Part of the earthen roof had caved in; dirt, ancient leaves, pine needles, and other debris lay mounded on the dirt floor. Otherwise, the place was abandoned. Aside from a badly rotted crate, not a stick of furniture inside. Ty started to turn away then turned back to peer through the window again.

A straw pallet lay against the cabin's front wall, to the left of the closed, badly bowed front door. The pallet wasn't as dusty and littered with grime as the rest of the cabin. It looked as though someone might have used it recently.

Ty winced against his confusion and nudged his hat onto his forehead to scratch the back of his head.

Why would the killer come here after killing Jake Battles? Maybe even have spent the night? Damned puzzling.

Ty mounted up and followed the trail of the horse and rider after man and horse had left the cabin. The trail angled wide of the Sunrise headquarters, skirting the periphery to the north. Whoever the rider was, he hadn't wanted to be seen. The trail angled up the next ridge. At the top, it swung straight west where, after two miles, it merged with the main trail out from Warknife and was promptly wiped out by the more recent tracks of wagons and horseback riders passing regularly along the Whiskey Creek trail.

Ty cursed.

CHAPTER 14

Town Marshal Chris Southern cursed and reined in his paint horse.

Riding beside him with his beaten and battered face and aching ribs, Brandon Waycross reined in his pinto and glanced at Southern. "What is it, Marshal?"

"I just had me a feelin' when we got back to the Anchor headquarters and there were no riders around, he was up to somethin'. *They* were up to somethin'—Stalcup and Cass Battles."

Young Waycross followed the marshal's gaze to the low rise a hundred yards ahead of them. A good dozen men were lined up, sitting their horses about ten feet apart in the blue-green mountain sage and scattered cedars. The two in the middle were the thick-set Con Stalcup in his brown Stetson and the rangy Cass Battles in a black cowhide vest and black hat with its band of studded silver conchos winking in the sunshine, two ivory-gripped Colts on his hips.

Spread out on the prairie beyond them lay the town of Warknife with the craggy dikes of the Demon River rising on its far side, roughly a half mile away.

Waycross turned to Southern. "Well," he said with a resigned air. "We almost made it."

Southern cursed again and spat into the sage and grama grass then ran his gloved hand across his mouth. He reached ahead for Ol' Suzy, slipped the big gut-shredder from its heavy leather scabbard. He rested the double bores across his saddlehorn then glared ahead at the riders lined out before him. Even from this distance, he could see their faces set in hard plains, eyes flat and mean beneath the shading brims of their hats. Only the horses moved, shaking their heads or switching their tails or trying to lower their snouts to crop grass before their riders jerked their heads back up with the reins.

Brandon Waycross glanced at the marshal again. "I'd just as soon not try to run for it. Truth be told, I'm too sore an' I'm tired of runnin'."

"Ah, hell, I'm not gonna run from Stalcup or Battles." Earlier, out of habit, Southern had slid Waycross's old Winchester carbine from the young man's saddle boot and slipped it into his own where it had resided with Ol' Suzy. Now he pulled it out and extended it butt-first toward Waycross. "If it comes to shootin', you might as well fight back."

Waycross looked at the rifle, glowering at it distastefully.

"Go on," Southern urged. "Take it. You have to fight back."

"All right." Waycross wrapped his gloved right hand around the neck of the old-model

Winchester. "I'm not much good at shootin', though, Marshal. I've never killed a man before, so . . ."

Southern looked at him again. Was he telling the truth or working a con on the old lawman? If he was working a con, he was the best con artist Southern had ever known, and he'd known a few. "Like I said, son," he said, "you have to fight back."

"I'll try."

"Take a couple down just for the satisfaction of it," Southern said, returning his gaze to the Anchor riders. "I might be able to empty a couple, three saddles with Ol' Suzy. I'd at least tramp up to St. Pete with a smile on my sour old mug."

The marshal nudged his paint on ahead. "Come on, boy."

Waycross gigged his pinto into motion and rode up alongside Southern. Together they dropped down the rise they'd been on, then climbed the steeper one ahead, the horses and riders facing them growing larger before them. One of the Anchor horses lifted its head and gave an anxious whinny. Finally, Southern and young Waycross crested the rise and stopped their mounts fifteen feet in front of Stalcup and Cass Battles, who regarded them with leering, crooked grins.

Southern raised Ol' Suzy's barrel and planted the butt against his thigh. With a hard, threatening grin of his own, he raked both heavy hammers back to full cock.

"Don't get your panties in a twist, old man," said the broad-cheeked, snake-eyed Cass Battles. The only way he favored his father was in his eyes. They were large and stony with a small fire of simmering emotion set back inside each one. Even in his old age, Jake Battles had been far more physically imposing with his broad, hard chest and wide shoulders. The man's enormous, rock-hard gut had given him the threatening aspect of a Brahma bull. "We ain't gonna take him from ya. Not yet."

He glanced at Waycross, then spat into the sage.

Stalcup said, "We're gonna give you a week." He slid his glaring brown eyes to Waycross. "If he don't hang in a week, we're gonna come for him an' hang him ourselves."

Southern opened his mouth to speak, but Cass Battles cut him off with, "He might have you an' half the women in the county hornswoggled with his moon eyes an' syrupy talk, but he don't fool me a bit. Never has, never will."

"That devil killed old Jake, Southern," Stalcup said, rising in his stirrups, his unshaven cheeks flushing with anger. "Shot him in the back and, when he saw me, he ran like hell!"

"I didn't," young Waycross said, eyes averted, slowly wagging his head, lips pursed. "I didn't shoot him. I didn't like him, but I didn't shoot

162

him. I couldn't kill a man. Not even Battles. Even if I could, I wouldn't do that to Ivy though he didn't treat her right, Jake didn't." He looked at Cass. "He didn't treat you right, either."

"Let's leave who or what my father was out of this, Waycross," Cass snarled. "He was my pa an' you killed him, and you're gonna pay for killin' him."

Southern almost laughed out loud. Cass wasn't one bit sad that the old man was dead. He was sad that his security was gone and that if he couldn't step up to the task at hand and run the ranch effectively himself—which, being cow-stupid as well as a part-time outlaw, a whore-mongering fool, and a drunkard, he probably couldn't—the Anchor would go under. He and his sister would be out in the cold, having to fend for themselves, which neither one had ever had to do.

What the hell had they been thinking—that old Jake would live forever?

Probably. Old Jake had somehow given the impression of being immortal. He'd been too tough and mean to die.

But dead he was . . . and his children were scared. His men would likely be looking for work soon, the Anchor now being essentially rudderless. But since they were more gun hands than ranch hands, and most had bounties on their heads, who besides Jake Battles, who'd taken pride in the rough nature of his payroll, would hire them? Out of long impulse, and because they'd been toughened and hardened by old Jake himself, they wanted revenge for his killing. However hard and mean he'd been, their employer had been taken from them, and it was in their natures to seek a reckoning.

"You have one week, Southern," Stalcup said. "One week!" He glanced around him, yelled, "You men—come on!" and booted his mount into a gallop past Southern's left stirrup.

The others including Cass Battles booted their own mounts into ground-chewing gallops, barreling on down the rise past Southern and young Waycross. When they'd gone, the marshal and the young horse tamer sat blinking against their sifting dust.

Brandon Waycross gazed over his shoulder at the Anchor men galloping in a long, shaggy line across the prairie toward the conical bluffs and slanted mesas of the Bear Paws then turned to the marshal. "I sure am sorry to put you in this position, Marshal. You're between a rock and a hard place."

"If you didn't kill Battles, you didn't put me in any position."

"You believe me yet?"

"Let's see what Ty Brannigan comes up with." Southern extended his open, gloved hand toward Waycross, and smiled meaningfully. Waycross looked at the carbine in his hand, considered it for a few seconds then flipped it in the air and caught it by the barrel. He extended it butt-first toward Southern.

"Be my guest. This forty-four carbine is why I'm in this situation in the first place."

Southern took the rifle and slid it down into his saddle scabbard.

"Come on, son," he said. "I'm hungry . . . thirsty."

Southern nudged his horse ahead toward town. Brandon Waycross followed suit.

MacKenna Brannigan checked her horse down suddenly and turned to her brother, who stopped his own horse and frowned at her curiously.

"Matt," she said, "you ride on back to the Powderhorn. I'll be back shortly."

"Mack, wait!"

But she'd already neck-reined her Appaloosa around and put the spurs to it and was galloping off down the right fork in the trail they'd come to, heading northwest toward the main trail that led to town. "I'll be back shortly," she yelled, throwing up her hand in a dismissive wave.

"Mack, you heard what Pa said! He doesn't want us out here!"

MacKenna had just barely heard her older brother's warning beneath the thuds of her galloping horse.

Matt's final warning came even more faintly to

her ears: "You're gonna be in a whole world of trouble, Mack!"

But she'd still heard it. And she knew it was true. Still, she did not switch course or even slow the Appaloosa's pace. Over the past twenty minutes since they'd left their father, she'd been pondering the matter of Brandon Waycross. More specifically the notion that the marshal, Chris Southern, was taking him to town.

MacKenna knew how much Brandon hated towns. Even one the modest size of Warknife. Even more than he hated being confined in town, he hated the notion of being confined in a jail cell. Even with the door open. She didn't know why this mattered to her after what he'd done to her, betraying her with Ivy Battles. But it did. She felt an overpowering compulsion to ride to town and see him and to let him know that she was thinking of him. She wanted to reassure him that her father would do everything in his power to find the real killer of Mr. Battles.

Her father had been a lawman of renown before he'd settled down to become a rancher and to raise a family. He'd tamed a half-dozen towns in Kansas and Oklahoma. If anyone could run Battles' killer to ground it was Ty Brannigan.

She needed so much to reassure Brandon of this.

Again, she wasn't sure why. In fact, she felt a little foolish. But damn her hide, she still loved the half-crazy man-child that was Brandon Waycross. And she had a feeling that despite his having cavorted and even having made a baby with Ivy Battles, that Brandon still loved her, too. When he'd finished breaking horses for MacKenna's father, he'd accepted a job doing the same for Jake Battles. That meant he'd been working close to the flirtatious Ivy, on her father's ranch, and he'd merely succumbed to a weak moment.

Should that one weak moment be such a deciding factor in their lives?

Did it need to be the reason that two people who genuinely loved each other should live apart, possibly each pining for the other until their last day on earth . . . ?

It just didn't seem right.

Still, Ivy was pregnant. Of course, her child should not have to grow up with the stigma of being a bastard, nor should Ivy have to live out the rest of her life with the stigma of being an unwed mother.

On the other hand, she was a Battles. Would anyone really find it all that surprising or odd that Jake Battles' daughter had birthed a child out of wedlock?

As she galloped along the main trail toward town now, MacKenna winced and shook her head, ashamed of the dark turn her thoughts had taken. Did she really love Brandon so much that she would want him to forsake his responsibilities to both the mother of his child and the child he'd fathered, as well?

Was that who she'd become?

She squeezed her eyes closed, lowered her head, and shook it. Enough thinking now, she told herself. Just get to town and be with Brandon. See how he is. You know what a loner he is, how alone he is in the world, with all of his family long dead. He probably feels as lonely now as he's ever felt in his life.

Horse and rider rounded a curve in the trail bisecting the broad, undulating prairie between the first front of the Bear Paws and the town growing larger and larger amidst the bluffs ahead of them. As Mack and the appy climbed a low rise, she saw the dust billowing ahead of her, on the other side of the rise, just in time. At the top of the hill, she checked her horse down sharply, drawing back on the reins and curveting the mount quickly, the horse giving a nervous whicker.

The first two riders of the gang ahead of her, climbing the rise from the other side, checked their own mounts down just in time, as well, or they would have run smack into Mack and the appy.

"Whoa! Whoa! Whoa!" intoned both Con Stalcup and Cass Battles as the horses of the riders directly behind them nearly rammed them from behind as their own riders drew hasty rein, followed by the exclamations of the men behind them, reining their mounts in quickly, as well.

They were closely bunched atop whickering mounts only a few feet down the rise below MacKenna.

She sat the Appaloosa on the top of the rise, glowering down at the men before her, her heart suddenly thudding fearfully. "What the hell are you lobos doing here?" she said sharply, holding the appy's reins up high against her chest. She sat blinking against her own dust and that of the Anchor riders ahead of her.

Anger mixed with fear inside her.

Stalcup and Battles gazed up at her, their own horses curveted and half-ways facing each other, the other horses and riders fanned out along the trail behind them.

Stalcup regarded her indifferently. Battles's hard eyes flashed lewdly. He grinned just as lewdly and leaned forward against his saddlehorn. "Well, well, well—look who's here. If it ain't the purty Miss Brannigan her own bodacious self!"

"I asked you a question," MacKenna snapped, her skin crawling beneath her shirt, where she felt Battles's goatish gaze raking over her.

"That don't mean we have to answer," Stalcup returned, canting his head to one side and narrowing his eyes at her. "You Brannigans think the world revolves around each and every one of you, always messin' in other folks' business, but it don't."

"Where's the marshal and Brandon?" Mac-Kenna said. If these men were out here, between Anchor and town, they could have intercepted the old lawman and his prisoner. MacKenna cast her gaze quickly down the hill to her right, halfway expecting to see two bodies hanging from a cottonwood standing along the creek down there, its breeze-brushed leaves glinting silver in the afternoon sunlight.

Relief touched her when she saw the cottonwood sporting no unnatural fruit.

That didn't mean another tree was not, however.

Battles glanced at Stalcup, grinned, then booted his piebald forward up the rise. He drew rein beside MacKenna, way too close to her for comfort, and dipped his chin to very obviously rake his gaze across her shirt again. "You look way too nice to always have your neck in a hump, Miss MacKenna. A smile instead of a frown would go so much better with the, uh"—he dropped his lusty gaze again to her shirt—"rest of you."

Stalcup chuckled.

Several of the men behind him loosed devilish laughs and annoying snickers. One of the horses, a white stockinged black, whinnied, and its rider leaned forward to pat its wither, keeping his own goatish gaze on the scowling Brannigan girl sitting the handsome appy on the rise ahead of him.

MacKenna glared at Battles, her jaws tight and her hard eyes narrowed as she said, "What did you do?"

"Who—us?" Stalcup said, arching his brows in mock innocence. He shrugged his beefy shoulders. "We didn't do nothin'."

Battles chuckled, keeping his gaze on MacKenna. "Con's right. We didn't do nothin'. Just sent a little message to that old blackbird of a useless lawdog's all. And to your former beau. You know the one. The one who impregnated my dear sis."

"What message is that?"

"He's got one week to fetch the judge and hold a trial," Stalcup said. "Then we hold our own trial. Out at Anchor."

"Says *who?*" MacKenna barked.

"Says *me!*" Battles said, tapping his chest. "It's my pa he killed."

"Why are you so sure?" MacKenna wanted to know.

"I seen him out there," Stalcup said. "There wasn't no one else."

"There had to be."

"Why did there have to be?" Battles said. "Just because you don't want to believe ol' doe-eyes is a cold-blooded killer?"

Was that it? MacKenna found herself vaguely wondering.

She tightened her back against her doubt, drew her shoulders back, and raised her chin. "Because he's not capable of doing such a thing. I know!"

"True, you know him better than we do," Battles said, chuckling again, devilishly. "But then, given what he did with my sweet sis when he was seein' you, you really don't know him all that well, do you?" He reached forward to slide MacKenna's long black hair back behind her right cheek.

She slapped his hand away, enraged, then reached forward and slid her Winchester carbine from its saddle boot. She cocked the rifle and aimed it at Battles's gut.

"Hey! Hey! Hey!" Stalcup intoned, holding one hand up, palm out.

"You ever touch me again, you weasel," Mac-Kenna barked at Battles, "I'll gut shoot you!"

She didn't give Battles a chance to respond. She reined the appy hard left, gave it the spurs, and galloped around the pack's left side then back onto the trail behind them. As she gained the bottom of the rise, she glanced over her right shoulder at them, all turning their horses now to stare after her, gazes suddenly vaguely incredulous.

All except that of Cass Battles, however. He was still grinning at her, his long devil's eyes narrowed, showing his teeth between stretched lips.

MacKenna cursed. She'd never hated any man as much as she hated Battles. She'd never had many dealings with him, but she'd run into him on the range from time to time, mostly during the fall gather, and she'd never liked the way he'd looked at her. She'd been able to read his mind. It wasn't hard to read the mind of a simpleton like Battles. Now she knew for certain why she hated him so badly.

Because she knew without any doubt that he, coupled with the cold-blooded Stalcup and their gang of hired killers, was capable of cold-blooded murder.

MacKenna glanced over her shoulder again.

The Anchor riders were riding on up and over the rise, away from her, dwindling from her sight, their dust rising behind them.

MacKenna off-cocked the Winchester, returned it to its boot, and nudged the appy into a faster run. Ten minutes later, she trotted the Appaloosa down Warknife's broad main street. She glanced to her right to see a big, moon-faced man with a beard and clad in a long, black duster step out of Logan's Gun & Ammunition Shop.

Lost in thoughts of Brandon Waycross, she turned her head forward and continued toward Marshal Southern's office. She did not see the two other men step out of the shop behind the big, bearded man. The big, bearded man wore a flat-brimmed, bullet-crowned black hat. The crown had a hole in it, up high and to the right. The second man, too, was big and moon-faced and clad in ragged trail garb. The third was small and with weak brown eyes but also with long, stringy brown hair, and a moon-shaped face. He wore a battered bowler hat, a hip-length, elk hide jacket over a hickory shirt, and baggy canvas trousers, the cuffs stuffed into stockman's boots worn to the texture of moccasins. Neither of the other two wore a beard, but no one could mistake all three men's close family resemblance.

The big, bearded man, who also had a scar running from the corner of his left eye clear down to the left corner of his mouth, cutting a grisly pink line through his beard, turned to the other two, arched his dark-brown crescent brows, and jerked his chin in MacKenna's direction.

She did not hear one of the others whistle softly under his breath.

Chapter 15

MacKenna reined her appy up to the hitchrack fronting Marshal Southern's long, low, wood-frame office and jail house. She strode up the three steps to the porch on which three chairs— two Windsors and a hide-bottom ladderback— were arranged around an overturned peach crate on which sat a checkerboard, neatly stacked red and black checkers, and an ashtray overfilled with the marshal's trademark wheat paper cigarettes.

MacKenna wrapped her knuckles on the door's upper glass panel then, not waiting for an invitation, turned the knob and stepped inside.

Her eyes went immediately to Brandon Waycross sitting in one of the four strap-iron cages lined up against the wall to MacKenna's right, two on each side of the door that led down into the basement cell block. It was in the basement where prisoners were housed when business was booming for Southern and his two deputies— usually on Friday and Saturday nights and on holidays or whenever a circus was in town. Southern kept a fairly tight rein on the town, following in the tradition of MacKenna's father back before she was even born, but, then as now, emotions erupted from time to time, and, then as now, men needed to be taken under rein.

Her eyes on young Waycross, MacKenna said, "Thank God!"

Lying on a cot in the cell just right of the basement cell block door, feet crossed at the ankles, Brandon lifted his head from his pillow. "Mack . . . what're you . . ." As he sat up, he winced as though against pain in his ribs. "What're you doin' here . . . ?"

"You're hurt!"

"It's nothing."

"Look at your face!"

MacKenna turned to where Marshal Southern sat at the large desk on the other side of the office, behind her. The lean, craggy-faced, gray-mustached lawman sat back in his swivel chair, facing MacKenna from the far side of the desk cluttered with papers and folders and large manila envelopes and age-yellowing wanted circulars. Boots crossed on the desk's edge, Southern was chowing down on the steaming plate of food he held on his chest, over the checked gingham bib he'd tucked into his shirt. His tan hat was overturned on the desk, beside another overfilled ashtray in which an ever-present lit quirley unspooled a thin stream of gray smoke into the room's dingy air.

Southern's also ever-present shotgun, the legendary Ol' Suzy, lay across a corner of the desk to his right. He'd just forked a big spoonful of roast beef and gravy-drenched mashed potatoes into his mouth when MacKenna had entered the office, and his right hand had reached at once for the shotgun until, identifying his visitor, he forestalled the movement.

Now, chewing, he sighed his relief and said, "Gave me a start, child!"

"I ran into the Anchor riders outside of town," MacKenna said. "I wasn't sure . . . you know . . ." She glanced over at Brandon, who dropped his feet to the floor and rose tenderly, pressing one hand against his ribs.

"No, they didn't throw us a necktie party," Southern said, stabbing his fork into another big chunk of nicely charred beef. "Wanted to give us a scare, I reckon. And a warning."

"I heard the warning."

"Yeah, well," Southern grumbled, slicing the meat chunk with his fork, then impaling it, smearing it around in the potatoes and gravy then shoving it into his mouth. "Wouldn't you know this had to happen when I'd sent my two deputies, Glenn Beach and Bob Early, over to Fool's Crow with a prisoner wanted by the reservation police. I'm hopin' they'll be back in a coupla days, but last I heard via the wire they got tangled up in some government red tape and it might take a while, and a federal judge, to get it sorted out. Sometimes the fates just laugh and laugh."

The marshal swallowed his food then leaned forward to pluck his cigarette out of the ashtray.

He took a deep drag, then tipped his head back, smiling dreamily, and sent the smoke pluming toward the ceiling.

"My God—you even smoke when you eat?" MacKenna said.

Southern looked at her, that dreamy, tobacco-induced smile still on his craggy, sun-burned face. "An intoxicating mix of flavors." He frowned. "Your pa with you, child?"

MacKenna shook her head then turned to where Brandon stood in the open door of his cell, frowning at her curiously.

"Shouldn't be out riding by yourself," Southern gently admonished her. "Not with the Anchor riders runnin' off their leash. Not with . . ." He let his words trail to silence.

"I know—those bushwhackers gunning for Pa. Ran into them out on the range."

Southern widened his eyes. "Anybody hurt?"

"No." MacKenna shook her head. Walking slowly toward Brandon, she glanced over her shoulder at Southern. "I'm not going to lie to you. I'm not supposed to be here, Marshal. I'll probably get the strapping I deserve. Haven't had one in a good five years now, but"—she turned her head back to Brandon—"I reckon I'm due."

She stopped in front of young Waycross and added with a distracted air as she gazed up at him, "I shouldn't have crossed Pa, but . . . I had to come see you, Brandon." Frowning, she shook her head. "Don't ask me why."

"You shouldn't have crossed your pa because of me," Brandon said, softly, reaching up and wrapping his left hand against the bars of the open cell door. "I'm not worth it."

"How bad are you hurt? Your face looks like hell."

"I'm fine."

"You don't look fine. One eye is swollen and . . ." She swung around to face Southern. "Shouldn't those men be arrested for this? Look at him!"

"All right, all right," Marshal Southern said behind MacKenna, with exasperation. He dropped his feet to the floor with a clang of spurs, set his plate on his desk, and swabbed the last of his potatoes and gravy from it with a ragged chunk of baking powder biscuit. "I got a woman at home who reads me from the book aplenty. Don't need another one here."

He rose from his chair, winked at MacKenna, donned his hat, plucked his canvas tobacco pouch off the desk by the ashtray, and strode out from behind his desk to the door and on outside, pulling the door closed behind him.

MacKenna turned back to Brandon who sighed as he opened and closed his hand around a bar of the cell door. "He's a good sort, Southern."

"It's nice of him to leave your door open."

179

"It is nice."

"I know how badly you hate being hemmed in, Brandon. Where did they find you?"

"I fell asleep along Bayonet Creek. Didn't hear them comin' till it was too late. Ringo, one of the ranch hands, tried to warn me, but I was too dang tired, too deep asleep. They surrounded me. I considered shooting it out, but, hell, one dead man's enough."

Young Waycross looked up at the hand squeezing the bar, flinched, and sighed. He lowered his hand, crossed his arms on his chest, leaned against the bars, and said, "Why'd you come, Mack?"

She shook her head sternly and lowered her gaze to his chest, for some reason unable to speak her next words to the soft, warm, brown eyes staring down at her, to the fine planes of the face, handsome despite the beating he'd taken . . . to the wing of brown hair curling down over his forehead and which, damn her, anyway, she wanted so badly to reach up and slide up off his forehead. "No. There's no more 'Mack.' I'm MacKenna to you now, Brandon. There is no more Mack. I didn't come here to try to restart our relationship. That horse has left the barn. You're going to marry Ivy Battles now."

"It kills you to say that, doesn't it?"

Instantly, as though a flash flood overtook an inadequate dam inside her, tears filled Mac-

Kenna's eyes and a sudden burst of emotion made her lips tremble. Her shoulders quivered and she heard herself say in a strangled little voice, "Yes!"

She squeezed her eyes closed, lowered her head, and sobbed.

Then his hands were on her arms and he was pulling her toward him and before she knew it, she was not resisting but stepping into him, lifting her head and opening her mouth to meet his as he lowered his face to hers.

His warm, full, masculine lips closed over hers, kissing her tenderly, with mounting passion. She groaned and sobbed as she returned the kiss while so desperately not wanting to but feeling a prisoner of her own emotion. Feeling as though she had no say in the matter.

"No!" she said suddenly, finally, reaching up with arms of lead, placing her hands against his chest, and pushing away from him, taking two steps back, out of his embrace. She gasped in horror of what she'd just succumbed to as she wheeled to face the opposite side of the room. She raised the back of her hand to her mouth, squeezed her eyes shut, and drew deep, even breaths, trying to reinforce that shattered dam inside her.

It would not be easy. She felt as though she were starting from scratch.

Tears continued to roll down her cheeks, then

finally, after a minute or so of steady, deep breathing, they stopped.

She jerked with a start as she felt his hand come down on her shoulder.

Again, she wheeled, this time to face him, to glare up at him. "Don't touch me. Don't touch me ever again!"

"I'm sorry, Mac . . . Kenna."

"I didn't come here for that." She tried very hard to keep feeling angry, nothing else. The anger had to push all the other foolish stuff away. "I came here because I knew you were alone, and you had nobody . . . nobody but her and she's not really all that much though you deserve her. I came here to let you know I was thinking about you. But only *thinking* about you. The *situation!* Nothing more. I don't love you anymore, Brandon. God, how could I?"

Yes, how could she? Why *did* she?

She had to suck back another sob that had started to roll up out of her throat. "I only came to assure you that my father and Marshal Southern will do all they can to get to the bottom of Battles's murder. That's all!"

She clenched her fists at her sides and resisted the temptation to stomp a boot down hard on the floor as though to punctuate her speech, to give not only the speech but her and Brandon's relationship a hard, final period. "I'm not going to see you again," she said, turning and taking long, hard strides to the door. "This was the last time."

She drew the door open quickly to cover the tremble she heard in her voice, felt in her heart . . . in her shoulders . . . knees.

Damn him for what he'd done to her. Damn her for still loving him despite what he'd done to her!

She stepped through the door, hesitated before setting her boot down on the porch. Marshal Southern stood with his back to her and slightly to her left, an unlit cigarette in his right hand. He was speaking to someone who was partly hidden by the marshal's tall, stoop-shouldered frame, but she could hear a slightly husky woman's voice. Around the marshal's right shoulder, MacKenna could see a thatch of red hair.

The woman's voice was saying, ". . . just wanted to let you know that I do appreciate you keeping an eye on my place, Marshal Southern. While I do have bouncers, they're no replacement for a man with real authority. I especially appreciate how you handled those four the other night." The woman glanced around Southern, her blue-eyed gaze finding MacKenna, her copper brows arching as though in surprise, eyes flashing appreciation at what they'd found standing behind the lawman. "Who's . . . this?"

The woman stared right into MacKenna's eyes with such intensity that MacKenna found herself feeling uncomfortable . . . feeling the need to look away. Which she did as she drew the door closed behind her, hearing the latching bolt click.

When she looked at the woman again, those lilac eyes were still glued to hers, as though plumbing the very depths of her. Did this woman know her? MacKenna began to think she did. Or thought she did . . .

Southern glanced over his right shoulder at MacKenna. A flush rose in his cheeks, behind his leathery tan. Then he turned, looking suddenly awkward, saying, "Oh . . . this . . . this, Miss Hayes . . . is . . . is . . ." The man frowned as though with deep consternation.

For God sakes, MacKenna thought, had he forgotten her name?

Pulling herself together, MacKenna stepped forthrightly forward, past Southern, and extended her hand to the lovely red-headed woman before her clad in what appeared a very expensive, hand-tailored gown of lime green silk and taffeta with white lace and brown trim. She wore a wrap of the same color around her otherwise bare, freckled shoulders, only partly concealing an opulent swell of freckled bosom inside a low-cut, form-enhancing corset.

The woman's perfume was rich with the smell of lavender and wild cherry blossoms.

"I'm MacKenna Brannigan," MacKenna said.

While she held her hand out to the woman, who MacKenna judged was maybe her mother's age or slightly older, the woman was slow to extend her own. She'd started to, but as soon as MacKenna had told the woman her name, the woman's beringed hand froze just after she'd started to raise it. She continued to stare into MacKenna's eyes. It was as though miniature lamps were lit inside the woman's own eyes, and her full, red-painted lips shaped a strange smile.

A slight flush rose into the fine, delicate lines of her freckled, alabaster cheeks.

Her smile broadened. She raised her hand, accepted MacKenna's own, and squeezed. Not shaking but just squeezing and holding the squeeze, still gazing deeply into MacKenna's eyes with that strange, unreadable smile.

"This, uh . . ." Marshal Southern said, half-raising his own left hand to indicate the woman before him, the consternated expression still in place on his face, "this is, uh . . ."

"Devon Hayes," the woman finished for him. "How nice to know you, Miss Brannigan."

CHAPTER 16

"Nice to meet you, Miss Hayes," MacKenna said, a little puzzled by the woman's reaction to her.

The woman continued to squeeze MacKenna's hand while gazing into her father's hazel eyes with her very luminous lilac ones that beautifully complimented the deep, lush red of her long, curly hair that tumbled across her freckled shoulders. The woman seemed deep in thought. Almost in a trance.

"I'm sorry," MacKenna said, frowning curiously. "Do we know each other, Miss Hayes?"

That seemed to snap the woman out of her reverie. She blinked, broadened her smile. An embarrassed flush rose in her cheeks, still firm and lovely despite her years. She released MacKenna's hand suddenly, self-consciously, and said, "I knew your father once . . . long ago."

"Oh?"

Marshal Southern, standing between the two women, to MacKenna's left, suddenly cleared his throat and dropped his gaze, flushing a deeper red than before. He toed a knot in a board of the porch floor, obviously uncomfortable.

Those haunting eyes were still on MacKenna's. "I take it he never spoke of me . . ."

"No . . . I don't . . . I don't think so," MacKenna

said, haltingly. Again, she frowned and canted her head to one side. "Should he have?"

Miss Hayes seemed to ponder that. She gave her head a quick shake and dimpled her cheeks with another smile. "Of course not. It was all so long ago."

"What was?"

"Hmm?"

"What was all so long ago?"

The woman's gaze lingered on MacKenna again, deeply pensive. "I'm sorry, Miss Brannigan. I've said too much, I'm afraid. A habit of mine." Those direct blue eyes traveled MacKenna's figure, clad in men's trail gear, as usual, from head to toe and back again. "My . . . you certainly are lovely. Breathtakingly so. I take it your mother is of . . ."

"Mexican descent."

"But you have your father's eyes."

"So I'm told." Suddenly self-conscious, MacKenna lowered her gaze to the porch floor.

"Well, then," Miss Hayes said quickly, turning to Marshal Southern as though she'd forgotten he was there. "I just came over to thank you for checking in on my establishment from time to time, Marshal. I hear there are a few parties of competing gamblers in town, and I wouldn't . . . well, I wouldn't . . ."

"You wouldn't want them exchanging lead in your fine establishment," Marshal Southern said, smiling down at the lovely woman. "Rest assured, I will do everything in my power to keep that from happening. As soon as my deputies get back from Fool's Crow, I'll send one of them over there to keep an eye on things. At the moment, I have a prisoner to watch."

"Very well. Thank you, Marshal." Miss Hayes reached out and gave the man's left forearm an affectionate squeeze. She returned her gaze a little hesitantly to MacKenna. A smile returned to her plump, red lips, but this time it was a rather weak smile, vaguely forlorn. Bittersweet? As though, long ago . . . too long ago for anything to be amended now . . . she'd missed out on an opportunity . . . ?

"It was very nice to meet you, Miss Brannigan. Maybe we'll run into each other again one day."

MacKenna smiled and shrugged. "I wouldn't doubt it. Warknife isn't all that big, and I get to town often, usually with . . ." She found herself letting her voice trail off. She frowned. Why had she had second thoughts about mentioning her father to this woman? Of course, it had been obvious what she'd been going to say, so instead of standing here stammering like a damn fool, she went ahead and finished the thought, smiling probably a little too brightly. "My father."

She just realized that she was feeling defensive about him.

"Of course. Good day, MacKenna. Marshal Southern . . ."

Miss Hayes stepped down off the porch, turned left, and began making her way east along the street, keeping to the boardwalks fronting the business establishments, attracting more than a few head-swiveling stares from the men milling around her.

MacKenna turned to Marshal Southern who stood, still holding the cold quirley in his long-fingered right hand, staring after Miss Hayes.

"Who is she, Marshal?"

Southern glanced at MacKenna. "Miss Hayes is one of the new owners of the Longhorn. Came up from Cheyenne. A woman of opportunity, I reckon." He gave a knowing smile.

"How did she know my father?"

Southern flinched at the question then turned his head to stare after the woman again. He stammered for a time and then he turned to MacKenna again and said, narrowing one eye, "I'm gonna let your father tell you about that, MacKenna."

MacKenna thought about that, her heart fluttering a little, anxiously. "Does . . . does Pa know she's here in town? Miss Hayes."

Southern drew a breath, let it out heavily. "Mack, I'm gonna let your father tell you about Miss Hayes. I will tell you one thing, though. Your father loves your mother more than anything in this world except for maybe you and your sister and brothers. Don't make too much of her." He lifted his chin to indicate Miss Hayes who was now lost in the crowded street. "She was a long time ago."

"I see." MacKenna chuckled, a little nervously. "Well, that's a load off."

Southern smiled at her, then turned to his office door. "If you'll excuse me, Mack. I'd best get back to work. You have a safe ride back to the Powderhorn. I'd escort you if—"

"No, no, I'm fine," MacKenna said. "At least I'll be fine until I get home." She was remembering that switching she might very well receive, and deserved. "You stay here with Brandon. Stalcup and Battles are notional. They might get to drinking tonight and have a change of heart and ride to town."

Southern frowned with concern. "They didn't pester you out there—did they, Mack?"

MacKenna smiled with pride. "Don't worry, Marshal Southern. I can take care of myself just fine." She glanced at the scabbard strapped to her saddle. "I know how to wield that carbine just fine. Ask Battles if I don't." She winked.

Southern laughed. "Don't doubt it a bit. I doubt they'll give me any trouble tonight, but I'll be here . . . with Ol' Suzy," he added with a wink and a grin, "if they do."

"Goodbye, Marshal Southern," MacKenna said,

stepping down off the porch and heading for the hitchrack.

"Goodbye, Mack."

MacKenna unlooped her reins from the rack, swung up onto the Appaloosa's back, and turned the horse out into the street after waiting briefly for a break in the wagon traffic. A dog came out and nipped at the appy's hocks as she put the horse into a trot, heading east toward the trail that branched off from the main one and headed south into the mountains, along Whiskey Creek.

MacKenna hardly noticed the dog, however, despite the appy's slight start. Her thoughts were with the lovely, lilac-eyed redhead who obviously still had feelings for her father.

Why had Tynan Brannigan never mentioned Devon Hayes?

Did he still hold a flame for her as she obviously still did for him?

It was a deeply unsettling thought. One that MacKenna had never had before regarding her father, one of the most loyal and honorable men she'd ever known. Did her father know that Miss Hayes was here in town?

Had they met?

If so, did MacKenna's mother know?

These troubling speculations persisted, preoccupying the girl's mind to such a thorough degree that she was only vaguely aware of turning off the main trail and heading south until movement on a bluff rising on her left snapped her out of it. It was like being pulled out of a waking dream. Suddenly, she was aware of her current place on the trail—she was roughly two miles south of town, following a long bend in the trail, with Whiskey Creek turning with the trail off its left side, beyond shrubs, cedars, and cottonwoods in which mourning doves and meadowlarks piped.

She lifted her head to peer up the bluff and suppressed a gasp when she spied a big, bearded man wearing a long, black duster and a bullet-crowned black hat sitting a gray horse on the bluff's crest. He was nearly straight above her, a hundred feet away, and he was staring down at her. He was silhouetted against the sun that was west-angling behind him, so she couldn't see him clearly.

But she remembered catching a glimpse of a big, bearded man in a long dark coat stepping out of the gun shop in Warknife just after she'd entered the town forty-five minutes ago. What had further distinguished him beyond his size and the beard was a grisly scar running down the left side of his face, clear from that eye to his mouth.

MacKenna checked the Appaloosa down and now sat holding one hand up against the sun as she stared up at the big man astride the gray.

"Hello, purty girl," the man said, his voice low and deeply resonant in the late afternoon silence, without a breath of breeze. He raised his voice with menace and mockery. "Sure a fine-lookin' piece of female flesh. You wouldn't be Ty Brannigan's daughter, now, would you?"

"Who're you?" Mack barked back at the man.

He grinned, shook his head, and made a lewd grunting sound, like that a man might make when savoring a plate of delicious food.

Before MacKenna could respond, the man neck-reined the gray back away from the edge of the bluff and disappeared, the horse's arched tail silhouetted against the cobalt sky the last thing MacKenna saw of horse and rider. Heart thudding, MacKenna stared up at the bluff. She was stiff with fear, and it was with effort that she reached forward with her right hand and slid her Winchester carbine from its saddle sheath angling up from beneath her right knee.

Feeling anger creep in, tempering her anxious-ness, MacKenna hardened her jaws and loudly racked a live round into the Winchester's action. She looked around, wondering if anyone else was out here, watching her.

Ogling her.

Not seeing anyone off the trail's left side, holed up in the trees and brush or on the lurk on the other side of the creek, she glanced up at the butte again. There was something about the large size of the man up there that seemed familiar to her. Familiar beyond having glimpsed him in town.

Had she seen him elsewhere?

Then, with a suppressed shudder, she remembered having the impression that the man she'd fired at in helping out her father earlier had been a man of considerable size, though he hadn't been bearded. She hadn't gotten a good look at him, but he'd moved heavily, climbed heavily into his saddle. And the back of the man she'd seen galloping away from her had been broad and thick—the back of a large, thick-set man clad in a long coat.

Not a duster. Maybe horse hide or something like that.

Were that man and this man connected?

Her hands shook as she squeezed the rifle. Some strange sense told her they were.

MacKenna removed her left hand from the rifle, keeping it free for the reins, and clucked the Appaloosa ahead, her heart beating quickly, hotly, nervously, angrily. She glanced up at the bluff that was falling away behind her now and said, "Show yourself, you cowardly devil! What are you running from? Are you afraid of a *girl?*"

Despite her anxiety, she'd pitched her own voice with mockery.

A crashing sound rose from the creek bed on her left. She gasped and turned that way, seeing brush move down near the edge of the water. A loud, coyote-like yammering rose from the same spot and, fear suddenly pushing out every other emotion inside MacKenna, she whipped her head forward with another gasp, crouched low, and put the steel to the Appaloosa, which whinnied shrilly and lunged forward into a ground-eating lope.

"Sorry to spur you that hard, boy!" the girl cried, squeezing her eyes closed as the horse shot up the trail, the horse's main buffeting against her face.

Another shrill, laughing, mocking cry rose behind her, accompanied by the rataplan of galloping hooves.

MacKenna did not look back. She knew the three stalkers were after her. She pulled her hat down tighter on her head to keep it from blowing off. After a couple of hundred, hard-pounding yards, she glanced over her shoulder, surprised to see the trail behind her empty. Puzzled but hopeful, she checked the Appaloosa into a trot, then, after yet another look over her shoulder, into a fast walk.

Nothing behind her but the two-track trail and low bluffs on one side, the cut of the creek a good distance from the trail now on the other side, the dark-brown water glinting in the gold and salmon hues of the late light.

Long, purple shadows stretched across the sage-peppered prairie.

She turned her head forward and saw the more

severe formations of the first front of the Bear Paws sliding toward her along both sides of the trail. She'd be home soon. She knew the trail by heart, knew the distances by heart. As soon as she took the next eastward curve in the trail and then followed it between two high, shelving sand-stone ridges leaning close against the trace, she would be only three miles from the Powderhorn headquarters. She'd be even closer than that if she took a shortcut well known to her and the rest of the family—one that was off-limits to wagons but anyone worth their salt on horseback could manage it just fine.

She glanced behind her once more. The trail was deserted. Only birds flitting between branches and her own curling dust.

Once again, relief rose inside her.

The men who'd frightened her had probably seen her coming, maybe even recognized her and decided to have some fun. Probably harmless fun to them but not to her. She was accustomed to being ogled in town. She'd started growing accustomed to it several years ago, when she was barely over twelve. At first, she'd found it flattering. But then, seeing a darkness in those admiring male eyes, it had given her a chill. There was admiration in those gazes, but there was goatish threat, as well.

Like the threat that had been in Cass Battles's eyes.

She'd once again experienced the dark side of male lust.

At least she had the carbine, Mack thought, squeezing the rifle's neck and pressing her finger reassuringly taut against the trigger. She was glad that Pa had taught her to wield it as well as he had. That was Pa. He knew the threat out here from animals as well as from men.

Thinking of men got her to thinking about her father and Devon Hayes again, and she was well on her way along the shortcut trail that threaded a narrow canyon between forested ridges when she realized she'd once again been so deep in thought for the past mile that she'd neglected to check her back trail.

Quickly, she turned her head to look over her shoulder.

Her gut tightened.

Not far behind her along the winding chasm, she saw three horseback riders through a screen of aspen leaves and pine boughs. They were murky, almost ghostly figures through the screening foliage. Walking their horses with menacing slowness, riding single file, casually sitting their saddles, they were just then rounding the bend that she'd come around only a couple of minutes earlier.

Heart once again racing, MacKenna turned her head forward and touched spurs to the Appaloosa's flanks. As she did, a man behind her laughed. A horse whinnied. Hoof thuds rose—a quickly rising rataplan.

"Should we take her now, Shep?" came a yell shrill with almost effeminate laughter.

A man yelled in a voice pitched with chilling, screeching mockery: "We're comin' for ya, little Brannigan girl!"

CHAPTER 17

MacKenna whipped her head forward and nudged the Appaloosa with her spurs. Again, the reliable mount laid its ears back, lowered its head, and shot up the trail.

MacKenna and the appy rounded another bend, and then the rocky trail rose straight ahead without another bend for a quarter-mile to the pine-stippled divide ahead. Behind her the whoops and hollers and the rataplan of horses' hooves grew louder. MacKenna could hear the creaking of tack, the jangling of bridle reins.

A narrow creek—virtually a freshet this time of the year—ran through a deep cut off the trail's right side, at the base of the southern ridge. MacKenna swung the horse down the bank and across the shallow water then up the opposite bank, wincing as brush clawed at her, one thorny branch clawing her right cheek. Once through the brush, she spurred the appy on up the ridge. As soon as the pines and aspens closed around her, she cast another wide-eyed look over her right shoulder.

One galloping rider and then another and then one more shot out from around the last bend in the trail and continued on up the rise, heading for the divide. Beyond the divide lay Powderhorn range. That route cut off from her now, MacKenna would have to find another way home.

Still, she heaved a shallow sigh of relief that she had, for the moment, eluded her would-be captors. She and the Appaloosa continued on up the ridge and through the pines that had concealed them from the stalkers. It wouldn't be long, though, before the three men would realize their quarry was no longer ahead of them.

Even simpletons, which something told Mac-Kenna these men were, could figure out that much.

The thought had no sooner passed through her brain than one of her stalkers laughed loudly, jeeringly, and bellowed with amusement, "Little vixen slipped away from us, boys. Come on!"

One of the other two gave a coyote-like, warbling cry and yelled, "We're right behind ya, Shep!"

As the appy lunged on up the ridge, picking its own way through the trees, MacKenna flinched when she heard splashing behind her as her hunters forded the creek. The splashing was followed by a great crashing and crunching of brush as the three men put their horses up the bank and began climbing the same ridge MacKenna was on.

"Oh, dear . . . oh, dear," MacKenna said as she whipped her rein ends against the Appaloosa's right hip, urging even more speed.

Her heart was a terrified child trembling inside her.

The horse gained the crest of the ridge, breathing hard. The top of the ridge was flat. It continued straight ahead to the south, as forested as the slope had been. Ahead, MacKenna saw a large, pale boulder sticking straight up out of the ground, amidst the pines. As she heard her stalkers angling toward her from her left, she stopped the appy behind the rock.

She waited, leaning forward, placing a reassuring, gloved hand against the appy's sweat-lathered neck. She pressed her forehead against the horse's mane. She, too, was breathing hard. She was sweating inside her wool shirt, and her heart was racing like some wild thing.

The drumming and crunching of the horses' hooves grew louder.

MacKenna heard the horses' strained breathing. She could hear the men's breathing, then, too. They were fairly panting like wolves on the blood scent.

Terrorizing her. That was their intention. To terrorize her and then overtake her.

Madmen!

She squeezed her eyes closed, slowly slid the Winchester from the saddle boot. Gritting her teeth and hardening her jaws, she clicked the rifle's hammer back to full cock. She held the Winchester in both hands, squeezing, hearing her stalkers grow closer and closer. Finally, they were right up on her, just on the other side of the boulder.

One of the men was making a strange sound—a garbled, mumbling, chuckling sound of great excitement. He was no doubt pondering what they would do with the "little Brannigan girl" once they'd caught her.

MacKenna stretched her lips far back from her teeth in dread, pressed her forehead and the brim of her hat even harder against the horse's neck. Her heart was beating so fast and hard she thought it would explode. She almost loosed a sob of holy terror but shook her head slightly, saying no to it, repressing it.

As the hoof thuds continued straight ahead of her, MacKenna lifted her head and opened her eyes. All three men were riding out from the other side of the boulder, maybe twenty feet just beyond her, angling off to her right and away through the tightly woven forest. The bearded man and one of the others, wearing what appeared a long elk hide coat, rode ahead of the third one, shorter and a little smaller than the other two and wearing a bowler hat and sun-coppered broadcloth jacket over a hickory shirt. The coat flapped out away from him, like wings, as he followed the others at fast trots through the trees.

MacKenna sat frozen in her saddle, watching

them. She felt as though a steel rod had been rammed up along her spine and clear up through the back of her neck.

Just keep going, she silently urged them. *Just . . . keep . . . going . . .*

As though the bearded man had somehow heard her silent plea, he checked his gray horse down abruptly. The man riding to his left stopped his own horse, then, as well, and curveted the mount.

"What is it, Shep?" yelled the third, smaller man in a slightly high-pitched, effeminate voice—though there was nothing effeminate about his moon-shaped face. He drew back on his own reins, then, as well.

The bearded, scar-faced man didn't say anything.

His eyes had found MacKenna from beneath the brim of his black, felt, bullet-crowned hat. A thong looped down from the hat to hang against his chest clad in sweat-darkened buckskin beneath the duster. He stared at MacKenna, expressionless. The other two followed his gaze. The face of the one nearest the bearded gent became flat and hard though his eyes glistened lustily.

The third man, who'd stopped his horse between MacKenna and the others, hooked a lopsided smile. "Why . . . there she is," he said in a soft, goatish voice.

The three were brothers. They had to be. They

looked too much alike not to be. Their faces were round, with large, round brown eyes. They looked stupid and mean as hell . . .

MacKenna thought her heart must have stopped. She couldn't feel it anymore.

Keeping his face expressionless, the bearded gent booted his horse forward, toward her. The man who'd been riding nearest him booted his steeldust forward, as well. When those two had ridden up even with the third man, who sat astride a claybank gelding, the third man nudged his own horse forward, too. He came on toward MacKenna, grinning, his brown eyes glinting beneath his battered bowler in the copper salmon rays of the dying sun.

MacKenna sat staring frozen in horror as her stalkers drew within forty feet of her. Within thirty feet . . . twenty feet . . .

Rage exploding inside of her, she raised the Winchester, screamed shrilly, loudly, the sound tearing out of her throat and vaulting toward the fading sky, echoing. It sounded like the angry, ratcheting cry of a hundred hunting hawks. She pressed the rifle's butt plate taut against her shoulder, lined up her sights on the bearded man quickly, and squeezed the trigger.

The rifle roared. The appy leaped beneath MacKenna.

She tightened her hold on the reins to keep the mount from pitching, then, seeing in the corner of her eye the bearded man tumbling down his gray's left hip, and hearing his indignant, guttural groan, she reined the appy around and galloped off around the rear of the boulder and into the forest to the east, heading in the direction from which her stalkers had come.

"Shep!" one of the men bellowed behind her.

More shots rose. A horse whinnied.

MacKenna put her head down and let the Appaloosa take her east at its own pace, leaping blow down and deadfall and weaving around trees. Her shoulders quivered not only out of fear of reprisal for what she'd done, but out of revulsion of what she'd done.

She'd be damned if she hadn't shot the big, bearded, scar-faced man plum out of his saddle! In her mind's eye, she saw him drop his rifle and throw his arms up and then fly down his horse's right hip. She shuddered again. She'd never shot a man before. Recently, she'd shot *at* a man, in his general direction. But that was only to scare him away from Pa.

But the big man with the beard—she'd lined up her sights on his chest and shot right *at* him.

She'd hit him, too.

Despite her automatic revulsion, the thought made her lips quirk a grin. He'd had it coming. That was for sure.

Again, she cast a cautious glance back over her shoulder, expecting to see the other two barreling toward her, triggering rifles. Surely, they'd come. And they'd be madder than hornets, too . . .

She jerked her head forward. A terrified scream vaulted out of her, and she drew back sharply on the Appaloosa's reins. A big man sat a big coyote before her, twenty feet away, between two lodgepole pines. His figure was obscured by the forest's deep shadows.

"MacKenna!" came her father's shout.

"Pa!"

Again, she rammed spurs into the appy's loins. The horse shot forward and she drew rein in front of her father, curveted the horse, leaned out over her left stirrup, and threw her arms around Ty Brannigan's thick neck.

"Oh, Pa!" she cried, finding almost over-whelming comfort in the presence of her father.

"I heard a shot!" Ty said, holding her taut against him. He gentled her back away from him, gazed into her face, his eyes cast with a father's terror. "What happened?"

"It was them," she said, her voice quavering.

"Who?"

"The three who were after you earlier. Least-ways, I think so."

"You sure?"

MacKenna nodded. "I saw them in town. Look, Pa, I know I wasn't supp—"

"No, you weren't supposed to ride to town, dammit, Mack." Ty cast his gaze over her shoulder, in the direction from which MacKenna had come. "Where are they now?"

"Back yonder. Not sure how far I rode. Maybe a half a mile. Maybe a mile." MacKenna paused, licked her lips then followed her father's gaze to the west. "I thought for sure they'd be after me by now." She turned back to her father. "I . . . I shot one of 'em."

Ty's eyes widened in surprise. "You did?"

MacKenna nodded slowly, still dazed at the gravity of what she'd done. "I . . . I might've killed 'im."

"Well, they need killin'. You wait here but keep that carbine handy in case they get around me."

Ty was about to rein away from his daughter but stopped when she grabbed his arm. "Pa, can't . . ."

He frowned at her. "What?"

"Can't we just go home? I'd . . . I'd really like to just go home."

Ty studied his daughter seriously. The light of understanding seeped into his eyes. He nodded. "Sure. We'll go home, honey. But you do know that's where you should have stayed."

"I know, Pa." MacKenna felt a knot of emotion in her throat. Not only had she likely killed a man, but she'd disobeyed her father. If she hadn't ridden to town, she wouldn't have gotten herself into the position she'd found herself in.

And Brandon Waycross had been right. He wasn't worth it.

Still, in spite of what had happened here this afternoon, she was glad she'd done it. She'd had to see him, and she'd seen him. She didn't think she'd have to see him again now. She thought that she'd closed the door on Brandon Waycross. She'd try not to think about him anymore.

But wasn't that what she'd thought after she'd met him on the butte last night?

"Come on, Mack," Ty said, reining his horse around, angling it down the slope toward the north, in the direction of the canyon trail MacKenna had left when she'd tried to elude her three stalkers.

MacKenna booted the Appaloosa into motion, riding up off her father's right stirrup. As they rode, Ty cast a cautious glance behind him then turned to MacKenna, a haunted look in his eyes. "I sure don't like that they came after you."

"I wasn't real thrilled about it, either." Mac-Kenna studied her father, saw the deep worry there. He'd thought that only he was in danger. But now he was realizing that his family—or at least MacKenna—was also in danger. Maybe they'd come after her only because she'd run them off earlier. Still, they were after her now, too. And maybe Matt, as well.

"Who are those devils?" Ty said aloud to himself, scowling down at his saddle horn in deep frustration.

"One called the big man Shep."

"Big with a beard and a scar?"

"That's him."

"Shep . . ." Ty said, scowling ahead, thoughtfully.

"Whoever they are, you sure musta got crossways with 'em, Pa."

"I must've. Somewhere . . . sometime."

"Pa . . . ?" MacKenna had to ask, because the question had been haunting her since she'd left town and not even her run-in with the three, moon-faced stalkers had seemed to snuff it out. "Did you know that Devon Hayes is in town?"

Chapter 18

The question came to Ty from his daughter's lips like a shovel slammed against his mouth. He turned to her in shock, feeling his lower jaw sag.

"I see," MacKenna said with a pale, dreadful look on her face. "You did know."

"Yes, I knew," he said, finally finding his tongue. "How did you know? How did you . . . ?"

"I met her at Marshal Southern's office."

Ty nodded slowly as he put his horse down the slope and into the canyon he'd left when he'd heard MacKenna's rifle shot. "I see." Bells were ringing in his ears.

"Does Mother know?"

Ty turned to MacKenna, who, riding to his right and also putting her horse down the slope and through the brush of the creek bank, leaning back in her saddle, the reins raised high, gave him a none-too-subtle-accusing look.

"No." The word was dull and flat on his tongue.

"Did she ever know?"

"About Devon?" Ty's guts twisted with guilt . . . regret. "No."

He should have told her. He wasn't sure why he hadn't.

"I don't know," he said, feeling as uncomfortable as his children must when forced to explain their behavior. "I guess I didn't think it important at the time. Your mother came two full years after . . . after Devon. Your mother so overwhelmed me that she sort of drowned out Devon's memory." His and MacKenna's horses splashed across the creek. The water splashed up cool against his pants. The light was fading fast, and it would be dusk soon. The mountain hollows were cold at night. "I don't think I've thought about her more than two or three times in all the years we've been married, your mother an' me."

"Miss Hayes still has feelings for you," MacKenna said, the last words of the statement coming out in a series of grunts as her horse lunged up the steep bank and onto the shortcut trail.

Ty climbed the bank, as well, and checked his horse down. MacKenna curveted the appy to face him, the breeze blowing her straight black hair back behind her smooth pale cheeks and clear, hazel eyes. Sometimes she looked so much like her mother when Beatriz had been only a few years older than MacKenna was now, that the vision of her twisted Ty's heart one quarter turn counter-clockwise.

It did now. So much so that it nearly brought tears to his eyes.

MacKenna had her mother's soulful eyes, as well, though MacKenna's were Ty's blue-green and not her mother's ink black. Still, they were

Beatriz's eyes, especially when that soulfulness was cast with accusing, as it was now. Soulful accusing.

Nothing made a grown man shrivel more!

"She couldn't," Ty said, shaking his head. "There's no way. It was too long ago."

"It's true, Pa. I may not be a full-grown woman yet, but I'm enough of a woman to be able to read the heart of another woman. It was in her eyes. She looked at me so strangely." MacKenna wrinkled the skin above the bridge of her nose and gave her head a quick couple of puzzled shakes. "As though she saw me as the daughter she'd never had. The daughter with Tynan Brannigan's eyes."

"My God!"

"What is it?" MacKenna asked.

"You are a woman, now, aren't you? How did that happen? Without me even knowing."

"I'm not so sure myself." MacKenna paused, keeping those eyes that looked jade now as a ray of saffron light strayed across them. "What are you going to do about her?"

Ty cast a cautious look up at the ridge. The gravity of the current conversation had not entirely distracted him from the threat of the three cutthroats. Turning back to MacKenna, he said, "I'm not going to do anything about her."

"Do you think she came here for you?"

"No. If she did . . . that would be foolish."

"I don't know, Pa. She looks like a determined woman to me."

"I reckon it takes one to know one, doesn't it?" Ty canted his head to one side and parried his daughter's none-too-subtle look of castigation with one of his own.

MacKenna was getting harder and harder to cow, however. She did not fade from his gaze. In fact, her mouth corners quirked a fleeting, proud grin.

"Come on." Ty turned his horse forward and booted it on up the trail with one more cautious gaze over his right shoulder. "It's gettin' late an' your mother's gonna be worried." He looked over at his daughter gigging her own mount into step beside him. "Let's keep that little incident concerning you and those three tough nuts from your mother, all right?" He didn't like keeping things from Beatriz, but she'd been through a lot in the past couple of days, and he wanted to protect her tender nerves.

He glanced at his daughter skeptically. "Did you really shoot the big fella with the beard?"

"I think I might have. Leastways, he fell from his horse. I must've hit him."

"Girl, I've said it before, I'll say it again—you got the bark on."

"I shot before I even thought about it, Pa. I just suddenly felt madder than a stick-teased rattlesnake!"

Ty laughed despite the gravity . . . and danger . . . of the situation MacKenna had found herself in. "One down . . . two to go. Maybe you took all three of 'em to the woodshed an' the other two have decided to pull their horns in. They might be headed back to town to buy tickets on the next stage out of Warknife."

Ty chuckled again, shook his head.

"Let's hope so."

They rode in silence for a time and then MacKenna looked over at her father again and said quietly, "Seems like we have a whole lot to keep from Ma, doesn't it, Pa?"

"Yeah, well." Ty's cheeks warmed with chagrin, and annoyance raked him. Who was the child and who was the parent here? Why did he seem to feel so much guiltier for what he'd done than MacKenna was feeling for what she'd done—namely, flagrantly disobeying his direct orders and riding to town to see Brandon Waycross?

"I think you'd better tell her, Pa," MacKenna told him, trotting her mount beside his. "It didn't seem to me like Devon Hayes thinks it's one bit important to keep your and her past relationship a secret. Ma's gonna find out sooner or later. And if it's much later than it already is . . . well, there might be hell to pay. And you know how she can make you pay it."

Ty winced as he and MacKenna topped the

breezy divide. "You got me there, daughter. You got me there . . ."

"Where ya hit, Shep? Where ya hit?" asked Buford Parmelee, swinging down from his horse and running over to where his older brother, Shep, lay on the ground groaning and grinding the heels of his boots into the forest duff.

"Where the hell's it look like I'm hit?" bellowed Shep, the largest of the three remaining Parmelee brothers. "This hole in my shoulder's big enough to drive a buckboard through!" He was not only the largest but the oldest—the one with a beard and a nasty facial scar he'd picked up sometime during his twenty-five years in the Wyoming Territorial Penitentiary near Laramie.

Of the three remaining Parmelee brothers, Buford was now the youngest and smallest. Jeoffords had been the youngest though not the smallest, but as of two days ago, Jeoffords was dead. Carlisle, who remained on his horse casting his enervated gaze between his wounded older brother and the rock from where the Brannigan girl had just blown Shep off his mount, wondering if he should get after the gun-savvy little vixen or stay here with Shep, was now the middle brother, between Buford and Shep, who was forty-six and angrier than an old wet hen at having been locked away for over half of those years. He'd still be locked away if two years ago he hadn't escaped from a crew of prisoners building a railroad trestle over Climax Canyon on the Wind River.

Carlisle wasn't quite as big as Shep, who'd honed his neck, shoulders, chest, and legs during the forced labor of digging mountain train tunnels. He'd honed his nasty disposition around those rocks and surly, club-wielding guards, and a good bit of solitary confinement, as well. Whoever had taken that knife to his face hadn't helped any.

Buford didn't know who'd given Shep the nasty tattoo. Shep had so far never mentioned the scar, which had likely been carved by an angry cellmate or a sadistic guard wielding a dull, rusty pig-sticker. Since Shep hadn't brought it up in the two months he'd been out, Buford and his other two brothers, one now dead, hadn't brought it up, either. Given Shep's sour moods and dark, glowering stares that grew sourer and darker when he hit the bottle, they thought it best to ignore it.

Jeoffords had been the youngest brother until two days ago. Jeoffords had fancied himself a gun-slinging cardsharp though neither his prowess with an ivory-gripped Colt or the pasteboards had saved him when he'd gotten high-headed and decided to try to take down the old former lawdog and town tamer, Ty Brannigan, alone. At thirty-five, Jeoffords had been the youngest, two years younger than Buford, thirty-seven, though it hadn't mattered all that much since Jeoffords had been only a half-brother and not genuine, full-blood kin.

And the three blood-brothers had never liked Jeofford's uppity mother.

Jeoffords had left a pretty, spare set of .45s and a folding Barlow knife with a naked lady carved into its handle. He'd also left his pretty young wife, Lisa. Jeoffords hadn't been all bad, though the full-blood brothers had never cottoned to him much because he'd thought he'd been better than they were, his mother having been from a land-owning line of South Georgia Piedmonts.

Still, since his father had been Wilfred Parmelee, he'd been a Parmelee. So his death would have to be avenged.

The Parmelees hailed from the mountains of Tennessee. Revenge was how things were done in Tennessee. It was in the Parmelees's blood. It was how they did things here in Wyoming, now, too. Revenge for dead family members, and revenge for a man losing half his life to a squalid prison. Ty Brannigan had been the Warknife lawman who'd put Shep away for cutting the throat of a circuit preacher with a broken whiskey bottle before raping the man's wife.

Now Shep was out after twenty-five long, hard years and a good dozen, ill-fated escape attempts. When he finally had escaped two years ago, he'd headed to the mountains of Colorado to let his trail cool. He'd returned to Wyoming a month ago with the vengeance fever fairly glowing in his eyes.

He'd spent those two years in Colorado robbing stagecoaches for stake money, and savoring . . . planning his revenge for twenty-five years gone. He'd just hoped Brannigan would still be alive when he got out. So he, Shep, could kill him slow.

A fair exchange, Shep thought, for the twenty-five years he'd never get back as well as the nasty scar on his face that had gotten infected and nearly killed him. The infection had done something to his brain. The infection and twenty-five lost years. But, then, the twenty-five lost years alone, not even considering the infection, would do anything to anybody's brain.

Now, by God, Brannigan would pay. And Shep's brothers were going to help him exact his reckoning, for that's what kin were for. Loyal kin, anyway. Jeoffords hadn't been loyal. He'd gotten high-headed and impatient and in a hurry to get back to the craps tables with Lisa, so he'd gone out alone to kill Brannigan and had received in return just what he deserved—hauled back to town lying belly down across his blood-smeared saddle.

The three blood brothers had had a good chuckle over that. That was a high-headed Piedmont for you.

"That looks awful painful, Shep," Buford observed, crouching and staring down at the blood oozing out around the gloved hand his oldest brother held taught against his left shoulder.

"Shep, you want I should go after that little trollop?" Carlisle asked.

"No," Shep said, shaking his head and grinding his teeth. "Save her for later . . . when I can enjoy what we do to her!" He groaned and tilted his head back until the cords stood out in his muscular neck like ropes. "Damn her purty hide!"

He thrust his left hand up at Buford. "Help me up, dammit. Carlisle, fetch my gray. I gotta get back to the cabin, get this bleedin' stopped. Dammit, I can't die! Not after all the years I laid awake dreamin' about what I was gonna do to Brannigan. That preacher's wife was waggin' it around like a damn flag. What's a man *supposed* to do? Soon as I follow her into her wagon, she starts screamin' rape, an' the old parson comes runnin' with a shotgun. Ah, hell—just get me on my damn hoss, Buford!"

"All right, all right, Big Brother," Buford said. "Carlisle's bringin' it now!"

When Carlisle had drawn Shep's horse up near where Shep and Buford stood, Buford trying like hell to keep his older, larger brother on his feet, Shep grabbed the reins out of Carlisle's hand.

"Help me now," Shep said, reaching up with his

left hand to grab the horn. "I'm so damn weak—*damn that girl's hide!*—I'm gonna need help into the saddle."

Carlisle scrambled down from his own horse, and he and Buford back-and-bellied their older, larger, grunting, and cussing brother up onto his beefy gray gelding, which he'd stolen from a rancher a few miles from where he'd escaped the prison work crew. He'd evaded the hunters and trackers and yowling blood hounds for three days before he'd secured the horse. After he'd secured the gray, he'd been as free as the wind and, tilting his head back, howled victoriously all the way back to the little shotgun ranch his brothers still ran with their old, decrepit father and Jeofford's pretty though sassy little wife, Lisa.

The ranch was near Rawlins, only a two day's ride straight north to Warknife up in the Bear Paws and west of the Wind Rivers. Shep had gathered possibles and guns and knives at the family ranch, then headed south to Colorado to let his trail cool.

"Let's go, boys," Shep said, when he'd taken up the gray's reins. He'd ripped off his neckerchief and stuffed it into the wound; he held it in place with his blood-soaked, gloved right hand. "I just hope that useless little tart of Jeoffords has some doctorin' skills," Shep said. "She has damn little enough of everything else, she better have some of *that!*"

Shep booted the gray into a full gallop, heading straight west to where he and his brothers and the pretty, sassy Lisa had moved into an old mining shack in a remote canyon at the base of a peak they'd learned from passing ranch hands was called Dancing Bear Peak because from a distance and at a certain time of day it resembled nothing so much as two bears dancing.

"She better at least have some *doctorin' skills!*" Shep roared, throwing his head back again on his shoulders. A little more quietly but with deep menace, he added, "Or so help me *God!*"

Riding behind him, Buford and Carlisle shared a dark, dubious look.

CHAPTER 19

Ty Brannigan heaved himself up out of the steaming copper tub in his and Beatriz's second-story bedroom in the lodge house at the Powderhorn headquarters.

He reached for a towel hanging from the wooden rack beside the tub and dried himself, starting with his hair and neck and then his chest and arms—going easy on the wounded left one, of course—and then his legs and, finally his back. He was groaning luxuriously as he ran the thick towel back and forth across his broad back, the flesh beneath the blades still layered with hard muscle, when the bedroom door opened, and Beatriz stepped inside.

She'd taken a bath before Ty had and was wearing a thick, cream robe. Her hair was bound atop her head in a blue towel turban. After her bath, as was her way, she'd gone downstairs to lay out everything she would need to prepare breakfast the next morning, and to make sure that each of the children, especially the two youngest ones, were settled in for the night. Sometimes Carolyn, a little on the nervous side, as was Beatriz herself, had trouble falling asleep right away and needed her mother's reassuring voice in her ear while Beatriz brushed out the girl's tawny hair, before she could succumb to the evening's slumber.

Still raking the towel across his back, Ty smiled at his lovely wife over the room divider that separated their sleeping part of the bedroom from the bathing and dressing area. His children's mother was still flushed from her own hot bath. "Is Carolyn settled in, honey?"

"Si, Carolyn is settled in." Beatriz closed the bedroom door then leaned back against it, crossing her arms on her chest. "MacKenna is the one I am most worried about tonight."

Her voice was firm, none too vaguely accusing. She narrowed one ink-black eye at her husband. The light of an amber lamp on the dresser to her left flickered in it.

Ty tossed the towel on a chair and reached for his faded red plaid robe that was also hanging from the rack beside the tub. "Oh?"

"Don't 'oh' me, Ty Brannigan. Something happened out there"—she lifted her chin to indicate the country north of the ranch, between the Powderhorn and town—"to MacKenna. Didn't it? She hardly said two words over supper, and that is not like her. She has a scratch on her cheek and I don't think she was just being careless. She is rarely that. She kept glancing at you . . . as though you two are harboring a secret from me. Which would be nothing new, of course."

Steadily, Beatriz's voice had grown louder

until Ty was sure it had penetrated the childrens' bedrooms. Her voice continued to grow louder as her passion built, and Ty found himself stealing against the onslaught he knew was building to a crescendo. "I don't like it when you keep the secrets from me, Tynan! I know you think you are protecting me from worry, but I am no fool! I know when something is wrong with my children, and I will not be treated like a silly child myself!"

"Easy, baby, easy," Ty said, walking toward her slowly, holding out his hands in supplication.

"Don't tell me that!" Beatriz said, raising her hands to clamp them over her ears. Her eyes blazed with anger. "I will not be told to take it easy. I want to know what is happening with this family. ¿*Entiendes*?" Can you understand?"

"I understand!" Ty placed his hands on her arms and drew her close against him. "I understand, baby."

"*Bueno*," she said crisply.

"Come."

Ty took her hand and led her over to the bed. He sat down on the edge of the big, red-canopied bed hand-built by the rancher himself with a thick red-plaid comforter and ornate posters carved and painted in the Spanish style—and patted the mattress beside him. "Have a seat."

It had been a Christmas present to his darling,

on their second Christmas together, with Matthew already a year old.

Beatriz stood before him, her left thigh pressing against his right knee, staring down at him, studying him skeptically. She wasn't sure she wanted to give in so easily, he knew. She'd been married to Ty Brannigan for twenty years. She knew all of his tricks and was wary of falling prey to one. He knew her well enough to know this about her. He also knew that because he knew her well enough to know this about her, he should also know not to hide things from her. She was smarter and wilier than he was, and trying to keep things from her hardly ever worked.

It only made her angry.

In his defense, it was in his nature to want to protect her. She was high-strung, and he didn't want her to worry. But she'd been right. He'd been treating her like a child, and she had every right to be angry.

Wouldn't he himself want to know everything that was going on with her and his children? Beatriz could handle life's harsh truths as well as he could.

"Sit down beside me, baby, and I'll tell you," he said, keeping his voice low so that it did not penetrate the children's rooms though they knew their parents were having a row.

That was all right. They were used to it. They

also knew that when you brought two strong-willed, passionate people like Ty and Beatriz Brannigan together, you could not expect there not to be rows. It was part of their passion for each other. Part of their love.

"All right," Beatriz said, finally, sitting slowly down beside him, keeping her own voice low now, as well. "I will yield to your wishes if you yield to mine." She turned to him, sandwiched his big, weathered face between her long-fingered, work-toughened hands, and slid her face up close to his. Her eyes were warm now, still admonishing but soft, waiting . . . "Tell me."

He told her first about his run-in with the three stalkers and about how Matt and MacKenna had heard the shooting and rode in to save their father's bacon, so to speak. Then he told her about MacKenna riding to town against his orders and running in to those very same stalkers who'd bushwhacked Ty on her way home.

He finished by telling Beatriz about Mac-Kenna's believing she shot one of the stalkers.

Beatriz arched a brow and widened her eyes, impressed. She nodded slowly. *"Buena."* She continued nodding appreciatively. *"Buena para ella . . ."* Good for her.

Ty smiled at his wife's reaction. "She's tough . . . and good with a carbine. I hadn't realized how good."

Beatriz caressed his cheeks with her thumbs.

"You taught her well, *mi buen hombre*. She is tough, like you."

"They are both tough—Matt as well as MacKenna." Ty pulled one of Beatriz's hands to his lips and kissed it. "Tough like both of us."

"You see I am not running around screaming like some tender-livered crone, mi amore. You can tell me what I need to know."

"Si, mi amore. I know. I know."

"Now tell me," Beatriz said, putting some steel in her voice, dropping her chin slightly, and gazing directly into his eyes. "What are you going to do about these men?"

She still had her hands on his face. He reached up and wrapped both of his hands around her wrists, squeezed them reassuringly. "I'm going to hunt them down and kill them . . . bury them in shallow graves."

"Ah!" Beatriz smiled as though thrilled. "Si, si—that is the hombre I married! The fierce town tamer, Ty Brannigan. I fell in love with you when I heard the first stories about you, from your time in Abilene, if you want to know the truth, mi amore. Before I even met the handsome town marshal of Warknife."

"Really?"

"Then, when you finally got around to introducing yourself with your hat in your hands—the big, rugged lawman-pistolero with hands like the heads of sledge hammers!" She smiled brightly into his eyes, her own black ones slanting up at the corners, one crossing slightly, beautifully. "There was nothing my poor father could do to keep me away from you!" She sat back and threw her head back, laughing in wicked delight. She had a lovely laugh, especially when she was laughing in wicked delight.

Ty smiled. "The poor man."

"Si. The poor man."

"Honey?"

She frowned, having spotted the sudden strain in his gaze. "Si, what is it, Ty?"

"I have something else I need to tell you."

Beatriz drew her head back, and her eyes grew incredulous. "Oh? Was there *more* trouble from these men?"

Ty winced. "Honey . . . this is a tough one."

"A tough one."

"Yes, a tough one." Ty leaned forward and entwined his hands together between his knees. "There's something I didn't tell you. I should have told you back when we first started courting, but it really didn't seem that important. *She* didn't seem that important."

Beatriz's eyes grew larger. The lamplight flickering in them resembled a hundred miniature bayonet blades—all aimed at Ty's heart. "*She* didn't seem all that important?"

Ty drew a fateful breath, let it out slowly. "There's a woman in town. I didn't know she was here until yesterday. MacKenna met her today at Chris Southern's office."

"MacKenna met her . . . this woman . . . at Chris Southern's office . . ." Beatriz stated the words as though trying to understand them fully and clearly. Her gaze was so direct, like her daughter's earlier, that Ty was having trouble meeting it. It was like two flames held up close to his eyes.

"Look, honey, her name is Devon Hayes."

"A most beautiful name."

"I knew her back in Abilene . . . before you and I started courting."

"How long did you know this lady with the pretty name, Ty?"

"Only about six months or so. She was an actress. A showgirl . . ."

"An actress . . . a *show*girl . . . ?"

"She had been part of a traveling theatrical troupe but she made such an impression that after she was in Abilene for a few weeks, she was hired full-time at the local opera house."

"Ah." Beatriz raised her brows, nodding. "I didn't know you'd courted such women, mi amore."

Ty smiled a little sheepishly, chuckled, squeezed her hand. "You wouldn't understand. This was Abilene . . . twenty-five years ago. A different time, a different place."

"A different man . . ."

Ty scratched the back of his head and stretched his lips back from his teeth. "You didn't ever run in such circles."

Truth be told, the upright and regal daughter of Diego Salazar didn't run in any circles. As beautiful as she'd been, after she'd returned home from Mexico after several years in academies for young women and finishing schools, she'd worked full-time for Diego in his bank, starting out as a bookkeeper then moving up quickly to loan manager, handling some of the largest accounts in Custer County. With the beautiful Beatriz Salazar handling loans, Diego had had no trouble in securing business relationships with rich and powerful ranchers and other moneyed businessmen.

He'd hoped his lovely daughter would marry one of them.

"How well did you know this actress, Tynan?"

Again, Ty winced. When she used his full first name, he knew he was in trouble. She was liable to blow her top and start spewing verbal lava again at any moment.

"Well . . ."

Beatriz placed his hand on her knee. "Yes . . . ?"

Ty turned to her. "We were going to be married."

Beatriz removed her hand from his knee and just stared at him in mute shock, mouth one-quarter open.

Ty returned his guilty gaze to his entwined hands. "It all happened so fast. I felt . . . I felt the weight of the years . . . I was already thirty-six . . . and I had no family . . . no prospects for one. I'd been so busy for the last ten, twelve years, working in Kansas and Oklahoma . . . Milestown . . . well, I started looking around. And . . . well . . . my eyes landed on this pretty actress I saw one night in a performance of Pocahontas at Donovan's Opera House."

"She was playing Pocahontas at Donovan's Opera House." Again, a statement, not a question.

"Yes."

"And you fell in love with her."

"I did."

"And now she's in Warknife."

"She is."

"And my daughter knew about her before I did."

Again, Ty flinched as though he'd been slapped.

Beatriz gave him another of her painfully direct, barbed gazes, her voice rising a little. "Why is this, Tynan?"

"I didn't think it necessary to tell you."

"Why didn't you marry her?"

"She left. One day she was in town, the next day she was not in town."

"Oh . . . very mysterious, this lady."

"Beatriz . . ."

"Have you harbored feelings for her all these years, mi amore? Is that why you didn't tell me about her?"

Ty turned to face her, took her hands in his, squeezed. "It's nothing like that, I assure you. After I met you, I forgot about her. You swept me away, my love. You were . . . are . . . the only woman I think about."

"There is more."

Ty frowned. "What?"

"There is more to why you didn't tell me . . . didn't even mention her name in passing to me in the twenty years we've been married." Beatriz placed a hand on his cheek. "Tell me."

Again, Ty frowned. He searched his mind for what she was talking about, but could find nothing.

"She hurt you," Beatriz said tenderly. "She embarrassed you. When she left."

"Ah," Ty said, lifting his chin then nodding slowly, returning his gaze to his wife, who, indeed, was far wiser than he. He felt his cheeks warm a little with the embarrassment she'd spoken of. "Si. I was ashamed. Humiliated. Me— the great Ty Brannigan, town tamer, lawdog . . ."

"*Abandonada*. By a woman." Jilted.

He smiled guiltily, nodded. "Si. *Abandonada*. That's probably why, soon after she left, I heard about the town marshal's job in Warknife and applied for it. It's a long way from Abilene."

"Tell me," Beatriz prodded, keeping her hand on his rugged face, "what do you feel beneath the shame?"

"What do you mean?"

"Is it love? Hatred? Or something in between?"

Ty looked around the room, as though for the answer his wife was looking for . . . and that he'd suddenly found himself looking for now, too . . . lay hidden in the shadows of the dresser or armoire, perhaps behind the brocade chair in the corner by the window, where he often sat at night when he couldn't sleep, the weight of the world . . . old memories of his more violent days . . . pressing down on him.

Finally, as the shadows inside his own mind took a more certain shape, he turned to his lovely wife. "It's far from love. It's far from anger now, too. I was angry for a time. Injured, I suppose, though I never let on even to myself. What I feel for Devon Hayes now, after all these years, mi amore, is absolutely nothing. I didn't mention her to you because I didn't want to needlessly complicate things between us. But I see now I should have told you about her."

"Si, you should have." Beatriz leaned forward and placed a tender kiss on his nose. "But now you have. Better late than never, eh?" She smiled.

"Yes."

"Will you see her in town?"

"Well, it's a small town."

"When you see her again, you tell her from me that you have a wild Mexicana for a wife, and if she tries to win you back after all these years, she will wake up some night with a stiletto in her guts!" She hissed, cat-like, and poked a finger between his ribs, twisting it as though it were the blade of a razor-edged stiletto.

Ty laughed and took his love in his arms, lay back and rolled over, on top of her, kissing her passionately, running his right hand across the lushness of her body.

Beatriz returned the kiss, groaning, running her hands through his hair. Suddenly, she opened her eyes. They were cast with concern. "Tynan— your arm!"

Ty grinned. "Can't feel a thing."

He opened her robe.

In the four other bedrooms up and down the second-floor hall of the Brannigan house, all four children had heard the row and had known what was coming. As loud as their parents' arguments nearly always were, the time afterward, when they each raised a flag of truce and prepared to make reparation, was often even louder.

The Brannigan brood each rolled onto their bellies with a bemused sigh, pulled their pillows over their heads, closed their eyes, drew some deep breaths against the loudening onslaught of their mother's love wails, their father's grunts and groans, and the squawk of strained bedsprings, and . . . one by one . . . they fell asleep.

Chapter 20

"Could just ride for home," Buford Parmelee muttered half to himself as he and his brother, Carlisle, approached the town of Warknife.

On this dark night weakly lit by a quarter-moon obscured by high, thin clouds, the town was little more than a ragged shadow spread across several low prairie swells before them. The moon glinted off of slanting, shake-shingled roofs and off the leaves of cottonwood trees pushing up close to the trail now as it became a street upon entering the town's southern outskirts.

Buford had muttered the statement half to himself, but his brother, riding ahead of him, had heard. Carlisle turned his head to one side, the brim of his hat casting a shadow across his face, blotting it out. That was just as well. Carlisle looked so much like Shep—a beardless Shep, that was—that he scared Buford a little. Buford knew he'd inherited the likenesses of each brother, but he wasn't nearly as big and strong, and he didn't think his eyes were as hard as either man's. At least, he didn't feel they were hard, though he thought he could use a dose of that hardness down deep in his soul, just so he could stand up to Shep, if for no other reason.

"What's that?"

Buford cleared his throat, hesitated. "I said we could just turn for home—you know, Carlisle!" He'd said the words louder than he'd intended, in a rush of desperation.

Carlisle halted his horse abruptly now and glanced around at the low-slung log shacks and stock pens that populated this end of the town on both sides of the street, some nearly overtaken by brush. A sprawling lumberyard sat up the street a hundred feet away, a large but uncertain shape in the darkness. The wan moonlight glinted dully off of the dark windows of the shacks facing east, to Buford's left. As he, too, looked around, he spied a cat hunkered low beside a rain barrel, watching the two men warily, eyes glowing copper in the darkness.

From somewhere in the buttes to the north, a nightbird hooted.

"Will you keep your damn voice down?" Carlisle admonished his brother, raspily. Again, he glanced around then returned his peevish gaze to his younger brother. "You wanna wake the whole damn town?"

"I'm just sayin' . . ." Buford said, just above a whisper now. He shrugged a shoulder, weakly. "That man we left back there in that shack . . ." he continued, a little guiltily, ". . . I'm startin' to wonder if he really is Shep Parmelee. He's mean an' ornery and downright nasty, Carlisle. Always climbin' my hump. Why are we riskin' our necks for him, anyways? All he does is call us girlish and stupid, gives us hell every time we turn around. He was even pinchin' Lisa's butt before Jeoffords died! Hell, I hardly even remember him from back before he went to prison. I don't know why we're riskin' our necks just so he can get revenge."

Carlisle put his coyote dun up close beside Buford's sorrel. Keeping his voice low, he said, "That's because you were barely ten years old when that judge put him away—for life! You'd have a chip on your shoulder, too, if a judge gave you a life sentence just for takin' what some little tart was waggin' in your face and then killin' some sky pilot who was out to fill you full o' buckshot! Some Bible-grindin' snake oil salesman who couldn't keep his alley cat wife on a leash!"

Buford fidgeted around in his saddle, again guiltily.

"That man back there in that cabin," Carlisle continued, raising an arm and extended index finger, pointing south, "is our blood brother. Jeoffords was only half, and he died tryin' to boast how tough he was. Damn foolish move. The way I see it, he got what he paid for. But Shep, he was a good man before prison. The way I see it, Brannigan took that away from him. Now, Shep's blood, you see. A Parmelee sticks with blood. *Fights* for blood! Understand, Buford? Besides, what're we gonna do—ride home an' tell Pa we left Shep up here to fend for himself—*with a bullet in his hide?*" Carlisle shook his head. "The old devil would take a bullwhip to us both, an' we'd deserve it."

Buford sighed. He was starting to come around to view the situation the way Carlisle saw it. He was right. Blood was blood. Shep might have been meaner than a sand rattler, but he was family. He was blood. He'd been wronged. That had to be made right. Buford felt especially guilty now. And cowardly for having said what he'd said about skinning for home.

That was not what a Parmelee would do.

Sometimes he felt bad for the weakness he felt inside himself.

"You got it, brother," he said now, keeping his voice low but putting some steel in it. He'd been cowed so many times since Shep had returned so unexpectedly from Colorado that he'd lost all of the steel in his voice and in his general countenance, he realized now. "I . . . I see it your way. Let's find that sawbones and get him out to the shack so he can tend Shep, get him back on his feet. Then all three of us Parmelees'll go after Brannigan and turn him into worm food. Hell, I'll lead the charge!"

"Now you're talkin'," Carlisle said. "Brannigan and that nasty little viper of a daughter of his, too."

"Her, too!" Buford said, forgetting himself and raising his voice again.

"Shhh!"

"Ah, hell—I'm sorry, Carlisle!"

"Come on—let's go lookin' for a pill roller before you wake up the whole town and the town law, to boot," Carlisle wheezed out. He turned his horse around and nudged it up the dark street.

He and Buford rode on up to the intersection of this secondary street and the main one and then turned a left onto the main one, riding slowly side by side, keeping to the street's shadows. They scoured the signs on the buildings to each side, looking for a doctor's shingle.

They rode all the way to the end of the street, where the town straggled back out into rolling sage prairie and, cussing to themselves, were about to turn around and ride back the way they'd come, certain they must have missed a medico's shingle.

"Every town has a doctor!" Carlisle wheezed out, stopping his horse.

"Must be on a side street," Buford opined aloud but keeping his voice down. "We're gonna have to scour the whole damn tow—"

"What the hell you two lookin' for?" came a man's slurred, nettled voice on the street's south side.

There was a saloon over there—the Chugwater Inn. The voice had come from the dense shadows in front of the small, low-slung watering hole, which was closed and dark. All of the saloon and parlor houses closed around one-thirty. That was the ordinance here in Warknife. A couple of stray rays of moonlight angled through the high, ragged clouds to illuminate the crude wooden sign hanging from chains beneath the roof over the saloon's front stoop.

Buford and Carlisle shared a glance. Buford's heart thumped anxiously.

Buford could tell by the expression on his larger, beefier brother's face that he was anxious, too. Still, Carlisle turned his head toward the saloon again and said into the shadows, "Sawbones. One of the hands is sick."

That was good, thought Buford. Let the man think they were ranch hands.

There was the pinging sound of a bottle falling over. Following the sound to its source, Buford thought he could see the vague outline of a man sitting back against the saloon's left front corner, beside a stack of empty whiskey crates.

"Dammit," came the man's curse. Louder, he said, "Straight on!"

"What's that?" asked Buford.

"Straight on!" came the man's voice, heavy with a building impatience. "Doc Hinkenlooper lives a quarter-mile outta town to the west. Little house in a grove of trees by the river. Now get the hell out of here. I need my beauty sleep!"

The man yawned.

Then came slow snoring.

Buford and Carlisle shared another look, this one a more agreeable one, brows arched.

"Come on," Carlisle said, and booted his dun straight on to the west. "Doc Hinkenlooper, here we come . . ."

A half a block east and on the other side of the street from the Chugwater Inn, Marshal Chris Southern stepped out of the murky shadows filling the break between a ladies' hat shop and a Chinese laundry. Stepping into the moonlight that was a little more intense now that the high clouds had moved out, he raised the quirley he held between the thumb and index finger of his right hand and tucked back against his palm, concealing the coal.

Turning his head to stare toward where the two strangers had ridden off in the night, Southern drew deeply, luxuriously on the cigarette and sent the smoke pluming over the moon-dappled street before him.

He frowned, puzzled, gazing westward.

Who were those fellas?

He wasn't sure because he hadn't seen them clearly in the darkness, but he thought they'd looked like two of the four strangers—one standing out because he'd been so much more dandified in dress and grooming than the other three, and now dead—he'd kicked out of the Longhorn several nights past.

That meant the two who'd ridden through town well after midnight, looking for the sawbones, were two of the four who were out to exact a reckoning or some such on Southern's friend, Ty Brannigan. The more Southern thought about it, taking one thoughtful drag after another off the quirley, he became more and more certain of it.

His heartbeat increased as his excitement grew.

Only two had come to town looking for the medico. That meant that the third one—the big man with the beard and the savage scar—must be in need of medical attention.

Southern took another deep drag off the quirley, then raised the half-smoked, twisted cylinder to study the coal, scowling. Should he follow the two over to the doc's now or wait until they rode back through town with the doctor in tow, presumably on their way back to wherever they were holed up with the big, bearded, savage-faced gent—and follow them?

That way he'd find all three and could start to get to the bottom of why their fancy-Dan compadre had bushwhacked Ty and MacKenna. He hated to use the doc like that, possibly endangering the man's life. On the other hand, the cutthroats needed Hinkenlooper. Doubtful they'd hurt him. Likely, they'd secure his services and set him free. Depending on how badly the bearded gent was injured, they might need him again. They might threaten the old man, warn him not to mention anything about the location of their hidey-hole, but that would likely be the extent of their menace.

Besides, Hinkenlooper was a tough old duck. He could take it.

Having made up his mind, nodding, Southern took one more quick pull from his quirley then dropped the butt in the dirt and mashed it out with his boot. He turned and tramped back through the break, heading toward his and Molly's little wood-frame shack a couple of blocks to the north, along a dry creek bed near the Demon River. He'd gather a little grub and a canteen as well as Ol' Suzy and saddle his horse. With luck, he'd be back at the mouth of that break by the time the two obvious cutthroats and Hinkenlooper pulled back through Warknife.

At least, he hoped they rode back through town . . .

Despite how exhausted he was, with his deputies gone and only him to watch over Brandon Waycross, Southern was glad he'd been out this late at night, which he usually wasn't. His part-time night deputy had just taken over for Southern, to watch over the jail's only prisoner, Waycross, when the local schoolteacher, Miss Langendorf, had tramped over to the marshal's office, clad in a hooded cape and shivering with fright. She'd claimed that a man or men had been skulking about her shrubs and peeking in her windows, and she'd wanted—no, she'd *demanded*—that Southern find the "diabolical depraves" and bring them to justice or at least make them stop.

Miss Langendorf, a nervous young lady from Denver, had made similar complaints in the past. Southern had doubted there would be any more to her current complaint than there'd been to her past ones and, having thoroughly investigated the yard around the school, in the back room of which the teacher lived, he'd found just that. No evidence of any skulkers.

He'd taken some time to drink a cup of coffee with the teacher and gotten her calmed down and even chuckling a little over her overly active imagination and bid her adieu. (He was glad that at least she had a sense of humor about herself.) He'd been on his way home for a few hours of shuteye, tramping through the break between the ladies' hat shop and the Chinese laundry, when he'd spied the two mysterious strangers riding through town and had overheard the conversation between them and the drunk outside of the now-closed Chugwater Inn. The drunk's voice Southern had recognized as belonging to the retired bronco buster, Clancy Adams.

At home, Southern managed not to awaken Molly while he gathered a few possibles in the kitchen—just a couple of biscuits, some jerky, and two apples, which he dropped into a small grubsack. Ol' Suzy in hand, he let himself back outside quietly and tramped over to the stable, where he saddled his blue roan gelding. He mounted up and retraced his footsteps until he was sitting Blue at the mouth of the break between the ladies' hat shop and the Chinese laundry.

He waited there a good ten minutes, unease building in him.

Surely, the two cutthroats had had time to gather the doc and be on their way back to their hidey-hole. The doc was old and slow, but, still . . .

Had Southern missed them?

He waited another ten anxious minutes, then, figuring the cutthroats must have chosen another route back to their hidey-hole, he booted Blue out into the street and turned him west. He'd head over to the doctor's place and try to pick up the cutthroats' trail from there. Blue had taken only three strides, however, before Southern reined him back around quickly and booted him back into the break between the two buildings.

He'd heard the clatter of buggy wheels and seen the vague outlines of approaching riders on the trail just west of Warknife.

A third of the way into the break, Southern stopped Blue and turned him back around to face the street, staying about ten feet back from the mouth of the break.

The thump of hooves and the clatter of buggy wheels grew louder until a horseback rider appeared, moving past the break from Southern's right to his left. The rider was followed by the doctor's beefy black, white-socked horse and the doctor's one-seater, canopied, red-wheeled buggy as well as the doctor himself clad in a bowler hat and tan jacket over his usual three-piece suit. In his early seventies, the doctor, a lifelong bachelor, sat slouched in the seat, reins in his gloved hands, looking tired and peeved about being awoken at the ungodly hour.

The buggy passed the break. It was followed closely by the second rider, a smaller man than the man riding lead.

As the horseback riders and the doctor passed on into the gloom to Southern's left, one of the men said, owlishly, "Come on—step it up there, old man. Gonna be light soon, dammit!"

The doctor muttered something in an angry tone but too quietly for Southern to hear above the thumping hoofs and clattering wheels.

The marshal gave the horseback riders and the doctor a five-minute lead, then booted Blue out of the break and onto their trail.

CHAPTER 21

Southern stayed well back behind the doctor and his two-man cutthroat entourage.

The country between the mountains and the town was open, interrupted only occasionally by gradual prairie swells. The stars were beginning to fade, and the faintest pre-dawn light was creeping into the eastern sky. If the lawman stuck too close to his quarry and the cutthroats were keeping a close eye on their backtrail, he might be seen. Unless they were total fools, or unless they weren't whom he thought they were, he had to assume they were occasionally perusing the trail behind them.

When the trio ahead of Southern entered the more broken country of the Bear Paws, and the trail along Whiskey Creek slipped into a canyon between steep slopes and high ridges, and the trail began to curve, sometimes sharply, Southern narrowed the gap between himself and his quarry. Good thing he did, or he likely would have missed seeing them swing to the right and follow a narrow canyon between shelving granite ridges to the west, beneath an especially high peak shouldering tall against the stars known as Dancing Bear Ridge.

By now, a good bit of gray light was bleeding

into the sky, softening shadows and extending visibility, so again Southern pulled back from the doctor and his outlaw entourage. Occasionally, the lawman could hear ahead of him the squawk of tack, the sharp hammering sound of one of the doctor's wheels striking a rock or pounding over a chuckhole. As the lawman rounded a bend in the ridge wall to his left, the country ahead of him opened into a brushy bowl. The trail cut straight across the bowl, crossed a narrow creek, and climbed a ridge of tan grass a hundred yards ahead. Just as Southern raised his gaze to the top of that distant ridge, he saw the doctor's carriage and the rider behind him drop down the ridge's opposite side.

Southern booted Blue into a trot. He climbed the ridge and checked the horse down about twenty feet from the crest. He swung down from the saddle, shucked his reliable Ol' Suzy from the saddle boot, and broke her open to make sure she was loaded.

Of course, she was loaded. He always kept Suzy loaded. He snapped the two-bore closed.

Something told Southern the cutthroats were near their destination. Southern had hunted and run cattle in these mountains for more years than he wanted to think about. He knew the Bear Paws almost as well as he knew the inside of his and Molly's own small house in town—well enough to know there was an old, abandoned mining shack on the other side of this ridge.

That was likely where the cutthroats were holing up.

Staying low, Southern climbed to within six feet of the ridge crest. He stopped, doffed his hat, got down on his old, aching knees, and climbed painfully up to within a couple feet of the crest. Dropping his head even lower and setting his hat down beside him, his chin raking the shin-high grass, he edged a look over the top of the ridge and down the other side.

The doctor and the two cutthroats were just then pulling up to the age-silvered log cabin that lay in the broad valley at the bottom of the ridge. The back of the cabin, which was flanked by a privy and a couple of roughhewn sheds, faced Southern, at the very base of the ridge. The doctor and his two companions disappeared around the cabin's right front corner as they pulled up to the door on the cabin's opposite side, out of the lawman's view. He'd just glimpsed one of the doctor's red-spoked wheels trimmed in the gray light of the full dawn now, and the rider following close behind him, and then they were gone.

Southern's old ticker picked up its pace.

He studied the slope before him. He had to get down to the cabin without being seen. That wasn't going to be easy. The slope's only cover were a few shadbark shrubs and some widely spaced, lichen-spotted rocks. There was a line of shrubs farther off to his left that he hadn't spied until now. In fact, that line started about ten feet down from the crest of the ridge and ran straight down the slope for a good half of the slope's length, almost abutting the cabin's rear left corner.

That was Southern's route!

He pulled his head back from the ridge crest, grabbed his hat, and crawled backward on his old, aching knees, wincing and grunting, for about ten feet before rising, doffing his hat, and taking Ol' Suzy lovingly in both of his gloved hands. He glanced down at his horse watching him from the base of the slope, twitching its ears skeptically.

"Stay, boy," Southern said.

The roan likely would. Blue had been trained to the ground rein.

The lawman started walking across the belly of the slope, paralleling the crest on his right. When he'd walked a good fifty yards through the grass waving now in a building morning breeze, brushing against the tops of his boots into which the cuffs of his denim trousers were stuffed, he turned right and climbed. Again, within a few feet of the top, he got down, removed his hat, and crawled until he could slide another cautious look down the other side of the ridge.

The cabin, bathed now in the full gray light of the dawn, was eerily silent.

So quiet that it made the morning bird song around Southern sound almost too loud. So loud it hurt his ears.

There was only one window at the cabin's rear, to the right of the narrow back door comprised of vertical, halved logs set above a deeply recessed patch of ground in front of it. A rusted steel chair and an overturned wheelbarrow sat to the right of the patch of ground, both obscured by the branches of an overgrown lilac that grew up nearly to the cabin's earthen roof. The window, cloudy with age, was sashed and missing one of its panes.

The lawman made a mental note to be especially quiet when he descended the slope. Through that gap in the window, the folks inside the quiet cabin would likely hear so much as a twig snap beneath a clumsy boot.

Hoping no one was looking out the cloudy window, Southern donned his hat, climbed to his feet, wincing again at the creaking of his old knees, and hurried over and down the crest of the ridge, moving quickly but quietly, looking for any obstacles he might trip over. After only a few long strides, he dropped down behind the line of shrubs, keeping the brush between himself and the cabin, and continued on down the slope.

He kept his ears pricked for any possible

sounds from inside the cabin that might indicate that he'd been spotted.

He cast occasional, cautious glances through the shrubs to gauge his distance between himself and the cabin. When he was roughly twenty feet off the cabin's rear corner, he stopped and dropped to a knee, turning an ear to the brush, listening for sounds coming from the cabin.

Nothing.

Still quiet in there. Eerily quiet.

He hoped like hell the doc was all right.

He'd just started to rise from his knee when a voice he recognized as belonging to Dr. Hinkenlooper said, "Hold him down! Hold him down! I told you it was going to take both of you to hold him down!"

A violent clamoring rose from inside the shack.

"He's awful strong!" came a girl's shrill voice. "Even with a bullet in his shoulder, he tried to savage me when you two left to fetch the doctor! I had to lay him out with an iron skillet!"

"Hold him down, dammit!" the doctor yelled, louder.

"We're doin' the best we can, you old pill roller. Just dig the damn bullet out!"

"I have it in my pincers," the doctor said. "Hold him down! He's gonna buck like a mule when I pull it out!"

Just then a great bellowing roar fairly exploded from the cabin.

The girl screamed.

A man's bear-like voice roared, "What—tryin' to kill me, you old devil!"

"Hold him!" the doctor cried.

There was a great struggling sound and then more clamoring.

A man yelled. And then another. There was a great thumping sound, as though of a body hitting the floor followed by another wail. That was followed by another, louder thumping sound, as though of another body striking the floor.

"Take *that,* you old devil!" came the bear-like shout again, so loud that it seemed as though it would blow the cabin's roof off.

"Don't!" the doctor cried. "I was only tryin' to save your—"

The doctor's protestation was drowned by a gun's roar.

Hinkenlooper groaned loudly.

"Christ!" Southern raked out and ran forward.

The revolver thundered again.

Again, the doctor groaned.

There were the thumps of heavy, dragging footsteps.

Another roar, and then another.

Southern ran faster but as soon as he'd picked up his pace, something reached up out of the ground, like a hand, to grab his right foot, pulling it back behind him as the rest of him flew forward and down. He dropped Ol' Suzy and struck the ground flat on his face, the powerful blow making his head swim and causing church bells to toll in his ears.

His poor, old knees felt as though rusty knives had been driven into them.

Again, came the thunder of the revolver from inside the cabin.

The heavy, dragging footsteps continued.

Shuffa-shuffa-thump! Shuffa-shuffa-thump!

As Southern rose onto his hands and knees, shaking his head as though to clear the cobwebs, there was one more gun roar.

"Ohhh, you devil!" the doctor bellowed.

Then there was a heavy, muffled thump as the doctor fell somewhere out of Southern's view.

Inside the cabin, the girl screamed again, louder and shriller this time: "Shep, you're pure loco an' poison mean, to boot!"

Running footsteps rose inside the cabin, their echoes chasing the echoes of the girl's raking scream. Southern had picked up Ol' Suzy, heaved himself to his feet, and was now running, knock-kneed and shamble-footed, out from behind the thicket and around the end of the cabin. He rounded the front corner just as the girl ran out the front door, leaping over the body of Doc Hinkenlooper, who lay half in and half out of the cabin, belly down and unmoving.

Southern stopped just off the corner of the cabin, regarding the girl with a dull curiosity. His vision was blurry and his head ached. He'd taken a good braining. Probably a concussion. He was having trouble raising the shotgun in his hands.

Had the crazy bastard really killed Doc Hinkenlooper?

The girl was a blond-headed blur as she hit the ground beyond the dead sawbones and ran, barefoot, at an easterly angle out away from the cabin, her long, flaxen hair blowing out behind her on the wind and glinting in the first rays of the morning sun breaking over the eastern buttes. As she ran, she held the hem of her gray wool skirt above her ankles, and the tails of her men's plaid shirt blew back behind her.

"Shoot her!" came the bear-like roar again from inside the cabin.

"Shoot her?" came another voice, tentative, quavering a little.

"Do it, Buford—prove your worth to me!"

"Shoot her, Buford!" came another voice. "Don't let her get away! She'll go to town an' blab!"

"Ah, hell!"

Southern had just turned his gaze back to the cabin's doorway as a medium-tall, pot-bellied man stepped through it and around the dead sawbones. Sure enough, he was one of the four Southern had confronted the other day in the Longhorn. This one was in his early thirties, moon-faced and dimwitted-looking, and with shoulder-length, straight brown hair. He was quite a bit smaller than the other two who shared his general features. A lot smaller than the bearded gent with the horrifically scarred face.

Standing to the left of Hinkenlooper, this younger, smaller man raised an old-model Remington and clicked back the hammer. He narrowed an eye as he aimed down the barrel, stretched his lips back from his grimy teeth, and fired.

Southern turned toward the running girl. She lurched to one side and screamed as the bullet plumed dirt just beyond her and a little to her left.

The shooter cursed, recocked the Remington, raised it again, extended it straight out from his right shoulder, and fired another round.

That round, too, merely plumed dirt beyond the girl growing smaller and smaller the farther she ran from the cabin.

"Stop!" Southern heard himself yell, trying like hell to raise Ol' Suzy.

For some reason, he couldn't get her any higher than his belly. She seemed to weigh as much as a smithy's anvil. Scowling in frustration, he ran his gaze up to his right shoulder and was shocked to see an extra lump poking up out of his jacket. Now he realized why he couldn't raise the shotgun.

He'd dislocated his damn shoulder!

The moon-faced man before him turned to him

suddenly, eyes widening in shock. "Hey," he called back into the cabin. "The old lawman from the Longhorn's out here!"

"Say *what?*" yelled the bearded man's bear-like voice.

Boots thumped inside the cabin. The man outside the cabin stood staring in shock at Southern, who gazed back at him, heart tattooing a frantic rhythm in his chest. He continued to squeeze the shotgun in his sweaty, gloved hands, but for the life of him he could not raise it.

A figure appeared in the open doorway, straddling the dead doctor. This man was bigger than the brother in the yard, but not as big as the bearded gent. He scowled at Southern, deep rungs laddering his forehead beneath the brim of his bullet-crowned, felt hat trimmed with a hawk feather poking up from the rawhide band.

"Why, it's the damn marshal from town!" he said, turning his head to yell back into the cabin. He smiled incredulously, looked at the shotgun the local lawman held frozen down near his waist, and shook his head. "What in the hell are you doin' out here, old man? Little far from your track, ain't ya?"

"Oh, for chrissakes, just kill him an' let me sleep!" yelled the bearded man in a voice not quite as loud as before. It had a weary pitch to it now. "Way too much commotion out here for a man to heal!"

This second, larger brother cocked the Winchester in his hands. He raised it to his shoulder and aimed in the direction of the girl, narrowing one eye as he gazed down the barrel. The man's right index finger drew back on the trigger. The rifle roared, orange flames lapping from the maw.

The girl gave a clipped, distant scream. The soft thump of her body striking the ground made its way to Southern's ears despite the church bells still tolling in them.

The larger of the two brothers outside the cabin cocked the Winchester, sending the spent round flying back over his shoulder to land with a clank inside the cabin behind him. He stretched his lips back from his teeth and turned to the still-frozen Southern. He kept his eyes on Southern but said to the younger brother, who eyed the marshal with wide-eyed incredulity, "Finish him, Buford. Do something right, for a change."

"Oh, God," Southern yelled silently to himself, staring at his shaking hands squeezing the suddenly not-so-trusty Ol' Suzy down before him. "This is how Molly becomes a widow."

Chapter 22

Ty swabbed the last of the egg yolk and bacon grease from his plate with the last of his baking powder biscuit, stuck the nicely favored chunk of bread into his mouth, and chewed. He paused in chewing to sip his coffee then sat back in his chair and reached into his shirt pocket.

He pulled out the two cigarette butts he'd found when he'd trailed the mysterious horse and rider out from Anchor to the Powderhorn and over to the Sunrise owned by Glenn and Sonya Thompson. The rancher frowned down at the feathered Indian head inked into the paper near the flattened-out butt.

"What do you have there, Ty?" Beatriz asked him from the other end of the table, frowning curiously over her steaming stone mug at him.

Their children sat to both sides of the long, heavy wooden table—Matt and MacKenna to Ty's left, the two younger kids, Gregory and Carolyn, to his right. All were still busily eating. Slouched in his chair, Gregory yawned often; the fifteen-year-old did not come fully awake until around nine or ten in the morning. It was currently only a little after six.

Ty held up one of the cigarette butts between his thick brown thumb and index finger. "I found this and another one just like it when I trailed the horse and rider this way from Anchor."

"What is so special about a couple of cigarette butts?" Beatriz asked.

She still looked flushed with satisfaction from the previous night, and her mostly black hair hung down past her shoulders after a recent morning's brushing. She still wore her nightgown, robe, and slippers. She would dress and put her hair up later, after she'd fed her family and they'd headed out to the chores Ty had assigned them. All except for Carolyn. The youngest girl would remain inside and help Beatriz in the kitchen and with other chores around the house.

Inside on a working ranch were as many chores as outside, and it kept the women busy.

MacKenna had been glad when Carolyn had become old enough to take MacKenna's place inside. From a very young age, the older girl's heart had yearned for the outdoors, where she preferred riding and working with the stock over cooking, dusting, beating rugs, and doing laundry. Fortunately, Carolyn was more of an indoor girl and didn't mind staying inside all day with her mother.

"They're ready-mades," Ty said. "Store bought."

"Like what my father smokes though I wish to all the saints in heaven he would give up that nasty habit!"

"Not only *like* what your father smokes, mi amore," Ty said, narrowing one shrewd eye at his lovely wife. "The very same brand."

Beatriz gasped, sat up straight in her chair, and slapped her open left hand down on the oilcloth-covered table hard, making the silverware jump and the mantles of the two lit lamps ring, the flames flicker. "Tynan Brannigan, you are not going to accuse mi padre of killing Jake Battles, are you?"

She gave a little flicker of a knowing, ironic smile.

Matt looked from her to his father and chuckled. "I doubt Grandpa ever had much to do with Mr. Battles. I heard Mr. Battles never trusted a banker a day in his life and kept all his money in his mattress."

Ty smiled. "That's an old wives' tale, son."

"Don't blame the wives, Tynan," Beatriz admonished him gently, dipping her chin and quirking her lips with another playful smile. She was always especially playful after a night like the one they'd shared. It was one of the multitude of things Ty loved about her—the gentleness that offset her harshness, the playfulness that tempered her firm practicality and Latinate self-righteousness.

"Old Jake stowed his loot in a safe," Ty told Matt. "I saw it once or twice when I was over at Anchor, planning roundups with the old devil."

Beatriz gasped.

Carolyn looked sharply up from her plate and turned her admonishing gaze to her father. "It's a sin to speak ill of the dead, Pa!"

"Thank you, child," Beatriz said, reaching over and caressing the back of her youngest daughter's neck while mock-glaring at Ty from the other end of the table. Part of her glare was not in gest, though, Ty knew. Beatriz was no longer a regular church goer for practical reasons—the nearest Catholic church was over in Cutbank, too far from the Powderhorn for regular attendance—but she'd attended regularly when she'd lived with her father in Warknife, riding over every Sunday in her father's chaise driven by Hector, their half-breed house boy. She still followed the rules.

MacKenna was gazing with interest at her father. "Do you think whoever killed Mr. Battles was smoking those ready-mades, Pa?"

"There's a good chance." Ty pocketed both butts. "I'm gonna ride to town and talk to Angus O'Reilly, see who else except your grandfather smokes that particular brand of quirley."

"You're going to town?" MacKenna said, widening her eyes in silent pleading.

"Yes, but you're not." How changeable, this girl, Ty thought. Only yesterday she'd been shut of Brandon Waycross. Now, only a few hours later, she wanted to see him again. The young man sure had a hold on her. As a father who did

263

not want to see his daughter hurt, Ty didn't like it one bit.

MacKenna drew her mouth corners down and lowered her head as though in prayer.

Ty looked at Matt and then at Carolyn and Gregory. "I want you all to stay close to home. No leaving the headquarters until further notice." He looked at Matt and MacKenna. "And you two keep your rifles handy and an eye skinned for those three you saved your father's hide from yesterday."

"What about you, Ty?" Beatriz said, concern in her gaze. "Shouldn't you stay home, too?"

"No." Ty shook his head. "I'm gonna track those devils down an' . . . ."

He let his voice trail off as he turned to Carolyn and Gregory, both staring at him with worry in their wide eyes.

"I'm gonna get 'em out of our hair once an' for all."

"Tynan!" Beatriz scolded him, sliding her eyes to their two younger children.

"They need to know what's goin' on, honey. They don't need coddling." Ty looked at his two youngest again. "Don't worry. Next time, I'll be ready for them. Carolyn, you stay in the house today. Gregory, don't stray far from your brother and sister."

"All right, Pa," Carolyn said, nodding slowly.

"All right, Pa," Gregory echoed his sister and,

toying with the fork lying on his empty plate, held his suddenly awake gaze on his father. "Pa . . . you gonna . . . you gonna kill those—"

"Gregory, that's enough! We will not speak of this at the table!" Beatriz scolded her youngest boy.

"Sorry, Ma," Gregory said, and scowled down at his plate.

Beatriz placed her hand on Carolyn's and encompassed both younger children with her reassuring gaze. "Don't worry, *mis hijos*. Your father is strong. He is accustomed to dealing with men like those he tangled with yesterday."

Gregory came alive again with, "MacKenna shot one of 'em! I overheard her tellin' Matt!" He grinned.

"Gregory!" Beatriz scolded him.

Ty smiled at MacKenna. "Likely scared 'em all off, too. Good shootin', honey. I know it's a sorry thing to have to do, but you had to do it. If you shot the leader, you might have cut the head off the snake and sent the others packing." He turned to Beatriz glaring at him from the other end of the table and gave a sheepish scowl. "Sorry, honey." He slid his chair back, placed his hands on the table, and heaved himself to his feet. "I'll be headin' out."

"Where to, Pa?" MacKenna asked.

"I'm gonna ride over and see if I can track those varmints from where you ran into them."

"I should go with you, Pa," Matt said.

Ty shook his head. "Not a chance. You're needed here." He glanced at the other three kids. "You all know your chores for the day. See they're tended." He looked at Beatriz. "I'll be back in time for supper."

She kept her worried, dark eyes on him, and nodded slowly.

Ty turned and left the kitchen. He gathered his hat, rifle, and saddlebags in the foyer, and stepped out onto the broad front porch. He'd just draped the saddlebags over his right shoulder when the door opened behind him, and MacKenna stepped out.

"Pa . . . ?"

Ty turned. "Yes, baby girl?"

"In all the excitement yesterday, I forgot to tell you that Con Stalcup and Cass Battles gave Marshal Southern only one week to try Brandon and hang him. Their words. After a week, they and their men will come for him."

"Ah, hell," Ty complained, running his thumb brusquely across his chin. "They know that's not enough time to get a judge here and to seat a jury. Not enough time for a full investigation into the murder."

"Of course, they know. They just want the satisfaction of hanging Brandon—out of pure spite!"

"Don't worry, honey. Southern will wire

the sheriff and the U. S. Marshal in Cheyenne. They'll likely send some men to watch the jail."

One week was likely not enough time to get enough men to Warknife to hold off the determined and lawless Anchor riders. The sheriff over in Cutbank was always short-handed and could probably afford to send only one or two deputies. Ty's words were hollow to his own ears, but he didn't want his daughter to worry.

"All right, Pa," MacKenna said, not buying it but nodding as though she did. She rose up on the toes of her boots and planted an affectionate kiss on his cheek. "Be careful. Since you've ordered us to stay home, you're not gonna have me and Matt to help you out of another tight one!"

Ty chuckled. "No, but you culled the herd for me, didn't you, baby girl?" He gave her chin a playful nudge with his thumb.

"I think so," she said, smiling proudly, lifting her chin. "Considering who it was, I truly hope I did!"

Ty squeezed her arm. "Later, honey." He moved down off the porch and over to where the horse he'd saddled earlier, his coyote dun, stood at the hitchrack.

A minute later, he was trotting the dun across the yard toward the open gate and the portal, glancing back over his shoulder to see that Beatriz had come out to stand beside MacKenna at the top of the porch steps. Beatriz had an arm around her daughter's shoulders.

Mother and daughter gazed with concern toward their husband and father.

Ty smiled and pinched his hat brim to the women. Inwardly, however, he cursed.

He'd hoped so badly to put this violent part of his life behind him. He'd thought he'd done just that way back twenty years ago when he'd gotten out of the lawdogging business once and for all and married Beatriz. The trouble was, he'd put too many enemies behind him, as well. But they didn't stay behind him. Every so often, even twenty years after he'd last made an arrest, those enemies came gunning for him . . .

Well, now he'd have to gun for these three and, if MacKenna's bullet hadn't given them a change of heart, put them behind him for good.

Again, as he jogged the dun out through the portal and into the open country, he cursed. A foul mood had fallen over him, a dark cloud of emotion.

Diego Salazar had been right. His daughter deserved so much more than the man she'd married—a man whom trouble dogged and would likely dog, endangering her family, for the rest of his life.

"Damn it all!" Ty said and booted the dun into a hard run as though he could outrun that cloud bearing down on him, heavy as an anvil on his shoulders.

He couldn't outrun it.

It stayed with him and even grew darker when he reached the spot where MacKenna had shot the stalker off his horse. Ty stuck his gloved right index finger into the rust-red spot on a sage shrub that marked where the man had fallen, and it occurred to him that he, Ty himself, was the reason his daughter had blood on her hands.

Of course, it was the blood of a black-hearted devil. Still, she had blood on her hands, and it was Ty's fault. The cutthroats wouldn't have been after Mack if they had not been after her father. They'd likely followed her out from town and, having seen that she was a pretty girl, had probably figured they'd have some fun with her—likely before sending her home belly down across her saddle to her father.

So, they were after Ty's family now, as well.

They had to die, no questions asked. Buried, as he'd vowed to Beatriz, in shallow graves . . .

He'd be damned if he didn't lose their trail, though, on the main trail out from town. It appeared the local stagecoach that ran up from Rawlins to Warknife had pulled through just that morning, obliterating the trail.

Ty did know one thing, however. He knew that all three were still alive, because it had been three horses he'd tracked from where MacKenna had shot one of them, and it didn't look like any of the three horses had been led. If she had, indeed, shot one of them, he must only be wounded. That meant there were three left to kill.

That was all right. After what they'd tried to do to MacKenna, Ty would enjoy the pleasure of killing all three. Maybe Mack's bullet had at least slowed them down.

Sitting in the middle of the trail between a slope bright with wildflowers and a shelving sandstone ridge, Ty looked around. He had no sense that he was being watched, but he hoped he was. He hoped the stalkers were close, watching him. He hoped they'd keep watching him, even follow him.

Follow him right into the trap he would set for them.

He gritted his teeth, hardening his jaws, at the thought then swung the dun around and booted it north toward Warknife where he hoped another dry run did not await him.

He wanted to find out who else besides Beatriz's father bought the ready-made Indian Feather cigarettes.

He'd swung the dun north just in time to miss the flash behind him of the morning sun off gun metal.

CHAPTER 23

Roy Cole sat back in Marshal Southern's swivel chair and studied the face of Brandon Waycross. The handsome devil of a horse gentler, and apple of the eyes of half of all the girls in the county, was just finishing up his breakfast, sitting at the edge of his cot, just beyond his cell's open door.

Handsome devil, that was for sure, Cole thought, though a thick wing of Waycross's wavy, dark brown hair hung down over his left cheek, obscuring his face.

An open cell door, Cole thought with one part of his brain while he studied the locally renowned and somewhat mysterious horse gentler. Now, what was the point in an open cell door? Or . . . what was the point of jailing a man if you were gonna leave his cell door open?

That there was what Roy Cole had been wondering ever since he'd entered the jail house at midnight to start his night shift, which he did from time to time, when Southern's two full-time deputies were otherwise occupied. Either Southern thought Waycross had killed Jake Battles or he didn't. If he did, he should close and lock the damn cell door. If he didn't, then he shouldn't have locked him up.

It didn't seem like all that much of a dilemma to Roy Cole.

But then, of course, Roy Cole was just the blacksmith here in Warknife. He wasn't a bona fide lawdog but only filled in when needed.

He had to admit, if only vaguely to himself, feeling a might jealous of the halfways sort of a prisoner he was here watching or, as Southern had said, keeping from getting taken out by the Anchor men and getting his neck stretched. Cole had never had much to do with the fairer sex. Or, more to the point, the fairer sex had never had much to do with Cole. He'd grown up down in the Never Summers, raised by an old drunk who'd prospected from time to time but mostly drank the tangleleg he distilled behind their dirt-floored, one-room cabin.

There weren't too many girls out that way, so Roy Cole had never learned how to behave around them properly. Even if he had, having taken after his father in the looks department, it wouldn't have mattered. Even a silver tongue couldn't make up for Cole's ugliness. So, he had neither a way with words for the ladies or the kind of looks that would turn their heads. At least, not turn their heads and cause them to make anything but sour, revolted expressions and quickly turn away and pick up their paces, in a hurry to be shed of him.

What would it be like to have the looks of

Brandon Waycross, Cole wanted to know, tapping his large, dirt-encrusted fingers on the arms of Southern's chair? To have half the county's female folk get all squirmy inside when you walked by?

Then it came again to Cole's brain.

The feeling that he'd seen Waycross's face somewhere before. Somewhere he wouldn't have expected to see it . . .

He finally decided to go ahead and say the words that had been on his mind all night.

"Hey, Waycross?"

The prisoner looked up from his plate, chewing, one brow arched.

"Where have I seen you before?"

"Huh?"

"Yeah . . ." Cole fingered the colorless spade beard hanging off his heavy, blunt chin. "I've seen you before. *Where?*"

"I don't understand, Mr. Cole," Waycross said, forking the last bite of ham and potatoes into his mouth then setting the empty plate down beside him on the cot. "You think we've met before?"

"Yeah . . . maybe." Cole tipped his head back and ran his thick, calloused fingers through his beard. "Somethin' like that. I just have this sense that . . ."

Waycross chewed the last of his food, swallowed, and frowned curiously through the cell's open door at Cole. "The sense that what?"

Cole narrowed one eye, shrewdly, as the recollection began to clarify in his head. Cole was not an especially smart man, though he was handy with an anvil and a smithy's forge. Not handier than most smithies, or any less talented. But what he did have was a good memory. Sometimes too good—especially when, say, he lay awake late at night and his mind started to cast buckets into the deep well of his past and he remembered the fierce beatings he'd taken from his drunkard father . . .

Sometimes, however, like now, that memory came in handy.

It was even something to be proud of.

A knowing smile slowly took shape on his thick, chapped lips on his doughy, large-pored, raw-featured face. The light of recognition glinted in his dark eyes, set deep beneath shaggy, sandy-colored brows.

He turned his head to face the bulletin board nailed to the wall right of the office's front door. Slowly, scowling at the wanted circulars tacked there, several layers of them, many yellowed and curled with time, he rose from the chair, making the chair squawk as he lifted his considerable weight from it. He strode over to the board and flipped quickly through the circulars, knocking several of them free of their tacks to wing wildly down to the floor around his thick-soled, hobnailed boots.

"What're you doing?" Waycross said, frowning and rising from the cot, his brows ridged with interest.

Cole didn't say anything as he flipped quickly through the circulars. Not finding what he was looking for, he looked around the room, muttering, "Where does Southern keep the old . . . ?"

His gaze landed on the wooden, army-issue ammunition box resting up against the wall behind the marshal's chair, sandwiched between two file cabinets. He walked over to the desk, swung the chair around to face the box, and slacked his big frame into it with a grunt. Leaning forward, he opened the box and riffled through the many old wanted circulars the marshal had placed there after removing them from the bulletin board. Most were brittle and yellow, curled at the edges, and smelled musty.

He grabbed up a thick sheath of them, set them on his lap and began riffling through them.

"What, uh . . . can I ask what you're doing, Mr. Cole?"

"Uh-uh," Cole grunted.

The big man licked his thumb and continued riffling through the dodgers, his heavy brows severely ridged.

"Gotta be in here somewhere," he said, breathing hard now with impatience as he shuffled through a second thick sheaf of wanted dodgers. "It was right up there on the board for over a year. That kid's handsome mug stared at me all night long! Name on it was . . . name on it was—"

He cut himself off abruptly as he stopped shuffling the circulars and stared down at the dodger staring up at him from his lap. His eyes slowly widened in recognition. A grin took shape on his thick-lipped mouth. His heart quickened as he stared down at the likeness penciled on the page before him, the face of a cunningly grinning, handsome young man set beneath the word:

WANTED
FOR ARMED ROBBERY—$500 REWARD.

Beneath the image of the handsome young man was the name: "BRANDON TALBOT of Laramie, Wyoming Territory."

Beneath that a description: "Six feet, lean, brown-haired, brown-eyed. Well-known for sweet-talking the girls. Runs with his bank and stage robber father Homer and brothers Willie, Lester, Pete and Mike, all killed during a bank robbery in Fort Collins, Colorado Terr. Don't let his looks fool you. Talbot is a deadly snake. Confront with caution!"

"Ah-ha!" Cole intoned, swinging around in his chair and raising the dodger up high to face the open cell. "I found—!"

He cut himself off, his delighted expression

turning instantly to shock when he saw young Waycross standing before him, scowling down at him. The horse gentler wasn't so handsome just now. His eyes were hard and flat beneath deeply furled brows.

"What'd you have to go and do that for, you big ape?" Waycross barked.

He hardened his jaws and pursed his lips as he raised the large marble paperweight that had been residing on Southern's desk and swung it forward and down against Cole's left temple with a loud *smack!*

The big blacksmith flew sideways from the chair to pile up with a groan at the base of Southern's desk. The darkness of unconsciousness washed over him, mercifully dulling the pain in his throbbing head.

Ten minutes earlier, Ty Brannigan rode into Warknife.

As he rode past the Longhorn Saloon on his right, a familiar voice washed out of the fog of his past. It was like hearing a chord from a once-favorite song played on a piano but completely out of context, at a far different time than when you last heard the song before, in a far different place. Ty turned his head to follow the voice to the large, three-story building's second-story balcony and picked out a head of copper red hair amongst the several, scantily clad blondes and brunettes milling there, smoking, talking, and laughing.

Devon Hayes, wearing a lacy, metallic green wrap over her shoulders and smoking a cigarette with a long, black cigarette holder, turned her head toward Ty. It was as though she'd sensed his presence, his gaze, having sensed *his* gaze. He checked down the coyote dun. He stared up at the woman, fighting the mixture of emotions rising in him, allowing only one—anger that she'd spoken to MacKenna, had given his daughter the impression that Devon still carried a flame for her father.

What was she up to?

Whatever it was, he didn't like it one bit.

He told her so with his eyes. He got the point across. Devon held his gaze for about five seconds and then slowly turned her head away and lowered her chin, smiling thinly and taking a short, pensive puff from the cigarette holder. One of the younger women standing with Devon on the balcony saw Devon's reaction, then turned her vaguely curious gaze over the balcony rail to the big man sitting the dun on the street before the Longhorn.

Ty rode ahead for another block, then swung the dun over to the left side of the street, to a small, neat, white-frame building bearing the shingle of ANGUS O'REILLY'S DRUGS & TOBACCO. He knew this was the only place in town that sold the Indian Feather ready-mades, because Ty's father-in-law, Diego Salazar, had mentioned it during one of their self-consciously congenial as well as desultory conversations on the front porch out at the Powderhorn, usually with a drink and a smoke or two before supper.

Angus O'Reilly, a lean man with neatly combed and pomaded brown hair and an ostentatious handlebar mustache with waxed and twisted upright ends, sat on the bench out in front of his store's large front, immaculately polished window. In the window were many shelves showing a vast array of colorful, stoppered bottles of all shapes and sizes as well as overturned canvas sacks spilling chocolate and hard-rock candy as well as peppermint drops and French kisses.

"Good day, Angus," Ty said, reining up in front of the hitchrack.

"Brannigan," O'Reilly said, setting to one side the newspaper, the *Warknife Caller*, he'd been reading while puffing his meerschaum pipe. "What can I do for you. One of the children's birthdays? Or maybe Beatriz's . . . ?" He gave a stiff smile, for he was a stiff man who ran a very neat store and had done so well back before Ty had retired his town marshal's badge over twenty years ago. Back then, he'd sold goods out of the back of a prairie schooner wagon—him and his enigmatic black partner, a former buffalo soldier.

The two still worked together, O'Reilly selling his medicines, elixirs, and candies as well as a fine selection of tobacco and occasionally hosting a local gypsy fortune teller. Bentley Hodges stocked the shelves, kept the place free of dust and rodent droppings and in generally good repair. Ty couldn't see the tall, slender black man, whose hair had gone gray years ago, but through an open front window he could hear him back in the building's bowels, sweeping. The two men lived together in a neat frame house on Second Avenue, with a well-tended yard, and while their relationship was often muttered about in speculative tones around town, they both commanded a genial respect as such that they were never pestered. At least, not as far as Ty knew.

Which was good. To each his own was Ty's way of looking at the world.

He'd always liked both men very much though he'd never shared more than a few words at a time with the famously tight-lipped Bentley Hodges.

"Nope, no birthdays," Ty said, swinging down from the dun's back. "The missus is next month. I'll probably be needing a box of those cream candies and some sugar plums. They both went over in a big way last year!"

"Well, you have to keep them happy, don't you?" said O'Reilly. He'd risen from his bench and stepped forward to knock the dottle from his pipe on the porch rail then fussily brushed the burnt tobacco off the rail and into the street with the side of his hand.

"She keeps me happy, and I keep her happy," Ty said, grinning. Then, guiltily remembering Devon Hayes standing on the balcony a minute ago, he felt heat rise into his cheeks as he added, "At least, I give it my best shot."

"We're all human."

"Yes. Some of us more human than others," Ty added, dryly. He pulled his right hand glove off with his left hand. He'd left the sling at home, the wound having healed sufficiently that he thought he could do without the support. He dipped his right hand into his shirt pocket, producing both of the cigarette stubs he'd found the previous day, and climbed the three painted board steps to the porch.

He opened his hand and held it out toward O'Reilly. "See those?"

O'Reilly gave him a skeptical scowl. "Cigarette butts?"

"Ready-mades." Ty plucked one of the butts up out of his hand and held it up between his left thumb and index finger, turning the inked figure near the drawing end toward the druggist. "Indian Feathers."

O'Reilly's frown deepened as he studied the butt, nodding once. "Ah."

"I'm assuming whoever smoked these," the rancher said, "bought them here."

"If they live around here, they probably did. I believe I'm the only one who sells that brand in Warknife."

"Who buys them from you, Angus?"

O'Reilly frowned again. "What's that?"

"Who buys them from you?"

Still frowning skeptically, O'Reilly turned his head to one side. "Why do you ask?"

"Jake Battles was killed."

"So I heard."

"I tracked a horse and rider off his place, from near where his body was found. I'm thinking that whoever that rider was might also be the man who shot Battles in the back. He left these two butts on his trail."

O'Reilly raised his brows, impressed by the information. "Oh, well . . ." He drew a deep breath as he stared down at the two butts in Ty's hand then lifted his gaze to the rancher, and gave a rueful smile, twisting an end of his handlebar mustache. "One of my loyal ready-made customers is your father-in-law."

Ty smiled. "Yes, I know. Let's assume Diego Salazar did not kill old Jake. Who else buys these from you?"

"Oh, well, not too many others." O'Reilly gazed off, thoughtfully, and continued to finger the waxed end of his mustache. "Norman Becker is one. Jed Lewis, the attorney. Whenever Hoyt Parker is in the area, selling horses or buying cattle, he buys them from me. And, to tell you the truth, Mr. Brannigan, I can't think of one other man."

Ty winced his disappointment, considering the information. Norman Becker, a former Easterner, owned a saloon and a freighting company here in Warknife but lived down in Laramie, in a big, stylish brick house. He traveled here only a few times a year, in a fancy chaise carriage and accompanied by several employees in three-piece suits, to check in on his business interests. Ty doubted he or either of the other two men O'Reilly had mentioned had had a bone to pick with Jake Battles, who did very little business with anyone, not having trusted anyone, and had opted to keep his money close to home. Even if the men O'Reilly had mentioned had had a reason to murder Jake, none of the three would have handled the messy business themselves. They all had the money to hire the job done for them.

"Well, damn," Ty said, taking a deep, frustrated breath.

"Oh, wait," O'Reilly said, with a droll chuckle. "I did have one other loyal buyer of the ready-made Indian Feathers." He turned to Ty, smiling.

"Who's that?" the rancher asked.

"Old Jake himself."

"What?"

"Sure, sure. Jake used to roll his own but when he got arthritis in his hands, I started selling him the Indian Feathers. Must be a couple of years back now. He quit buying them, though, after his heart episode and his lungs got bad. Doctor's orders. The doctor had ordered him off drink and tobacco long ago, but after Jake's heart and lung problems started to worsen, he stopped buying even the ready-mades though I know from Bernard Weaver he did not give up his Scotch whiskey!"

O'Reilly winked and smiled.

Bernard Weaver owned the Territorial Hotel here in Warknife, which boasted one of the finest saloons in this part of the territory. Ty assumed that Jake was likely buying his whiskey by the case from Weaver, a crusty old sot himself and one of Battles's few friends. At least, one of the few that Ty knew about.

"So, Jake smoked them, eh?" the rancher said, frowning deeply, trying to add that information to the fact that whoever had murdered Jake— at least the man most likely to have murdered him—also smoked the Indian Feathers.

He didn't have long to ponder the information.

Just as wild, galloping hoof thuds grew in the street to his left, a man shouted, "Stop him! Stop that devil! That's Waycross—he's escaped the jail!"

Ty turned his head and widened his eyes in surprise to see—sure enough—Brandon Waycross galloping hell for leather from the direction of the town marshal's office. Young Waycross was crouched low in the saddle and savagely whipping his rein ends against the big buckskin's hips, weaving through the mid-day traffic and evoking many shrill curses and angry shouts as well as threatening fist shakes. He almost ran down a lady crossing the street. She screamed, whipped around, and ran out of the hard-charging buckskin's way, losing her picture hat then tripping over the hem of her long skirt, and falling.

When he was twenty feet from where Ty stood on the druggist's stoop, Waycross's gaze found the rancher.

"It ain't true, Mr. Brannigan!" he shouted as he whipped past the drug and tobacco store in a blur of fast motion. "Whatever Cole tells you, *it ain't true!*"

He galloped around a stalled mining dray and braying mule team and then he was gone.

Chapter 24

Ty cursed and ran down the druggist's porch steps and into the street, gazing off toward where young Waycross had just disappeared beyond his own heavy dust cloud, men still cussing the kid's back in his wake.

"Someone get after him! That's Brandon Waycross! He's wanted for murder!"

The indignant, deep-throated shouts had come from behind Ty. He whipped around now to see the big, beefy blacksmith, Roy Cole, limping toward him and holding a big, brown hand over his left temple. Cole's long, stringy, reddish-brown hair hung down along both sides of his beefy, blunt-featured face. In his other hand, hanging down against his left leg, he held a sheet of paper that fluttered in the breeze as he continued limping toward Ty.

The big man glanced to his right, stopped, and shouted, "Larson! You an' Swenson get after him!" He whipped the hand holding the paper forward, in the direction in which Waycross had vanished. "There'll likely be a reward in it for you. He smashed me in the head, laid me out cold for a whole minute when I was in the official capacity of *deputy town marshal!*"

The thuggish, indignant Cole swept the thumb

of the hand holding the paper across the badge on his grimy, smoke- and sweat-stained blue wool tunic.

The two men he'd addressed were standing out front of the Half-Moon Beer Saloon, both holding frothy beer mugs in their fists. They glanced at each other quickly then just as quickly set their beers down on a bench in front of the saloon and started toward two horses tethered to the hitchrack before them.

Ty thrust his left hand out commandingly. "Go back to your beers, gentlemen!" Though he hadn't been the law in Warknife for twenty years, he still commanded authority in these parts. Joe Larson and Bill Swenson, who mostly worked roundups and calving seasons, swung back around and returned to their beers.

Roy Cole, who'd stopped on the street about twenty feet west of Ty, scowled angrily at the rancher. "That renegade clubbed me over the head and *ran!* When I was in—"

"I know, I know," Ty said. "When you were in official capacity as Deputy Town Marshal." He stopped before the man who stood even taller and wider than Ty himself. "Why'd he run?"

"Cause I showed him this!" Cole raised the paper in his hand.

Ty took it, looked down at it, muttered the words as he read them. " 'Wanted for armed robbery . . . five hundred dollars reward . . . Brandon

Talbot of Laramie, Wyoming Territory . . .' "

He quickly read the rest, lowered the paper to his side, and turned to stare east, the direction in which Brandon Talbot, alias Brandon Waycross, had just disappeared, riding hell for leather, which was how Con Stalcup had seen him leaving the scene of Battles's murder.

Still holding his hand to his bloody temple, Roy Cole said, "I stared at that handsome mug drawn there on the circular for nigh on a year, a coupla years ago, while I was workin' nights at the jail, an I reckon it burned into my brain. When I was starin' at Waycross sittin' in that jail . . . why, I remembered." He gave a shrewd grin that caused his ruddy, indelicately carved cheeks to swell inside his beard. "Brandon Talbot . . . that's who he is. Why, he's nothin' but a bald-faced liar. Prob'ly rode up here to hide out in the mountains . . . and spark a whole new set of girls."

Ty turned his gaze to Cole. He hardened his jaws, suppressing the urge to smash his fist into the man's repulsively twisted, grinning mouth. The blacksmith knew as well as Ty did . . . likely as well as everyone in the county did . . . that one of those girls Talbot had sparked was MacKenna.

Ty drew a deep, calming breath, raised the dodger again, read it again, and looked up when galloping hooves and clattering wheels sounded beyond him to the west. A box wagon was thundering toward him, two beefy sorrels in the traces, chomping the bits as they galloped hard, growing larger and larger before Ty and Cole, who stepped to one side to avoid being flattened.

As the wagon roared by—a supply wagon with the single word ANCHOR painted on its side panel—Ty recognized the two men in the driver's box as Anchor riders. The wagon was mounded with feed bags. One turned to Ty, fire in his eyes beneath his black Stetson's brim, and said, "We had a feelin' he'd run," the man spat jeeringly at the rancher. "We'll be headin' back to Anchor to inform the boss an' Cass Battles!"

As the man who'd spoken turned his head back forward, the other man, the one driving, turned his head to yell over his shoulder, "And you can bet when we catch him this time he'll *hang!*"

That man turned his head forward and whipped the reins violently over the sorrels's backs. The horses and the wagon and the two Anchor hands dwindled off into the distance of the street that had frozen in the aftermath of Waycross's jail escape. All faces were now turned expectantly toward Ty and Cole, as if wondering what their next moves would be.

Ty wondered that himself.

He glanced toward the jail house, then turned back to Cole. "Where's Southern?"

Cole shrugged his heavy shoulders. "I'll be hanged if I know. He or one of the other deputies usually relieves me at eight, but I ain't seen hide nor hair of any of 'em. I need to have a nap and some breakfast and get to work in my shop!"

Ty frowned. "Well, that's damned peculiar."

"Peculiar about Doc Hinkenlooper, too!" came another voice beyond Ty.

The rancher shunted his gaze westward again to see a man in cowboy garb sitting a cream horse, roughly fifty feet away, the horse turned sideways in the street. Ty recognized the rider as Dale Petry, foreman out to the Hatch Ranch, twenty miles west of town.

"What's peculiar about the doctor, Dale?" Ty asked.

"He ain't home, an' he knew that Mrs. Griswold's water was about to break. The midwife is with her now, but she sent me to town to fetch the doc." The stocky, middle-aged man with a gray walrus mustache and wearing a butterscotch Stetson with a funneled brim shook his head. "He don't answer his door, and I checked the shed out back. His buggy's gone!"

The lines across the cowman's forehead grew deeper as he studied on the situation. Both the town lawman and the doctor were not where they should be.

"I just hope Mrs. Bjornson can handle the delivery—that's all I got to say!" said Dale Petry as he reined his cream back around and booted the mount into a westward lope.

Ty turned to Cole. "Anyone else in the jail?"

"Nope."

"Then go have your nap and breakfast and get to work in your shop. Southern will no doubt be along soon. I'll ride over to his house and check on him. Molly might be feeling poorly, and he hasn't been able to get away just yet."

Just yet.

Hell, judging by the sun's westward lean, it was edging into the afternoon.

Concern and befuddlement raking Ty, he folded the wanted circular neatly and shoved it into a back pocket of his buckskin trousers. As he did, he remembered what O'Reilly had told him about Jake Battles himself having once smoked the ready-made Indian Feathers.

Could it be only a coincidence that the killer had left Indian Feather butts behind on the night he'd shot Battles from bushwhack? Only a coincidence that the man who'd shot Jake—or had probably shot him if Talbot hadn't done the dirty deed despite his not being whom he'd been saying he was—also smoked the ready-mades?

The rancher's head was spinning. He felt a deep compulsion to get out to Anchor again and to do some more snooping around despite Brandon Talbot formerly known as Brandon Waycross now looking guilty as hell since he'd conked Cole on the head and broke jail. Yet Ty felt a deep concern for Chris Southern as well as the doctor. Hinkenlooper might have gotten called away in the middle of the night. Hell, sawbones often were. The medico might have gotten himself tied up and unable to get away from a dire medical situation.

That would explain the sawbones not being home.

But what about Southern? If he was home, he would certainly have sent word to Cole by now that he'd be late getting to his office.

Those questions bouncing around in the rancher's head, he swung up onto his dun's back and reined away from O'Reilly's drugstore and tobacco shop. As he did, the proprietor stood before him atop his stoop, twisting a waxed end of his mustache again and frowning with deep concern. His former buffalo soldier associate, clad in a neat white apron that matched his head of snow-white hair, now stood just behind and to one side of O'Reilly, leaning on a broom, also frowning curiously at the rancher.

"Ty . . . what the hell's going on?" O'Reilly asked. He shook his head slowly. "Something . . . something's not right . . . is it . . . here in town?"

Ty reined his horse to the west, also shaking his head and muttering, "Seems that way . . . seems that way." He put the steel to the dun, which lunged into a lope to the west, and added silently to himself, "And it's not just here in town!"

As he swung down the next cross street that led north, Ty reflected that he couldn't remember having so much on his plate even back when he was actually wearing the badge of Warknife town marshal. Back in those days, however, the town had still mostly been going through the slow transformation from an old hide hunter's and fur trapper's camp to a bona fide ranching, farming, and mining supply hub. It had been more dangerous and violent, for sure—at least, until Ty had put his tried-and-true skills of town taming to work—but simpler. There'd been no stage line yet, certainly not as large a population as it boasted now.

Now there were more people, more complications . . .

It didn't, of course, help that he himself boasted a checkered past—thus the men stalking him.

Thus Devon Hayes . . .

He shook his head to clear the conflicting mental clutter from his brain and reined up in front of Chris and Molly Southern's neat wood-frame house. The structure, which Ty had helped his old friend build after Southern and Molly had moved to town from their ranch and Chris had taken over as the town's main lawman, hunkered under the drooping branches of several box elders and cottonwoods at the end of the lane and only a stone's throw from the Demon River. Sunlight dappled it through the branches, glinting lemon off the dark windows.

A cat meowed. Ty peered over the picket fence

ringing the house to see the Southerns' big tabby cat, Sammy, slinking down the porch steps to the narrowed, cobbled walk that led to the front gate.

"Hello, Sam," the rancher said as he opened the gate and stepped through it.

The tabby hurried up to him and pressed its fat, furry body against Ty's right leg, purring. The rancher paused to give the cat a quick scratch then stepped around it, down the cobbled path, and up onto the porch. He'd just raised his hand to knock when the front door opened. Molly Southern stood before him, brown hair liberally streaked with gray pulled back in a tight bun, and gazed up at him with deep lines cut across her forehead.

"What is it, Ty?" she asked, a sheen of tears shimmering in her eyes. "What's happened?"

"What?" Then he realized that she thought he'd come bearing bad news. "Oh, no, no, no, Molly," he said, hugging the small, frail woman, clad in a plain gingham dress and with a crocheted cloak wrapped around her shoulders. "It's nothing like that. No bad news. I came here looking for Chris, but I take it he's not here—am I right?"

Ty released the woman and she stepped back, tipping her head back to gaze up at him, relief tempering the concern in her gaze. "No, he's not." She squelched a sob, and more tears shone in her eyes. "Oh, Ty—I thought for sure they'd sent you with bad news for me." She brushed a hand across her trembling lips. "I don't know what I'd do without that old rascal!"

"Where do you think he is? Any idea?"

"No, but he must have come home last night sometime, while I was asleep. He left a mess in the kitchen as he usually does. He dropped an apple on the floor and some biscuits are missing. So are his saddlebags, which means he rode off somewhere. Oh, Sam—leave Ty alone!" she scolded, looking down at Sammy rubbing his hefty body up against the rancher's leg again, purring up a storm. Looking up at the rancher again, she said, "I take it you have no idea, either, Ty?"

"No, I don't." Ty looked down at the cat still rubbing against him and pondered the situation of the missing lawman and sawbones and shook his head.

Damned strange.

Was the fact that both were missing at the same time a coincidence?

Ty stooped to give Sam another obligatory scratch then straightened again. "Don't worry, Molly. I'm sure he'll be back soon."

"That old devil," said Molly Southern, scowling with feigned anger and shaking her head, her voice quaking with emotion. "He'd better get his skinny carcass home soon or I'll give him the strapping of his life!" She raised her small, blue-veined fist and shook it.

"Just desserts!" Ty said, chuckling. He pressed his lips to the old woman's temple. "Please, try not to worry, Molly. I'm sure he'll be along soon."

Sensing Ty was about to leave, she grabbed his arm and gazed up at him with a beseeching look. "Stay for coffee?"

He squeezed her hand. "I can't. I have a full day, I'm afraid."

She pursed her lips and nodded. "I understand." She feigned a smile. "How's Beatriz?"

"Just fine."

"The kids?"

"They're good, too."

"I want to have that clan of yours back for supper again soon. I so love having a houseful of the wild Brannigan clan!"

"Be careful what you wish for, my dear." Ty crouched to give her wrinkled cheek another affectionate kiss. "Goodbye now, Molly. Try not to worry."

He set his hat on his head, swung around, and started across the porch.

"I won't!" Molly crowed behind him. "I'm done worrying about that old devil!"

She slammed the door as though in anger, but Ty winced as he stepped back down the porch steps and into the yard, knowing she was badly worried and that he'd done nothing but aggravate that worry by coming looking for Chris and not finding him here.

He pushed back out through the gate and looked around, heavy with weariness and concern.

He'd come to town in hopes of solving one mystery only to find two more mysteries cluttering his already cluttered mind.

"Where are you, Chris?" he muttered to himself, looking around at the cottonwood branches in which robins and chickadees flitted and sang. "Where are you, doc?"

CHAPTER 25

With a weary sigh, Ty grabbed his reins off the rack fronting the Southern house and mounted up.

He rode back into the heart of town and checked the town marshal's office, just in case Chris had returned. He had not. Standing on the stoop fronting the office, Ty looked around, perplexed, wondering what to do now, feeling helpless.

He couldn't track either Chris or the doctor. Their trails would be cold by now.

About all he could do was wait.

There was something he could do while he waited, however.

He mounted back up and rode over to the Longhorn, swung down from the leather, and tied the dun's reins to the rack. Inside, only about a third of the tables were occupied. Five or six men, all businessmen whom Ty knew, stood at the long bar running against the wall to his left. As he stood scanning the room, all faces turned toward him and held, eyes cast with mute interest.

"Ty," one man said by way of greeting, cordially dipping his chin.

Several others nodded, muttered their own greetings.

"Hello, there, Ty," said the bartender, Norman

Willewaug, standing behind the bar in a black foulard tie and crisp red vest, towel draped over one shoulder, hands on the bar before him, sharpened matchstick protruding from between his lips. He'd been a barman in one watering hole or another in Warknife for the past twenty years at least. He was tall with a wasted, pock-marked face and neat black mustache stitched with gray. "A little early for you, isn't it?"

Ty walked over to the bar, picked a six-foot gap between Merlin Dempsey, barber, and Walter Nobles, part owner of the largest lumber yard in town. He set his left elbow on the bar's edge and leaned his head over his shoulder toward Willewaug. He could feel all eyes in the room still on him.

Word had gotten around about him and Devon Hayes. That they shared a history.

Quite an interesting story, he supposed. Fodder for the local gossip mill.

"Whiskey," he told Willewaug.

"Comin' right up, Ty," the barman said, his voice a little too congenial. He turned and pulled a bottle of Irish whiskey off a high, back bar shelf, plucked a sparkling goblet off a pyramid to Ty's right, poured it level with the rim and slid it expertly across the bar until it came to a halt directly in front of the rancher with nary a drop tumbling down the side.

"Thank you mighty kindly, sir," he said in a

feigned jovial tone. He wasn't feeling one bit jovial. He tossed the man a silver half-dollar.

"Anytime, Ty," Willewaug said. "Shall I leave the bottle?"

"Nah. Only time for one. Just wanted to oil my tonsils, is all," he lied. He'd only ordered the shot in an attempt to make himself look less conspicuous.

"Any sign of the marshal?" Of course, that story had gotten around, too. Everything got around fast.

"Not yet."

"The doc?" asked Merlin Dempsey, a bald, dapper little man standing to his left, the man's bowler hat lying on the bar beside his beer perched on a folded newspaper.

"Him, neither."

"I'll be damned." Willewaug smoothed his mustache down with two fingers.

A conversational hum had risen from the tables behind Ty.

Good. He'd been waiting for the busybodies to resume their business.

When the barber slid his beer off his newspaper and leaned forward, adjusting his glasses and gazing down at the print before him, Ty summoned Willewaug by raising his left hand from the edge of the bar.

Willewaug leaned toward him, confidentially.

"Miss Hayes in?"

He'd made the query just above a whisper. Still, Dempsey glanced toward him.

Willewaug shook his head. He kept his own voice low as he said, "Around an hour ago, she told me she was gonna ride out on her barb horse. Looked a little troubled, needed a break. Probably stressed—you know—running a new business alone until her partner gets here. When she gets like that, she usually saddles ol' Warrior and rides out for a little jog along Whiskey Creek. Seems to clear her mind."

He winked and smiled then moved off down the bar to fill an order.

Ty absently turned the shot glass in his hand. Forty-five minutes ago, eh? He'd ridden into town around that time. He and Devon had shared a meaningful look around that time, him on the street, her on the balcony with several of her painted ladies fluttering around her. She must have ridden out right after that.

Oh, well. He didn't really need to see her, anyway. She'd received the silent message he'd sent with his eyes.

Stay away from my family.

Ty tossed back the shot, nodded goodbye to Willewaug and Dempsey, and headed for the door to several more verbal salutes issuing from the tables around him. He went outside, untied the ribbons from the rack, mounted up, and rode back over to the town marshal's office.

Still, Chris wasn't back. Ty considered checking the Southern house again, and reconsidered. If Chris still hadn't returned, the rancher's over administering presence would likely only make Molly even more upset than she already was. Ty sighed as he stepped back off the stoop of the town marshal's office.

There was only so much he could do. Here, regarding Southern and the sawbones, he had no leads as to their whereabouts, so his hands were tied. He felt the pressing need to get back out to the Powderhorn, to check on his family. There were three cutthroats riding the range, after all, and they'd attacked—or at least they'd tried to attack—MacKenna the day before. Ty wanted to assume that by Mack having wounded one of those men, she'd read to them from the book and they'd reconsidered just how badly they wanted to kill Ty and terrorize his family.

But that was likely just wishful thinking. At least, he'd have to assume it was.

He had to get home.

That thought in mind, he stepped into the leather, turned the dun into the street and booted him into a trot, weaving through the afternoon traffic, throwing up his hand to return greetings yelled at him from both sides of the town's main thoroughfare. He'd lived in the area long enough to know a good chunk of the population. There were damned few folks he didn't know in these

302

parts. He was lucky to be getting out of town without having been shanghaied into a long, windy conversation or two, as was often the case.

His grim, distracted demeanor had likely saved him the trouble.

At the edge of town, he turned the dun south onto the Whiskey Creek Trail. He by turns trotted and walked the horse, wanting to get back home as quickly as possible without unnecessarily tiring the mount. Also, having in the past been the hunted as well as the hunter of men, he knew to leave some bottom in the beast he was riding in the event that extra energy proved needed.

A half hour later, he was well into the canyon cut by the creek, riding into the mountains and nearing the turn off to the Powderhorn trail. He rounded a bend in the trace and saw a horse and rider stopped on the trail maybe a hundred yards ahead of him. The horse and its rider clung to the shadows along the left side of the trail, so Ty could see only a vague silhouette above where sunlight glinted off the bit in the horse's teeth.

Abruptly, the rider swung the horse off the trail's left side and into heavy brush.

Ty blinked, shook his head, not sure he'd seen what he thought he'd seen. No, he'd seen it, all right. It had been almost like an image from a dream, but there'd been a horse and rider on the trail, all right. They'd been sitting there, stock still, facing him, and then they'd turned and disappeared into the shadbark, hawthorn bramble, and cottonwoods.

Whoever that rider was, he was right skittish.

Why?

One of the cutthroats?

"Gid-up, there boy!" Ty said, putting the steel to the dun. The horse lunged into a hard gallop, which was what the rancher had been saving it for.

When he reached the spot where the rider had slipped off the trail, he put the dun through the brush and descended the steep bank, the brush clawing at him from both sides and nearly dislodging his hat. When he reached the bottom of the cut, he shucked the Henry from its sheath and reined the horse to a stop, looking around.

The crunch of brush and thud of hooves rose on the creek's far side and above him. He looked that way to see the rider through the screening trees and shrubs climbing the opposite bank toward a bald ridge jutting like an arrowhead over the creek, a hundred feet above the man.

"Gy-ahh!" Ty spurred the mount into and across the shallow creek, the water splashing high around him, the sunlight painting rainbows in it. It dampened his trouser legs.

He gave the horse its head when he reached the opposite ridge, letting the horse pick its own way up the steep incline through more thick brush. The dun, like the rider's horse, followed a deer path, lunging up and forward, clawing at the steep terrain with its front hooves and pushing off the ground with its rear ones. Brush crunched madly. The horse blew hard, the bit rattling in its teeth. Ty crouched low, holding his hat on his head with the hand holding the reins, holding the Henry by its neck with his other hand.

When he was fifteen feet from the ridge crest looming above him, beyond the brush and scattered cedars, a horse whinnied sharply and a woman screamed shrilly.

Ty frowned as the dun made the last few lunging leaps up the ridge. What the . . . *who* the hell . . . ?

The horse made the last lunge up and over the lip of the ridge. Ty drew sharply back on the reins and stared straight ahead, brows ridged sharply with confusion. He'd thought he'd been chasing a man . . .

But only a horse stood before him, facing him from fifty feet away on the bald ridge crest carpeted in short brown grass, sage, and pale rocks. The horse whickered edgily, switching its tail angrily. It was a handsome strawberry roan barb with a silky blond mane and tail. The horse was staring at something on the ground between it and Ty.

Shutting his gaze back toward himself, Ty saw the tightly coiled snake, head pointed toward the barb, button tail raised and quivering.

Quickly, Ty raised the Henry to his shoulder, cocking it, and sent the snake spasming bloodily in two separate pieces, its mouth ripping into the ground as though into the flesh of its killer.

Ty looked at the barb. He looked around for its rider.

"Devon?" he called, tightly, incredulously. He'd heard a woman scream, and Willewaug had said she rode out on a barb.

"Down here!" Yep, it was her, all right.

Following the voice, Ty shuttled his gaze to the right.

He could see nothing but the southern edge of the ridge and the canyon trailing off below and, to the left and running from north to south, Whiskey Creek ribboning along the canyon's center.

"Ty—I'm down *here!*" Devon's voice came again, shriller this time.

The rancher cursed and swung down from the saddle. He dropped the dun's reins, walked over to the edge of the ridge, and stared down the sheer drop before him.

Devon sat staring up at him from a six-foot, gravelly shelf jutting out from the belly of the cliff roughly twenty feet down from the top. She wore a white silk blouse with puffy sleeves, a pearl necklace, a long, slitted leather riding skirt and high-topped, black paten riding boots. The blouse was badly rumpled and pulled down to expose one freckled shoulder. Her thick, curly copper hair hung in a mess about her shoulders. Sand and bits of grass clung to it. A black felt hat lay crown down on the ground beside her. It was trimmed with a single, blood-red feather.

Devon's right leg was curled beneath her. Her left leg stuck straight out in front of her. She leaned back on her hands, wincing and slitting her eyes painfully, the jade orbs glinting in the sunlight. Obviously, the horse had thrown her when it had seen the snake.

"Are you hurt?" Ty asked.

She tucked her upper lip under her bottom teeth in a grimace and nodded. She glanced at the booted foot sticking straight out in front of her. "Ankle."

"I'll get a rope."

Cursing silently to himself, Ty walked back over to his horse. He grabbed the dun's reins, led him to the edge of the cliff then turned the mount so that his head faced away from it. He removed the coiled lariat from the saddle, tied one end around the horn, then dropped the coil over the side of the cliff. The end along with four or five extra feet dropped onto the ledge beside Devon.

"I'm coming," he said with a sigh.

Again, she grimaced up at him, her expression one of agony mixed with deep chagrin. "I'm sorry," she said softly and lowered her eyes.

Ty turned to the dun. "Stay right there, boy."

He patted the horse's left hip then grabbed the rope. He pulled it taught, wrapped his gloved hands tightly around it, and then, turning toward the horse, backed down over the edge of the cliff.

He paid the rope out slowly, wincing at the pain the maneuver kicked up in his wounded left arm. The wound was healing well—he no longer wore the sling—but it was still tender as hell. Using it the way he was using it now wasn't doing it any damn good.

Slowly, he lowered himself down the edge of the cliff, sort of walking down the sheer wall before him. He glanced down to see Devon gazing guiltily up at him. She had a vaguely haunted look in her eyes. Embarrassment and humiliation mixed with the guilt. He couldn't help being affected by that look. She didn't want to be here any more than he wanted her here. That, in turn—her knowing how much he didn't want her here—kicked up his own guilt though he wasn't sure why.

When he gained the shelf on which she sat, he released the rope, turned to her, and dropped to a knee, resting his hands on his thighs. "How bad?"

She drew a deep breath. "I don't know if it's sprained or broken, but I can't put any weight on it. I tried to get up, and the pain made me so dizzy I was afraid I'd fall over the edge of this"—

she glanced around, her hair billowing out away from her shoulders—"whatever this is."

Ty glanced over the shelf. The canyon bottom was still another forty or fifty feet below him. A small tributary trailed down the narrow, secondary canyon directly below to the broader, main canyon to the west, where Whiskey Creek ran from north to south.

Ty glanced up at the cliff before him over which the rope hung. "Well, the only way out of here is up." He took the rope, fashioned a loop, and slip knotted it. "You're going to have to stand."

"I'm sorry, Ty," she said again, grimacing again guiltily.

"Why'd you bolt?"

"I knew you didn't want to see me. That look you gave me in town said it all. Believe me, I didn't want to run into you out here, either. I thought you were still in town!"

"Yeah, well, I live out here, you know."

She gave a throaty groan of deep frustration.

Ty rose with a sigh, extended his left hand to her. "Let's get you on your feet. I'll look at that ankle once we're out of here."

"You don't have to look at it. I'll ride back to town and have the doctor look at it."

"No, you won't."

She looked at him.

"Hinkenlooper's not in town," Ty said. "At

least, he wasn't in town as of an hour ago. If that ankle needs tending, the only one around to tend it is . . ."

Devon scowled at him, incredulous. "Who . . . ?"

"My wife."

Chapter 26

"Oh, no," Devon said. "I'd rather take my chances right here!" She patted the ground beside her, then arched a curious brow at the rancher. "Does she, uh . . . know . . . about us?"

"Now she does. She should have known a long time ago, but . . ." Ty let his voice trail off and extended his hand to her again. "Come on. We're burning daylight!"

"Is she anything like your daughter, this wife of yours?"

"The apple did not fall far from the tree."

"I'll take my chances right here—thank you very much!"

"Come on," he said with a sardonic snort.

"All right."

She placed her left hand in Ty's left. Standing off her left shoulder, he placed his right hand under her right arm and gently pulled her to her feet. "Oh, God!" she groaned, falling backward into him until he thought she would throw them both backward off the ledge and into the canyon below.

The rancher grabbed her around the waist and heaved her upright, stepping forward and away from the edge of the shelf. She flopped back against him, her legs weakening. "No, no—don't pass out!" he said in a pinched voice. "I can't get you out of here if you pass out."

She drew a breath, stiffened in his arms, swallowed, blew a lock of hair away from her mouth. "I'm all right. I'm not . . . I'm not going to pass out." She chuckled. "I don't think . . ."

Standing behind her, he dropped the loop of the lariat over their heads and drew it taut at their waists, just above the buckle of his cartridge belt.

"Lean back," he said. "Let your feet hang loose."

"That shouldn't be a problem."

"Let me and the horse do the work."

"That shouldn't be a problem, either." Devon turned her head sideways to look at him behind her. "Ty, I really am sorry about this. It was a fool stunt. I saw you, and I panicked. I feel very badly about—well, about coming here and making you . . . and your daughter and now probably your wife, as well . . . uncomfortable. I hope your wife—what's her name?"

"Beatriz."

"Pretty."

"Funny—she said the same thing about you."

"Hmm." She pondered on that for a few seconds. "I hope Beatriz understands that I have no ill-intentions. I have to admit to, well"—she turned her head forward and shook it resolutely— "no, never mind." She glanced over her shoulder at him again. "My intentions here are purely business. I have no designs on you."

Ty reached up and shook the rope against the wall of the cliff before him and looked up toward the ridge. "Let's go, Rowdy. Forward slow!"

Devon glanced over her shoulder at him again, one brow skeptically arched. "Rowdy?"

Ty's cheeks warmed a tad. "MacKenna named him when he was still a colt and she was still in pigtails." Ty grunted as the rope drew taut and the horse started to pull him and the woman upward, Devon giving a gasp of surprise and placing her hands on his thighs as her feet left the ground.

"Easy, easy," he said, holding the rope in both gloved hands above her head and beginning to slow-walk them both up the face of the cliff. "That's how it's supposed to go."

"You've done this before?"

"A couple of years ago, MacKenna fell down an old mine shaft when Matt was teaching her how to ride."

Up the cliff they went slowly, Devon practically sitting in the rancher's lap, the toes of his boots pushing off the wall before them.

"Matt's your son, I take it?"

"Yes."

"MacKenna—she sounds like quite the adventurous child."

"That's one way of putting it," Ty said with a

dry laugh. "She's a handful. Always has been, always . . ."

"Always will be," Devon said, chuckling now herself.

They were halfway to the top.

The horse pulled ahead a little too quickly, and Devon reached back around with a start, grabbing Ty's cartridge belt.

"Easy, Rowdy, easy—slower, boy!"

"She aptly named him."

"Oh, yeah."

They came to the lip of the ridge.

"A little farther, boy," Ty said as his head rose up above the ridge crest.

The horse pulled him and Devon up onto the lip of the ridge and they fell together on their sides, Ty rolling and sliding them both away from the edge, his arms around Devon's waist. "Whoah, boy! Whoah!" he said, pulling back on the taut rope.

Forty feet beyond him and Devon, the horse stopped, shook its head and switched its tail.

"Back!"

The horse backed up two strides, slackening the rope.

"Stop!"

The horse stopped and stomped its right rear hoof as though to punctuate the maneuver it was proud to have performed so winningly.

"Good, boy!" Ty said. "Good Rowdy!"

"Good Rowdy," Devon said, a little breathless, as Ty slipped the loop up and over their heads and tossed it away.

He looked at Devon sitting before him. She had her eyes on him, as well. Their gazes stayed locked for two or three seconds though, as suddenly uncomfortable as the rancher was feeling, it seemed more like twenty or thirty minutes.

He turned away, feeling warm blood diffuse in his cheeks.

Flushing, Devon sucked a sharp breath through her teeth and reached forward, placing a hand on her right ankle. "It's really hurting now."

"I can see it swelling in your boot." Ty maneuvered himself over to the ankle in question, lifted it gently onto his left thigh. "Going to have to take the boot off."

Devon looked at him, tentative. "Ty?"

He looked back at her. "Don't." She shook her head. "Just get me on my horse."

"With a broken ankle?"

"I can ride."

"I can't let you ride all the way back to town."

Ty placed his left hand on the heel of the boot and gently pulled.

"Oh!" she gasped, her face turning pale as she threw her head back on her shoulders, her curly red hair spilling onto the ground. "Oh, *Lord—!*"

"Hurts pretty bad?"

"Y-yes!"

Ty lowered her foot to the ground. "All right—we'll take the boot off after we get to the Powderhorn."

Devon dropped her chin and glowered at him wide-eyed. She slowly shook her head. "I am not going to your family's ranch!"

Ty drew a deep breath, shook his head. "I don't see that you have any choice. That boot has to come off and that ankle—if it's broken, and I think it is—will have to be set. It's only another mile to my headquarters, almost six miles to town."

Devon threw her head back on her shoulders again, turning pale all over again. "Oh, *God!*"

"Beatriz is a damn good medico. Raising me and four kids, she's set plenty of broken bones, even tended some snakebite. You'll be fine."

"She'll stick a stiletto in my guts!"

Ty laughed. "Funny—that's how she put it!"

"Oh, *God!*"

Ty climbed to his feet. "Fiery Mexicana, my gal. But she'll wait at least until after she's set that ankle." He crouched and placed his hands under Devon's arms. "On three, I'm going to pull you up and set you on your horse. One . . . two . . ."

"No—wait!"

"Three!"

He drew her up sharply.

She gasped and sagged back against him, turning her head to one side, resting back against his chest.

"Ah, hell," Ty grumbled.

Out like a blown lamp.

Oh, Lordy, Ty thought, his old lover hanging limp in his arms. What am I gonna do now?

He looked around feeling a keen edge of frustration poking his loins like a rusty pig sticker.

He looked at Devon's horse standing thirty feet away, reins hanging. Ty assumed the mount had somehow avoided being bitten by the viper, for it showed no signs of swelling or misery, and it would by now. The handsome barb merely regarded the big man holding its unconscious rider in his arms skeptically, occasionally switching its tail at pesky flies as was his own dun standing nearer and craning its neck to gaze back at the two curious folks standing behind him.

One standing, rather. The other was being held up by the other one, the woman's head resting back against the man's chest.

What a pickle, the rancher thought. Not only was he going to have to take his former lover—whom Beatriz had known nothing about until two days ago after twenty years of marriage following two years of courtship—back home with him, he was going to have to ride into the Powderhorn compound with said former lover riding double on the dun with him!

Ty knew the first thing Beatriz was going to ask, and understandably so: What had the two of them been doing together in the first place?

It wasn't going to be all that easy to convince her that today's reunion had been coincidental. He already knew that Beatriz harbored suspicions that their reunion in town the other day had not been coincidence. Nor that Devon's appearance in Warknife was one bit coincidental. Ty had to admit that he wasn't so sure it was, either.

Anyway . . . all this pondering was doing nothing but delaying his getting the woman onto his horse and over to the Powderhorn where Beatriz could treat that ankle. Maybe that was intentional. He wasn't looking forward to riding through the Powderhorn headquarters gate with his former lover on his saddle and in his arms.

"Hello, honey—look who I ran into! Could you set her ankle?"

As if he didn't already have enough on his mind.

What a pickle!

He picked Devon up in his arms, wincing at the pain in his left one. He walked up to the dun, grabbed the reins and set his charge on the saddle. Holding her steady with his right arm while grabbing the cantle with that hand—at least as steadily as he could in such an awkward position—he toed a stirrup and swung up onto the dun's back, behind the saddle and the woman. She seemed to be coming around now, groaning and moving her head.

Ty neck-reined the dun around and walked him over to the woman's fine barb, who shied just a little at the strange horse and strange rider. Ty managed to reach down and grab the reins with his left hand. Leading the barb by its reins and sort of cradling Devon on the saddle before him, he booted the dun eastward along the crest of the bluff. He'd been up here before and knew there was an easy way down to the tableland on the bluff's far east side and that he could hook up with the trail leading to the Powderhorn headquarters if he angled southeast across the tableland, toward the bald-topped, conical formation of Mount Baldy looming in the far distance.

Devon came awake with a start, gasping and jerking upright in the saddle, throwing her hands out to each side as though she thought she were about to fall.

"Easy, easy," Ty said, keeping his right arm snaked around her right side, his left hand, the one holding the reins of her horse, on her elbow. "You're all right."

"Oh, God," she said with an embarrassed groan, "I passed out!"

"That you did."

She set her left hand on the saddlehorn and pressed the fingers of her right hand to her right temple. "Never could handle pain very well." She glanced over her left shoulder at the man behind her, grimacing. "I'm so embarrassed!" She turned her head forward and dropped her chin to look at the horse she was on. "And I'm on your horse! Please, Ty—let me at least ride my own horse. I can manage!"

"I got a feelin' you maybe can't. Besides, we're here now, and the less you move around on that ankle, the better off you're going to be. Just rest easy. We'll be to Powderhorn in a few minutes."

Again, leaning forward against the horn, she pressed her right hand to her temple. "I'm so embarrassed. And I'm about to meet your wife!"

"That you are."

She glanced over her shoulder at him again. "Isn't there anyone else out here who could set that ankle."

"I'm sure most of the ranch women out here can set a broken bone, but Beatriz is the closest one. Makes sense this way despite the . . . um . . . obvious discomfort."

"Oh, God."

"Yeah, well. Seems you wanted to meet my family."

She frowned over her shoulder at him. "What?"

"MacKenna. In town."

"Oh. That." Devon turned her head forward

again. "That was accidental but . . . I'm not going to lie . . . I was curious. I saw you in her eyes."

Neither one said anything again until they came to a two-track trail angling east, and Ty turned the dun onto it, heading for the Powderhorn headquarters.

"All right," he said, "since we have some time to kill, why don't you go ahead and tell me. I gotta admit, I was damned curious. But only for a while, you understand. After you disappeared the way you did, so suddenly, I stopped thinking about you."

"Yeah, well, I didn't stop thinking about you."

"Why'd you leave? I'm only mildly curious, though, you understand."

Devon drew a deep breath. "Of course , . . mildly curious."

"Why?"

She didn't say anything but kept her head aimed forward. He couldn't see her face from his position, of course, but he imagined that she wore a pensive expression, probing with her emotions back to another time . . . another place. Abilene, Kansas, over twenty years ago . . .

"It was fear," she said finally, then glanced over her shoulder at him again. "Fear of being married to a good man. Fear of losing myself in you."

He gave her a skeptical look.

"Well, you remember . . . I wanted to be a bona fide stage actress. Not just a showgirl, which was essentially what I was in Kansas. Of course, it never came to much, but back then I still had my ambitions."

"I never would have kept you from attaining your dreams."

"I knew you wouldn't. Still, I guess I was worried I'd lose my edge . . . my hunger. I'd been hungry for so long. Remember, Ty, I came from a very bad place—a no-account gambling father in Missouri, a former schoolteacher mother who had not been able to stand up to him. We moved and moved . . . to the next town . . . the next gambling parlor. When I started filling my dresses out, I started dancing, learned to play the piano. Ran away from my no-account parents— they were both drunkards by then and living in squalor in Deadwood—and joined a traveling acting troupe."

She looked over her shoulder at him again, scowling. "What you offered me was so different. So much better, of course." She gave a dry chuckle. "I think I became afraid of it. That I couldn't live up to it. Or maybe that I would get too comfortable with it and give up my dreams. My dreams were the edge I'd had since I was a young girl growing up in squalor. They were what kept me going. Wanting to sing and dance, to make men admire and want me. I built a future in my head. I wasn't sure what life would be like without that. I guess I couldn't imagine it. What

I could imagine frightened me. I didn't think I could live up to it."

She paused and stared straight out over the dun's ears. "I panicked. One day I was walking by the train station. I started trembling, and my heart started racing. I couldn't catch my breath. Suddenly, I realized I was walking into the station and I was buying a single ticket to St. Louis."

"You might have told me."

"I didn't know what to say. Besides . . ." She let her voice trail off.

"Besides what?"

She looked at him, her eyes wide and grave. "I loved you. I believe now that I probably feared that most of all. I loved a good man. And he loved me."

She chuckled again, dryly. "Imagine that!" She paused then continued with, "I've been married three times since Abilene, Ty. Can you believe that?"

He didn't know how to answer that, so he said nothing.

"Three worthless men. Just as worthless as my father. But, you see, I was more comfortable with them than I was with you, despite my genuine love for you—a strong, good, quiet man. I didn't love them. I *thought* they'd loved me, but I don't think they did. In fact, now I know they didn't. I'd fallen prey to the same thing my mother had—big personalities, big promises, pockets full of easy money. The adventure of moving from place to place, singing and dancing in some of the finest dance halls and opera houses in the Rockies, my being lavished gifts upon by moneyed mining and railroad moguls."

"It's certainly not the life I could have given you."

"No. Neither one of us would have been happy. But do you know what?"

"What?"

She looked at him again. "Not a day went by I didn't think of you and feel ashamed for how I'd abandoned you. You didn't deserve that."

"No, I didn't."

"I'm glad you forgot me. Well, maybe not deep down I'm not, but I deserved to be forgotten about. I'm so glad you married a good woman, have a nice family, a successful ranch . . . a happy life. That said," she added after another pensive pause, "I lied when I said you weren't at least part of the reason I came to Warknife."

Ty stared down at her, frowning, not sure he wanted to hear what she had to say next.

"When I was given the opportunity to buy into the Longhorn, you played a part in my final decision."

"I shouldn't have."

"No, I know. But I'm not going to lie to you anymore." Again, she looked up and over her shoulder at him. "You did."

He didn't respond to that because then they were passing under the portal and through the Powderhorn headquarters' main gate and into the yard. Beatriz was just then crossing the yard from the barn, carrying a pail of fresh milk for butter, heading toward the main lodge, the front porch of which young Carolyn was sweeping in her slow, daydreamy yet methodical way, the hem of her cream day dress swishing about her legs and gold-button ankle boots. Hearing the hooves of the approaching horses, Beatriz stopped, turned around, and raised a hand to shield the westering sun from her eyes as she studied the two riders on the dun.

Carolyn turned to them, too, and stopped sweeping.

Ty reined the dun to a halt a few feet just inside the yard.

Beatriz and Carolyn stared at him, frowning. Their eyes took in the woman in front of him. MacKenna had been leaning forward against the corral, watching Matt work with a young bronc at the snubbing post inside. As she, too, turned her head toward her father and the redhead on the dun, she turned her body full around and stepped slowly out away from the corral, staring hard at the newcomers. Matt turned from where he'd been working with the bronc and took in the pair now, as well, frowning curiously, maybe a little skeptically.

As though sensing something amiss, Gregory pushed his dung- and hay-mounded wheelbarrow out of the barn, released the handles, straightened, and stared toward the object of the rest of his family's interest. He thumbed his leather-billed immigrant hat up off his forehead and said softly, "I'll . . . be . . . ."

Devon stiffened and lowered her gaze as though in shame to the saddlehorn.

She sighed deeply.

"Here we go," Ty said, and booted the dun toward his wife.

CHAPTER 27

Ty reined up in front of Beatriz.

"Honey," he said, "this is Devon Hayes. She took a tumble. I think she has a broken ankle."

He could have been introducing any stranger in need of help. Beatriz must certainly have been shocked, but her expression did not betray any emotion at all. She dropped her pragmatic, dark-eyed gaze to Devon's left ankle hanging over the stirrup fender. "I see."

She set down the pale of milk and, keeping her eyes on Devon's ankle, yelled, "Carolyn, get upstairs and turn the covers down on your grandfather's bed. MacKenna, fetch my medical kit to your grandfather's bedroom then stoke the stove, heat water, and gather cloths. Also, fetch the bottle you provided for your father the other night. The bottle in my kit is low." She raised her eyes briefly to her husband and added tartly, "If there's anything left in it."

Carolyn jerked to life so suddenly, she dropped the broom to the porch floor with a sharp *crack!*

MacKenna said nothing. She just swung toward the house and long-strode across the yard, swinging her arms down swiftly at her sides, keeping her incredulous, none-too-vaguely curious gaze on her father.

"Anything I can do, Ma?" Matt called from the breaking corral, still holding the colt's halter rope.

"If the ankle is broken, I will need splints."

"I'll fetch the ones you used on pa two winters ago when Wiley threw him!" Gregory yelled from the front of the barn. "I know where they are!" He swung around and ran into the barn's deep shadows.

"Matthew," Beatriz said, "fill the wood box in the kitchen then tend these horses!"

"You got it, Ma!" Matt said, removing the rope from the colt's hackamore and then shuttling his own curious gaze to his father.

Beatriz turned to her husband. "Don't just sit there like a lump on a log, mi amore," she said, widening her eyes with urgency, then gesturing wildly with her hands. "Get Miss Hayes up to your father's old room!"

Ty had been so flabbergasted by the matter-of-fact way his beloved had reacted to the fact that he'd shone up here with his former lover—sharing the same horse, no less—that he'd sort of fallen into a disbelieving stupor, sitting there with one arm around Devon, his other hand on the dun's reins. Now he jerked with a start nearly as violent as Carolyn's had been, almost throwing both himself and his red-headed charge from the saddle.

"You got it, honey!"

Devon glanced skeptically at him then turned and lowered her head to Beatriz. "I am so sorry to be such a burden, Mrs. Bran—"

"Ty, quick, quick, before the ankle swells any further!" was Beatriz's only response to that. She swung around, picked up the milk pail, and strode toward the porch steps.

Ty swung down from the dun's back. He reached back up for Devon who turned to face him, glancing at his left arm. "How's that arm holding up?"

"Don't worry about me," Ty said, reaching up to take her left hand in his, then sliding his hand up her arm. "You heard the lady—let's get you into the house. Easy, now. Easy." Slowly, she slid down into his arms.

He gave a grunt as he adjusted her weight in his arms, holding her against his chest, trying not to remember one night, years ago, when he'd once carried her into an Abilene hotel room in similar fashion. He could feel Devon's eyes on his face, looking up at him. He wondered if she was remembering that same night, hoped she wasn't.

He swung around and headed for the porch steps.

Beatriz had just gained the porch. Now she glanced over her right shoulder at him, meeting his vaguely truckling gaze with a dubious one of her own. He felt the urge to assure her that there'd been nothing amiss in his having run into his former lover out on the range, that it had been merely a strange coincidence albeit more improbable than most coincidences. But then, reciting that explanation silently to himself as his boots thudded on the porch steps, and hearing how hollow the words sounded, he found himself no longer in any real hurry to provide the explanation.

He gained the porch. Just as he did, Beatriz opened the lodge's stout oak door and stepped inside, pushing the door wide, then holding it open for her husband and Devon. Beatriz averted her chill gaze as, holding the door, she thrust her other hand out to indicate the staircase rising in the foyer's late afternoon shadows, about twenty feet from the door.

Ty felt himself cringe guiltily as he brushed past his wife with his former lover in his arms, strode through the foyer, then mounted the steps. Devon clung to him, her arms around his neck. He could feel her heart beating through her back against his chest. He couldn't help feeling sorry for her. No woman, not even one who'd left a man she'd presumably loved without explanation, should have to endure such embarrassment.

Humiliation.

On the other hand, Ty wasn't in the best position, either. At least, he was on home ground. Devon was a fish out of water out here. A fish out of water and quite possibly in enemy territory.

But then, maybe they were both in enemy territory.

Again, he found himself anticipating getting Beatriz alone and explaining to her what had happened despite how lame he knew the explanation was going to sound. If the shoe had been on the other foot—if Beatriz had found herself in a similar situation, riding home on the same horse with a former lover—would *he* believe *her?*

He mounted the second-floor hall. His late father's bedroom was the first room on the hall's left side. Carolyn was just inside the room, holding the door open and thrusting an arm out, much like her mother had done, to indicate the room before her. As though Ty didn't know which bedroom his father slept in.

Both of his girls had so much of their mother in them, it was downright frightening.

"Here we go," he said, trying to lighten the mood but hearing a nervous edge in his voice as he stepped into the room, past his daughter.

Carolyn looked up at him, frowning curiously. "Who . . . who . . . ?"

"Later, cupcake," Ty said as he gentled Devon onto his father's old bed.

Beatriz had come up the stairs behind them. Now MacKenna was there, as well, following her mother into the room. Beatriz glanced at Ty and said, "You—out. I will tend this lady's ankle and we will both be needing privacy as I do so."

What? She didn't want Ty seeing the lady's ankle?

"Honey, I think you're gonna need help cutting that boot off."

"MacKenna will help me cut the boot off," Beatriz said, accepting the canvas medical kit from her daughter.

Stepping up to the bed, MacKenna looked down at Devon. She slid her gaze to her father, arched one skeptical brow, shook her head once, slowly, darkly, then returned her gaze to her father's former lover.

Devon had seen the look that MacKenna had shot her father. Now she looked up from between the two Ty women at Ty himself. She appeared to turn a shade paler than before.

"You'll be fine," Ty said, grinning down at her as he swung toward the door.

Devon grinned back. Hers looked as stiffly artificial as his had felt.

Ty left the room and started down the stairs. Halfway down, he found himself chuckling.

"What's so funny, Pa?" Gregory asked him as Ty's youngest son entered the foyer, carrying the two splints that Matt and Beatriz had fashioned for Ty's own broken ankle two winters ago when he'd been stupid enough to ride a half-broke bronc on an elk hunting trip and had been laid up in bed two months for his foolishness.

At least it had been winter and not roundup or

branding, or his goose really would have been cooked.

"Nothing, son," Ty said, brushing his fist across his mouth but unable to squelch one more laugh. "Just the dark gods havin' themselves a good laugh at my expense is all . . ."

Gregory gave him a dubious look, shrugged, then headed upstairs with the splints.

Hearing Matt filling the wood box in the kitchen, Ty went out onto the porch. He propped the front door open with a brick to let out the heat from the range. He took a seat in one of the chairs out there, hiked a boot on a knee, removed his hat, and hooked it on the extended knee. He leaned back in his chair and fished his makin's sack out from beneath his shirt. He pulled out a wheat paper, troughed it between his thumb and index finger, and dribbled the chopped Durham into the trough.

He wagged his head at the recent turn of events that for some reason he was starting to see as comical. If ever the gods had wanted to torment a man for keeping secrets from his wife, those gods were having one hell of a good time right now. Hell, Ty would sit out here and enjoy a cigarette.

It might be his last one . . .

He chuckled again then twisted the cylinder and fired a match to life on his thumbnail. He lit the smoke and, puffing the cigarette, remembered what he'd originally gone to town for this morning.

This morning.

Boy, that seemed a long time ago now.

He reached into his shirt pocket, pulled out the two cigarette butts with the Indian stamped on the paper, and stared at them lying there in the palm of his hand.

Jake Battles had smoked the same brand.

He closed his hand around the butts as his mind drifted off to Chris Southern, Doc Hinkenlooper. Both men were probably back in town now. Sure, sure. They'd each been pulled away for benign reasons. Still, Ty worried . . .

Then his mind drifted to Brandon Waycross—*Talbot,* rather—and his heart picked up its beat.

Tomorrow, he decided, he'd ride over to Anchor, try to get Con Stalcup and Cass Battles to call off their dogs. That wouldn't be easy. They had likely already heard about the bounty on Talbot's head. That bounty and the fact that young Waycross had drifted up here to the Bear Paw country and changed his name would be all the proof Stalcup and Battles needed that he'd killed Jake. Of course, it was no proof at all, and Ty had his doubts. Just because he'd once robbed banks with his family didn't mean he was a cold-blooded killer.

Of course, it was going to be a heavy lift to convince Stalcup and Cass Battles of that, however.

Ty looked down at the two cigarette butts in his hand again.

Stalcup and Battles were likely on Waycross's trail by now.

"In such deep thought, mi amore."

He turned his head sharply, surprised to see Beatriz standing just outside the front doorway, turned toward him, her arms crossed on her chest. Ty's cheeks burned with chagrin. He rose clumsily, kicked his chair with a boot heel, saying, "Honey, now . . . I can explain. It's not what it . . . it's not what it looks like."

Beatriz lowered her chin and walked toward him, looking up at him from beneath her dark brows, smiling coyly. "I know, mi amore." She placed both hands on his chest, shoved him back down in the chair. "She told me what happened." Beatriz climbed slowly into his lap, draping her long legs over an arm of the chair, turning toward him, sandwiching his big face in her hands. "I never doubted you, mi amore. No man would be so foolish as to bring his *current* lover to his wife for tending."

"No." Ty kissed his lovely bride—yes, still lovely after all these years. "How is she?"

"It's only a sprain. A bad sprain but a sprain nonetheless. I wrapped it tightly, and she will need to rest it for a day or two."

"Here?"

"Yes, here. I told her not to put any weight

on it for at least a day. Two would be best."

Ty winced.

"Don't worry," Beatriz said, pecking his lips and nudging his chin playfully with her thumb. "It will be nice to get to know her." She smiled.

He frowned, incredulous. "It will?"

"Si. I would like to get to know the woman my man loved before me."

"She's not at all like you."

"I know. You are a man of wide-ranging tastes."

"Not anymore, my love."

"No." It was Beatriz's turn to frown. "What were you thinking so hard about that you didn't even hear me come out? The past? What might have been, or . . . ?"

"No, not the past. Not Devon. Nothing like that. I'm sorry, honey, my head is so full, it feels like it might very well explode!"

Beatriz turned, lay back against him, and gently kissed his neck. "Tell me."

He told her about learning that one of the few men in the area to smoke the Indian Feather ready-made cigarettes had been old Jake Battles himself. He told her about the mysterious case of the missing town marshal and the missing doctor and finished up with the biggest news of all—that Brandon Waycross had escaped from the jail and that his real name was not Brandon Waycross.

"What?" Beatriz and another female voice intoned at the same time.

Footsteps sounded from inside the lodge, growing louder until MacKenna stepped out onto the porch and turned to face her father and mother. Mack held a steaming china cup and saucer in her hands. Since the rustic Brannigans rarely used china except on special occasions, Ty figured the cup must be meant for Devon lying in his father's old bed upstairs.

MacKenna regarded her father in wide-eyed shock. "H-his name isn't . . . Brandon Waycross?"

"Ah, hell," Ty said, raking a big hand through his hair. "I didn't want you to hear that, honey. At least not that way."

Quietly, her hazel eyes cast with shock, MacKenna said, "If his name isn't Brandon Waycross . . . what is it?"

Ty drew a deep breath, let it out slowly. Beatriz had turned around to stare at him, waiting, her expression almost as shocked as her daughter's.

"His real name is Brandon Talbot. He's from Laramie."

Frowning, puzzled, MacKenna shook her head. "Well . . . why . . . why the made-up name . . . ?"

Ty glanced at Beatriz, confounded.

Beatriz placed her hand on his arm. "Mi amore, your daughter is strong enough to hear the truth. She *deserves* to hear the truth."

"Gracias, Madre," MacKenna said.

Ty switched his gaze to her. "Hales from a family of bank robbers—his father and several brothers. His father and brothers were shot down during a robbery in Colorado. Brandon got away."

MacKenna looked down at the steaming liquid in the china cup, frowning, then looked at her father again. "So, he came up here . . ."

"To avoid the law."

"How did you learn this about him, Pa?"

"Roy Cole found an old wanted circular with Talbot's likeness on it." Ty gave an expression of deep regret and sympathy. "I'm sorry, honey. He lied to us all."

"He escaped from Mister Southern's jail?"

"Yes."

"Does Anchor know?"

"They likely do by now. There were a couple of Anchor men in town when he busted out and stole a fast horse. I think it was Avery Cutter's big buckskin. He may have made up a last name, but Brandon does have an eye for good horse flesh." He'd also been genuinely good at gentling horses, the rancher silently noted to himself. That was something you couldn't fake.

"Which way was he headed?"

Ty frowned, a little puzzled by the question. "West."

"Toward the Wind Rivers."

"I suppose so. Why do you ask, honey?"

MacKenna looked down at the cup in her hands again then turned toward the open door. "I'd best get this tea up to Miss Hayes."

"Wait," Ty urged. "Hold on, honey!"

But MacKenna was already gone. Ty heard his daughter's boots on the stairs.

Beatriz had turned toward where her daughter had disappeared, as well.

"You know somethin', honey," Ty said to his wife, scratching the back of his head, his brows ridged with consternation, "That child bedevils me no end."

"Always has," Beatriz said, placing a kiss on his cheek. "Always will." She rubbed in the kiss with her finger then added knowingly, "Like her father, your daughter has her mysteries, Tynan."

CHAPTER 28

Ty had a quick supper and then saddled a fresh horse and rode back to Warknife. He wanted to inform the staff and working girls at the Longhorn Saloon that Miss Hayes was injured but safe and that she'd be staying a few days at the Powderhorn while she recovered.

He didn't bother worrying anymore about throwing more grist into the Warknife gossip mill. It was way too late to worry about that.

For her part, Devon had wanted Ty to send for a buggy from town to retrieve her that very night but yielded to Beatriz's stern warning that while the ankle was merely sprained, it was sprained badly enough that any strain on it within the next two days would make it worse. It might even cause a fracture. Beatriz thought it best that Doc Hinkenlooper ride out to the ranch to inspect the badly swollen ankle himself, to make sure it was indeed a sprain and not a fracture, before Devon put any weight on it.

After putting the folks at the Longhorn at ease, Ty checked on Chris Southern and Hinkenlooper and was deeply disgruntled to learn that not only had neither man shown up in town but that Southern's wife, Molly, was fit to be tied, as the saying went, with worry about her mysteriously missing husband. She told Ty that Chris's two deputies, Glenn Beach and Bob Early, had finally returned from Fool's Crow. Both men had each led a small posse out to track the old lawman down but having found no sign before dark, had returned, crestfallen, to give Molly the grim news that Chris was still missing.

Ty comforted the poor, sobbing woman the best he could, and assured her that Chris would likely show up before morning with a perfectly reasonable explanation for his unexpected disappearance.

Hollow words, he knew. But it was the best he could do.

He, too, was badly worried about his old friend as well as Hinkenlooper. He was convinced that both men had likely ridden out of town together. Why was anyone's guess.

Ty kissed Molly's cheek, donned his hat, mounted up, and rode back out to the Powderhorn in time to catch about four hours of shuteye. He rose at the first faint blush of the false dawn in the bedroom windows, about a half hour ahead of his family, and dressed quietly while Beatriz slept, breathing softly into her pillow.

At least, he'd thought he'd arisen before his family. He was surprised when he walked into the kitchen to make a sandwich for his grub sack to find MacKenna sitting at her usual place at the eating table. She was fully dressed in her usual range gear including bull hide chaps, checked shirt, and neck-knotted bandanna. Her black hat sat on the table near her right elbow. Her long, black hair shone from a recent brushing and was tied into a long queue falling straight down her slender back.

A lamp burned on the table before her.

"Good morning, baby girl. You're up kinda . . ."

As she turned to face her father, he saw the wanted dodger on the table before her. The same circular he'd stuffed into his back pocket in town.

Ty slowed his pace as he approached the table, gazing confoundedly down at the yellowed dodger, Mack's former beau's likeness staring up at her with eyes far sharper and more cunning than the eyes Ty remembered seeing in the face of Brandon Waycross.

"Where did you find that?" Ty said, patting the back pocket in which he'd stuffed the circular.

"I found it on the floor upstairs in the hall, outside your and Ma's room." MacKenna blinked slowly, glowered up at her father, nearly closing one eye.

"I'm sorry, Mack. I wish you hadn't found that."

"I wanted to see it for myself." She shook her head slowly, gazing down at the dodger. "What a liar!"

Ty squatted beside her, wrapped an arm around her, tipped his head against hers. "Dammit all . . ."

She placed her hand on his knee with affection. "You can't protect me forever, Pa. What's more." She turned to give him a grave look. "You don't have to. I'm tough. I'm strong. I'm a Brannigan."

Ty smiled and kissed her cheek. "I wish your grandfather could see you now."

She returned his smile. "Why are you up so early?"

Ty straightened, sighed, and walked around the table toward the cupboard in which Beatriz kept the bread, cheese, and the rich Mexican sausage she ground and spiced herself. "I'm gonna ride over to Anchor. Want to check on a few things."

MacKenna scraped her chair back and rose. "I'm going with you."

Ty turned to object then closed his mouth.

"I need to get to the bottom of who he is, Pa," she said with firm resolve, narrowing her eyes determinedly. "I need to know who Brandon Talbot really is. I need to know if he's a killer. I need to know just how badly I was misled!"

Ty could tell by the expression on his daughter's lovely face and in her lake-clear hazel eyes that she, indeed, was riding along with him. He owed her that much for keeping secrets from her. So did Talbot.

They'd leave a note for her mother.

"Tell me somethin', Mack," Ty said a half hour later, as he and MacKenna rode cross-country

343

toward Anchor, "how come you're so sure Brandon is headed for the Wind Rivers?"

"He told me he learned how to gentle horses from Henry Two Kills. Mentioned him often. Said this Two Kills fella was like a father to him. I forgot all about it until you said he left town riding west. I knew right then he was headed for Two Kills's cabin in the Wind Rivers." MacKenna glanced at her father. "At least, I have a feeling that's where he's headed. He'll need supplies, and he'll likely get them from Two Kills."

"Henry Two Kills, eh?" Ty raked a thumb along his jaw and gazed northward. "Old Henry lives up high, above Elk Creek and the falls. Old shotgun ranch. Haven't been up that way for years." Two Kills was an old half-breed who kept to himself. He used to trap wild horses and break them for the army.

"Do you know where he lives, Pa?"

Ty nodded. "Been through there a time or two, huntin' outlaws in the old days. Ate a meal or two with old Henry, bunked on his floor. This was long ago. If he's still there, he'd be as old as the mountains themselves."

"Brandon said he was getting up in years but still going strong, though he wasn't trapping horses anymore."

"Yeah, those days are over, I'm sure. Whoa—wait, hold on!"

They'd just crested a low ridge. Ty stopped the leggy cream he was riding, giving the dun and the roan a badly needed rest. Riding to his right, MacKenna stopped her own horse. They both stared down into the next valley where five horseback riders sat in a ragged circle, smoking and talking.

Ty saw that one was the lanky, ostentatiously attired Cass Battles with his twin, pearl gripped Colts holstered down low on his thighs. He was smoking a cigarette while talking with the four others, one of them also smoking, while another was just about to take a drink from a canteen.

The man who raised the canteen to his mouth tipped his head back. As he did, his gaze apparently found Ty and MacKenna sitting their horses on the ridge. He lowered the canteen, glanced at Battles and the other three Anchor hands, moving his lips, catching the others' attention. Then they all swung their heads around and lifted their gazes to the ridge.

Ty glanced at his daughter. "You stay here, baby girl. I'm gonna ride down and have a palaver."

"Be careful, Pa. I don't trust Cass Battles farther than I could throw him uphill in a stiff wind!"

"Me, neither." Ty clucked to his horse and the cream stepped down off the ridge.

As he rode slowly down the ridge, holding the reins loose in his left hand, leaving his right one free for the Colt holstered on that hip, just in case, the five Anchor riders swung their horses around to face him, sitting stirrup to stirrup roughly six feet apart. Ty didn't like the dark looks in the faces before him, nor the belligerent ridges of their brows.

Especially Cass Battles's brows.

Ty had never liked young Battles. Not the least reason why was because some years earlier, when MacKenna had just been starting to fill out her shirts, he'd caught young Battles casting her craven looks during roundup. Ty had ridden over and told the kid, who was maybe sixteen or seventeen at the time, to keep his eyes off his daughter.

Young Battles had cast him a toothy sneer, curling one half of his upper lip, and said, "That girl was made for lookin' at. Gets better to look at every damn—"

He hadn't finished the sentence before Ty had slung his right, gloved hand out and forward, smashing it across young Battles's right cheek with a sharp cracking sound. The kid's hat tumbled off his shoulder to the ground. He yelped, grabbed his cheek, glared at Ty, and reached for the Remington he had holstered at the time on his left hip, for the cross-draw. Ty, who'd known the move was coming, already had his own Colt in his fist, hammer cocked, the barrel aimed at young Battles's belly. Though only sixteen, Battles was already known as a firebrand who'd drawn on several men in the past.

That day he closed his hand around the Remington's walnut grips but left the piece in its holster. He glared at Ty, showing his teeth like an angry cur.

Shrill, cackling laughter had lifted from the ridge behind and above young Battles. He swung his head around in time to see his father sitting a horse atop the ridge, Jake's stocky, big-gutted visage silhouetted against the sky. Jake laughed wildly, guffawing loudly, and slapped his thigh then swung his horse around and disappeared down the other side of the ridge.

His laughter had dwindled slowly on the late-summer breeze.

Ty refreshed his mind with the cautionary memory as he drew rein now before the Anchor men.

"You're on Anchor range, Brannigan," Cass Battles said, his gray eyes cold and mean. He flicked his gaze up toward where MacKenna sat her Appaloosa atop the ridge. "You and your daughter."

"We come in peace," the rancher said. "Just wanted to talk with you about Brandon Waycross."

"Now, we both know that ain't his real name, don't we?" Battles stuck his cigarette between his lips, rose up in his stirrups a little, reached into a back pocket of his black denims, and pulled out a folded sheet of paper. He unfolded it and held it up for Ty to see. It fluttered in the wind. Battles poked a gloved finger at the name near the top, just below WANTED: "Brandon Talbot," he said as smoke slithered out of his mouth around the cigarette, with sneering, jeering exaggeration.

Ty gave a wry snort. Cole had obviously found another copy of the same circular Ty had taken and ridden out to Anchor to hand deliver it to Cass Battles. Half the town of Warknife—hell, half the county—felt subservient to the Battles family, for some reason. Likely just afraid of the biggest bully on the block, which had been old Jake, Cass, and Stalcup and their entire bunkhouse. Also, Cole was likely sporting a sizeable chip on his shoulder after getting that nasty bump on his head. That was probably enough for him to want to see Talbot hang.

"Do you have him?" Ty asked.

"No, but he headed west from town," said the man on the pack's far left. Ty recognized him as one of the two men who'd been in town yesterday with the buckboard when Waycross had busted out of jail. "Headed into the big mountains, most like."

Battles removed the cigarette from between his teeth and cast the man a sidelong, reproving glance, narrowing his eyes. "I'll do the talkin' here, Ringo."

Ringo Wayne, a gunman out of Texas, flushed and gave a cordial dip of his chin, keeping his own flinty eyes on Ty. "You got it, boss. I was just sayin' . . ."

To Ty, Battles said, "I sent the rest of the men out trackin' him last night. If they don't have him yet, they will soon. We're headed that way now." He drew deeply on his cigarette and said as he exhaled the smoke, "He'll likely be trimmin' some cottonwood along the Demon River by sundown." The Demon flowed out of the Wind Rivers to the west, edging around Warknife in the north.

"Why don't you pull your horns in? I don't think he did it."

"The hell! You seen the dodger. The man's a blue-faced liar!"

"He may be a liar and even part of a bank robbing family, but I don't think he murdered your old man."

"What proof do you have?" Battles said.

Ty opened his mouth to speak. He glanced at the cigarette Battles was just then taking another puff off of and closed his mouth. The cigarette was a ready-made. Ty narrowed his eyes at the smoldering cylinder.

An Indian Feather?

He couldn't see any markings on it. If the Indian was there, Battles's gloved right thumb and index finger were covering it up.

"You got none," Battles said. "So get the hell off my range, Brannigan. You know Pa's orders? Shoot trespassers on sight." He grinned devilishly as he flicked his gaze again to MacKenna sitting her appy at the top of the ridge behind her father. "Wouldn't want us to shoot you, would you?" His grin broadened, his eyes sparking with goatish male lust. "Leave your daughter all alone out there . . . ?"

He cast that leering grin toward the men sitting their horses to his right. "I know the fellas here wouldn't mind partaking a little of that stuff up there—eh, boys?"

Rage burned suddenly in the rancher's belly. He felt the blood rush to his face, his heart quicken, skip a beat.

Returning his gaze to Ty again, Battles said, "We all been sorta wondering about her. Wonderin' what sorta fun Waycross was gettin' when he was breaking horses for you."

Heart thudding, Ty glared back at the man. He had his right hand on his right thigh. Felt it slide as though of its own accord toward the Colt holstered nearby. Battles's eyes flicked down to the rancher's hand. He tossed away his cigarette and set his own right hand on his own right thigh, near the pearl grips of the Colt jutting up from his black, hand-tooled, tied-down holster.

Battles grinned. "Think you're still faster'n me . . . town tamer?"

350

The rage burning through Ty was causing him to throw caution to the wind. At the moment, he wanted nothing more than to blow this man's head clean off his shoulders. He didn't care about the risk. It was five against one. If he did manage to clear leather first and blow Battles the third eye he so richly deserved, the other four would likely clean his clock.

And then they'd go for MacKenna.

CHAPTER 29

Ty knew he should try to tamp the situation down, but the rage blazing inside of him wouldn't let him. He kept remembering that goatish glint in Battles's eyes when he'd looked up at MacKenna sitting her horse on the ridge.

His thudding heart slowed. The younger man still inside him, the cool, calm, collected lawman who'd faced down many men in the streets of Hayes, Abilene, and elsewhere, returned. Maybe not in total. No, there was no denying the passage of years. But he still had something that Cass Battles did not have.

Experience.

He was not the fastest gunfighter. He never had been. But a soothing calm had nearly always melted away the nerves that usually fired in most men at such a time as this, when their lives straddled the line between the sod and the grave. No, he wasn't particularly fast. But he was calm and he was true.

He glanced at the other four riders. All but one slid a nervous gaze quickly between Ty and young Battles. The other one, the second man who'd been in town yesterday, grinned in mute delight, his own hand sliding along his thigh toward the worn, walnut grips of the hogleg jutting from the soft, brown holster he wore high on his right hip and which had the initials, L.J., stamped into it. That was for Leonard J. Reed. Ty knew most of the hardcases on Battles's role.

"If you're gonna pull that smoke wagon," Ty said sharply through gritted teeth, "then pull it, you copper-riveted tinhorn!"

Battles' eyes flashed wide in sudden indignation. He hardened his jaws and closed his hand around the pearl grips of his right-side Colt. As he did, Ty curveted his horse with one hand while clawing his own Colt Navy .44 from its holster.

Battles fired a might ahead of Ty. But Battles' bullet merely nipped the nap of Ty's buckskin shirt, on his left side. Ty's bullet plowed into the inside of Battles's right elbow. Battles screeched and dropped his gun then, crouching forward over his wounded arm, glanced at the other four riders and wailed, *"Kill the lowdown dirty son of a bitch!"*

Ty slid his Colt to his left and blew the man who'd been sitting directly to Battles's right out of his saddle before the man had his own Colt even halfway out of its holster. Pulling his feet free of his stirrups and throwing himself from his saddle, to the left, Ty avoided a bullet from L.J. Reed—one that likely would have taken him through his brisket.

He struck the ground hard—that was the only way a man his age landed anymore, hard—then raised his Colt again and blew L.J. off the back of his horse's arched tail. The other three men fired but their horses were pitching too violently for accurate shooting. One bullet plumed dirt and sage to Ty's right, only inches from his right arm, while the other one barked off a rock a little beyond and to the right of the first bullet.

Ty aimed at one of the two men fighting their horses and cursing and recocking their pistols, but held fire when a puckered, blue hole appeared in the dead center of the forehead of the man he'd been aiming at.

Courtesy of MacKenna. Had to be.

The man's head snapped violently back on his shoulders. As the flat crack of his daughter's rifle reached Ty's ears from behind him, the head-shot man's whinnying horse swung sharply to one side, throwing the man forward and through the air over where Ty lay in the dirt and sage. He landed just beyond the rancher and rolled.

The other man's own horse swung completely around. When it turned so that horse and rider were pointed at Ty again, Ty aimed the Colt quickly and watched in satisfaction as his bullet puffed dust from the man's dark-red corduroy shirt, clipping the edge of the lapel of his black bullhide vest.

The man cursed as the bullet punched him back in his saddle. The man dropped his gun and rolled down the side of his horse to land with a heavy thud. His pitching horse kicked him in the head with one scissoring rear hoof, turned full around again and galloped off to Ty's right, angrily shaking its head and trailing its reins along the ground to each side, stepping on them and making them leap.

Ty sat on his butt, staring into the dust and smoke wafting before him.

Slowly, he lowered his own smoking Colt.

Battles's four hands lay around him, unmoving. Battles himself was gone. He'd galloped off during the melee. Ty looked toward the northeast, which was the direction he'd glimpsed the man heading in. Battles just then slipped into an evergreen copse carpeting the side of a ridge, and was gone.

Galloping hooves rose behind Ty.

He turned see MacKenna riding toward him, holding her Winchester carbine in one hand. "Pa!" she yelled as she approached, eyes wide with concern. "Pa, you all right, Pa?"

Ty cursed.

His daughter having to save his fool hide was beginning to become a damn fool habit.

He shoved his Colt into its holster and grabbed his left arm with his right hand, groaning. "I'm all right, baby girl. Just a little worse for the wear, is all."

MacKenna sheathed her carbine, swung down from the saddle, and marched over to him, scowling angrily now. "Damn fool stunt, Pa!"

"What stunt?" Ty said, incredulous.

"I saw what you did. You challenged him, didn't you? Cass Battles!"

"The hell I did!"

"You sure didn't try to back water. I could see that much even from the ridge, and I heard most of what you said. Cass threatened me, and you decided you were going to—what? *Take on all five of those Anchor men?*"

Kneeling beside her father, MacKenna was red-faced with exasperation.

Ty grinned at her. "I knew I had my own personal Annie Oakley to back my play. And back it you did." He glanced over his shoulder at the man whom MacKenna had shot out of his saddle. "Good work, honey. I'm sorry you had to do it. But good work."

MacKenna regarded her father reprovingly, shaking her head. "If this is how you are now, pushing sixty, I'd hate to have seen what you were like thirty years ago!" She paused, glanced at his arm. "Now, you've gone and opened that wound up!"

Ty had been staring at something on the ground ahead of him, pensive. Now he glanced at his arm, saw a few spots of blood staining his sleeve over the wound. "It'll close up again on its own, though I gotta admit I haven't been too good to this wing of late."

He returned his attention to the cigarette Cass Battles had dropped.

"What're you looking at?" MacKenna asked him.

Ty started to push himself to his feet. His hip barked like an angry dog. He gave a frustrated chuff and dropped back down to the ground again.

"Now, what's wrong?"

"Old age." Ty thrust his right hand toward his daughter. "Be a good girl and help this foolish old bag of bones to his feet."

"You're lucky I'm not burying you," she said as, rising, she grabbed Ty's hand and pulled him to his feet with a grunt.

Ty limped over to where his hat had fallen. He picked it up, dusted it off, reshaped the battered crown, and set it on his head. He walked over to the one-and-a-half-inch length of cigarette, picked it up, and studied it closely.

"Well, I'll be damned."

"Don't tell me it's time for a smoke break."

He turned and held the stub up and down between his thumb and index finger so that the Indian Feather logo faced his daughter. "Look at that."

MacKenna frowned. "The same brand of cigarette you found where Mister Battles's killer fired on him . . ."

Absently pocketing the quirley, Ty turned to

stare off in the direction Cass Battles had ridden. "Exactly."

"Are you thinking Cass Battles killed his own father?"

Ty nodded slowly. "That's what I'm thinkin', all right."

"But, why? Why would he do such a thing?"

Ty continued staring toward the northeast, which was not the direction of the Anchor headquarters. "Hard to say. On the other hand, nobody much liked Jake Battles. I have a pretty good suspicion that included his own kids." He turned to MacKenna frowning. "But Chris Southern said that Cass was in jail in Chinook when his father was murdered."

"Couldn't be him, then—could it, Pa?"

"I don't know. Somethin' tells me it was. And the direction he's headed is right suspicious, too."

"Why's that?"

"Anchor is straight south. He's headed northeast. Same direction that rider who left the Indian Feather butts was headed after he'd left Anchor and the scene of old Jake's murder." Ty had turned to stare after Battles again, pensively caressing his chin. "Damned suspicious . . ."

The firebrand being guilty of murder might also have been the reason young Battles had been so willing to pull iron on Ty, who was investigating Jake's murder.

Ty jerked off a glove, stuck two fingers between

his lips, and whistled for his horse. "I'm gonna get after him."

"Wait, Pa," Mack said.

"What is it?"

"If you're sure it was Cass who killed his father, we have to get to Brandon before the rest of the Anchor men find him!"

Ty switched his gaze to the direction in which Cass Battles had disappeared, and glowered his frustration, chewing his upper lip. MacKenna had a point. It would be a crying shame if the Anchor riders hanged young Talbot if, as Ty was pretty damn sure, the real culprit was Cass Battles. Talbot may have been a robber and a liar, one who'd broken MacKenna's heart, but he didn't deserve the kind of punishment Stalcup's men had in mind for him.

"All right, baby girl." Ty gave Mack a direct, admonishing look. "But there's gonna be no 'we' about it. I'll ride into the Wind Rivers and try to find Talbot before the Anchor men do."

"Pa, you're gonna need help! You know I can hold my own in a lead swap!"

Ty wagged his head. "Not a chance. Not if hell froze over and the devil got icicles in his beard! You're riding back to the Powderhorn and you're gonna stay there until I return with young Talbot." He dipped his chin, ridging his brows severely, commandingly. "You mind me now, little miss, or I will give your backside a tanning.

The kind your ma used to give so you won't be able to sit down for a week!"

MacKenna's face crumpled in frustration and she sagged back in her saddle. "Oh, Pa!"

"You mind me, young lady."

She sighed, letting her shoulders sag, and stared at her father in defeat.

Ty gazed back at her, silently amazed. He'd be double-dee damned if even after all she'd learned about the so-called "Brandon Waycross" the young man still didn't have a hard pull on her. Ty would have been worried about her if he hadn't more and more of late been realizing how strong she was. Brannigan strong. When you coupled that with Salazar strong—well, then, you had a formidable young lady on your hands.

One who also had a keen sense of justice not unlike that of Ty's own.

If there was even an inkling of a chance that Mack's former beau was innocent of the crime he'd been accused of—well, then, he simply had to be saved from the Anchor vigilantes.

But Ty would let MacKenna have no part of that. She'd been in enough danger over the past several days.

"Go on home, now, honey," Ty said softly, gently, knowing he'd broken her heart. "Stay there until I get back. Keep everybody to home."

"What will I tell Ma?"

"Tell her the truth." Ty was done holding

things back from his wife, who deserved to know everything he did. "But reassure her I intend to take no chances with the Anchor riders. That's rugged country up there. I can steer clear of the Anchor men while making my way to Two Kills's place."

"You'd better, Pa," MacKenna said, suddenly turning the tables again, becoming the parent. "Don't take any chances." She glanced at the four dead Anchor men lying in heaps behind her then turned back to Ty. "*We* may have taken down four of them and put another out of commission, but there's still a good ten or so left, and you know what they are. Cold-steel artists—every man-jack of 'em."

"I know." Ty smiled at her emphasized *we*. "Go on home, baby. I'll be back in a day or two."

MacKenna pursed her lips in a grimace of sorts and neck-reined the appy around, directing it toward the Powderhorn. "I'm gonna hold you to that, Pa." She nudged the mount with her spurs.

Ty walked over to the cream and swung up into the leather.

"Wait," MacKenna said, suddenly reining her Appaloosa back around and galloping over to rein up beside her father. She leaned out from the right side of her saddle and threw her arms around Ty's stout neck, hugging him tightly. She planted a kiss on his cheek and gazed into his eyes, deep lines carved across the almond skin of her forehead. "Thank you."

Ty smiled, kissed her cheek. "Not a problem, honey."

"Good-bye, Pa."

"Goody-bye, honey."

MacKenna reined the appy around again and booted it into a hard gallop around the dead men and then on toward the home ranch.

Ty took a few seconds to watch her dwindle into the distance before him, dropping gradually into a canyon, her queued black hair bouncing against her back. When she was gone, missing her already, Ty reined the cream around, directed it northeast, and booted it into a ground-devouring gallop toward the ermine peaks of the Wind Rivers and Henry Two Kills's cabin.

CHAPTER 30

MacKenna dropped down into the draw, stopped the appy, and swung down from the saddle.

Hating herself for what she was considering, for her father certainly deserved a better, more obedient daughter, she clambered up the side of the grassy ridge she'd just descended, following the trail of bent grass left by her horse. She bent forward to grab tufts of brome and needle grass and sage to help with her ascent of the steep slope.

When she neared the crest, she stopped, doffed her black hat, and held it down beside her. She edged a look up over the lip of the ridge, casting her cautious gaze back in the direction from which she'd come. She watched her father's broad back narrow gradually as he and the cream galloped at a northeastward slant away from where MacKenna crouched just beneath the lip of the draw. Smaller and smaller the jouncing horse and rider grew until they topped a low ridge, crested it, and dropped down the other side, first the horse and then the rider disappearing from the girl's view.

MacKenna returned the hat to her head, swung around, and slipped and slid back down the steep slope, muttering under her breath, "Forgive me, Pa."

She wanted to follow her father's orders. She really did. She just couldn't do it. Her heart was a wild horse galloping inside her. It was that wild black stallion that she and her father had watched as they lay belly down and side by side against the side of the ridge several days ago, just before all of the current trouble had exploded seemingly all at once. That stallion inside her would not be tamed.

MacKenna could not find it inside herself to ride back to the ranch and just sit there idly waiting for her father and Brandon Talbot to return. She would not follow her father into the Wind Rivers. That she would not do. She would not go that far in disobeying his wishes.

But she had to do *something*. And that something had come to her even before she and the appy had started descending the draw.

She would follow Cass Battles and, if possible, run him to ground and drag him kicking and screaming, if it came to that, back to Warknife and into Marshal Southern's jail. Cass could not be allowed to ride free while the man accused of Battles's crime was set upon by the Anchor wolves.

MacKenna swung up onto the Appaloosa's back.

Nope. She just couldn't let it happen.

She had to do something. And run the damnable, cow-stupid, lusty, and back-shooting

Cass Battles to ground was exactly what that something was.

When she was through and if Pa still wanted to tan her hide, she'd go out and pick the stoutest, longest willow switch she could find!

"Hyah, boy!" she urged, nudging the appy with her spurs.

Horse and rider lunged up the steep ridge and galloped back around the dead men again, angling toward the northwest. Mack cast her guilty gaze to her right, to the northeast, the direction in which her father had ridden. She muttered what to even her own ears sounded like a hollow apology.

She turned her head forward and felt her lips shape a guilty but eager grin.

Mack had little trouble following Cass Battles.

The Anchor firebrand had left a clear trail of broken bromegrass and sage as well as hoof prints where the ground was softer. Even a good bit of blood from his wounded arm spotted the brush he'd ridden over. The trail was clear enough that MacKenna was able to follow at a fast, steady pace.

So fast and so steady, in fact, that as she rode around the left side of a large lodgepole pine standing alone near the crest of a low ridge, she reined her mount down abruptly. She jerked back on the reins, then swung the mount around and put it up close to the tree's tall, straight trunk, where several boughs screened her from view from where Cass sat his chestnut gelding only thirty or so yards straight ahead of her, at the crest of the ridge.

Mack used her left hand to shove a bough of the lodgepole aside and cast her gaze toward Battles just as he lowered his canteen from his lips, then threw his head far back and launched an enraged, pain-racked wail toward the clear, cobalt Wyoming sky arching over him. The wail echoed, causing several crows to light from the lodgepoles and cedars around the wounded firebrand, cawing their annoyance.

A squirrel high in the branches of MacKenna's screening tree chortled angrily.

MacKenna slid her right hand toward the rear stock of the carbine jutting from her scabbard strapped over her right stirrup. She could take him so easily. She glanced at her hand and then at Battles who sat his horse facing away from her, crouched forward and to his right, cradling his wounded right arm in his lap.

MacKenna looked at her hand again. It trembled with indecision. Should she take him now or wait?

So easy!

She reached forward and placed her hand on the carbine's stock then looked up suddenly with a gasp as hooves thudded and tack squawked ahead of her. Cass was just then booting his horse down the other side of the ridge, horse and rider quickly dropping from view.

MacKenna removed her hand from her rifle.

Best to wait and see where he was headed, though MacKenna thought she knew. They were nearly to the headquarters of Glenn and Sonya Thompsons' Sunrise Ranch. That's where Mack's father had said the killer's trail had led from the sight of Jake Battles's murder. Why Cass would be heading for the Thompson place was anyone's guess. Mack booted her horse forward, hoping the guessing would soon be over.

She slowed her horse near the crest of the ridge, peered cautiously down the other side. Battles was just then reaching the valley floor and turning his horse to follow a trough between ridges, to the east. When he was out of sight, angling along the curving bottom of the trough to the north, MacKenna put her horse down the ridge. She continued following Battles until she looked up to see him just then cresting the ridge that stood directly south of the Thompsons' place.

Sure enough, Mack thought as she put her own horse up the steep, grassy ridge, letting the pinto choose its own way around the widely scattered pines. He was heading for the Sunrise.

Was he somehow in cahoots with Glenn and Sonya Thompson in the murder of his father?

MacKenna shook her head, frowning. That didn't make any sense. The Thompsons were a keep-to-themselves, childless couple with very little land and a small herd, a few chickens, and pigs. Mack couldn't believe they'd had anything to do with anyone, much less Jake Battles, whose Anchor ranch lay on the other side of Powderhorn range from their little spread. Battles wouldn't have put the squeeze on them the way he often did with the other ranchers around him. The Sunrise was too far away.

What could they and Cass Battles possibly have in common?

MacKenna halted the pinto several yards from the crest of the ridge, tied the reins to a cedar branch, and fished her spyglass out of a saddlebag pouch. She walked up the slope, keeping her head low. Several feet from the top, she removed her hat, tossed it down beside her, dropped to her knees, and crawled to within a foot of the ridge crest.

She removed the spyglass from its soft leather sheath, raised it to her right eye, and adjusted the focus until the back of the Thompson cabin, set fifty yards or so from the base of the ridge, swam into focus.

So did Cass Battles, who just then bottomed out in the Sunrise headquarters and walked his horse slowly toward the cabin, which was flanked by a sizeable garden, the arrow-straight vegetable rows separated by just as arrow-straight irrigation ditches.

MacKenna frowned, deeply curious, as she stared down the ridge through the spyglass. Her curiosity grew as Battles walked his horse around the garden, between a privy and a woodshed sheathed by deep, green shrubs. The perfect garden was fronted by a circular patch of flowers ringed by stones all of the same cream color and size. MacKenna recognized the flowers as irises, her mother's favorite.

MacKenna's frown grew more severe as Cass Battles slanted his horse purposefully toward the flower patch—it had to be a purposeful move because he so easily could have avoided it—and walked it right through it, trampling the precious irises!

MacKenna lowered the spyglass from her face and gave a deep, guttural cry of fury. She raised the spy glass again just as Battles walked his horse out of the torn flowers. She heard herself mutter, "Why did you do that, you unheeled *pendejo*?"

That was a word she'd learned from her grandfather when she'd visited Diego Salazar in his bank in town one day and she'd heard the hot-tempered, gray-headed, old man yell the epithet at the back of a customer stomping angrily out of his office. MacKenna had cajoled the old man, a sucker for a pretty face—especially when said face belonged to his granddaughter—into translating its meaning to her, which had made her cheeks warm.

They were warm now, too, though not from muttering the epithet but from her anger at Cass Battles, who just now drew rein in front of a window in the house's rear wall. One of the torn irises, a deep-purple beauty, clung to his horse's right rear hoof. Battles peered into the window then booted his horse up to the next one, peered into that one, then booted the horse on up to the third and last window in the house's back wall. He removed his hat, waved it in front of the window several times, obviously trying to draw the attention of someone inside.

Which he must have done.

He turned his horse around and rode toward the back door at the far end of the house. He wasn't halfway to the door before the door burst open and a plump woman in a tight-fitting, cream day dress with printed brown flowers, her brown hair in a bun, stormed out of the house, closed the door, and then stomped barefoot up to Battles's horse, gesticulating angrily with her hands. MacKenna was too far away to hear what Sonya Thompson was saying to Cass Battles, but the woman was obviously angry, all right.

Several times, she glanced at the house's rear windows.

Cass Battles remained on his horse, and he

and Mrs. Thompson were obviously having a conversation—or an argument, rather—until Battles sagged far to the right and sort of half fell from the saddle. Sonya cupped her hands over her mouth in terror, cast another anxious look toward the house's rear windows, then hurried over to where Battles was sagging back against his horse.

He was obviously close to passing out, likely from blood loss.

Mrs. Thompson wrapped her left arm around Cass's neck and then, glancing back over her shoulder toward the cabin's windows—looking for *Mister* Thompson, no doubt, MacKenna thought with a wry chuff—she led Battles around the garden's far side. She and the wounded man, who walked as though drunk, leaning heavily into the woman, angled off into the trees and brush that separated the house from what appeared a much smaller, dilapidated, age-silvered cabin sitting near the base of the ridge MacKenna was on.

Soon, as they approached the front of the cabin, they slipped out of Mack's field of vision. She lowered the glass, frowning. They must have gone inside.

A few seconds later, Mrs. Thompson ran back out of the cabin, retracing her steps to the back of the one she and her husband were living in. Battles' horse remained ground reined where he had left it. Now, with yet another wary glance toward the cabin's windows, Sonya grabbed the reins and led the horse back the way she'd led Battles. She led the horse around behind the cabin and tied it to a tree. Moving quickly, looking pale and frantic, she hurried back around the side to the front and disappeared out of Mack's field of vision again.

She'd no doubt gone back inside the old shack. To her lover?

Is that what was going on here? Were Cass Battles and Sonya Thompson lovers?

MacKenna lowered the spyglass and worried her bottom lip with her finger, her heart quickening.

There was now ample proof that Brandon had not killed Jake Battles. Cass Battles had killed his father. He'd been the one hunkering in the brush near where his father had been shot. He'd been the one who'd ridden here to the Sunrise Ranch after he'd killed old Jake. The cigarette butts and the trail his father had followed to the Sunrise, and the trail MacKenna had just followed to the Sunrise now, too, were proof of Cass's guilt.

Weren't they?

MacKenna was no attorney, but it was obvious enough that Battles had killed his father and had let Brandon take the blame. Not only that, but he'd tried to run Brandon down and hang him!

What MacKenna should do now was ride to

town and tell Marshal Southern about what she and her father knew about Cass Battles.

Was that what she was going to do?

No.

She winced, shook her head again, used her right index finger to roll her bottom lip down, then let it roll back up again.

No. She couldn't do it. She had to know if Sonya Thompson was somehow tied into the murder, as well.

But why would she be?

Maybe old Jake had discovered his son cuckolding Mister Thompson and . . .

Oh, hell. Jake Battles had never cared before about who his lusty dog of a rotten son was panting after, married or not. MacKenna had it on good word that Cass Battles had sparked many married women in the past. His father had likely known, but old Jake had done nothing about it.

Still, Mack's curiosity was a mad dog chomping into her ankle, not willing to let go until she'd trekked down the ridge to that shack and done a little investigating. Then, if it didn't look like she'd get herself or anyone else killed, she might just tattoo Battles's head with her rifle butt, tie him belly down across his saddle, and haul him back to town and to Marshal Southern's jail.

MacKenna crabbed backward down the slope, grabbed her hat, set it on her head, rose, and shucked her carbine from her saddle boot.

Holding the rifle down low by her side, she walked up to the crest of the ridge. Crouching, staying low, she angled down the hill to her right.

She weaved her way through the trees that slanted their shadows across the belly of the grassy slope. When she gained the base of the ridge, she stepped carefully through discarded boards and logs and other debris partly concealed by the heavy shrub growth behind the little shack, to the shack's rear wall. There were two windows in the rear wall, one to her far right, another to her left as she approached the shack between the two windows, not wanting to be seen from inside.

The one to her right was partly broken out. The one to her left was cracked and badly warped and soot-streaked but intact. She edged over to it, doffed her hat, and edged a peek inside. The images before her were blurred by the warped, dirty glass, but she could see that Cass Battles sat on the floor just beyond the window. He leaned back against the wall, near the closed front door. He was on a straw pallet. Mrs. Thompson sat beside him, her legs curled beneath her, leaning toward Battles as she removed his shirt.

"Oh, Cass!" Mack could hear Mrs. Thompson saying. "You shouldn't have come here!"

Battles turned toward her. His voice was loud and pitched with anger. "Where the hell else was I s'posed to go? Ride all the way to town and bleed out halfway there?"

Sonya shushed him desperately and left off removing his shirt to clamp her right hand over Battles's mouth, leaning out to her right to cast her gaze through the wide cracks between the vertical planks of the door. MacKenna heard her say, "Glenn's inside. He's on one of his miserable benders, hasn't done a lick of work in over a week!"

"He can go to hell! Baby, you have to tend my arm!"

"Darling, you need a doctor!"

Battles leaned even closer to the woman, grabbed her arm with his left one, and shook her violently. "Go to the house and get a sheet. A big one. And a bottle. Surely there's enough hooch in there!"

Before Sonya could respond, there sounded the raking scrape of a distant door opening.

A man's angry voice shouted, "Sonya! Sonya, where the hell *are* you? Is he *back?*" That last part was bellowed so loudly and with such rage that MacKenna herself gasped and closed her hands over her mouth. She lurched with another start when the enraged voice came again with: "I told you what was gonna happen to *both* of you if he ever came back!"

CHAPTER 31

It was a rough country Ty was traversing, carved by the winding course of an ancient river as well as a wet tributary of the Demon.

It was not easy riding. There were better trails in this neck of the Wind Rivers. But he figured this more problematic route along the Demon's Sister River, through steep canyons beneath towering, rocky, pine-peppered ridges and moody gray crags should keep him hidden from other riders—namely, the Anchor men led by the cagey and determined Con Stalcup, who was bound and determined to exact revenge for the murder of the man who'd employed him for the past fifteen years, as were those fogging the sage behind the Anchor foreman.

Ty figured he had the advantage of knowing where young Waycross was headed. Or had been headed the day before. No doubt having taken care to cover his trail, he was likely at Henry Two Kills's cabin now unless he'd already stocked up on supplies and pushed on, either north into Montana or south into the Colorado Territory. Two Kills's cabin was only a few miles from the range's western edge, once you crossed a vast plain of mountain sage broken by slanting dykes then rose up into rocky, pine- and fir-choked canyons in which the air was pleasantly cool and winey.

At least, Ty hoped he had the advantage over Anchor and that the Anchor riders didn't know about Two Kills's old horse ranch at the far northeastern end of Sheepeaters' Gulch, at the bottom of a bone-littered, boulder-strewn buffalo jump once used by the Shoshone and Arapaho people who had roamed this remote neck of the mountains.

Ty doubted the Anchor men knew about Two Kills's place. He'd met very few people other than long-time residents of this country who knew about Henry, much less had visited his place. Henry came to town only once or twice a year—a short, bandy-legged, taciturn old man clad in ancient buckskins and Indian-beaded shirt and with long, white hair and a bib beard that hung nearly to his flat belly hardened by all of his years trapping and breaking horses for the army. The last time Ty had visited the old hermit's cabin—years ago now—Henry had had a pet badger named Pete who kept a check on the rodent population around Henry's ranch and whom Henry occasionally teased with a cottonwood stick just for fun until Pete got fed up and sulked off under the porch of Henry's ancient log cabin to curl up and tend his nerves.

No, only long-time residents knew about Henry, and damn few of them except the shop owners Henry did business with in town from time to time. None of the Anchor riders had been in the Bear Paw and Wind River country long. Ty knew the bulk of them were gun-hung tough nuts doubling as occasional cow nurses from Oklahoma and Texas. Of them, Stalcup had likely been in this country the longest—fifteen years. Ty doubted Stalcup, who hailed from Arizona, knew about Henry. He'd have had no reason to, and probably no occasion to, either. Stalcup rarely strayed from Anchor, never far from old Jake's side.

Ty crossed a low divide, paused beside a lightning-split, wind-twisted cedar growing up out of a cracked boulder, and scanned the vast, broken country around him. The cool wind was blowing; he held his hat down on his head and squinted against the brassy, lens-clear sunlight. He was glad to not see any movement or dust curls on the ridges or slopes of the badlands splayed out around him like a lady's fan, with the Demon's Sister River white-foaming and thumping loudly as it roared down its stony bed along the canyon's far right side, at the base of the southern, pine-clad ridge.

Then Ty did spy movement. He slid his hand toward the Colt on his right hip, then stopped. Only a coyote slipping through the twisting trough between slanting, stone dikes, a dead jack-rabbit hanging from its jaws. Possibly scenting the man and horse perched on the divide, the brush wolf turned sharply, shifted the rabbit in its jaws, and disappeared into the misty shade cast by a slant-topped, cabin-sized boulder.

Ty booted the cream, whom Carolyn had named Pearl despite its being a gelded male, ahead along an old horse trail following the course of the roaring river. Not far ahead, the canyon narrowed to a bottleneck and the cliff wall rose a good, sheer two hundred feet on the left side while on the right the canyon wall became a gradually sloping boulder field. That was the old bison jump. The floor of the canyon and the crease between the boulders were virtually paved with ancient bones crushed and eroded by the floods and winds of time.

As Ty rounded a long bend in the sheer granite wall on his left, Henry Two Kills's old ranch shifted into place before him. The humble outfit, a handful of small log buildings including Henry's cabin, a lean-to stable, and two unpeeled pine pole corrals, sat in a broad horseshoe of the river that filled the canyon with a steady, echoing roar. The ranch was backed by a shelving mountain slope carpeted in the lush blue-greens of pines, spruces, and firs.

An idyllic setting but a remote and lonely one, as well.

Ty put the cream up another low rise and drew rein, gazing ahead at the old outfit that Henry hadn't named but only called "his little outfit." There was no portal or entrance gate. The old horse trail led straight on into the yard which was shaded by several shaggy pines and firs. Ty's attention was drawn to a low rise flanking the cabin on the right. Atop the rise, a lone man appeared to be working with a shovel.

The man was flanked by a horse—a buckskin lazily switching its tail.

Frowning curiously, Ty nudged the cream ahead. The horse had taken maybe a half dozen strides before the man on the rise behind the cabin, glanced toward Ty, glanced away, then jerked his head back to gaze directly at the man on the cream horse riding slowly toward him. He held the shovel at a downward slant across his thighs, then abruptly dropped it, walked over to the buckskin, and shucked a rifle from the scabbard.

Cocking the rifle, young Talbot walked forward, keeping his gaze on Brannigan who now angled the cream in the direction of the rise the young horse gentler was on. Talbot stopped at the edge of the rise and stood there, gazing toward his unexpected visitor. The hot afternoon wind blew his longish, curly, dark-brown hair back up over his head. It grabbed at the untucked tails of his red, Spanish-cut shirt. It blew the buckskin's tail back toward the pine-clad rise beyond it.

He held the cocked rifle—an old-model

Spencer, Ty saw as he drew within fifty yards of the base of the rise—low across his thighs. That was Henry Two Kills's old repeater. Talbot didn't seem in any hurry to use the rifle, so Ty left his own guns in the leather. Maybe Talbot's professed skittishness about guns had been as much of a lie as his last name had been, or maybe it wasn't. Ty decided to give the young man the benefit of the doubt.

Another in a long line . . .

The wind kicked up dust and pine needles and blew it around the canyon, making an eerie moaning sound. Ty squinted his eyes against the grit peppering his face as it curled up from behind him.

He reined up at the base of the apron slope and gazed up at Brandon Talbot for a few seconds, then booted the cream up the side of the slope. At the top, he drew rein to the right of the man he'd known for the past three years as Brandon Waycross.

The horse gentler did not turn to look at him but remained standing at the edge of the slope, gazing back down the old charnel ground of the canyon and its ancient, bone-paved riverbed. The wind continued to blow his hair back behind him.

Ty gazed at the hole the young man had dug despite his battered ribs and was now filling in. A five-length of cottonwood stick protruded from the ground at the head of the apparent grave. Ty recognized the stick as the one Henry Two Kills had used to tease his badger, Pete.

He turned to Brandon and frowned. "Who's the grave for?"

Keeping his attention on the canyon, the young man said, "Henry."

"What happened?"

Brandon turned to him now with a wry half-smile. "I found him lyin' beside that firepit out front of his cabin, where he used to sit of a night, drinking his homemade wine and teasing Pete with that stick." He canted his head toward the stick poking up out of the ground fronting the grave. "Had his throat torn out."

A soft chortling sound rose to Brannigan's right. He turned his head to the badger, black-faced and with a slender white stripe running down its forehead, slouched in the shade of a flame-shaped rock twenty feet away. Pete regarded Brannigan with his menacing dark eyes, lifting his upper lip to show his small, razor-edged front teeth.

"Easy, Pete," the rancher said. "You're among friends here."

"Is he?" Brandon asked.

Brannigan turned to the kid who was looking at him over his left shoulder.

"That's the thing about badgers," Brandon said, keeping that ironic smile on his mouth and glinting in the warm brown eyes that had made so many girls tumble for him, heedless of the safety of their own hearts. "You just never know if they're your friend or your enemy. You can try to make one your friend, but you gotta treat 'em right. Go pokin' a stick at 'em, they might just bite ya. Tear your throat out, even."

He squeezed the rifle he held across his thighs, opened his hands, squeezed again.

"That's the way of badgers, though, isn't it, Talbot? They never try to be anything other than what or who they are. Can you say as much?"

Talbot turned his head back forward to gaze out over the canyon again. "No, no, I can't. But, then, I didn't have no choice in the matter."

"In the matter of robbing banks or running away and changing your name?"

"Both." Brandon turned to Ty again now. "I didn't have no choice. My pa and my brothers forced me to ride with 'em. But I never robbed any bank, Mister Brannigan. You have to believe that. I refused to rob or to shoot anybody. I only held the horses. You have to understand. We were dirt poor. The larger outfits down there in Wyoming . . . they burned us out. We were homeless. Penniless. Hell, they even shot our horses."

A sheen of emotion shone in the young man's eyes as he gazed up at Ty. "They even shot our horses! You gotta understand—horses mean more to me than people! So, when Pa and my brothers wanted to go after the banks run by the ranchers who burned us out . . . and I only had to hold the horses we robbed from one of the men who burned us out . . . sure, I went along with it."

He paused, stared up at Ty, and added softly but with his gaze sincere, even grave, "But I never shot anyone." He looked down and kicked a rock over the edge of the rise. It thumped, bouncing. "After that last job . . . when the law was layin' for us, an' Pa and my brothers were killed, I ran like hell and I kept on runnin' until I got up here. Figured I'd be safe in the Bear Paws, as remote as they are. A good long ways away from Laramie . . . them corrupt ranchers. So, yeah . . . I changed my name. I looked up old Henry. He and my old man were friends . . . fought for the Confederacy during the war. Went west together. Robbed banks together before settling down. Wyoming wasn't remote enough for Henry, though, so he headed here."

He looked down at the cabin then turned to Ty once more. "Both men could read an' write. Right learned men, my pa and even old Henry, who was half-Chocktaw but raised by a minister who taught him his numbers and letters. They kept in touch over the years. I read the letters. Henry's life, livin' way out here, gentling horses, appealed to me. I thought I might visit him sometime and . . . well, I reckon I got the chance."

He turned full around to gaze down at the grave.

"And now he's dead. Bit by his own badger." He glanced at Pete who now lay apparently asleep in the shade cast by the flame-shaped rock. "Shouldn't have teased him."

Ty looked at Pete and then back at Brandon. "Did you really love my daughter?"

Brandon looked at him quickly, his eyes sincere. "More than you can ever know." Angrily, he kicked another rock down into the yard. "What can I tell you? I'm a damn fool."

"Well, not when it comes to horses," Ty said.

"No." Brandon looked up at the rancher again. "Horses are easy."

"I know you didn't kill Jake Battles."

Brandon frowned at him but didn't say anything, the wind blowing his hair.

"Cass Battles shot him."

"Cass?" Brandon's brows ridged as he jerked his head back in disbelief. "Why?"

"I hope to find that out before too long. I think he headed for the Sunrise Ranch."

"Ahh . . ."

It was Ty's turn to frown. "What does that mean?"

Brandon smiled knowingly. "Mrs. Thompson has quite the reputation. Leastways, she did back when she was a schoolteacher."

"Ahhh." Sonya Thompson had taught the kids of area ranchers at the little schoolhouse on Raven Creek, not far from the main trail into

Warknife, until she'd accepted the hand of Glenn Thompson. "So, they have a history."

"So I've heard."

"Uh-huh."

Brandon shook his head slowly, stubbornly. "I'm not going back to town, Mister Brannigan."

"What—you're gonna keep running? Come on back to town and let me help you clear your name. We'll have us a palaver with Chris Southern." If he'd made it back to town himself by now, Ty added silently to himself.

"What about the Anchor riders?"

"They're out here looking for you." Ty swung his head around to gaze back down the canyon and at the rims rising in the west and east. "We'll skirt around them, get back to town, and clear your name. Throw the real killer behind bars."

"Stalcup might just have a thing or two to say about—"

Brandon stopped when the rataplan of many galloping hooves reached his and Ty's ears.

Ty turned to see a long line of riders galloping along the canyon's western rim—ten, at least. All were silhouetted menacingly against the broad, blue Wyoming sky. They were heading for the main route into the canyon.

"Ah, hell!" Ty said, grimacing at the oncoming riders.

Brandon turned to him, smiling like the cat

386

that ate the canary. "Like I was about to say, Con Stalcup might have something to say about your plans, Mister Brannigan!"

Young Talbot threw his head back and laughed.

CHAPTER 32

"I told you what was going to happen to you both if he ever came back!"

Glenn Thompson's shouted words echoed around inside MacKenna's head as she stared in horror through the cloudy window into the cabin. Sonya Thompson had closed her own hands over her mouth in shock and sagged back against the wall, to MacKenna's left, her brown eyes wide and round.

"Oh, you think so, do you?" Cass Battles bellowed as, also sitting with his back against the wall, he slid his pretty, pearl-gripped Colt from the hand-tooled holster on his right thigh. "We'll see about *that!*"

"Battles, that you?" came Glenn Thompson's voice again, louder this time. He was walking toward the little cabin. MacKenna could see the man through the gaps in the logs of the cabin's front wall, just beyond Battles, where the chinking had disintegrated.

MacKenna's heart thudded.

"Oh, God!" she muttered into her hands. "Oh, God! Oh, God! Oh, God!"

Cass Battles cursed and, gritting his teeth in anger and likely against the pain in the arm MacKenna's father had blown a bullet through, he got his feet beneath him and, shoving his shoulders back up hard against the wall, using the wall to help hoist him to his feet, he started to rise from the floor, grunting, his red face swelling, veins standing out in his forehead. He held the Colt barrel up in his gloved left hand which was coated with the blood from his wounded right arm.

"Havin' another little student and teacher study session, eh, Battles?" bellowed Thompson. He was nearly to the front door now. MacKenna could see him through the gaps between the logs.

She stood with her boots stuck to the ground in horror, knees feeling like mud.

Battles completed the complicated maneuver of gaining his feet. He cocked the Colt and turned toward the closed door.

"No!" Sonya cried, leaping to her own bare feet. "Darling, please!" She rushed past Battles to the door.

Just as she closed her hand around the knob, a raking shout came from the other side of it, shrill with mocking fury.

"Darling, please!"

Sonya had just started to pull open the door, had drawn it maybe two inches from the frame, when a thundering blast sounded, making the window in front of MacKenna rattle in its frame, making MacKenna's ear drums shudder and ache. She watched through the window, stupefied, as Sonya

Thompson was suddenly blown straight back away from the door to slam up against the wall and window in front of MacKenna.

Sonya stood with the back of her head pressed up against the cloudy window, three inches from MacKenna's shocked, wide-open eyes. So close that MacKenna could see the woman's pale scalp through the partings in her hair where it had been drawn up into the tight bun at the top of her head. Sonya stood there for five or six seconds before her head slowly slid down the window and out of sight.

It was followed by the thump of her plump body striking the cabin floor.

Frozen, knees quivering, heart racing, Mack stared through the window.

Cass Battles stood with his back to the window to MacKenna's left, near the front of the cabin. He stood looking in his own brand of wide-eyed shock at Sonya piled up on the floor at the base of the wall. The door stood halfway open, a pumpkin-sized hole in it. Wood from the door lay strewn around the cabin, between MacKenna and the opening in which Glenn Thompson now stood, extending a long-barreled shotgun straight out from his right side, level with his waist.

Gray smoke slithered from the right barrel yawning blackly at MacKenna.

Thompson gazed coldly over the extended shotgun toward his wife.

Battles suddenly swung himself to his left, toward the now-open doorway, swinging the cocked Colt that way, as well. Shouting, *"You damned old drunken fool!"* He aimed the Colt at Thompson's belly. The gun roared and bucked in Cass's left hand.

Thompson's eyes widened in shock as he stumbled backward. The shotgun in his hands thundered again, the buckshot whipping past Battles' right side to smash into the wall somewhere to Mack's right with a heavy thud. Thompson took another stumbling couple of steps backward, his shirt on fire from the flames from Battles's gun. He looked down at the flames, slapped at them with his hands then turned and ran in a shambling fashion straight out away from the cabin, yelling.

Battles took two long strides through the cabin door, stopped, aimed the Colt straight out from his right shoulder, and fired. The bullet parted the rancher's hair at the back of his head. He flew forward with another scream, hit the ground, and rolled. He came up on his back. The flames had been snuffed by the ground, but his shirt was still smoking.

Battles whipped around, his intense amber eyes immediately meeting the terrified eyes of MacKenna staring through the window. Battles gave an evil, leering smile then cocked the smoking Colt in his hand and raised it.

MacKenna gasped and drew her head straight down below the window a quarter second before Battles's Colt roared and the bullet tore through the window with a menacingly soft pinging sound before thudding into a pine behind the cabin.

MacKenna dropped to her knees, shaking, horrified, head swimming from the shock of all that she had witnessed in a little over a minute.

"Miss MacKenna!" Battles bellowed, his voice pitched with mocking and black menace. "Did you follow me, you little polecat?"

Footsteps sounded, growing louder. As he headed toward her from the side of the cabin, Battles's boots crunched brush, kicked an airtight tin with a clanking sound, knocking it against the cabin with a duller clanking sound. MacKenna drew a deep breath, gathering her wits. Hands shaking, she quickly racked a live round into her Winchester's action and swung herself and the rifle to her left just as Battles appeared off the cabin's left rear corner, turning toward her with a bright-eyed look of holy murder.

MacKenna shot him.

He'd been about to trigger his own extended Colt, but Mack's bullet knocked him off balance and he triggered his own weapon into the corner of the cabin, to her left.

"Oh," Battles said through a heavy grunt,

stumbling back and sideways. He got his boots tangled up and he fell on his right side, on his wounded arm.

He gave a girlish screech and rolled onto his back, quivering.

MacKenna drew another calming breath and heaved herself to her feet, pumping another round into her Winchester's chamber. She walked over to where Battles lay in the brush that was stained red from the bullet she had fired into his belly, just below his breastbone. Blood pumped from the hole in his black shirt. Grunting and cursing under his breath, he looked up at MacKenna. His eyes rolled around; there was a faraway look in them.

MacKenna was in such shock it took her nearly a minute to find the question that had been preying on her mind.

"Why?" she said, shaking her head in total befuddlement. "Your own father . . . ?"

Battles's grimace turned into a smile. "The old bastard said if I got thrown in jail again . . . he'd . . . he'd write me out of his . . . will." He stared up at MacKenna, swallowed. His face acquired almost a peaceful look now. "Got out . . . a day . . . early . . . came back and gave the old hog walloper . . ." His expression became a grimace again as pain racked him. He coughed; blood stained his lips. "Gave him one he couldn't digest!"

He coughed again, gave a deep, ragged sigh, turned his head to one side, and lay still.

Mack glowered in disgust, shook her head as she glared down at the dead man. "And Brandon just happened to be there . . . perfectly placed . . . to take the blame . . ."

She resisted the urge to give him a hard kick.

What was the point? He was dead.

What he'd told her was enough to clear Brandon's name.

Reluctantly, she turned her attention to the Thompsons. She still couldn't quite believe what she'd just witnessed. The carnage she'd witnessed. She turned and looked up along the side of the cabin. She could see Glenn Thompson lying on his back roughly a hundred feet from the cabin. He was dead.

What about Mrs. Thompson?

MacKenna should check to make sure. The poor woman likely was—the blast had taken her from point-blank range—but MacKenna couldn't just ride away without making sure.

She drew another calming breath though it didn't do much to calm her and walked up the side of the cabin. She turned at the front corner and walked to the door. She stood in the open doorway, gazing inside, instantly feeling sick to her stomach. She turned away, crossing her arms on her belly, afraid that she was going to be sick. She desperately didn't want to be sick.

She knew if she started, she might never stop.

That Sonya Thompson was dead there could be no doubt.

MacKenna knew that something should be done with the poor woman's body—the men could go to hell—but there was nothing she could think of to do. She certainly couldn't take time to bury her. Later, when she'd helped clear Brandon's name, she and her father and brother would return and give Sonya a proper burial. MacKenna didn't care what happened to Battles and Glenn Thompson. As far as she was concerned, the wolves and coyotes could have them.

But Mrs. Thompson should have a proper burial. She may have had poor taste in men, but she should still be given a proper burial.

As far as Sonya's poor taste in men, MacKenna could relate.

Still fighting back the bile rising in her throat from all the carnage she'd witnessed out here, she drew several more calming breaths then brushed her gloved fist across her nose, set her rifle on her shoulder, and walked back down the side of the cabin. She glanced one last time at Cass Battles lying dead in the grass, gazing almost serenely at the sky, then continued on past the cabin.

She climbed the slope, angling over to where she'd left her horse.

"Easy boy, easy boy," she said as she approached the Appaloosa who eyed her warily, having heard the gunfire and likely having winded the carnage.

She removed the reins from the tree she'd tied them to, slid the Winchester into the boot, and mounted up. She looked around for the fastest route over to the Whiskey Creek Trail, which would take her to town. She needed to tell Marshal Southern, if he was back in town—and he must be by now—what had happened out here today. She chose a crease between haystack buttes in the northwest and booted the appy toward it.

She put her prized mount into a fast gallop through the crease then slowed the horse when she gained the Whiskey Creek Trail. She gave the horse a breather, trotting it along the trail as they headed north toward Warknife. As she passed a crossroads and continued north, the sound of snapping twigs and thrashing brush rose on her left. She reined the appy to a sudden halt and cast her gaze into a thicket of wild rose and hawthorn at the mouth of a very slender canyon between steep-sided buttes. The brush ran about twenty feet back into the canyon.

The thrashing and snapping sounds continued.

MacKenna could see a large, murky figure back inside it, maybe ten feet away from her.

Suddenly remembering the men who had been after her father, one of whom she'd wounded, her heart picked up a fearful pace once more. She reached forward and slid the Winchester from its scabbard. She'd just pumped a round into the chamber before the figure burst out of the brush and onto the trail just ahead of her.

A horse and rider!

The man was slumped far forward in his saddle. So far forward that his gray, hatless head rested on his horse's neck. The horse side-stepped, whickering edgily. MacKenna's lower jaw dropped as she studied the horse, gradually coming to the realization that its slouching rider was none other than . . .

"Marshal Southern!"

Chapter 33

MacKenna booted the appy up beside the nervous gray and placed her hand on the lawman's right shoulder. The second her hand touched his shoulder, which felt unusually lumpy to her touch, he lifted his head with a loud, pain-racked groan, tipping his head back and squeezing his eyes closed.

"Ah, Christ!"

It was then that she saw the blood staining the man's shirt and vest. In addition to having a dislocated shoulder, he'd been shot low in the chest . . .

My God, would the carnage never end?

Marshal Southern opened his eyes, turned his head toward MacKenna. He studied her closely. It appeared to take him a moment to realize who he was looking at.

"Mac . . . Kenna . . . ?"

"Marshal Southern, what happened to you?"

He winced, gave his head a single shake. "Those . . . animals . . . after your pa . . . they killed Doc Hinkenlooper . . . shot me. Left me for dead. I reckon I thought I was dead. Managed to crawl back to my horse . . . into the saddle. Musta passed out." He looked around, blinking, scowling. His craggy cheeks were pale and gaunt. "Where am I?"

"On the Whiskey Creek Trail. Not far from Powderhorn. Can you ride?"

Southern looked at the reins he held in his gloved hands, shrugged. "I reckon I *been* ridin' . . ." He paused, cast his washed out, pain-racked gaze northward, toward town. "Poor Molly. She must be worried sick."

"I'll get word to Mrs. Southern just as soon as we get you patched up, Marshal. Do you want me to lead your horse or can you steer?"

Southern looked at the ribbons in his hands, slid them toward MacKenna. "You'd best take them. I'll concentrate on stayin' in the saddle." He looked at MacKenna, desperation mixing with the pain in his eyes. "I can't die, Mack. I'm not afraid of dyin'. It's . . . Molly."

"You're not gonna die, Marshal—not if I have anything to say about it." MacKenna took the reins from the man. "You hold on real tight, now, hear?"

Southern wrapped his hands around the horn, looking very woozy. But then, Mack was surprised he was conscious at all. He must have lost quite a bit of blood.

MacKenna booted her Appaloosa ahead then turned to watch the gray as she gently tugged on its reins, wanting to make sure that the old marshal did not tumble out of his saddle when she got his horse moving. He lurched back slightly but remained on the mount, head lowered, eyes closed. When she was confident he was not going to tumble off the horse, she booted the appy into a little faster walk, glancing back to see how the lawman was doing.

He looked frail and unsteady, but at least he remained mounted. His lips were pursed, and his jaws were taut with determination. He felt like hell, but he was bound and determined to remain in his saddle for the sake of his wife, Molly, if for no other reason. Mrs. Southern was a sweet old woman whom MacKenna adored as did everyone who knew her.

Mack was amazed at the old man's grit as well as at his devotion to his wife. Shot in the chest, his shoulder likely dislocated, he'd still managed to flee his attackers, climb onto his horse, and try to get back home. He must have lost consciousness while trying to do so. The horse had probably been confused and frightened by its unconscious rider and the smell of blood; that was maybe why it hadn't headed back to town on its own. Maybe wolves or coyotes had been drawn by the smell of blood and that had further frightened it.

As MacKenna rode, heading toward the Powderhorn trail, she considered what Southern had told her about the men who were after her father having killed Doc Hinkenlooper. Another nice old man. Now he was gone. MacKenna supposed that was partly her fault. The killers must have fetched the doctor from town to tend the wound of the man Mack had shot and killed him maybe to keep him quiet about what he'd seen and where he'd seen it.

Rage burned in her. She shook her head slowly, hardening her jaws.

Who were those men? Why did they have such hatred for her father?

MacKenna hoped to find out and to help her father send the scurvy rats to their rewards in hell . . .

She turned onto the trail that would take her and the marshal to the Powderhorn and cast another cautious look back over her shoulder. Southern was leaning far out to one side, sort of sagging, as though he was about to unseat himself.

"Marshal!" MacKenna checked the appy down to a stop.

She'd just started to step down from her saddle when Southern suddenly drew himself straight again, with a start, opening his eyes. He gave a grim smile. "I'm all right, Mack. Keep going. Keep going, child. Get this old worthless bag of bones to your mother. Beatriz will know how to keep my old ticker ticking."

"Are you sure?" MacKenna asked, remaining in the saddle. "I could ride ahead and get the wagon."

"I'm sure, child. Get me to your mother."

Roughly fifteen minutes later, MacKenna led the gray through the Powderhorn portal and the open gate, yelling, "Ma! Ma! Come quick! Marshal Southern is wounded! Matt, help me!"

Matt, working with the colt again in the breaking corral, dropped the halter rope and came running. Just as he crouched through the corral, the house's door burst open and Beatriz Salazar stood on the porch in a bright red dress over which she wore a red and white checked apron, a porcelain green bowl in her hands, rimed with crusted biscuit flour. She wore a flower smudge on her right, almond-colored cheek and a lock of hair that had fallen from the bun atop her head hung down beside it.

"¿Qué le sucedió al mariscal Southern?" Beatriz called. What happened to Marshal Southern?

MacKenna swung down from the leather and opened her mouth to speak but the old marshal spoke for himself, in a voice low and raspy with pain. "This old fool took a bullet in the chest, Beatriz. Don't ask me why I ain't dead. Too damn ornery, I suppose!"

He pulled his right boot out of the stirrup and started to fall straight down to the ground and would have if MacKenna and Matt hadn't been there to catch him.

"Easy does it, Marshal!" Matt said. "Easy does it, now!"

"Ah, hell!" the old lawman carped.

Matt had grabbed Southern under the man's

arms. Now he stood him upright, and MacKenna said, "Can you walk or should we carry you?"

"I can walk . . . with help."

As MacKenna and Matt turned the old man around and began to guide him gently and slowly toward the house, Gregory and Carolyn ran out of the house to stand beside their mother, staring in shock at Matt, MacKenna, and Marshal Southern.

"What happened to Marshal Southern, Mama?" Carolyn asked.

"He's been shot. Gregory, Carolyn—you both know what to do. *Vomanos*!" Beatriz clapped her hands together, and the two younger children headed back into the house, Gregory lumbering behind his fleeter-footed younger sister.

MacKenna and Matt guided the old man slowly up the porch steps. He managed to lift each of his feet up the steps but by the time they'd reached the top of the porch, he was pretty much hanging slack in the two younger people's arms.

As he approached Beatriz, who'd stepped aside to let him and Mack and Matt pass, he stopped and said wearily, "I'm very sorry, Beatriz."

"Don't be silly." She stepped before him, placed her hands on his arms, and glanced at the bloody wound in his chest. She winced, shook her head, pecked the old man's leathery left cheek, and glanced at her children. "Get him into the kitchen. Put him on the table. We're going to have to fetch Hinkenlooper."

"Doc Hinkenlooper's dead, Ma," MacKenna said as she and Matt led old Marshal Southern through the open door and into the house. "I think the marshal's gonna be all up to you!"

MacKenna saw her mother's face blanch a little. Mack knew her mother could set bones and suture cuts but digging out bullets was another matter altogether.

Beatriz was thinking the same thing as she stepped over the threshold and into the foyer just as MacKenna and Matt led the old marshal into the kitchen. Seeing a figure on the stairs ahead of her, she stopped and turned the brunt of her attention into the foyer's deep shadows.

Devon Hayes stood on the second step up from the bottom. She was fully dressed, and she had a crutch under each arm. They were the crutches that Ty had used when he'd broken his ankle two winters ago. They'd been leaning behind the door of Killian Brannigan's old room. That was where the woman had found them.

"Dios mio!" Beatriz intoned. "What are you doing, Miss Hayes? That ankle—"

"Is better," the red-haired, jade-eyed woman said. "At least good enough for me to lend a hand rather than just lie around up there like a lump on a log."

Beatriz shook her head. "No, no, no. You must rest!"

"Ever performed surgery before . . . dug a bullet out of a man's hide?"

Beatriz gave a fateful sigh, shook her head, raised her hands and let them flop back down against her apron. "No."

"I have." Miss Hayes shaped a slow smile.

"I doubt Stalcup is gonna do any listening until he's done some shooting, and by then it's probably gonna be too late for both of us!" Ty said. "Mount up!"

"Ah, hell, they have us, Mr. Brannigan!" Brandon Waycross alias Brandon Talbot said, staring toward where the dozen or so Anchor riders were swinging down off the north ridge of the canyon, following a switchback trail toward the canyon floor. Their dust shone pink in the late-afternoon light behind and above them.

"There!" one of them yelled beneath the rataplan of galloping hooves, pointing. "On the bluff behind the cabin!"

Ty swung up into the leather and turned to where Brandon stood, staring toward the oncoming Anchor riders, still holding his old-model Spencer rifle down low across his thighs.

"Fork leather, boy!" Ty said. "I didn't ride all this way just so's you could commit suicide, and that's just what you'll be doin' unless you climb onto that horse and follow me!"

He swung his mount around and booted it on

down the rise. He glanced over his shoulder and was relieved to see young Waycross swinging up onto his stolen buckskin's back. "All right, all right—I'm right behind you!" he said, booting his horse down the rise and into the sifting dust of Ty's dun.

"They're runnin' for it!" the rancher heard Con Stalcup shout behind him.

He swung his mount east, away from the cabin, and put the steel to him.

He galloped along the base of the canyon's north rim, remembering from one of his rare previous visits out here that a narrow side canyon to the main one would take him east along the floor of another ancient dry watercourse and into an area known as the Buffalo Canyons. Henry Two Kills had once tracked a bear he'd shot into the canyons and had been amazed at its breadth and depth as well as by all of the ancient, wind- and water-carved caves that ringed it.

Ty had been just as amazed when Henry had shown it to him. There was not one but two buffalo jumps in there as well as many gaudy rock paintings that had indicated the canyon area had once been sacred ground to the ancient ones who'd lived here long before the white man had come.

Plenty of good places to fort up and hold off the Anchor men, as Ty remembered.

He glanced back to make sure Brandon was still

behind him. The kid was. So were the Anchor riders, roughly a hundred or so yards behind Ty and his unlikely charge galloping just off Ty's cream's right hip. Young Talbot was crouched low in the saddle, chaps flapping, his hat brim basted against his forehead by the wind. He glanced over his shoulder, looked at Brannigan, and gave his head a fateful wag.

"They mean business!" the younger man said. "And to hell with their horses, I reckon! Gonna run 'em to death!"

Ty turned his head forward, giving an ironic chuff. The kid was about to be run down by a wolf-like pack of killers who intended to play cat's cradle with his head but he seemed more worried about how they were treating their horses.

Yeah, Ty could see what MacKenna saw in him. Ty was glad to know once and for all that Brandon Waycross . . . no, Talbot . . . wasn't a killer. He'd sort of known that all along, even after he'd learned he wasn't who he'd been pretending to be, but the rancher felt better having the young man's innocence confirmed.

If Ty died helping him, at least he'd know he'd died helping an innocent man.

They started into the diverging canyon, which was roughly a hundred yards wide and did not look like a diverging canyon from Ty's current vantage because there was a long island of ancient, pines dead ahead, obscuring the fact that the canyon continued once you made your way around either end of the pines. Ty wouldn't have known about the side canyon if Henry hadn't shown him.

Apparently, Henry had shown Brandon the canyon, as well, for as Ty cast one more look back over his shoulder at the younger man, Brandon smiled his understanding.

They rode around the pine island's south end and then into the diverging canyon continuing beyond the pines. The first stretch of the canyon was narrow, its floor stippled with sage, rock, and prickly pear with occasional shrub thickets growing up along the base of the canyon walls. Gradually, the walls of the canyon pulled back until Ty and Brandon were galloping through a vast natural amphitheater, with the dark mouths of caves showing amongst pines and firs on the granite ridges to Ty's right and left.

Behind him came the gun cracks of the Anchor riders, echoing off the canyon walls. Bullets tore into the sage to Ty's right and left. He turned to see the Anchor men closing on him and Brandon, the riders savagely whipping their rein ends against their horses' hips and withers, crouching low and grinding their spurs into the mounts' flanks.

Apparently, their animosity toward young Talbot knew no bounds. They wanted to finish the hunt right here. Not only had their boss been murdered, their livelihoods imperiled, but they felt as though they'd all been duped by both Talbot and Ty, whom they saw as uppity for extending his reach into the local law business.

And into Anchor business.

"I'll be hanged if they ain't shootin' for keeps!" Talbot said, flinching at a bullet that screeched past his head and spanged off a rock ahead of him.

"Up that rise!" Brannigan yelled as he directed his horse around the east side of a pedestal rock standing in the middle of the canyon.

The rise in question was dead ahead as he straightened his mount on the north side of the pedestal rock. The slope of the rise was relatively gentle and stippled with rocks, boulders, cedars, and pine. At the top of the rise, two rectangular cave openings sat side by side, roughly a hundred feet down from the very top of the sheer, cracked and crenelated granite and limestone ridge rising above the dark cavern mouths.

"You sure?" Brandon called behind him. "They could keep us pinned down up there until we've snapped off all our ammo. And I have damned little ammo, only what's in Henry's old Spencer!"

"Don't worry, kid," Ty said, casting a quick, reassuring smile back behind him. "I got it all planned out!"

Then a bullet plowed into his horse with a sickening *thunk!*

The cream screamed, dropped, and rolled.

Ty did the same.

Chapter 34

Ty rolled to a stop, cursing, dust wafting around him.

"Mr. Brannigan!" Talbot yelled, reining his own horse to a stop.

Gritting his teeth at the sundry aches and pains in his battered body, including in his wounded left arm, Ty waved him on up the hill. "Keep going! I'll be right behind you!"

Talbot thrust his left hand toward him. "Climb up! We'll ride double!"

"Get moving, kid!" Ty said.

He didn't need to say it again. Just then a bullet hammered the slope just inches from the buckskin's left rear hoof. The horse gave an indignant whinny and lunged into an instant gallop on up the ridge. Brannigan hurried over to the wounded horse then stepped back as the animal heaved itself to its feet in a great, billowing cloud of dust, snorting and blowing.

Ty saw a bloody patch along the side of the animal's right rear leg, just above the knee. Just a graze. As the horse snorted again and turned away, getting ready to run as more bullets peppered the slope around it and its rider, Ty reached out and slid the Henry from the saddle sheath. The barrel had just cleared the leather

411

before, giving a shrill, angry whinny, the cream lunged into a gallop off across the belly of the ridge, angling down toward the canyon floor.

Pumping a live round into the Henry's action, Ty swung around, dropped to a knee, and sent three rounds caroming down toward the Anchor riders who were just then approaching the base of the slope fifty feet away. One of his bullets blew a hat off a man's head. The man gave an indignant yell and leaped from his saddle. Another round caught another rider in the man's right thigh. That man yelled, dropped the rifle he'd been wielding, and slapped his gloved hand over the wound, reining his horse to a halt with his other hand.

The other riders checked their own mounts down quickly at the base of the slope. Shouting, they leaped from their saddles, rifles in their hands, and ran toward the rocks and boulders scattered along the slope's base.

Ty rose, turned, and ran up the slope, sweating and breathing hard, his lungs hurting now, as well, joining the misery of the rest of him. He followed a zigzagging course to make himself a harder target. Still, several bullets came damn close to coring him. One nipped his right boot, a menacing sensation that urged him into even more speed. He gained the top of the slope and hurled himself into the cave, rolling into the safety of the cavern's deep shadows.

He turned to see Brandon lying prone on the cave floor, facing the entrance, the Spencer in his hands.

Guns barked at the base of the slope. Bullets kicked up dust, pine needles, and rock shards at the lip of the cave. The grit blew into the cave, peppering Ty's and Brandon's Stetsons.

Ty lowered his head against the onslaught, grimacing against the pain in his old, tired, aching body.

"You all right, Mister Brannigan," Brandon asked. "That was a nasty tumble."

"I've felt better, but I'll live."

"Not if they have their way," the kid said, smiling and canting his head to indicate the Anchor men, whose rifles were barking feverishly, continuing to hammer the slope at the lip of the cave.

Anger burned through Ty. He set his rifle down, lifted his head, cupped his hands around his mouth, and yelled, "Hold your fire, Stalcup! *Hold your damn fire!"*

Several more bullets came whining up the slope, striking the ground in front of Ty and Talbot and peppering their hats with dirt and sand. Then Stalcup yelled beneath the din, and the shooting dwindled to silence.

Stalcup yelled, "Pinned down up there, Brannigan! You might have the high ground, but it's gonna be dark in a couple of hours!"

Ty knew what the man meant. Under cover of darkness, the Anchor riders could slip out from behind the covering rocks and steal invisibly up the slope to both sides of the cave and shoot inside at much better angles than the one they had now, firing up from the bottom.

Ty set his rifle down and cupped his hands around his mouth. He yelled, "Brandon Waycross might really be Brandon Talbot, but he didn't kill Jake Battles. Cass did!"

His only response was silence and the breeze stirring amongst the rocks.

At the base of the slope, a man laughed. Another chuckled.

"What's so damn funny?" Ty inquired through his hands cupped around his mouth.

"I know!" came Stalcup's response.

Ty frowned curiously at young Talbot lying beside him. The kid gave a wry snort and scratched his chin. "Had me a feelin'."

Ty was incredulous. Frowning deeply, he turned to the downslope again and shouted, "You *knew?*"

"Sure," Stalcup returned, amusement in his voice. "I saw Cass crossin' the stream with his tail between his legs. He got outta jail in Chinook a day early."

It was Ty's turn to give a caustic chuff. "But you blamed Brandon, anyway . . . ?"

"Ah, hell," Stalcup yelled up the slope. "Old

Jake was gonna write Cass out of his will. Who would have run Anchor after the old man was dead? He was gonna be dead soon, anyway. His lungs was full of cancer. He wasn't right in the head. Hadn't been for months!"

Brandon gave a mirthless laugh then cupped his own hands around his mouth and yelled over the lip of the cave and down the slope, "And you thought you were gonna marry Ivy, too—eh, Con? She had a change of heart after I came along."

Brandon glanced at Ty, gave a guilty shrug of a shoulder.

Ty glowered at him.

There was a brief silence except for the wind and the ticking of blowing grit.

Then a man chuckled snidely.

Beneath the wind, Ty heard Stalcup say quietly but tightly, "Shut up, Anderson." Then he shouted up the slope, "Yeah, that might've been part of it. Gotta admit, it was nice seein' you there, so easy to take the fall." He chuckled. "What can I say? Ivy's young and she cuts a fine figure."

Another man laughed lustily.

"And she's going to have a nice inheritance," Brandon added.

"That, too." The foreman's voice grew louder, more insistent. "Kid, it's nothin' personal, all right? We're just tryin' to save our jobs, is all.

Brannigan, it's nothin' personal. But I'm gonna give it to you straight. You two ain't gettin' out of here alive!"

"Yep, that's what I thought," Brandon said, stretching his lips back from his teeth. He glanced at Ty.

"See, I told you they wasn't gonna listen to reason, Mister Brannigan."

"You were right, kid."

Stalcup shouted up the slope again, his voice shrill with impatience and rage. "Come on out, Brannigan! This is your own damn fault! You shouldn't go stickin' your nose in where it don't belong! Come on outta there! Why prolong the matter?"

Brandon gave Ty another of his ironic, knowing smiles. "They need to keep us quiet, Mister Brannigan."

"Yep, knowin' what we know—they sure do. Stalcup wants to keep Cass in charge so he can keep his job and marry Ivy."

Brandon opened his mouth to speak but Ty cut him off quickly, pressing a finger to his lips. He'd heard the faint crunch of gravel under a stealthy tread. Now he lifted his head, brought up his rifle quickly and fired into the belly of the Anchor rider who'd just stepped in front of the cave from its right side, bringing a Winchester carbine to bear, grinning.

Ty's bullet punched him back off his feet.

His unshaven face acquired a shocked look. He yelled and then he was gone.

The man had struck the slope but hadn't rolled once before Ty's second bullet found the second man on the slope to the right of the falling one, who'd just been straightening and raising his Yellowboy repeater. The second man snapped off a single, wild shot before he was following the first man down the slope, rolling wildly, kicking up dust, losing his hat and his rifle, which clattered over rocks.

Ty and Talbot lowered their heads quickly as the thunder of barking rifles rose from the rocks at the base of the slope. Ty jerked on Talbot's arm, canted his head toward the shadows farther back inside the cave. He and the kid crabbed backward on their bellies. When they were fifteen feet back from the slope, they rose.

"Come on," Ty said, donning his hat.

Talbot frowned. "What?"

"Follow me."

"What? *Where?*"

Ty beckoned and continued walking into the cave's deep shadows. He paused to strike a match, held it out before him. The flickering, watery light showed the dark mouth of a low, narrow off-shooting passage.

Behind him he heard the ringing of Talbot's spurs as the kid followed him into the passage, both men crouching, for the ceiling was low. Ty let the match go out when a misty, dawn-like light appeared farther on down the corridor.

"What the hell . . . ?" the kid said incredulously behind him. "The cave has a back *door?*"

"Sure does," Ty said as the gray light grew before him. He grinned over his shoulder. "Told you I had it all figured out."

"Damned impressive, Mister Brannigan. Damned impressive." Talbot chuckled.

"Thanks, kid."

"What's the plan?"

"You'll see."

The light grew ahead of Ty. It grew and grew, and the low circular opening grew larger and larger. The ceiling dropped a little, however, so by the time he and the kid reached the cave's back door, petroglyphs showing brightly in the stone walls to each side of them, they were practically doubled over, their hats in their hands. Finally, the narrow corridor drew back behind Ty and the kid and they stood on a gravelly trough with a seven- or eight-foot rise ahead of them and from which a large spruce jutted.

Ty glanced at young Talbot. "Come on."

Holding his rifle in both hands across his chest, he walked to the bank, climbed it, sidling between the ridge's south wall and the prickly branches of the spruce, the cool wind of the late afternoon filling his nostrils with the tang of the spruce. Just beyond the spruce, he swung right, following the base of the sheer, stone ridge wall for a hundred feet. He and the kid were heading toward the slope that had fronted the cave, but now they were on the slope's far southern edge.

As they walked slowly, both holding their rifles at the ready, Ty noted that the gunfire had died. There were only the early evening sounds now of birds and the lightening wind buffeting the branches of the pines and aspens climbing the ridge on their left, just beyond a narrow draw choked with rocks and boulders. Many of the rocks and boulders were also decorated with the colorful paintings carved by the ancients—mostly stick figures wielding spears stalking stick, four-legged animal figures, some large and shaggy and with curved horns. The sun was painted brightly above the men and the animals they hunted—sometimes lemon yellow, sometimes blood red.

When they arrived at the front of the bastion of granite in which the cave had been carved likely by what might have been an underground stream at one time, Ty stopped. Brandon stopped just off his left flank.

Ty looked down the slope but several boulders lying straight ahead of him, on the down slope, blocked his view of the slope's base. Edging a look around the corner of the stone bastion on his right, he could see several feet of the declivity dropping away from the cave. The part of the slope he could see was vacant. Only rocks and tufts of sage, some scraggly cedars and Ponderosas.

"Brannigan!" Stalcup shouted. "We're gonna wait you out!"

Silence.

Ty glanced at Brandon and canted his head to indicate the draw dropping away on his left. The kid nodded. Ty turned to his left and climbed gingerly down the side of the draw, wincing at the hitch in his hip caused by his tumble with the cream.

"We got all the rest of the day, Brannigan!" the foreman shouted again, his voice growing testy, impatient. "All the rest of the day! After dark, we're gonna shoot you outta there!"

Ty and the kid made their way down the draw that dropped with the slope on their right and that was concealed from their view by big spruces and boulders.

A little while later, Stalcup shouted again, "All right, Brannigan! This is ridiculous! Just throw those rifles out and come outta there. Why prolong this thing!"

By now, Ty and the kid had come up behind the Anchor riders, the eight or so remaining men hunkered behind three separate boulders dead ahead of them. Stalcup was on one knee behind a boulder to the far right of the other seven men. The foreman was holding his Winchester across his knee and peering around the left side of his covering boulder, gazing up the slope toward the cave that Ty and Brandon had vacated twenty minutes ago.

"Yeah," Brannigan said, gritting his teeth with anger at these men who'd kill him in cold blood. Who'd hang an innocent man just to protect their jobs, allow Stalcup the woman he wanted. "Why prolong it?"

Each man jerked with a sudden start.

They all turned their hatted heads sharply to the two men flanking them. Ty and Brandon each were partly covered—Ty by a Ponderosa pine, Brandon by a small boulder to Ty's left.

"Drop them or die," Ty said, giving a savage grin. "It's as simple as that."

All seven men, all down on one knee, shared conferring glances, their eyes dark beneath their dusty hat brims.

Stalcup gave a wry smile, gave his head a single, fateful wag. "Back door, eh?"

"Back door," Ty said. "You're not so lucky."

Stalcup looked at one of the men kneeling behind a boulder to his left. "All right," he said, again fatefully, sighing. "Fellas, I reckon we done been—"

He cut himself off as he swung toward Ty, bringing his rifle around, his eyes widening beneath severely ridged brows. He fired but not until after Ty's bullet took him through the dead middle of his chest, throwing him back violently

421

against the boulder. He stood leaning back against the boulder, groaning, his hat tumbling from his head as he ground the back of his head against the boulder, writhing in agony.

He opened his eyes, dropped his chin, glaring at Ty. "You go to hell!" he grunted.

He tried to raise his Winchester again but didn't get it above the level of his gun belt before Ty shot him twice more in the chest, once to each side of the original wound.

"You first," Ty said.

Stalcup's rifle tumbled from his hands as he dropped straight down the face of the boulder to his butt, leaving a broad streak of bright red blood on the rock face above him. He lowered his head to his chest, as though he were drunk and it was time for a nap, legs straight out and spread wide before him.

Ty turned to the other seven men. None had made a move when Stalcup had. Now they stared in shock at the dead foreman. Brandon was holding his Spencer on them.

Slowly, by ones and twos, they turned to Ty, their eyes dark, fearful.

The man kneeling behind the same boulder as Stalcup, on the boulder's opposite side, threw down his rifle. "I'm out," he said.

He raised his gloved hands and glanced at the other Anchor men kneeling behind two other boulders beyond the dead Stalcup.

"What about you?" Ty asked them, sliding his Henry over to cover them.

One cursed and angrily tossed away his carbine. Then the others did, as well.

"Now the gun belts," Ty said.

When they unbuckled their gun belts and tossed them away, they stood, raising their open hands.

"Now what?" asked a man whose name Ty knew was Cedar Anderson. He was a short, wiry man with cold blue eyes set to either side of a raptorial nose, and a low-crowned black Stetson.

Ty said, "Now get on your horses and ride the hell out of this country. Don't ever let me see you anywhere near the Bear Paws again." He hardened his eyes as well as his jaws. "I will kill you on sight."

They widened their eyes in surprise, glanced around at each other, keeping their hands raised.

"Well, what are you waiting for?" Ty bellowed. "Haul your freight the hell outta here!"

To a man, they swung around and fairly ran out into the canyon where their horses milled separately, reins dangling. Ty could see his cream and Brandon's buckskin out there, too.

Silently, he and Brandon watched the Anchor men mount up and gallop off down the canyon, back in the direction from which they'd come.

Brandon turned to Ty, one brow arched in question.

"Yeah," Ty said. "They should all be behind bars. But they're more trouble than they're worth. And, hell, I reckon they were just riding for the brand."

"You'll get no argument from me," the kid said, turning his head to stare after the last of the fleeing riders. "I'm just glad it's all over. I never have cottoned to necktie parties." He glanced at Ty again, narrowing one eye and crooking his mouth corners in a grin. "Especially ones held in my honor."

Ty smiled.

"Come on, kid." He shouldered the Henry and started to walking, limping, toward his grazing cream. "We got a long ride ahead of us. I gotta get home. And you best get back to Ivy."

Brandon Talbot sighed, nodded, and started forward. He sighed again as though steeling himself against an uncertain future—one that included a young wife and a baby. "I reckon you're right."

"You can do it."

"I know it," Brandon said, hurrying to catch up to Ty. "And I will."

He bunched his lips and nodded decisively.

When he caught up to Ty, he looked up at the taller, older man. "But . . . what about that reward on my head?"

"Don't worry," Ty said. "Marshal Southern and I will figure something out."

Marshal Southern . . .

Ty just hoped the old lawman was still in one piece.

Chapter 35

Beatriz shouldered open the front door of the Powderhorn lodge house and sidled out onto the porch with a tray on which sat a small silver coffee server, two china cups on china saucers, and a small plate bearing two muffins. Near the muffins was a silver bread knife and a china saucer filled with freshly whipped butter.

Sitting on one of the several wicker chairs haphazardly arranged on the porch to her right, her crutches leaning against the side of her chair, Devon Hayes turned to Beatriz, arching her brows in question.

"After that," Beatriz said, walking toward the pretty redheaded woman, the silver coffee server steaming before her, "I think we each deserve a snack."

"After that" had been in reference to the surgery Miss Hayes had performed on Marshal Southern, digging the bullet out of his lower chest while Beatriz and MacKenna had assisted. Matt and Gregory had stood nearby, ready to hold the wounded man down if he awoke. Fortunately, however, the marshal hadn't regained full consciousness during the procedure after having passed out as soon as Matt and MacKenna had laid him down on the table.

"That looks wonderful," Devon said, smiling as Beatriz set the tray down on a small wooden table on the porch near her guest. She glanced up at Beatriz, her eyes suddenly concerned. "Did Matt and MacKenna get the marshal upstairs all right?"

Beatriz sat down in the chair across the table from Miss Hayes. "Si, they did. The marshal seems to be resting comfortably."

"That's good to hear." Devon sat back in her chair. "If no infection sets in, he should be all right. The bullet didn't seem to tear him up that bad, though I can't understand how he's still alive, having lost as much blood as he did."

"That's an easy one." Beatriz smiled as she leaned forward to pick up the server and tilt it over Miss Hayes's cup, filling it with the steaming black brew. "Love."

"Ah," Miss Hayes said. "Love."

"Si." Beatriz filled her own cup then set the server down and regarded the redhead speculatively. "Where did you learn how to perform surgery like that, if you don't mind me asking? That certainly wasn't your first time. You seemed to know exactly what you were doing."

Devon set her cup and saucer on her knee. "One of my former husbands was a doctor. By the time I knew him, he was really more of a gambler, but I helped him dig a few bullets out of men. Mostly his friends." She gave a grim twist of her mouth.

"He didn't have the most wholesome of friends."

"I'm sorry to hear that."

"Don't be. Reginald was a card sharp. One who cheated. That's how he died . . . cheating the wrong man in Nacogdoches."

Beatriz gasped, placed her splayed hand over the bodice of her dress.

"Yes, my life has been rather shocking at times," Miss Hayes said, smiling guiltily. She sipped her coffee, looking thoughtfully off toward the barn. "Never was good at choosing the right man after . . ." She let the sentence trail off, shaking her head slightly as though to dismiss the thought, then took another sip of her coffee.

"After Ty?" Beatriz asked, tearing open one of the muffins and picking up the knife to butter it.

Miss Hayes smiled, then took one more small sip of her coffee and turned to Beatriz. "Yes. After Ty." She reached over and placed her right hand on Beatriz's left wrist, giving Beatriz a direct look with her cat-like, jade eyes framed by all that curly, deep-red hair. "Please don't worry, Beatriz. I'm not here to take him from you."

Beatriz gazed back at her. She had to admit, she'd been wondering just what the woman's intentions were. "You're not?"

Miss Hayes smiled again, gave her head a quick shake. "No." She drew a breath and stared off toward the barn again, her eyes again thoughtful. "I have to admit that I've thought about him over the years. I also have to admit that he was one consideration in my coming here. In buying the Longhorn in Warknife."

"He was?"

Miss Hayes turned to her. "I knew he was here. I'd heard he'd moved here not long after . . . not long after I fled the notion of marriage." She looked off again, a sadness showing in her eyes, then turned back to Beatriz again. "I won't lie to you. I regretted it. Leaving him. I also won't lie that I haven't thought of what it might have been like . . . if I'd stayed with him. Of the family we might have had." She smiled and looked down at the coffee cup on her knee. "Now I know."

When she looked up again, there were tears in her eyes. "Having seen your lovely family, now I know."

Beatriz felt a tender smile shape her lips. She reached over with her own hand, placed it on Miss Hayes's right wrist, gave it an affectionate squeeze. "You know what I think, Miss Hayes?"

"Please, Devon."

"You know what I think, Devon?"

"No. What's that, Beatriz?"

"I think we're going to be friends, you and I."

Devon smiled, blinking tears from her eyes. They rolled down her cheeks, glinting in the late light angling over the Powderhorn headquarters yard. "I'd like that." She laughed, brushed tears from her cheeks. "I'd like that very much!"

MacKenna pushed through the lodge's front door and stepped out onto the porch, happy to see her mother and Miss Hayes sitting in chairs to her right, seemingly having a pleasant conversation. Seeing them getting along so well, she hated to interrupt.

But she had to.

As Matt stepped out of the house behind her, MacKenna cleared her throat and stepped tentatively toward her mother. "Ma? I hate to interrupt . . ."

"Si, si," Beatriz said, turning her head to face her daughter. She frowned when she saw the Winchester carbines in both MacKenna's and Matt's gloved hands. They each had a pair of saddlebags draped over their shoulders and a bedroll clamped under their left arms. Their Stetsons were on their heads. "What is it, children? Where are you going? Remember, your father said that . . ."

"We know what Pa said, Ma," Matt said, flanking MacKenna. "But that was before . . ."

He let his voice trail off, deferring to his sister.

Both Beatriz and Miss Hayes slid their concerned gazes to MacKenna.

"We were so busy with the marshal," MacKenna said, "that I didn't have time to tell you about pa. He rode into the Wind Rivers."

Beatriz's puzzled frown deepened. "Why would he—"

"He rode there because I knew that Brandon had ridden there. You see, Ma, I found out for certain-sure that Cass Battles killed Mister Battles."

Beatriz gasped and closed her hand over her mouth in shock.

Miss Hayes just stared in deep puzzlement and consternation at Mack, likely not knowing much about the Battles situation. Mack didn't want to tell her mother that she had killed Cass Battles. She didn't want to tell her about anything that had happened over at the Sunshine Ranch. She would eventually, but even if the horrific words could find their way to her mouth, there wasn't time.

"The Anchor riders are after Cass. Pa's gonna be alone against them, if they catch up to him and Brandon. Now, he strictly forbade me to ride out after him, but . . ."

"Go!" Beatriz said, rising from her chair and throwing her right arm out toward the barn. "It is late but go! Find your father!"

MacKenna glanced up at her brother standing behind her. Matt nodded. They hurried down off the porch steps and strode to the barn.

MacKenna and Matt didn't reach the Wind Rivers before good dark closed over them. They rode for another hour but when the country started to break up around them, making for tricky travel, they set up a night camp in a pine grove near the Demon River.

"Not sure what we're doin' out here, Mack," Matt said as they sat around the fire. Having warmed and eaten a can of beans, they were now sipping coffee. "Neither one of us knows where this Henry Two Kills cabin is."

Mack sat several feet away from the fire, gazing back in the direction from which they'd come. She sat with her knees raised, elbows resting on them. Her coffee steamed in the darkness.

"Brandon told me it was just north of Bailey Peak," she said, staring into the darkness beyond the fire. "I figure if we can get close, we might hear gunfire. If it comes to that." She blew on her coffee and sipped it. "Hope it doesn't, but if it does, I'd like to be close enough to lend a hand."

"Yeah, well, I reckon this beats moonin' around home, waiting for him," Matt said. "Wondering . . ."

MacKenna could hear him poking a stick around in the fire.

"Say, what are you starin' so hard at over there, sis?" he asked.

"Not sure."

"What's that?"

"Not sure," Mack said, louder. She frowned. "I swear, I'm more like Pa every day. He's always said he's got a sixth sense for trouble." Her frown deepened. "I swear I got an uneasy feelin'."

"Really?"

"Yeah."

"What do you think it's about?" Matt asked behind MacKenna.

"Not sure. It's just that for the past hour or so that we were ridin', I felt like someone was followin' us."

"Pa's bushwhack—?" Matt cut himself off sharply. "Oh . . . wait."

MacKenna looked over her right shoulder at him. "What?"

Matt was standing now, holding the stick he'd been probing the fire with, staring off to the south.

MacKenna swung her head around to follow her brother's gaze. Her eyes widened when she saw a small orange glow off in the distance and up a slight rise.

"A fire?" MacKenna said.

"What else could it be?"

"It wasn't there just a few minutes ago."

"No, this is the first I've seen of it."

MacKenna gained her feet, careful not to slosh the hot coffee over the lip of the rim and onto her fingers. She walked a few feet out in the darkness, staring at the fire. It was a couple of hundred yards away.

"Just some drover, probably," Matt said.

MacKenna felt a prickling at the back of her neck. She'd felt it before when they'd been riding. It had grown more severe when Matt had pointed out the fire to her.

She walked over to where she'd leaned her rifle against a Ponderosa and picked it up. "Matt?" she said, turning to her brother standing to her left.

Matt turned to her.

"I'm gonna check it out."

CHAPTER 36

"What?" Matt frowned. "Why?"

"Pa's sixth sense is grieving me. Just wanna check it out. I'll feel better."

Matt grabbed his own rifle. "I'll come with you."

"No. Stay here. It might be a trap."

"MacKenna, you listen to your big brother." Matt ridged his brows and tightened his voice, his face flushing with anxiety. "I'm not gonna let you go over there alone. If you're goin', I'm goin'."

MacKenna thought it over, nodded slowly. Maybe they both should go. They were safer together than apart.

"All right."

"We walkin' or ridin'?"

"Let's walk. Make less noise."

"All right."

"Let's go," Matt said, and started walking forward.

Hearing the murmur of the river on her left, MacKenna walked forward, as well. She stayed about ten feet to Matt's right, holding her rifle like he was holding his, down low so the light from the star or the thumbnail moon wouldn't reflect off of it. Their father had taught them both well.

They moved down the slight rise their own camp was on and out of the pine woods, on down to a flat area before another rise halfway up where the other fire flickered and glowed, growing larger with each step the sister and brother took as they moved toward it.

"Mack?" Matt said to MacKenna's left, keeping his voice low.

"What is it?" Mack whispered.

"Could be Pa."

MacKenna shook her head. "It's not."

Matt glanced at her. "How do you know?"

MacKenna hiked a shoulder, kept her gaze forward as she walked. "I just know."

"You're soundin' kinda strange, sis."

"I feel strange," MacKenna said.

The prickling at the back of her neck grew as she and Matt climbed the next rise, heading toward another stretch of woods forming a wedge as it drifted down from the top of the next ridge. The fire appeared to have been built in the middle of those pines and aspens.

MacKenna felt the urge—as strong as the initial urge to check out the strange fire—to turn back around and return to her and Matt's own camp. Something would not let her do that, however. Something told her that she and Matt might not be any safer over there than over here.

If there was a threat out here—and that prickling against the back of her neck told her there indeed was—they'd best confront it straight on rather than let the threat confront them later on, maybe when they'd both drifted off to sleep.

Slowly, walking side by side, holding their rifles low, they entered the woods, stepping carefully over deadfall and blowdowns.

MacKenna's heart thumped heavily against her breastbone. Her hands sweated inside her gloves, her right hand holding the carbine around its receiver. The fire grew before her, shunting shadows this way and that. It was only sixty or so feet away now. She could see nothing, no one, around it.

Matt raised a hand and stopped. MacKenna stopped, then, too.

"What is it?" MacKenna whispered to him.

Keeping his head turned forward, Matt called, "Hello, the camp . . . ?"

No response.

MacKenna turned toward the fire again. The fire flickered before her, its glow dulling as it used up its fuel, growing a little smaller now, dimmer.

Matt looked at MacKenna. He frowned and shrugged, perplexed.

MacKenna returned the shrug then turned her head to look around them. "Watch your back, Matt," she said, turning full around to make sure no one was trying to sneak up behind them.

Matt looked around, too.

When they were relatively certain no one was near them, they continued walking forward even more slowly and quietly than before, though there was no way, unless you were an Indian in moccasins, to move in total silence in woods carpeted in weeds, dead branches, old leaves, and pine needles.

They moved up to within twenty feet of the fire and stopped.

They looked around the camp.

No. It wasn't a camp. There was only the fire here. No gear. No horses.

No men.

Just the fire.

"Must've pulled out," Matt said softly.

"Wait." MacKenna traced a broad curve around the fire, moving up on the other side of it to a large, teardrop-shaped rock.

Something was on the rock. It glittered in the firelight.

She picked it up, held it up in the palm of her hand, showing it to her brother.

MacKenna stared at the bullet, her heart thudding, skipping beats.

"Come on, Mack," Matt said, his voice low and dark. "Let's get the hell out—*ohhh!*"

"Matt!" MacKenna cried, watching her brother stumble forward, drop to the ground, roll once and lay still.

A figure now stood where Matt had been standing.

A much bigger man than Matt. A big, bear-like man with a thick, brown beard into which a grisly scar curved down from the big, moon-faced, bear-like man's left eye, beneath the brim of his bullet-crowned black hat. The man's right arm was in a sling, angled across his broad chest, beneath the right flap of his open, black duster. In his left hand he held the rifle whose butt he'd rammed against the back of Matt's head.

"Hello there, little Brannigan girl!" the man fairly roared, his deep voice echoing. He grinned a grisly, death's head grin, showing a mouthful of rotten, crooked teeth. "Did you miss us? I know *I* sure missed *you!*"

Two other men stepped out of the trees flanking him.

One was nearly his size. The other was much smaller and with bulging eyes in his own moon face. But both men looked enough like him to be closely related. Holding rifles up high across their chests, their eyes flashing lustily in the firelight, they, too, grinned at MacKenna.

"Drop that rifle, little girl!" yelled the second largest of the three men, jutting a warning finger at Mack.

MacKenna tried to raise the carbine but her hands were shaking. Somehow, she lost the damn thing, heard it clatter onto the ground at her feet.

Her fear running wild, she gave a shrill scream, swung around, and ran into the darkness beyond the fire.

"Oh, no you don't! You ain't gettin' away from me—not after what you done to me, little Brannigan girl!"

Heavy footfalls rose behind Mack as did the wild whoops of her three pursuers.

"No!" Mack screamed, hating the fear she heard in her frightened little girl's voice.

With Matt unconscious, she was alone out here. Alone with three wild lobos hot on her heels. Unless she could outrun them, she was going to die.

The big man might have been big, but he could run. Mack heard his heavy foot thuds growing louder behind her as well as the crunching and snapping of branches beneath his boots, his raspy breaths raking in and out of his lungs. The others weren't as fast. They were a little behind him. Mack could tell that by the sounds of their own running footfalls.

Those two were howling like moon-crazed coyotes. The big man wasn't yelling. He was running and breathing hard, sort of grunting with each labored breath, his fury and goatish lust fairly exploding out of him.

Mack was going to die but only after he'd . . .

She whipped a terrified glance over her shoulder. He was closing on her—a huge, lumbering figure silhouetted in the darkness only a few feet behind her, scissoring his one good arm, lifting his knees high with every lunging stride. The moonlight flashed in his flat, dark, animal-like eyes and in his rotten teeth revealed by his eagerly stretched-back lips.

Mack turned her head forward.

Too late.

Both feet were suddenly ripped out from under her by a fallen tree in her path. She hit the ground just beyond it, rolled, then, fear driving her, she quickly gained her feet and started running again—

Straight into a yielding figure, who lurched backward against Mack's momentum.

"No!" Mack cried as a big hand wrapped around her right arm.

"Take her!"

The hand jerked her back behind the man whose hand it was—a big man with a familiar voice.

Warmly familiar.

Then Mack saw Brandon Waycro—er, Talbot—step out from behind a tree, grab her, and pull her back behind the tree with him.

Ty raised the rifle in his hands, cocking it, aimed straight out from his right shoulder.

Rage flamed hotly inside him as the big man running toward him stopped suddenly only a few feet away. The big man stopped so suddenly he nearly fell forward, propelled by his own momentum. He jerked his left arm up like a wing. His eyes and mouth opened wide, in shock to see the man standing before him, bearing down on him with a cocked Winchester.

"Shep Parmelee," Ty grated out through gritted teeth, then twitching a demonic smile. "Should've figured it was you, judging by the description. As ugly a man as ever lived . . . even before the scar."

"Hold on, now, Brannigan!" Parmelee cried, holding up his hand holding the rifle. "Don't shoot—I—"

"I know what you were going to do to my daughter!" Ty shot him, blowing the top of the man's head off from nearly point-blank range.

One of the other two snapped off a quick shot from where they stood ten feet behind where their brother had fallen. The bullet whipped past Ty's left ear to slam into the tree behind which Brandon had taken MacKenna.

Ty pumped a fresh round into his Henry's action and started to aim the rifle but eased the slack in his trigger finger when a rifle thundered off to his right. One of the men standing before Ty yowled and dropped. The rifle thundered again, flames lapping in the darkness.

The other Parmelee brother grunted and flew

backward, hitting the ground with a resolute, snapping thud.

Ty turned to see Matt step out of the darkness, ejecting the spent round from his Winchester's breech. He'd lost his hat, and his hair was in his eyes. He walked slowly toward Ty, frowning curiously, shaking his head.

"Pa . . . ?"

"Pa!" MacKenna cried behind Ty.

He turned. His daughter ran into his arms as Brandon stepped out from behind the tree. MacKenna hugged Ty tightly, pressing her cheek against his chest. Her body quivered with fear.

Ty wrapped his arms around her, swallowing her up against him, returning her bear-like hug.

Matt stepped up to him and Mack, giving a guilty little smile as he caressed the back of his head.

"You too are in big trouble," Ty said, squeezing his daughter in his arms. "Big, big trouble."

"I know, Pa," MacKenna said, keeping her cheek pressed up hard against his chest. "I'll pick a nice, big willow switch. The biggest one you've ever seen!"

Ty couldn't help but snort a laugh then raise his right arm to include his son in the hug.

William W. Johnstone is the *New York Times* and *USA Today* bestselling author of over three hundred books, including the bestselling series Smoke Jensen: The Mountain Man; Preacher: The First Mountain Man; Flintlock; MacCallister; and Will Tanner: U.S. Deputy Marshal, and the stand-alone thrillers *Black Friday*, *Tyranny*, and *Stand Your Ground*.

Being the all-around assistant, typist, researcher, and fact-checker to one of the most popular Western authors of all time, J.A. Johnstone learned from the master, Uncle William W. Johnstone.

He began tutoring J.A. at an early age. After-school hours were often spent retyping manuscripts or researching his massive American Western history library as well as the more modern wars and conflicts. J.A. worked hard—and learned.

"Every day with Bill was an adventure story in itself. Bill taught me all he could about the art of storytelling. *'Keep the historical facts accurate,'* he would say. *'Remember the readers, and as your grandfather once told me, I am telling you now: be the best J.A. Johnstone you can be.'*"

Visit the website at www.williamjohnstone.net.

Center Point Large Print
600 Brooks Road / PO Box 1
Thorndike, ME 04986-0001 USA

(207) 568-3717

US & Canada:
1 800 929-9108
www.centerpointlargeprint.com